Blueprint for the Heart

Restoring Madison, TX

Book One

Laura Finger

Olivia in the foyer and cut herself off, eyes narrowing. "Sorry. Didn't mean to make a scene."

Olivia summoned a smile, the one she'd practiced in the restroom mirror at the Houston conference center before her final interview with the trust. "No trouble at all," she said, though her voice skittered up a half-octave. "I'm so sorry about the water. They warned us, but I thought we'd have pressure back by this morning."

Brian attempted a forgiving shrug, but his lips made a thin, bloodless line. "We have to be on the road, anyway. San Antonio's only a few hours."

The woman squared her shoulders. "We'd just like to check out, please. Is there someone we can talk to about a refund?"

Olivia's hands found each other in front of her, fingers locking as if she could brace herself against the flood of apologies rising in her chest. "Of course. I can process that now. If you have a second, I'll print you a receipt."

They did not have a second. The couple migrated to the porch, pausing only long enough for the man to mutter a half-hearted thank-you. The woman didn't look back.

Olivia closed the door behind them with a soft click, the noise already swallowed by the hammer-drill chorus from the courthouse. Through the wavy glass of the sidelight, she watched the guests hoist their bags over the trench and head for the parking lot, navigating the obstacles with the brisk efficiency of people who had learned never to expect more than the minimum. When they finally disappeared behind the glare of a cement mixer, she let her head thump against the doorframe and counted to five.

A part of her wanted to chase after them—explain, plead, bribe with a free stay and a bottomless carafe of decent coffee—but the rest of her knew the futility. The online reviews would be savage; the reservations calendar was already anemic.

For months, Olivia had been running uphill against a landslide of bad luck and worse timing, but today the slope felt vertical.

She made her way to the reception desk, its mahogany top burnished to a wet shine by generations of careful hands. She pressed her palms flat against the wood, letting the cool grain ground her while she waited for the tremor in her chest to subside. Her grandmother's brass desk bell sat at one corner, polished to a mirror. For years, she'd watched her abuela ring it for emphasis while negotiating with vendors or settling the arguments of guests who expected the impossible. Sometimes, when Olivia was a little girl, she was allowed to press it herself, a privilege reserved for the trusted.

Now the bell seemed pointless, a prop in a play no one had come to see.

She inhaled, slow and deliberate, and surveyed the foyer: crown molding dusted with white, a runner rug tracking footprints from the door to the stairs, a pile of unread brochures sliding off the end table. She'd chosen everything here—every paint swatch, every reproduction sconce, every oddball curio rescued from the thrift stores and estate auctions of three counties. None of it mattered to the people who booked a night and left before breakfast, or who checked in only to check out as soon as the jackhammers started.

She was halfway through composing a refund email when her phone buzzed. The screen showed a local number, but not one she recognized.

She let it ring. The desk bell remained unstruck.

Her throat burned. She blinked at the screen until her vision cleared, then typed a reply that was quick, professional, and so neutral a stranger could have written it: Apologies for the inconvenience. Please allow 3-5 business days for the refund to process.

She pressed send, leaned against the carved edge of the desk, and let herself stand there, unmoving, until the ache in her chest dulled to a manageable throb. Outside, the jackhammers screamed on, disassembling the center of her world one pulverized stone at a time.

❧

Six months earlier, Olivia stood in the glass-clad box of Alexander Stirling's Houston office, rehearsing her pitch in the span of time it took for his executive assistant to fetch a tray of drinks. The view from the twenty-third floor was as far from Madison's crumbling courthouse as it was possible to get —everything below washed in sun-glinting traffic and steel, skyscrapers rising like the business end of a graph. Alex Stirling's domain was open plan and relentlessly expensive, the conference room's floor-to-ceiling windows reflecting the city back at itself in dizzying layers.

"You're early," Alex had said, appearing at the threshold with his shirt sleeves rolled up, no tie, the image of a man who'd conquered something and now wondered what else remained. "Have a seat, Olivia. Do you want coffee, water—something stronger?"

Coffee, please, she'd answered, and then regretted it because her hands would shake. She sat at the glass conference table, knees pressed together under her dress, and tried not to leave any smudges on the immaculate chrome. The model of the Limestone Inn was already waiting at her place: a laser-cut balsa miniature with delicate fretwork, each dormer and spindle rendered in perfect scale. Her own handiwork, assembled in a fevered three-night sprint after learning she'd made the last cut for the Stirling Madison Preservation Trust's shortlist.

The trust might have been a peace offering from Stirling to cover up past sins towards the populace of Verde County, but

Olivia was damned determined that she would make the best of the offer.

Alex thumbed the inn's turret with the care of a chess player. "You did this yourself?"

"I did," she said, and then, because the pause after was too long, added, "My father was an engineer. I got the patience from him, I think."

"Impressive. Is that color accurate?" He turned the model so the porch faced him, scrutinizing every detail.

"Mostly. I'm restoring it to the original paint—pale yellow with white trim and green accents. There's an entire section in the plan for using historically matched pigment. I can show you."

He grinned, eyes crinkling at the corners, and gestured for her to continue. "Walk me through it."

She started with the history: the Kendrick house, built 1891. Four owners, two major renovations, not a single square foot of the original longleaf pine lost to termites. When she got to the Mexican-American stonemasons who'd built the foundation—names half-erased by time but preserved in a few smudged payroll ledgers—she saw Alex's attention sharpen.

"Most of the labor that built Madison came from Tejano families," she said, steering clear of the PowerPoint and speaking directly. "It's not in the courthouse tour, but it's in the bones of every building downtown. I want to use the Limestone to showcase that. Each guest room will be named after a craftsman or a family, and each will have a story panel in both English and Spanish. The community events will feature local historians and descendants—"

"Why?" Alex interrupted, but not unkindly. He leaned forward, folding his hands on the table. "Why does that matter for an inn? What do you think the guests are looking for?"

Olivia hesitated. The right answer was in her notes somewhere—about brand differentiation, about appealing to heritage travelers, about the growing market for "experiential hospitality"—but what came out was the truth. "Because if we don't, no one else will. And because my abuela always said that when you welcome someone under your roof, you owe them the truth of who you are. My grandfather made sure to note every man who toiled and sweated in the creation of the property for the Kendrick family. I want people to see the real Madison. Not just what's in the brochures."

Alex nodded, slow and deliberate, like he was turning her words over in his head to see if the edges fit together. "Tell me about the numbers," he said.

She flipped to the spreadsheet, hands steady now. Bookings, projected occupancy, off-season rates. She had answers for everything—contingency plans, the marketing rollout, the breakeven point right after month twenty-two. She even had an explanation ready for the black eye on her financials: the failed Houston B&B partnership with Muriel, the embezzlement, the bankruptcy filing, and how she'd rebuilt her credit one micro loan at a time.

He listened without blinking, then asked, "And if the courthouse renovation overruns? Or if the historic district doesn't come back the way you expect?"

She'd prepared for this, too. "We pivot to long-term stays. Target the courthouse clerks, the seasonal workers. Host destination events—weddings, writers' retreats, local conferences. I know it's not as glamorous, but I can keep the lights on."

Alex's smile was thin, but not unsympathetic. "And you'd be running it yourself?"

"Every day," she said. "It's my life now."

He looked at her, really looked, and for a moment the office's icy calm faded, replaced by the warmth of two people who recognized the same stubborn streak in each other. "You know, I thought this would be about spreadsheets," he said. "But it's about legacy, isn't it?"

She wanted to nod, or to smile, or to tell him that yes, it was all she'd ever wanted, but her throat closed up, and she managed only a quiet, "Yes."

He sat back, weighed her for another long second, and then reached into the file folder at his elbow. "All right. Here's what I'm offering." He slid the paperwork across the table. "It's a loan, not a grant. But it's low interest, and the first two years are interest-only. The trust will own the property as collateral until you're paid up, but you'll have full autonomy on restoration and operations. You in?"

She could barely process the words—her plan had been to negotiate, to plead for better terms, to promise the moon—but he was giving her everything she'd dared to hope for, and more.

"I'm in," she said, the words tumbling out before she could second-guess herself.

He stood, and she stood, and they shook hands over the tiny model of her future.

On the way out, the elevator walls reflected her in ghostly, overlapping silhouettes. She pressed her palm to her chest, felt the hard gallop of her heart, and wondered how long it would take for this victory to feel real.

THE SUN HAD SHIFTED WESTWARD, spotlighting the courthouse dome like a precious artifact in a museum of construction wreckage. After the guests peeled out of the lot and Olivia finished scrubbing her face in the kitchen sink, she gave herself a two-minute window for self-pity, then cinched her hair into a low knot and headed back outside. She'd meant to catch the site foreman during the lull between shifts. Instead, she found herself face-to-face with a stranger standing astride the sidewalk cut, clipboard in hand and expression blank as printer paper.

He didn't look like a construction worker. For one thing, his shoes were too clean—black oxfords, scuffed only at the heel, standing out on the dirt-caked concrete like punctuation marks. He had ironed his navy button-down shirt meticulously, and his dark slacks had a single, precise crease down each leg. Over one shoulder, a battered leather messenger bag with a Texas Historical Commission patch sewn crookedly to the flap. He wasn't tall, exactly, but he gave the impression of height by the way he held his posture—shoulders squared, chin parallel to the horizon, eyes level with her own.

"Excuse me," she called, with enough volume to startle a pigeon off the courthouse eave. "I'm looking for Mr. Gonzales —the foreman?"

The man pivoted using only his feet and smiled a tiny, quick smile. "He's at lunch. May I help you?"

His voice was clear, clipped, every consonant filed to its proper length. Olivia felt herself straighten in response.

"Maybe you can," she said. "Are you with the Commission?"

He nodded, producing a laminated ID that he held between two fingers. "Andrew Kim. Preservation architect, site manager for the Phase One exterior. And you're Olivia Cuellar, right? Owner of the Limestone?"

He said it like a fact, not a question, but she gave a wary yes, anyway. In a sea of workers dominated by Hispanic features, she noticed something that hadn't occurred to her before; he was Asian. Given the history of the community, throwing in yet another flavor of "outsider" signaled trouble in Madison.

He offered a handshake, which she took only after a half-second pause. His grip was dry, brisk, businesslike.

"What can I do for you, Ms. Cuellar?" he asked, returning

to his clipboard with a flourish that made it clear he had not built his adult life around small talk.

She pointed her chin toward the blockaded porch. "Can you tell me why my sidewalk has been torn up for a week, and nobody warned the businesses?" I've lost four bookings since Monday. People don't want to carry their luggage over a trench."

Andrew glanced at his clipboard, then up at the worksite. "That's the gas main reroute. It wasn't on the original timeline, but after we exposed the old pipe, we had to bring it up to code. It's a safety issue."

"Would've been nice to get an email," she said, feeling her pulse pick up. "I'm supposed to host a rehearsal dinner next Saturday. Are you saying I should cancel?"

He didn't flinch, but he did pause—a microsecond, almost imperceptible, but Olivia caught it. "No, ma'am. The crew will have it poured and cured by Thursday. The detour is inconvenient, but it's temporary. The long-term improvement will increase the value of your property."

She bit down on her first response, which was not fit for daytime TV. "And what am I supposed to do until then? Hand out hard hats at check-in?"

He blinked, once. "I can provide you with the current project schedule. If you like, I'll ask the team to mark the safe path with cones. We can post additional signage for your guests." He delivered the offer in the same monotone as everything else, as if he'd already categorized her complaint and moved on to the next item on his mental checklist.

Olivia folded her arms. "Have you ever actually stayed at a B&B, Mr. Kim?"

His eyebrow quirked, just barely. "Yes. Many times. Most places I work, actually."

She felt the ground shift under her feet, not in the literal sense, but in the sudden realization that she might be up against someone who not only understood her pain, but had probably diagrammed it in PowerPoint. She couldn't help but stare, assessing him despite her determination to keep their conversation professional. His broad face and curling black hair weren't exactly displeasing, but she was there for business, not to admire a fellow import from outside of Verde County.

"Then you know how important first impressions are," she said, her tone sharpening despite herself. "Right now my reviews are trending toward 'total disaster zone,' and if it keeps up, I'll be out of business before your crew finishes the curb cut."

He nodded, the gesture grave. "That's not our intention. I'll talk to Mr. Gonzales and see if there's a way to expedite the approach. Maybe a temporary bridge. In the meantime, if you have specific complaints, please document them. We track all stakeholder impact for the grant audit."

Stakeholder impact. Olivia tried to imagine her abuela using the phrase and almost laughed. Instead, she said, "You really like your forms, don't you?"

His mouth twitched. Not a smile, not quite. "Documentation is how things get fixed."

She stared at him, trying to decide if he was a robot or just a different species of human, and realized that he was probably just as worn out as she was—maybe even more so. The world was full of people who cared too much and wore it like armor.

"Fine," she said. "I'll send you my list." She pivoted on her heel and started back toward the porch, but then paused, her hand on the duct-taped warning sign. "Are you going to be here tomorrow?"

"I'm here every day," he said.

"Good. I'll have coffee on at seven." She didn't wait for a response, but she could feel his eyes following her retreat.

Inside, she let herself lean against the door for a long moment, feeling both victorious and completely, utterly defeated. The trench was still there, but at least she'd named it out loud. Sometimes that was the only power you had.

THAT NIGHT, the kitchen of the Limestone felt more like an operating room than the heart of a home. Olivia had lined up her ledgers, her business plan, and her battered laptop along the scarred length of the butcher-block island. Next to her coffee mug, a bottle of ibuprofen and a squeeze-stress ball shaped like a cowboy boot—both necessary, neither sufficient. The house was quiet but not silent; every so often a foundation-shudder from the square would send the refrigerator into a nervous rattle, or the water heater would emit a protesting knock.

She tapped the calculator with her left index finger, letting the click-clack set a rhythm. She'd been through the projections a hundred times—enough to know, even before the construction, that the margins were as thin as tissue. Now, with four cancellations in a single week and no new bookings to replace them, the runway to profitability was shrinking by the hour.

She ran the numbers again. If she slashed the event budget, cut the fresh-flowers subscription, and renegotiated with the laundry service, she might, maybe stretch through October. If the wedding party next month didn't bolt. If the building inspectors kept their promises. If. If. If.

It was the same fragile line she'd walked in Houston—just-in-time invoices, robbing Peter to pay Paul, waking up every night with her pulse in her throat. She remembered the moment Muriel had come clean, how the confession had felt at first like a relief, and then a void. She wondered if she was hard wired to fail at this, if ambition was just a polite synonym for delusion.

She stared at the monitor, the cash flow table marching her toward an inevitable deficit. There was an email from Alex in her inbox, a single line checking in—How's week two? Need anything?—but she hadn't answered. She didn't know how to say what she really felt: that she suspected he'd seen this coming, maybe even counted on it. That the trust's loan was a way for him to buy a badge of virtue, rescue a local landmark, and show the town his heart had grown three sizes since his very public debacle. Failing to buy up and transform Madison's historic German Quarter smarted for Stirling in ways more than financial.

She wondered if he pitied her. She wondered if she'd rather he did.

Beyond the window, the courthouse square was an empty grid of lampposts and chain-link shadow. The only movement came from the flashing hazard beacons on the backhoe, strobing every few seconds across the glass. In the reflection, Olivia looked spectral—a floating oval of face, hair coiled in a half-collapse, the pale triangle of her blouse suspended over the gleam of the countertop. Behind her, the inn's rooms were dark. Upstairs, her small staff made every bed, placed every mint on its pillow, and waited for guests who might never arrive.

She set the calculator down and pressed her palms to the island, feeling its solidity beneath her. Trying to channel the memory, she remembered how her grandmother ran a boarding house. She let the memory warm her, just for a second, and then let it go.

Olivia reached for the stress ball, squeezed it until the little foam spur creased white, and closed her eyes. Outside, a distant dog barked. A car passed on Travis, taillights red as a warning.

The doubt gathered behind her eyes, dense and formless as storm clouds. For a heartbeat, she let it all in—the fear, the fatigue, the certainty that she was always one misstep from the same ruin that had found her before. Then, methodically, she slid the cash flow spreadsheet into a folder, stacked the invoices by due date, and clicked off the desk lamp.

She stood in the dark for a long moment, watching the window until her own reflection faded and the courthouse lights came on, one by one, across the square. She could still see the dust clouds in the air, which were now edged with orange, making them almost pretty.

She told herself one more time that tomorrow she'd find a way. She'd always been good at tomorrow. It was tonight that gave her trouble.

Chapter Two

Her arms ached from an early morning spent scouring fingerprints off the lobby's marble-topped console, then standing on a step stool to brush pollen from the cornices. The only guest remaining in the inn—a retiree from San Antonio with a folding bicycle and a penchant for grapefruit halves—had already checked out, leaving the place so silent that Olivia could hear the shiver of her own breath in the foyer. The building inspector was late, which did nothing to lower her pulse. She straightened the guest book, then the stack of business cards, then the guest book again, all while watching for the glint of an official truck through the window's shifting dust.

She was in the kitchen, aligning the glass canisters on the counter, when a knock rattled the back door. Not the front—never the front; the best way to put an owner off balance was to come in through the servants' entrance, her dad used to say, and this one must've read the same playbook. Olivia wiped her hands on a towel and steeled herself before opening the door.

The man on the stoop was compact, sturdy, his polo shirt

tucked tight into cargo pants that suggested utility more than style. He wore the resigned expression of someone who'd already delivered two bad verdicts this morning and wasn't looking forward to a third. In one hand, a digital clipboard; in the other, a go-cup of coffee that steamed slightly in the humid air. He glanced past her into the kitchen before offering a curt, "Ms. Cuellar?"

She nodded. "That's me. You're right on—well, you're here."

He didn't laugh, didn't even smile. "Shouldn't take long." He slipped a plastic bootie over each shoe and stepped inside, scanning with the rapid, birdlike movements of a man who had been trained to see only flaws.

They began in the kitchen. Olivia had spent two weekends and her last thousand dollars sanding, painting, and mounting hardware on the cabinets. It looked fine at a glance—"Instagrammable," her best friend Elena Rodriguez had declared at the launch party—but as the inspector moved through, he rattled the stove, opened the dishwasher mid-cycle, and ran a fingertip along the seal of the industrial fridge, which she'd scored for a bargain on Facebook Marketplace. He murmured, "No commercial hood?" and typed something. As Olivia shifted from one foot to another silently, he unscrewed the aerator on the faucet, and squinted. She groaned silently as he found a chipped tile in the prep area and took a photo.

He didn't comment until he reached the pantry, where he flicked the light switch several times, then peered into the ceiling fixture. "You have knob-and-tube up there?" he asked, already knowing the answer.

"I'm upgrading next quarter," she lied. "It's on the schedule."

He grunted, and moved on. In the dining room, he measured the distance between table edges, then the width of the double doors. He checked the fire extinguisher, nodded, then popped open the service closet to inspect the breaker panel.

Olivia followed at a respectful distance, arms folded to hide the tremor in her hands. She tried to interpret the man's every micro-expression—was the tight mouth good, bad, or just his face? Had she made the right call in sanding down the breakfast nook instead of fixing the back stoop? Would he be happy with honest intentions, or did he thrive on ruining small businesses with legal threats?

They climbed to the second floor, the site of last year's "emergency" bathroom renovation. Olivia had replaced the 1970s avocado fixtures with secondhand porcelain, painted the walls an inoffensive gray, and installed grab bars in the ADA suite. The inspector walked the space in silence, occasionally tapping a wall or measuring a doorway. In the hallway, he crouched to examine the old radiator covers, then made a sour face and typed for a solid minute.

By the time they returned to the lobby, Olivia's optimism had ossified into a knot at the base of her skull. She tried to break the tension with a smile. "So, how did we do?"

The inspector didn't answer immediately. He transferred several images and notes from his tablet to his phone, then scrolled with his thumb. He glanced up at her, then back down. "Can we sit?" he said, gesturing to the small round table near the window.

She pulled out a chair for him, then sat across, her knees suddenly unsteady.

He began, "Ms. Cuellar, I'll be straight with you. I've seen worse." His voice was oddly gentle, as if prepping her for hospice. "But the kitchen is going to need serious upgrades before you can serve anything beyond cold breakfast. You'll need a vented commercial hood, upgraded suppression, and a full health code retrofit. Fifteen thousand, minimum."

Olivia tried to breathe, but it came out in a shallow hiss.

She nodded, pretending to jot notes on a napkin, though the pen didn't move.

"And the bathrooms—" He paused, thumb flicking the screen again. "ADA requires all public restrooms to be fully compliant. Stalls have to meet size specs, doors need to be widened, and the sink in the second-floor suite is about an inch too high. Your grab bars are fine, but the turning radius in the hallway? It's not enough. You're looking at another ten thousand to bring it all up to code."

It was like being punched twice in the chest. Olivia fought to keep her face neutral. "I thought—" she began, but the words turned to paste on her tongue. "I thought the bathrooms were fine. I used the state guidelines."

"State's less strict than county," he said, not unkindly. "You need to follow the local codes for all public accommodations. They changed last year after the lawsuit in San Saba County. I can send you the relevant sections."

Oh, that's fine. As if I need something more depressing to read. Perhaps at night when she lay wide awake, mentally calculating her losses before giving up and reaching for her phone to do the actual calculations on her calculator app. "Thank you," she said, because it was all she could say.

The inspector finished his coffee in a single swallow. "I'll give you thirty days to submit a work plan. You can operate in the meantime, but if there's a complaint or a surprise inspection, the penalties can be severe." He stood, snapped his tablet into a holster at his belt. "If you have any questions, my cell's on the card. I recommend Brown & Sons for the hood—they do good work and don't gouge."

Houston levels of "gouge," or Madison levels? Still, she stared at him in mute resignation, unwilling to let a syllable pass her dessicated lips.

He left by the same back door, leaving the kitchen colder and smaller than before.

Olivia waited for his car to turn out of the drive before she sat again, this time letting her head drop into her hands. The numbers battered her consciousness: fifteen thousand for the kitchen, ten for the bathrooms, plus whatever horrors the knob-and-tube would unleash when she finally hired an electrician. Alex's loan had given her breathing room, but she'd already earmarked it for roof repairs and a marketing blitz to salvage the summer season. There was nothing left for emergencies, and this wasn't an emergency—it was an extinction-level event.

Her phone buzzed in her pocket. A calendar alert: "Lunch with Elena - 12:30." If she canceled, she wouldn't be long for this world. Despite an angelic appearance, Elena was vicious when thwarted.

She lingered in the kitchen until the shadows lengthened. From the window, she could see the courthouse square, now a slurry of mud and plastic fencing. The mockery of order, she thought, like pretending your house was still a home when the roof had blown away.

She made herself a cup of tea, watched the bag bleed color into the water, and wondered how many days she could stay afloat. She had always been good at tomorrow, but this was the first time she doubted it would ever come.

The phone started its rampage just after three. Olivia was halfway through an email to Brown & Sons, subject line "Urgent: Range Hood Estimate," when the first ring sounded in the reception area, sharp as a smoke alarm. She silenced the computer and hurried down the hall, heart already stuttering with the premonition that nothing good ever came in the middle of the afternoon.

"Limestone Inn, this is Olivia," she said, pushing brightness into her voice.

A woman's voice, flat and nasal, came on immediately. "Hi. I need to cancel my reservation for next Thursday. My husband has a sensitivity—" she paused, searching for the right word, "to noise. I didn't realize there would be a jackhammer going every morning at seven. We'll find somewhere else, thanks."

Olivia started to say something, to promise it would be better next week, but the line had already gone dead. She scribbled a note on the reservation sheet: "CXL 3:03 pm. Reason: Construction." One cancellation. Probably not the last.

She'd barely made it back to the office before the phone rang again. This time, it was a man, his tone too friendly, the way customers sometimes were when they intended to escalate. "Olivia, hi! We're the Hausers, supposed to check in Saturday for the writers' workshop? Anyway, we're really sorry, but we've decided not to risk the drive from Austin. The last group said the street was impassable and there was, um, dust everywhere. Is that... how it's going to be?"

Olivia hesitated, tempted to fudge, then said, "They're promising to have the primary access open by the weekend. The crews usually wrap up by late afternoon, and I can—"

"Ah, okay, I get it," he said, voice already receding. "It's just, my wife has allergies and the last time— Anyway, if it's really a hassle, you can just put us down for a refund. Thanks so much, and let us know if it gets better!"

He hung up, and Olivia logged the second cancellation. Her hand trembled as she pressed the receiver back into its cradle.

The third blow came via email, just before four: "Regret to inform you that our family must change our travel plans. So sorry! Will leave a good review anyway—your staff was lovely." No signature, just a Gmail address and the pale blue misery of a reservation block blinking itself out of existence in the booking software.

Olivia stared at the screen, watching the calendar go from patchwork to nearly blank. The cancellations had started slowly—one every couple of days, easy enough to backfill with last-minute travelers or the odd overbooked wedding party. But today, three in a single span, and not a single new booking to offset them. She checked the forecast for next week—rain, possibly thunderstorms—which meant the construction would drag on, maybe worsen, the mud turning everything outside into a pit.

She thought about Alex's loan, the interest payments, the way the numbers on her spreadsheet didn't seem to listen to optimism or pep talks. She thought about her grandmother's voice, the "no hay mal que por bien no venga" that usually buoyed her through bad luck. This time, the saying tasted like chalk.

Her cell buzzed on the desk, a text from Elena: "Dinner at Mom's? She's making caldo." Olivia sighed, knowing she wouldn't be able to hide anything from Elena. Or Marta.

Outside, the street was empty except for a single worker in a high-visibility vest, shoveling loose gravel into the yawning mouth of a curb cut. Olivia watched him work, steady and slow, filling a hole that looked a little bigger every time she checked. She imagined herself at the bottom, waving up at the surface, waiting for someone to notice she was missing.

The landline rang again. This time, she let it go to voicemail.

❧

By nine, the inn was as quiet as a tomb. Olivia padded barefoot through the parlor, the guest rooms, the back staircase, switching off lights as she went. The silence felt medicinal at first, a balm after a day spent getting battered by voices and verdicts. But as she made her way to the office, it pressed in on her, the way the Texas heat pressed against windows after sundown: thick, persistent, impossible to ignore.

She sat at the antique desk—a solid, roll-top behemoth inherited from her father—and opened the battered MacBook that had survived the last months in Houston. The spreadsheet glared at her: one column for expected revenue, one for expenses, one for "Unforeseen Catastrophes," which she'd started as a joke but now filled with alarming precision. She scrolled to the bottom, where a single cell blinked red: "Loan Payment #1, due in 60 days: $800."

She stared at the number until it blurred, then scrolled back up to the calendar, where she'd circled the same figure in a trembling hand. $800. She'd run the numbers a hundred times; with full occupancy and two catered events, she could cover it with room to spare. With half bookings, she'd need to raid the maintenance fund and hope the roof didn't cave in. With zero bookings—like the current forecast—she'd be three months from foreclosure, and maybe thirty days from the first shame spiral.

She traced the payment date with her finger, remembering the way Alex Stirling had slid the paperwork across the glass table in his office. His generosity, his belief in her—it had felt like oxygen at the time. Now, it pressed against her ribs. She couldn't call him for help; she couldn't ask for a second favor. The contract was clear, and so was the subtext: "You're the best shot we've got, Olivia. Don't make me regret it." Two failures from Houston trying to make amends in Madison. But where Alex had an out and a wife who could pull him from the brink if he failed again, Olivia had no one. There were barely any Cuellars still living in Madison who she could turn to.

The words echoed the same way Muriel's had, the day she

admitted to draining their Houston partnership dry. "I needed the money, Liv. I thought you'd figure it out." The betrayal had hollowed her out, left her suspicious of every promise, every handshake. Alex was no Muriel, but the lesson stuck: trust, but always have an escape route.

A warning ping: new email. She opened it. Another cancellation, this one polite but curt. "We wish you the best in your renovations, but at this time we must withdraw our reservation. Good luck!"

Olivia laughed, a brittle sound, and moved the message to a folder labeled "Missed Connections." She considered pouring herself a drink, but the thought of waking up dull-headed and unprepared was too much to risk. Instead, she pulled up the file with the original business plan, scanning through the color-coded tabs. She'd built the model herself, every assumption backed by market research and survey data, every cell filled with the kind of hope only the desperate could muster.

She adjusted the variables: dropped occupancy to 20%, tripled the cost of emergency repairs, erased the "Events" income altogether. The red on the screen metastasized. She toggled back and forth, watching the numbers worsen with every click, until the future she'd spent years building was reduced to three months of runway, a line graph angling downward toward zero.

She closed her eyes and tried to summon her grandmother's voice, the one that had pushed her through midterms and heartbreak and the aftermath of Muriel's betrayal. "No hay mal que por bien no venga." Every disaster brings a blessing. But what was the blessing in this? A clean slate? Another lesson in humiliation?

She set her jaw. No. Not this time. Even if she failed, it wouldn't be for lack of fight.

Olivia opened the "Unforeseen Catastrophes" tab and, in

the margin, typed: "Find a way." Then she saved the document, closed the laptop, and let the office fall into darkness.

Tomorrow she would start again. For now, she let herself sit in the quiet, heartbeat steady, waiting for the first crack of morning to edge the world back into possibility.

Chapter Three

Determined to face this latest thorn in her side, Olivia arrived at the county annex ten minutes early, circling the gravel lot twice before committing to a parking space by the drainage ditch. Her Mazda's tires crunched over the loose stones, the sound obscenely loud in the stillness. The courthouse itself loomed across the square, domed and besieged, but it was the spartan concrete block of the Verde County Services Building where the meeting would play out. A battered traffic cone propped the front door, as if to say that even official business here was subject to the laws of erosion and neglect.

She killed the engine and sat for a minute, gathering herself. Her hands shook on the steering wheel, a faint tremor that reminded her of the first time she'd been summoned to the principal's office in elementary school. Olivia had no real reason to be nervous, as Judge Williams assured her that the unanimous vote had appointed her to the Courthouse Renovation Committee, but she couldn't shake the sense that her presence was temporary, conditional, a test of how well she could walk the line between local and outsider.

The entryway smelled of lemon disinfectant and scorched coffee. She signed her name on the clipboard at the security desk, then trailed down a corridor lined with faded campaign posters and community resource bulletins. A fluorescent hum set her teeth on edge. At the end of the hall, the meeting room: a windowless box, brown carpet patterned in a geometric motif that hadn't been in style since Ann Richard's days as governor. Someone had set out folding chairs in rows, but most of the attendees clustered near the folding tables at the front, elbow to elbow over stacks of binders and bottled water.

Olivia recognized most of the faces—some from childhood, others from more recent Chamber of Commerce breakfasts, or from their frequent appearances in the opinion section of the Madison Weekly. There was a pecking order to these things, and Olivia, despite her birthright, knew she'd landed somewhere below the salt.

Teresa Alvarez was already at the front, her blue dress suit a shade too electric for the gray walls, her hair coiled tight as a whip. Olivia nodded as she entered, got a once-over in return, and then a smile—thin, precise, barely stretching the corners of her mouth.

"Ms. Cuellar," Teresa said, emphasizing the surname in a way that was both greeting and warning. "I wondered if you'd make it. Traffic from the square is a mess."

"Managed to slip around it," Olivia said, matching the smile but keeping her teeth hidden. "I'm early, right?"

"Always a good impression." Teresa flicked a glance toward the knot of men at the table, her voice dropping. "Some people seem to think that's enough."

Olivia ignored the dig, moved to the edge of the room, and found herself an empty chair. She busied herself with the handout packet—pages and pages of site plans, grant applications, and agendas. At the top, her own name, spelled correctly for once. She wondered whether Teresa had taken the time to proofread it personally.

As the room filled, the noise level rose: scraping chairs, the slap of manila folders, the low murmur of small-town gossip disguised as networking. David from the hardware store greeted her with a lifted eyebrow, then sat next to an older man in a bolo tie who looked like he'd spent his whole life waiting for a government job to retire from. Near the coffee urn, two women in matching "Friends of the Library" fleeces whispered over a box of donuts.

Judge Williams entered precisely at six, the room settling like a snow globe set on a shelf. The judge wore her habitual uniform—dark slacks, a pale silk blouse, and a string of freshwater pearls—but tonight she twisted her hair up, which added an inch to her height and an air of implacability to her profile.

She opened the meeting with brisk efficiency. "Let's call the roll," she said, and did so without looking at the paper in front of her. Olivia's name came third, after Teresa and the city manager. When she answered, Judge Williams offered a brief, approving nod.

"First order of business: introduction of our new committee member, Ms. Olivia Cuellar, owner and operator of the Limestone Inn."

There was a polite round of applause, but Olivia caught the fractional delay in Teresa's clapping, as if she were waiting to see how hard everyone else would commit before joining in.

"Welcome, Olivia," said a man from the far end of the table—a retired plumber who had been on every town committee since the Eisenhower administration. "You must be proud to carry on your family's tradition."

"She's not exactly a legacy, is she?" Teresa interjected, her voice pitched low enough for the entire room to hear but soft enough to feign innocence. "Didn't you spend a decade in Houston, dear?"

Olivia met her gaze, kept her own voice level. "Fourteen years. But Madison's always been home. My abuela ran a boarding house off Travis Street for forty years."

"That's right." The plumber leaned forward, eager to reassert control. "I remember your grandmother. Strong lady. Ran a tight ship, I'll tell you that."

Teresa gave an affected little sigh, as if the committee's standards were sliding by the minute. She turned to the judge. "I just hope that—given the sensitive nature of the courthouse's history—everyone at this table is prepared to put Madison first. It's easy to be dazzled by newcomers and fresh perspectives, but tradition matters."

Judge Williams let the silence stretch a fraction too long before responding. "That's why Olivia's here. We want all stakeholders represented—business, heritage, and the future. I expect everyone to give her the same respect you'd give any committee member."

There was a ripple of assent, but Olivia could sense the outlines of a battle already drawn: the Old Guard, wary of outside interference, and the scattered cohort of progressives and pragmatists, eager to prove that tradition and change didn't have to be enemies.

The meeting slogged through the first hour—updates from the construction crew, a review of where they stood in with the Texas Historical Commission in the courthouse renovation program, a discussion about whether to keep the current landscaping or rip out the rose bushes in favor of native grasses. Olivia kept her input measured, nodding when asked, scribbling notes when not. She resisted the urge to check her phone, even when it buzzed twice in her pocket with texts from Elena.

It was during the budget review Teresa struck again.

"I'm just saying," she said, "that if we're going to approve another forty thousand for the design firm, we should have more than a three-page summary of their progress. Some of us aren't accustomed to signing off on things sight unseen."

The city manager shifted in his chair. "They submitted the full report last week. They also emailed it to everyone on Friday.

Teresa's eyes flicked to Olivia. "Well, maybe some of us aren't as glued to their screens as the younger generation. But I'd like to see hard copies. It's too easy for things to get lost in translation."

Olivia felt the eyes on her, the implication that she was the root of digital decay in Madison's civic process. "I printed mine out," she offered, sliding the stapled sheets across the table to Teresa.

The older woman hesitated, then took them with a tight-lipped "thank you." The message was clear: civility could be weaponized, and the only thing more dangerous than a direct insult was a polite one.

The rest of the meeting passed in a blur of bureaucratic jargon. Olivia stopped taking notes and started counting the number of times Teresa undermined her with a single well-placed "dear" or "young lady" by the end.

People filtered out in clusters, stopping for postmortems in the hallway. Teresa gathered her things with deliberate slowness to force Olivia into a private audience.

"Ms. Cuellar," she said, turning with the full force of her attention. "A word, if you have a moment?"

Olivia braced herself. "Of course."

Teresa stepped in close, lowering her voice to a confidential murmur. "You seem like a bright woman, Olivia. But Madison is not Houston. People here have long memories. I hope you understand that your appointment isn't... universally popular. There are some who think you got the seat because of your connection to the trust, not your qualifications."

Olivia blinked. "I don't have any connection to the trust. I applied for funding like anyone else. The committee voted—"

Teresa held up a hand. "Perception is everything. I'm just saying, if you want to be effective here, you should be careful whose side you're seen on. This isn't the city. Out here, allegiances last generations."

Olivia could have argued. She could have pointed out that it was Teresa's own sister who'd lost the committee vote, or that her "objectivity" was as transparent as the lemon-scented glass doors. But she said only, "Thank you for the advice."

Teresa's smile returned, sharper now. "I'm sure you'll do fine. Just... don't expect a honeymoon."

She swept out of the room, leaving Olivia to gather her papers in the sudden silence. The air felt thin, denuded of oxygen by the effort of keeping herself composed.

On her way out, Olivia stopped in the lobby, hands braced on the metal rail of the staircase. She took a moment to breathe, to listen to the after-hours echo of county business winding down. The judge passed by, pausing on the landing above.

"You did well in there," Williams said. "Don't let Teresa rattle you. She means well, in her way."

Olivia smiled, not trusting herself to speak.

"It'll get easier," the judge promised.

Olivia nodded. She wasn't sure she believed it. But as she stepped out into the dark, she realized she hadn't checked her phone all night, and the tremor in her hands was finally gone.

THE FOLLOWING THURSDAY, Olivia found herself back in the same conference room, its recirculated air and fluorescent lighting now familiar enough to induce a kind of low-level nausea. The agenda this time was meatier: introduction of the preservation architect, review of the master plan proposal, and a public Q&A that promised to devolve into a complaint session if experience was any guide.

The room was half full when she entered, most of the faces unchanged from last week. Judge Williams presided at the head of the table, reviewing notes with the single-minded focus of someone determined to outlast her opposition by sheer force of will. Teresa Alvarez sat two seats over, her lips pursed as she worked a Sudoku in the margin of the printed agenda. Even the "Friends of the Library" contingent had claimed their patch of chairs and were already deep in whispered consultation over the snack schedule for next month's book sale.

At 6:05 sharp, the judge tapped her pen against a water glass. "Let's bring this to order," she announced, voice cutting cleanly through the din. "Tonight, we have the pleasure of meeting our lead preservation architect, Mr. Andrew Kim."

There was the usual rustle as people straightened in their seats, some out of habit, others in a perfunctory show of respect. Then Andrew stood. He wore a pair of wire-rimmed glasses that seemed determined to slide down his nose at every opportunity. His shirt was a deep blue, the sleeves rolled to the elbows, revealing forearms corded from actual labor. He carried a leather messenger bag that looked as if it might double as a survival kit. He smiled, polite but not warm, and advanced to the front of the room.

"Thank you, Judge Williams," he said. "Good evening. My name is Andrew Kim. I'm a third-generation Texan and the preservation specialist for Crain, Rutherford & Associates out of Dallas. We've consulted on historic courthouses in over a dozen counties, but I have to say, the Verde County Courthouse is a jewel. The stonework alone is world class."

He spoke in quick, clipped bursts, every sentence trimmed of excess. Olivia recognized the cadence—she'd met enough engineers and restoration folks in her father's orbit to know that efficiency was a religion with these types.

Andrew opened his laptop and projected a series of images onto the wall: detailed scans of the courthouse facade, cross-sections of foundation cracks, thermal renderings that revealed where the old insulation had all but evaporated.

"As you can see, the structure's original bones are intact, but there's severe mortar loss throughout the south wall. That's priority one. We'll need to stabilize before any cosmetic work. Inside, we've mapped all the original finishes and identified which were covered up by later renovations. The goal is to bring the public areas back to the 1910 layout, while making sure we hit all the ADA and life safety requirements of modern code. It's doable, but there will be tradeoffs."

He advanced to the next slide—a Gantt chart so dense with overlapping color bars it looked like a game of Tetris gone to hell.

"The timeline is aggressive," he continued. "Phase One, stabilization and envelope, six to eight months. Phase Two, interior restoration, another ten months. We could finish in under two years if the weather holds and the contractors cooperate. But, and this is crucial—downtown will be affected. There's no way to sugarcoat it. We'll have scaffolding and lane closures, and access to some businesses will be rerouted for weeks at a time."

At this, a groan rippled through the room. Someone in the back muttered, "Figures," and another voice—possibly David from the hardware store—said, "Guess there goes my foot traffic."

Andrew paused, hands folded over the top of his laptop. "We're working with the city to minimize disruption, but preservation is messy. If you want it done right, there's no shortcut. I'll take questions now."

A silence, heavy and expectant. Teresa was the first to speak.

"You mentioned you're from Dallas," she said, chin raised slightly. "Are you in any way affiliated with Mr. Stirling's operation? The trust, or any of his, ah, investments in Madison?"

Andrew blinked, nonplussed. "No, ma'am. Stirling Group is based in Houston, not Dallas." He failed to hide a smile at his amusement at her inability to distinguish between the two metropolitan behemoths that dominated the state. For a Dallisite or a Houstonian, it counted as a cardinal sin, one that Olivia bit the inside of her cheek to keep from laughing at. "Our contract is with the County and funded by the Texas Historical Commission. Mr. Stirling's interests are outside our scope."

"That's not what I heard," Teresa pressed, arms crossing with the finality of a courtroom verdict. "His name is on every other project in town. Seems like a conflict."

Andrew shrugged, a gesture so minimal it was almost an exhale. "If the County wants to review our disclosures, I'm happy to provide documentation. My job is to preserve your courthouse, not broker real estate deals."

That got a round of snickers from the library ladies and a grudging nod from the plumber.

Olivia watched the exchange with a kind of fascinated dread. She could see the argument forming on Teresa's face—the urge to pick apart every detail, to push for the weak spot in the armor. Andrew, for his part, was unruffled, answering each question with the calm assurance of someone who knew that, ultimately, stone and mortar didn't care about local politics.

She raised a hand.

Andrew turned to her, waiting. "Ms. Cuellar?"

Olivia hesitated a beat, feeling the weight of every eye.

"Can you be more specific about the 'affected' access to downtown? How long, realistically, will my guests be climbing over trenches and dodging caution tape?"

Andrew gave a tiny, appreciative nod. "Fair question. Once stabilization begins, the main entry will be closed for two months. You can access the location through the east side, but they will periodically close it while we reconfigure the scaffolding. We're working with the city to install temporary walkways, but yes, there will be days when it's an obstacle course."

Olivia grimaced. "That's going to kill my spring season."

He didn't sugarcoat it. "I'm sorry. If there were a way around it, I'd say so."

Judge Williams interjected. "Is there any leeway on the start date? Can we push construction until after the peak tourist months?"

Andrew checked his notes. "We can shift by a month or two, but if we wait past May, the temperature spikes and we risk mortar curing issues. Delays get expensive fast. The grant from the state is contingent on keeping the schedule."

More muttering, this time less hostile and more resigned.

Andrew ran through the remaining slides: cost projections, contractor bids, the color palette options for the restoration. A barrage of technical jargon accompanied each point, but he distilled every answer down to its plainest form.

By the end of the presentation, Olivia felt both better and worse—impressed by Andrew's competence, but sobered by the magnitude of what lay ahead. The committee, meanwhile, had split down visible lines: the progressives and restoration fans applauding the detail and ambition, the skeptics retreating into their chairs, already rehearsing how they'd explain this to their friends at the breakfast table.

After the last question, the judge called a five-minute recess. Andrew packed his laptop with methodical care, then made his way to the back of the room, where Olivia was refilling her cup from the coffee urn.

"Ms. Cuellar," he said, voice low. "If you want, I can review your business's access points and make recommendations. Sometimes it helps to have an advocate on the inside."

Olivia blinked, startled by the offer. "Thank you," she said, uncertain if it was genuine or just good optics. "I might take you up on that."

He nodded once, then moved on, pausing only to answer another volley of questions from a city councilman who wanted assurances about ADA compliance.

Olivia sipped her coffee, bitter and burnt, and let the realization sink in: whatever she'd thought this committee would be, it was now her life for the next two years.

As the group reconvened, she caught Teresa's eye. The older woman gave her that same, unreadable smile—the one that said, I warned you. Welcome to the front lines.

❧

The next morning, Olivia sought refuge in the Special Collections department of the Madison Public Library, one of the last places in town where the air was reliably cool and the only sound was the whisper of turning pages. She also had special access, since Elena was the archivist who guarded the priceless documents like a dragon defending a horde of golden coins. The reading room occupied the building's original footprint—a soaring neoclassical shell, with wainscoting so dark and glossy it looked perpetually damp. Olivia remembered it from childhood as a place of near-religious hush, where the town's elders convened over ancient newspapers and teenage volunteers dared each other to sneak past the reference desk.

Today, only the two inhabited the space. At a far corner table, Elena hunched over a stack of archival folders and muttered at her laptop screen. Olivia hovered in the doorway, let her pulse slow, then navigated between the study carrels.

Elena glanced at her and lifted a hand, fingers smudged with graphite. "You look like hell," she said, sotto voce.

"That's because I spent the night with Teresa Alvarez's voice in my ear," Olivia replied. "I may need to borrow your noise-cancelling headphones for the next meeting."

Elena snorted, then motioned for her to sit. She wore her hair pulled back in a loose braid, streaks of silver visible even in the dim library light. Her round glasses magnified the bags under her eyes, but her smile, when it came, was genuine. "So, how was the firing squad?"

"Efficient. Teresa kept her claws retracted mostly, but she's definitely on a mission. The new architect—Andrew Kim—presented the master plan. He's good, but... it's going to be a mess. They're talking six months of downtown under wraps."

Elena grimaced. "Gretchen's going to lose her mind. She walks to the bakery every day after school. Are you ready for months of complaints about the detour?"

"I'm bracing myself," Olivia said, then leaned forward, voice lowering. "Honestly? I don't know if the business will survive that long. The last round of cancellations nearly killed my operating budget. If they shut down the square, I'm toast."

Elena reached over, squeezed her hand. "You'll find a way. You always do."

"Maybe," Olivia said, not believing it. "I just wish the rest of the town wanted this as much as the committee does. Half the people at the meeting acted like we were selling off the courthouse brick by brick."

"That's because they don't see the inside," Elena said, nodding toward the folder labeled "Verde County Court: 1901-1960." "They see the dome, the clock, the lawns for homecoming. They don't care about the wiring, or the plumbing, or the asbestos tiles in the basement. Out of sight, out of mind."

A laugh echoed from the story time area. Elena shot a dirty look their way while Olivia let her gaze drift to the mural on the far wall—bluebonnets and cowboys, painted in the earnest primary colors of a grant-funded project from the 80s. "Do you ever wish you could just freeze the town the way it was?"

Elena shook her head. "No. But I wish we could have a say in how it changes. That's what bugs me. They talk about community input, but really it's just people with money and out-of-town firms making the calls. Like Stirling. He's not even from here, but he's shaping the whole place to fit his ideas."

"Speaking of," Olivia said, "I heard Teresa try to connect the new architect to Stirling, just because they're both from out of town. You'd think he was some kind of Bond villain."

Elena's eyes narrowed. "That's not far off."

Olivia raised a brow. "Is there something I should know?" Elena and Caleb had successfully fought off Stirling in his attempted takeover of Madison's historic German Quarter, but bad blood remained amongst them. Elena kept her eyes and ears open for any future hints of impropriety from Stirling.

"I did some digging," Elena said, dropping her voice further. "Stirling's trust is technically hands off on the courthouse, but he's been lobbying the city council about what happens with the square once the renovation is done. There's talk about converting the old jail into an 'event center'—read: wedding factory. And guess who already bought the lots on either side?"

Olivia sat back, exhaling. "Let me guess. Not the Kiwanis."

"You got it."

The front door rattled open, and Caleb Bauer entered in full chef regalia—apron still dusted with flour, cap askew, face shining with the heat of the bakery kitchen. He crossed to their table and dropped into a seat, fanning himself theatrically.

"Ladies," he said, voice pitched just above a whisper, "I have two minutes before I have to check the second proof. Gretchen says hi, and also, she wants to know if you're going to the Fall Festival."

Olivia smiled. "Tell her I wouldn't miss it."

Caleb grinned, then focused on Elena. "Did you tell her about Stirling's latest conquest?"

"She already knows," Elena said, rolling her eyes. "He's taking over the courthouse next."

"Of course he is," Caleb said, and for a moment the three of them sat in a bubble of shared exasperation, no further explanation required.

Olivia reached for her bag, pulled out the committee handouts, and slid them to Elena. "Here's the full master plan. Maybe you can make sense of the bureaucratese."

Elena flipped through the pages, nodding. "I'll read it tonight. Gretchen is at a sleepover, so I can have an uninterrupted date with local government."

Caleb glanced at his watch, then pushed away from the table. "Duty calls. Don't let them bulldoze the library before I get back, yeah?" He gave Elena a peck on the cheek and left, waving to the toddler on the rug as he went.

Elena watched him go, absentmindedly twirling her engagement ring, then looked back at Olivia, her expression softening. "Are you okay?"

Olivia hesitated. "I don't know. I thought being on the committee would mean I could actually do something, make a difference. But it feels like I'm just a seat warmer. The actual decisions are happening somewhere else."

"They always do," Elena said, tapping the folder. "But it

matters that you're there. Even if you're the only one asking questions."

Olivia smiled, the tension in her shoulders easing just a little. "Thanks."

They sat in companionable silence for a while, the low hum of the library restoring some measure of calm. When Olivia finally stood to leave, she felt steadier, if not exactly optimistic. The world outside was still a battlefield, but here, at least, she could breathe.

She paused at the exit, glancing back to see Elena already deep in the master plan, pencil in hand, lips moving as she read. For a second, Olivia saw not just her friend, but the thread of connection that ran through every room in the town —the shared history, the grudges and jokes and stubborn loyalty.

She pushed open the door and stepped into the morning light, ready to face the next round.

❧

That Saturday, the town assembled for the first of many planned "Community Conversation" forums. The high school auditorium hosted the event—a relic from the WPA era, with wooden seats that squeaked if you so much as shifted your weight, and a lingering odor of varnish and gym socks. Olivia arrived early, hoping for a good seat near the back, only to discover the place already half full. The social infrastructure of Madison was on full display: church deacons in the first two rows, the Lions and Kiwanis packed in clumps along the aisles, and a smattering of high schoolers orbiting the donut table like shy comets.

Beneath the faded velvet curtains on the stage sat a podium, with two massive poster boards flanking it, displaying renderings of the "Restored Courthouse: Vision 21st Century."

Olivia scanned the crowd, noting a familiar line of division: at the far left, the "change is good" contingent—mostly newcomers, young families, business owners like herself. On the right, a wall of folded arms and cowboy hats, many belonging to the same men and women who had voted down the last school bond in a landslide. She spotted Elena and Gretchen midway up the aisle, waving her over with discreet urgency.

"You made it," Elena whispered as Olivia squeezed into the seat beside her. "We were taking bets on whether you'd get cold feet."

"I'm here for the spectacle," Olivia said. "How long before someone brings up the Texas Historical Commission's 'agenda'?"

Gretchen, who had become tall and willowy overnight, snorted. "My bet is five minutes after Judge Williams starts talking."

On cue, the house lights dimmed, and the county judge stepped up to the microphone. She radiated command in a tailored navy suit, hair pulled back so tight it gleamed. For the first few minutes, her remarks were pure boosterism—the courthouse as "the center of Verde County life," the importance of preserving heritage for future generations, the "tough but necessary choices" ahead. Olivia recognized the phrases, having helped ghostwrite a few for the committee's press release.

As the speech rolled on, the mood in the room shifted. When Williams referenced "the generous grant from The Texas Historical Commission and private matching funds from local business partners," a ripple of murmuring ran through the right side of the auditorium.

"We all know what 'matching funds' means," a man

behind Olivia muttered to his neighbor. "Means my property tax goes up, same as always."

There was applause from the left and scattered clapping from the center, but the right flank remained unmoved. Olivia saw the familiar faces: Teresa Alvarez, stone-faced and alert, and several of the old-timers from the breakfast circuit, some whispering behind their hands, others simply glowering.

The floor opened to public comment, and immediately a man in a denim jacket seized the microphone. "I don't care what Austin says," he declared. "They're not going to tell us how to fix our own buildings. Every time the state gets involved, it costs three times what it should. Why not hire locally? We built it in the first place, didn't we?"

Scattered shouts of "Yeah!" and "That's right!" from the wings. Judge Williams let him have his moment, then thanked him for his "perspective" and called up the next speaker.

A woman in a cardigan spoke of her pride in Madison's history, but worried about "revisionist elements" erasing the parts some found inconvenient. Another man, voice trembling, asked if the money wouldn't be better spent on "something for the living, not the dead."

Olivia felt the words as a tightening in her throat. She wanted to stand up and argue—explain the necessity, the risk of letting the building collapse, the way heritage could actually make the future possible instead of suffocating it. But she didn't. She just sat and listened, absorbing the current of unease that ran below every speech.

After an hour, the judge wrapped things up. "We're listening," she said. "We'll take your concerns to heart as we move forward. This is your courthouse as much as mine."

The lights came up, and the crowd immediately fractured into dozens of small, urgent conversations. Olivia lingered in her seat, unsure whether she felt hope or something like defeat.

Elena bumped her shoulder. "You want to get coffee?"

"Yeah," Olivia said, blinking back the heat in her eyes. "Yeah, I really do."

They stepped into the lobby, where old friends and new adversaries brushed past each other in uneasy truce. At the far end of the hall, a group of men, all wearing matching ballcaps, cornered Jude Willliams, all talking at once. She met Olivia's gaze over their heads and gave a quick, tired nod of acknowledgment.

"Did you hear the guy going about the 'revisionist history'?" Elena asked as they made their way out. "He sounded like your uncle after the family reunion tequila."

"I'm pretty sure he is my uncle," Olivia said. "Or at least a first cousin twice removed."

They laughed, and for a second the tension lifted.

Outside, the air was thick with the promise of rain. Olivia looked back at the auditorium, its pale bricks gleaming under the sodium lights, and wondered if she'd ever truly belong on either side of the divide. Maybe that was her job, she thought —to stand at the fault line, holding the edges together, even if it meant being pulled in two directions at once.

She squared her shoulders, took a deep breath, and followed Elena into the night.

Chapter Four

As she slid onto the last wooden pew at Our Lady of Guadalupe Church, Olivia realized the lingering incense stung her eyes more than she'd admit. The sanctuary held only a third of its capacity—just enough to amplify every cough, every sniffle, every scrape of a boot against tile. From her angle, she could see most of the congregation: ranch hands in plaid, old women in lace veils and orthopedic shoes, two high schoolers who alternated between checking their phones and exchanging daredevil glances. Every head in the nave seemed to know exactly who she was, and exactly what she'd come back for.

She'd grown up on these benches, learning first the discipline of stillness, then the art of invisibility. But in Madison, no one ever truly vanished, especially not the girl who ran off to Houston and came home with a business plan instead of a fiancé or a degree in nursing. The moment she'd entered the vestibule, an invisible string had tugged all the old ladies' gazes toward her, knitting their whisper-web tighter. Even the Jesus above the altar—gaunt, lacquered, perpetually bleeding—seemed to arch an eyebrow.

Mass unfolded in its usual pattern: ritual, refrain, the over-caffeinated pitch of Father Miguel's homily. He spoke about new beginnings, about embracing the stranger and forgiving the prodigal. Olivia wondered, not for the first time, if he wrote his sermons with one eye on the back pew and the other on her abuela's memorial plaque by the font. She tried to keep her attention forward, tried not to look at the cluster of grandmothers holding court just three rows ahead.

The service ended with a quick smattering of applause—this was still rural Texas, after all—followed by the slow roll of parishioners out into the humid morning. Olivia hung back, pretending to study the stained glass over the side altar. She recognized every blue-and-gold panel: St. Michael spearing the serpent, the Immaculate Conception, her favorite, St. Francis grinning at a retinue of birds. The saints always looked more at home here than she did.

She made it to the vestibule, hoping to slip out before anyone tested the depth of her piety, but Doña Carmen had already stationed herself by the wooden doors, a floral-scented sentinel with a mission. Carmen's hands were curled around the handle of her cane, knuckles bloodless, eyes sharp as a whittling knife. Olivia gave a small, polite smile, then immediately regretted the show of deference.

"Olivia Cuellar," the old woman intoned, as if reading from an indictment. "We have not seen you in a long time."

Olivia tried to hide the flinch. "Yes, ma'am. It's good to be home."

Carmen clucked her tongue, not unlike a hen chastising a chick for leaving the yard. "You left us. Now you want to come back and profit from our stories?"

It was so direct that for a second, Olivia wondered if she'd misheard. Then she caught the glance Carmen shot toward the row of holy water fonts, where two of her lieutenants stood with pursed lips and folded hands.

She forced a soft laugh. "I'm just reopening the B&B. It's what I've always wanted—"

The cane tapped once against the floor, the universal sign for cutting the crap. "Your abuela hosted people because she had no choice. She didn't make a show of it. Didn't go running to Austin or Houston for help."

Olivia felt her jaw tighten, the pulse in her neck picking up speed. "The building needed work. I had to get a loan."

Carmen's eyes narrowed. "From a stranger. From Alex Stirling. Another outsider buying up Madison."

The last word landed with an audible thud. Olivia tried to summon the PR answer she'd used with the Chamber of Commerce, the one about partnerships and preservation and keeping history alive, but here, under the cross-eyed scrutiny of the original Madison matriarch, it turned to chalk in her mouth.

The women at the holy water had stopped pretending not to listen. Olivia could feel their attention like a cold draft down her back. Carmen leaned in, her breath a blend of rose-water and coffee.

"You should know," she said, voice barely above a whisper, "that not everyone is so quick to forget. Or forgive."

She left the words hanging, then pivoted with surprising grace for someone pushing ninety, her cane clicking a syncopated exit across the flagstone. Olivia watched her shuffle off, unsure whether to follow, apologize, or melt into the floor.

She lingered by the font, dipping a finger in the cool water more out of habit than faith, and glanced around the emptying vestibule. She realized then—not as an epiphany, but as a bone-deep certainty—that she could build the most beautiful inn in the county, paper every wall with memories and artifacts, and still never be allowed all the way back in.

Outside, the sun had burned through the morning fog, casting the parking lot in hard light. Olivia blinked, steadying herself on the heavy wood of the door. Her hands felt oddly numb.

She imagined all the stories about homecoming: how people would welcome her back as a prodigal, or at least as a curiosity. She'd never pictured this—her motives interrogated, her ambition mistaken for greed, her entire past reduced to a single, selfish act.

The harshest part was knowing it wasn't untrue.

She walked to her car in silence, the voices of the parishioners trailing her like a second shadow. It was barely nine-thirty, and she already wanted to turn around, drive anywhere, be anyone else.

But the day was just starting, and so was she.

BY THE TIME Olivia reached the church steps, the first wave of parishioners had already colonized the courtyard and parking lot, their voices rolling in low, intersecting currents. The deacons and altar boys loitered by the statue of La Virgen, while families formed tight, migrating pods around tables laden with pan dulce and Styrofoam cups of Folger's. Above it all, the bell in the squat white tower marked time in grudging, metallic increments.

Olivia paused at the edge of the plaza, hesitating. She knew it would look weak to turn and leave so quickly, but she also knew the cost of standing out here, exposed. She lingered by a planter filled with marigolds, one hand pretending to check her phone, the other fidgeting with her car keys.

She didn't have to wait long. A pair of women in matching windbreakers drifted into her orbit, one of them giving her a quick, up-and-down scan before leaning toward her friend.

"It's her, right?" the first stage-whispered. "The one from the news."

The second nodded, lips pursed. "Houston scandal. They had to close the whole place down, I heard."

Olivia let the words pass over her, but they landed anyway—tiny darts, each finding the gap in her armor. She'd heard a thousand versions of her story since coming back, each more warped and simplified than the last. The reality was less sensational, but truth rarely survived more than a mile down Highway 90.

She shifted her gaze to the play structure, where a clutch of kids in sandals chased each other around the rubber mulch, their feet slap- clapping as they ran. Behind them, two old men—both veterans of the Friday-morning men's group, both in hats advertising wars they probably never fought—stood sentinel, arms crossed, eyes following Olivia's every move.

"That's Cuellar's granddaughter," one of them muttered, not even trying to lower his voice.

"She's the one who's fixing up the bed-and-breakfast," the other replied. "But you know she's not doing it for the town. She's got investors. Outsiders."

The first man snorted. "Her grandfather would roll over in his grave to see this."

There it was: the ultimate censure, reserved only for those who had truly disappointed the dead.

Olivia resisted the urge to walk faster. Every step felt like an audition, every smile a test of whether she could still pass as one of them. When a young mother with a stroller glanced her way, Olivia forced a greeting, hoping it would short-circuit the rumor mill. Instead, the woman's face closed up like a window slammed against a coming storm.

At the edge of the lot, she stopped, her car the only import in a sea of battered Chevys and Fords. She fumbled for the unlock button, suddenly conscious of how her every movement was both public and suspect.

A voice behind her: "Ms. Cuellar?" She turned to see the

parish council president, a man with a hairline as thin as his patience, approaching with a clipboard and the rictus smile of someone about to ask for a donation.

"Good to see you back," he said. "I hear you're working on the old Kendrick place."

Olivia nodded, trying to keep her tone light. "I'm trying. If the contractors ever finish tearing up the street."

He chuckled, too loud. "Well, folks around here miss the tradition. It's not the same, you know, with a stranger running things." He left the words hanging, a dare she couldn't take without confirming his every suspicion.

"I'll do my best," she said, then excused herself, claiming an urgent errand.

She slid into the driver's seat and let the door thunk shut. For a moment, she just sat, feeling the burn of every eye on her back. The keys dug into her palm. She remembered sitting here as a teenager, waiting for her father to finish a last-minute confession, dreaming about the day she'd leave this whole town behind.

Now she was back, and it felt like being sentenced to exile in her own life.

She closed her eyes, inhaled the chemical tang of air freshener and old upholstery, and wished, not for the first time, that she'd been born with thicker skin.

Or maybe no skin at all.

LAS COLINAS WAS ALREADY in full lunch swing by the time Olivia arrived, the door chimes barely audible over the overlapping conversations and the sizzle of onions on the flattop. The air was thick with cumin and fried masa, and somewhere in the kitchen Elena's mother, Marta Rodriguez, was belting out a corrido at maximum volume, as if daring the clatter of the dining room to drown her out.

Olivia made for the corner booth, the same one she'd haunted with Elena every Saturday in high school, back when the biggest scandal in her life was getting caught skipping catechism. She slid onto the cracked vinyl, letting the tabletop's old soda-ring scars anchor her to a version of herself that hadn't yet learned to flinch.

Within minutes, Elena materialized, hair still damp from a morning run, eyes red-rimmed but bright. She dropped into the seat across from Olivia, breathing hard like she'd just sprinted the distance from the library.

"You look like you've seen a ghost," Elena said.

"Just Doña Carmen," Olivia replied. "Close enough."

Elena snorted, flagging the server for coffee. "Let me guess: she threatened to organize a boycott? Or was it the 'you've shamed your ancestors' speech?"

"Both, with bonus points for reminding me I'm not a real Cuellar."

The coffee arrived, scalding and strong. Elena watched as Olivia tried, and failed, to open a packet of sugar without spilling half of it on the table.

"Want to talk about it?" Elena asked.

"I'd rather talk about anything else," Olivia said, though she wasn't sure that was true.

They sat in comfortable silence for a while, Elena sipping her coffee, Olivia counting the cracks in the Formica. The restaurant filled and emptied in waves, each table another microcosm of town politics: farmers in their feed store caps, insurance ladies in pastel cardigans, a trio of high school teachers hunched over the daily specials. Through it all, Marta circulated like a minor deity, dispensing both food and unsolicited advice with equal fervor.

When she finally reached their booth, she set down two

plates of enchiladas, a basket of chips, and a bowl of salsa so aggressive it doubled as a decongestant.

"You eat," Marta commanded, pointing her spatula at Olivia. "You look like a plucked chicken. Bad luck to do business on an empty stomach."

Olivia managed a weak smile. "Thank you."

Marta softened, just a little. She tapped Elena on the wrist, then leaned in. "Don't let those old biddies get to you. They'll forgive anything as long as you show up for the tamale fundraiser. Or the parish raffle."

Olivia tried to laugh, but it came out thin. "I'm not sure they want my money."

"They want everyone's money," Marta said. "And they want to see you sweat for it." She straightened, patted Olivia's hand with surprising gentleness. "You just work hard. They'll come around."

With that, she swept off, leaving the scent of chili and a faint trail of reassurance in her wake.

Elena waited until Marta was safely out of earshot, then dug into her food. "You know she's right. It's all about actions. They don't care about press releases or ribbon-cuttings. They want to see you up at dawn, rolling tortillas, mopping floors, bleeding for it."

Olivia picked at her enchiladas, appetite flattened by anxiety. "I don't know if I have it in me," she said. "It's not just the gossip. I keep thinking... what if I'm actually doing what they say I am? What if this is just Houston all over again? Failing, but slower."

Elena put her fork down, her expression shifting from teasing to serious. "That's not who you are."

"How do you know?" Olivia whispered. "Maybe I'm just better at pretending."

For a moment, neither of them spoke. Then Elena reached across the table, took Olivia's hand in both of hers.

"Because you could have stayed in Houston. You could have run from all of this. Instead, you came home, knowing exactly how hard it would be."

"That doesn't make me a hero. It might just make me stupid."

Elena grinned. "Welcome to Madison. Home of the gloriously stubborn."

A fresh wave of customers swept in, and Marta reappeared, seating a family with three shrieking toddlers in the booth behind them. She shot Olivia a quick thumbs-up, as if to say, See? Survive this, and you'll survive anything.

Olivia tried another bite, found it tasted less like ashes and more like memory. She watched Elena finish her plate, envied her the certainty with which she faced the world.

"I just wish I knew how to fix it," Olivia said.

"You can't fix people," Elena said. "You can only show them who you are, one day at a time."

The check came tucked under a napkin, along with a hand-scrawled note from Marta: "You make us proud, mijita. Even when you mess up."

Olivia folded the note, tucking it into her wallet. She realized that, for the first time all day, her hands weren't shaking.

They lingered for another hour, talking about everything but the inn. When Olivia finally stood to leave, she looked back and saw Marta watching her from the kitchen pass, arms folded, lips pursed in a smile that was equal parts hope and challenge.

Outside, the sun was high and bright, the air sweet with the promise of rain. For the first time in weeks, Olivia felt almost ready to step into the day, even if it meant doing so alone.

❧

AT DUSK, the courthouse square was an abandoned set piece—scaffolds thrown like the skeletons of tents after a dust bowl circus, chain-link fencing bowing in at the softest spots, a drape of caution tape fluttering yellow-black in the faintest breeze. Olivia parked a block away and walked the last stretch, past the statue of Madison's first county judge (the nose chipped off, as always, by some anonymous senior prank), past the portable toilets with their doors rattling on windless hinges.

She ducked under a sagging section of fence, boots sinking an inch into the churned-up clay, the color of blood after a hard rain. The silence was total except for the echo of her own steps and, from somewhere deep in the undercroft, the slow drip of water onto stone. The construction crew had left hours ago, their cigarette butts and lunch wrappers the only sign of recent life.

The half-built limestone wall ran the length of the north façade, mortared unevenly, as if the workers had lost faith halfway through and started laying each stone just to get it done. Olivia ran a gloved hand along the surface—so new it bit her skin with a thousand tiny grains—and imagined the patience it would take to sand each joint to perfection. The small specks of remaining limestone dust swam in the air, catching the light. She leaned in and inhaled the subtle acrid scent of the stones that she always swore she could smell despite her grandfather's assurances that she was imagining it. Above her, a length of rebar jutted out, already rusting, casting a crooked shadow that looked like a hand clawing at the evening sky.

She made her way toward the main entrance, stepping over broken cinder blocks and the coiled intestines of old wiring. The double doors had been removed, replaced by a sheet of plywood stamped with the lumberyard's brand and a warning: DO NOT ENTER—SITE UNSAFE. Olivia smiled at the irony, then slipped through the side, careful not to snag her jacket on the nail-heads sticking out at odd, predatory angles.

Inside, the rotunda was a gutted echo chamber. Someone had scrawled a smiley face in the dust on the floor. Above, plastic mesh netted off the dome, exposing its inner ribs, which splintered where last year's freak hailstorm nearly caved it in. Olivia tilted her head back and traced the light where it leaked through, forming a pale, uneven halo around the shell of the old county seal. Like every government seal in Texas, it was a version of the beveled star that came from Sam Houston's coat button. An homage to Sam in every iteration.

She circled the interior perimeter, her boots sounding hollow against the stripped boards. In the corner, an upside-down bucket, a pair of gloves forgotten beside it, and the shattered handle of a trowel. Olivia picked up the gloves, recognized the initials—G.G.—spray-painted across the back in white. Gonzales, the foreman. She wondered if he'd noticed she was always one day behind, always trailing the real work by just enough to feel like a trespasser.

Near the far wall, a collapsed archway marked the entry to the old clerk's office. Olivia crouched beside it, running her fingers over the cold, sharp edges where the stone had split. She plucked a fragment, pocketed it—habit from her days in salvage. She examined the rest of the collapse: twisted nails poking out of what had once been crown molding, a chunk of marble baseboard that still held the ghost of a hundred years' worth of scuff marks. If she closed her eyes, she could almost hear the stamp and shuffle of clerks on the other side, the faint arguments of lawyers from two generations ago.

She straightened, dusted off her jeans, and stared up at the remains of the staircase. The top half was gone, ripped out for code compliance, but the lower run held steady, as if daring anyone to trust it. Olivia put a foot on the first step, pressed down. Solid. She climbed halfway up, using the banister for balance, and peered into the rafters.

The water damage had turned the wood to sponge, splitting the main beam above her. She made a note to herself: reinforce here, replace the secondary bracing, don't trust any of the old anchor points. She pictured the trusses, the load calculations, the way everything would have to interlock perfectly or else fail all at once. The thought was both terrifying and—if she was honest—exhilarating.

She descended, careful, and pulled her notebook from her backpack. Hands already grimy, she snapped a pencil from behind her ear and sketched. Not the picture-perfect courthouse from the restoration grant; not the sepia version on the town letterhead. This one was truer: scaffolds still in place, scars visible, every joinery line circled and annotated with what it would cost to fix. She made lists in the margins—stone, grout, steel, man-hours, money she didn't have yet—and drew a rough outline of the courtroom window she wanted to rescue from the demo team.

As a girl, she sat beside her grandfather, her unsure fingers sketching out what she saw, while he simply indulged her as she completed what amounted to work in her childish estimation. The urge to sketch, to document, handed down from one generation to another in the dusty workroom.

A gust of wind whistled through the open arch, carrying with it the grit of lime and old insulation. Olivia squinted, brushing hair from her face, and tried to imagine what the finished building would feel like: not flawless, but lived-in; not a replica of the past, but a rebirth with every imperfection accounted for.

She closed the notebook, slid it back into her pack, and stood for a while in the middle of the shell. Light from the streetlamps outside slanted through the open walls, casting her shadow across the dust and rubble. She rolled her shoulders, feeling the weight of the day in every muscle.

This is what it would take, she thought. Sweat, sleeplessness, pain that settled in the bones. A willingness to keep working long after everyone else had gone home, or given up. She'd have to prove herself one beam at a time, not just to the town, but to the ghosts in the mortar and to the version of herself who still believed in starting over.

The last of the daylight vanished, leaving only the glow of her phone's lock screen and the moonlight through broken glass. Olivia headed for the exit, her path marked by footprints that would disappear by morning, erased by the next storm or the next round of heavy boots.

She squared her shoulders and walked into the night.

Chapter Five

By sunrise, the street out front of the inn looked like it had survived a slow-motion tornado. Olivia braked to a crawl, squinting through the murk of overnight dust that still drifted in suspension. It wasn't the usual parade of orange cones or a fresh excavation that caught her eye, but a wall of what looked, for a half-blind second, like a primitive barricade—three chest-high heaps of red, ancient-looking brick stacked along the walk in no discernible order, with stray bricks scattered in the grass like landmines. She coasted past, glancing for a second at the courthouse square, which was empty save for a single, slumped over city worker asleep behind the wheel of a loader. As she rolled up to the curb, her hands reflexively tightened around the wheel, like she might throttle the dashboard into giving her an explanation.

The Mazda's door stuck on the first try, then gave way with a rubbery pop. The air was already thick with the metallic tang of earth and something older, a burnt-iron scent that had no business in a century-old B&B. Olivia stepped around the first mound of brick and crouched to inspect it. Each one was the color of dried blood, stamped on the face with "THURBER" in block capitals so deep you could lose a dime in the groove. Even with the mortar still crusted to their backs, the bricks radiated a grave sense of purpose—a kind of sullen dignity that made it clear these weren't the generic pavers you could buy at Lowe's by the pallet.

She let out a slow whistle and brushed the grit from her fingers. There was no note, no explanatory sign, no evidence anyone had even considered how these would look to guests trundling their roller bags to her front door. The only clue was a laminated placard zip-tied to the newel post of the porch, the kind reserved for city notices and tree-removal warnings. Olivia ripped it loose and read:

"NOTICE: HISTORIC STREET PAVERS—TO BE SALVAGED AND REPURPOSED PER COUNTY RESTORATION GUIDELINES. TEMPORARY STORAGE. DO NOT DISTURB."

"Bullshit," she muttered, then looked up and down the block to see if the prank had an audience.

There was no one. Even the morning dog walkers had retreated to safer neighborhoods, leaving her alone with three tons of misplaced history.

She shouldered her bag and sidestepped the disaster, but the bricks didn't leave her alone. By the time she reached the porch, her shoes were rimmed with brick dust, which left a rusty trail on the white wood steps all the way into the foyer.

Inside, the inn was the opposite of outside: chilly, still, and, for now, perfectly under her control. She made it three steps toward the reception desk before the phone started ringing.

The first call was from David at the hardware store, who never bothered with hello.

"Are you the one who's got the Thurber bricks on the lawn?"

Olivia pulled the receiver to her ear, tucking the spiral cord under her chin. “It wasn’t my idea. I found them piled on my front lawn this morning.”

A pause, heavy with judgment. “People are saying you’re pulling up the street to sell souvenir bricks. That true? Have you no sense of shame?”

She felt a spike of heat in her throat. “No, David. The city dumped them here. You think I have time to pry up Main Street before breakfast service?”

He grunted. “Well, people are pissed. Those bricks are history. The shale in those is irreplaceable. Are you planning to sell off the very soil of this state, one brick at a time?”

The line went dead.

Olivia was no idiot. She’d sat through every section on Texas history before the Madison Independent School District deigned to cut her loose with a diploma in one hand and a homecoming mum in the other. Part of her education in the venerable history of her own state included being dragged across the downtown streets to peer at the red bricks under her tennis shoes. The community funds purchased the bricks, and the finest brick manufacturer in the United States, a Texas company, supplied them.

She had time to fill the percolator and hit send on an invoice before the phone rang again. This time, it was a woman’s voice—sharp, nasal, the sort Olivia associated with school committees and the Junior League.

“Ms. Cuellar? Are you aware that the bricks out front are irreplaceable? The Mexican laborers who built this town made them. My great-grandfather drove the wagon to Thurber to pick up the bricks himself.”

Olivia drew a breath, then another, searching for the right mix of polite and unassailable. “I’m aware of their history. I didn’t touch them. Please call the city manager.”

“Oh, I already did,” the woman snapped. “He said the work crews followed your instructions.”

"That's not—" Olivia started, but the caller was gone.

She let the phone ring three times before picking up the next. By that time, she set her voice as calm as marble.

"Limestone Inn, Olivia speaking."

A beat, and then a familiar, deliberate drawl. Teresa Alvarez, head of the courthouse committee and unofficial grand inquisitor for the town's social order.

"Good morning, dear. Quite a display out front. Is this a new marketing strategy?"

Olivia closed her eyes and pressed her free hand to her forehead. "No, Teresa. Some mistake. The city—"

"Well, whatever it is, I'm sure you'll handle it." Their words were dipped in honey, but the message underneath was clear: one more strike, and she'd be out.

She hung up, letting the phone's click echo in the empty hall. A second later, the landline lit up again. She let it ring, counting off the seconds like she was defusing a bomb.

Outside, a pair of early risers with matching Labradoodles slowed to stare at the brick pile. The older of the two leaned in for a better look, then gestured at the inn with a pointed, unmistakable shake of her head. Olivia watched through the lace curtains, then let the edge fall back into place.

Olivia'd been in Madison for less than a year and already her name was on the tip of every tongue—sometimes for the right reasons, more often for the wrong. She thought about the calls, the way the story had already spread and warped by the second ring. As for the bricks? She knew how easily a single misstep could mar a legacy that had survived a century of wear, and how quickly the town's memory could rewrite her as a vandal instead of a caretaker.

She grabbed her cell, thumbed in the number for the county office, and braced herself for the bureaucratic labyrinth to come. But before the call could connect, the inn's phone erupted again—this time with the insistent, doubled tone of an incoming fax.

She stared at the machine, watching as it spit out a single sheet. In bold, unsparing type, the headline:

ATTN: OLIVIA CUELLAR—CEASE AND DESIST REMOVAL OF HISTORIC MATERIALS IMMEDIATELY.

Below a blurry paragraph of legalese, half of it obscured by a misaligned toner cartridge.

She laughed short and sharp and then ripped the fax in half.

When the phone started up again, she let it ring until the machine picked up, her own voice promising a callback she had no intention of making.

She stood in the middle of the foyer, surrounded by silence and the faint scent of lemon oil and brick dust, and realized that she had finally achieved what she'd always wanted: a place in history.

She just hadn't expected it to look like this.

SHE PUNCHED in Andrew Kim's number so hard the glass on her phone registered a tremor. He picked up on the second ring, the background noise of construction winding down just audible behind his clipped greeting.

"Andrew Kim," he said, as if the surname alone would insulate him from what was coming.

"Andrew. It's Olivia," she said, then, before he could reply, "Did you authorize the ceremonial dumping of a century's worth of Thurber brick on my lawn, or is this just another historic district tradition nobody bothered to warn me about?"

A pause. In the background, a power tool screamed, then stopped. "I'm not sure what you—"

"Don't," she snapped. "Three tons of street brick. Right in front of my inn. With a city notice tied to my porch like I'm the one who asked for it."

Another pause, this one long enough to let the silence needle at both ends. "That wasn't supposed to—" he began.

"Supposed to what? Magically float to the job site after dark? Because what it actually did is make it look like I'm robbing the town blind and using it to build my own little empire." Olivia heard her voice rising, each word a brick in its own right.

"I apologize," Andrew said, the words falling flat, probably the first of a half-dozen he'd rehearsed in his bureaucratic sleep. "There must have been a miscommunication with the transport. The bricks were scheduled to be moved to temporary storage at the county yard, not your property."

"Well, the entire local rumor mill disagrees. I've had six calls before 8:00 a.m. accusing me of everything short of arson. You know this is a PR nightmare, right?"

"I do," Andrew replied. "And I take responsibility. I'll call the site supervisor right away. We'll have the bricks removed before noon."

"Not good enough," Olivia said, trying and failing to keep her hands from shaking. "You don't get to vanish behind a clipboard while I get tarred and feathered in the town square. You're going to fix this—in person. Today."

She expected another slippery attempt at deflection, maybe some passive-aggressive mention of how tight his schedule was or how she was "making it personal." Instead, he sighed, and in that sigh she heard a note of actual fatigue, maybe even regret.

"I'll be there in twenty minutes," he said.

She was still composing her next line when he hung up.

Olivia set the phone down and paced the length of the lobby, one hand pressed flat to her sternum. She could feel her pulse against the fabric of her blouse, the ache of anger compounded by a humiliation so fresh it still stung. On the street, a city pickup had replaced the dog-walking pair, idling at the curb while a worker in a reflective vest took pictures of the bricks from every angle.

She wondered how many other businesses were fielding calls this morning, how many of the town's small disasters were ever really accidents, and whether she would ever, in her life, get through a day in Madison without being summoned to answer for something beyond her control.

The phone rang again, and for a wild second she considered hurling it into the brick pile and letting it ring itself to death. Instead, she picked up, this time using her customer service voice.

"Limestone Inn, how can I help you?"

A man's voice, older, thick with the rolling cadence of a lifetime spent talking over farm equipment. "You know you can't keep those," he said, skipping pleasantries altogether. "They're town property."

Olivia counted to three. "Yes, sir. The city's already working on relocating them."

He grunted. "Shoulda left 'em where they was."

She managed not to slam the phone, though it took every ounce of muscle control she had.

She sat at the reception desk, letting the building's stillness seep back into her bones. For a moment, she closed her eyes and pictured what the day could have been—eggshell sunlight through the lace curtains, the smell of coffee and bleach, maybe even a single morning without catastrophe.

She heard distantly the crunch of gravel out front. The Mazda again, or maybe Andrew's truck. Olivia squared her shoulders and waited, rehearsing her opening volley.

She would not let him off the hook. She would not apologize for the city's screw-up, or for caring more about history than the people who supposedly owned it.

She was tired of taking the blame.

Andrew's pickup arrived twelve minutes after their call, rattling to a stop with a throat-clearing rumble that seemed calculated to draw every curtain on the block. Olivia watched him from the foyer, arms crossed, jaw set; she noted the rapid, careful way he gathered his tools and marched up the walk, avoiding the bricks with an unconscious precision, like he'd spent a lifetime sidestepping hazards.

He wore the same navy shirt from their first encounter, sleeves already rolled, the collar faintly darkened with sweat. The messenger bag, patched and battered, was slung across his back. For the first time, Olivia noticed the small nicks and flecks of paint on his hands, the ink lines that bracketed his nails. He looked like a man permanently haunted by blueprints, too accustomed to building things in his head to ever be fully present in his body.

"Good morning," he said, voice even but tight. He glanced at the brick piles, then at Olivia, and she caught the flicker of something like embarrassment—an emotion she'd never seen him admit to in public.

She offered no greeting, just a quick tilt of her head toward the disaster zone. "You want to explain?"

He started to answer, but just then the city truck revved, and the worker—tall, broad, sunburned across every visible surface—stepped out and joined them on the sidewalk. He looked at Olivia, then at Andrew, then at the bricks, and shook his head.

"Someone's got their wires crossed," he said, clearly

enjoying the show. "We were told to get 'em out of the right-of-way. Didn't say where."

"Who gave the order?" Andrew asked, tone already shifting into professional triage.

The foreman shrugged, pulling a folded printout from his back pocket. "Email from City Engineering. Said the bricks are historical, can't go in the landfill, stack 'em at 'designated safe location.' Figured the B&B was as good as any, since it's next on the paving schedule."

Olivia snorted. "Perfect. I get to babysit town artifacts on top of everything else."

The worker grinned. "You want 'em gone, you gotta talk to the county. I just follow orders."

Andrew stepped in. "We'll coordinate with the city yard, have them moved this afternoon. In the meantime, I apologize for the inconvenience." He said it as if he'd been programmed to repeat it in five different languages, but there was a note of genuine contrition behind the corporate script.

The worker shrugged again and retreated to his truck, leaving the two of them alone among the relics.

Olivia took a breath, willing her voice to steady. "I hope you realize that this is going to fuel every conspiracy theory about me in a ten-mile radius."

Andrew nodded, gaze fixed on the pattern of the brick stamp. "Thurber's not easy to come by. Most towns ripped them up in the seventies and paved over with asphalt. The Brick Plant hasn't even been operating since the 1930s. These are original—probably laid by the crews that built the courthouse."

"I know," Olivia said, more sharply than she intended. "My abuela used to tell people the bricks were tougher than the families walking on them. That they were proof you could survive being buried, as long as you held onto your name."

Andrew met her eyes, and for the first time she saw he

understood. Not just the technical history, but the weight of legacy. "You know, they laid these under the Fort Worth Stockyards, too. These aren't my first Thurber bricks, or my first rodeo." His attempt at a joke fell flat as Olivia scowled at him, her nerves frayed by the morning's events.

"We'll get them handled," he said, softer now. "And if anyone tries to blame you for it, I'll take the hit."

She almost laughed, then caught herself. "You really think that'll work?"

He hesitated, then offered a half-smile that was equal parts sheepish and stubborn. "No. But it's worth a try."

She watched him work the rest of the morning: on the phone with city offices, mapping the timeline of when the bricks would be moved, inspecting the porch and sidewalk to ensure the drop-off didn't cause any damage. He moved with a careful, economical purpose, as if a committee had approved each gesture and cost out to the cent. But whenever he thought she wasn't looking, she caught him sneaking glances at her—curious, maybe even admiring, in a way that made her wonder if he'd been sent here just to test her composure.

By noon, the city had dispatched a second crew, this one with a flatbed and a supervisor in a clean golf shirt. They loaded the bricks, row by row, with the reverence of pallbearers. The supervisor apologized in his own way, and then the truck was gone, the front lawn left scraped but intact.

Andrew lingered, clipboard in hand, looking at the patch of lawn where the bricks had been. He turned to Olivia, as if searching for the next line in a script neither of them had agreed to read.

"I'll make sure the report blames it on the city," he said. "And if anyone wants to make a scene, I'll take the heat."

She watched him for a long second, weighing the offer. "Why are you being so decent about this?" she asked, surprised at how raw her own voice sounded. "I've been nothing but a pain in your ass since you showed up."

He shrugged, then glanced away, as if the answer was obvious. "You care. Most people don't. They complain, but they don't care what happens to the town. Or its history. That matters."

She felt something shift, a click in her chest like a door unjamming after too many years painted shut.

"You're still a pain," he added, so quietly she almost missed it.

She almost smiled. Almost. "I've been called worse."

He nodded, the line of his mouth quirking just a little, and then he excused himself—something about a meeting with the ADA consultant, an urgent need to measure the slope of the courthouse ramp before the afternoon storm. He left the inn without another word, but as he rounded the corner she caught him glancing back, just for a second, as if to check that she was still watching.

Inside, the phone was silent for the first time all day. Olivia made a cup of coffee and sat by the window, watching the empty sidewalk as the sun burned off the last of the morning's haze. The story in town would keep mutating, she knew; by dusk, someone would have her selling bricks on eBay, or rebuilding the inn's fireplace with stolen heritage.

But she had survived worse than gossip, and there was a kind of peace in knowing the truth—if only for herself.

She thought of Andrew, his measured voice, the way he'd stood up when it counted. For the first time, she wondered what else they might have in common besides the burden of fixing other people's mistakes.

She sat for a long time, the coffee cooling in her hands, and in that moment, she let herself believe that people could survive some disasters. Maybe even redeemed by them.

❧

BY TWO, the inn's front walk looked as pristine as a crime scene after the cops had finished with it. Olivia was halfway through a pan de polvo and an overdue expense report when she heard the deliberate, two-tap knock she now recognized as Andrew's. He waited on the porch, face tilted to the sun, as if the light might somehow bleach the morning's embarrassment out of existence.

She debated not answering—then let the screen door slam behind her as she joined him. He didn't say hello, just gestured at the now-empty yard.

"I'm sorry about the chaos," he said, and then, after a beat, "You handled it better than most."

Olivia shrugged, unable to muster much sarcasm. "You should see my Yelp reviews."

He smiled, then grew serious. "I have a favor to ask."

She raised an eyebrow. "Already? Most people wait at least a day before requesting my services as a public scapegoat."

Andrew glanced at his shoes, then met her gaze. "I need help to connect with the local families. Especially the older ones. There's a... legend, I guess, about the courthouse. That some of the stonework has hidden maker's marks—names or initials from the original masons. I want to document them before restoration covers it up for good. But I don't have the language, or the trust."

She thought back to the morning's parade of phone calls, the way even the most progressive locals still drew a hard line between "our" history and the versions preserved by outsiders.

"Why do you care?" she asked. It came out sharper than she meant, but the question was sincere.

He hesitated, picking at the seam of his messenger bag. "My grandfather was a cabinetmaker. Came over after the war, worked for thirty years doing custom work in gated communities across Dallas and Forth Worth. Hell, the whole damned Metroplex, come to think of it. He signed everything. Not on the front, but on the backs of shelves, inside drawers—little marks you'd never see unless you tore the thing apart. I didn't know until I started helping him with a restoration in Dallas, and we found a dozen of his signatures inside an old judge's chamber. He always said, if the world won't remember your name, leave it somewhere for the next person to find."

Olivia absorbed the story, feeling its weight settle alongside her own family's tales. She could picture her abuela rolling tortillas for some long-dead judge, never knowing her name might someday matter more than his.

Andrew went on, voice soft. "I think the courthouse has signatures like that. But I need someone who knows the right questions to ask. Who people will talk to."

"You realize you're asking me to help you break into a closed society," she said. "My grandfather was the supervisor for the work crews, but I'm 'the snob who ran off to Houston first opportunity I got'."

He nodded, unfazed. "I realize. You're the only one who could."

She leaned against the porch post, considering. "Who's on the list?"

He pulled out a sheet—typed, double-spaced, annotated in red. Half the names were familiar from church, the other half from the perpetual circuit of civic events and fundraisers. At the top: Carmen Maldonado, self-appointed matriarch of the Madison old guard, notorious for her memory, her mean streak, and her annual victory in the tamale contest.

Olivia groaned. "You want me to go see Carmen? She tried to excommunicate me after Mass."

"I can go alone," Andrew said quickly, "but I'd rather not make a scene."

She laughed, brief and bright. "That's the whole point. With Carmen, a scene is mandatory."

He smiled. "Will you come?"

She should have said no. She owed nothing to Andrew, and even less to the town that had so eagerly made her the villain of the day. But she could feel the pull of obligation—the sense that, if she didn't do this, the story of the courthouse would be written in the same erasures that had already erased her own family's contribution.

"Fine," she said, grabbing her jacket. "But if she throws me out, you're paying for lunch."

They drove in Andrew's pickup, the cab filled with the scent of black coffee and air freshener that failed to mask the underlying tang of old paper and tools. He drove with both hands at ten and two, scanning the horizon like he expected a rogue city inspector to leap out and flag them down.

"You know what you're in for, right?" she asked as they hit the county line. "Carmen is like a walking Wikipedia, but with a lot more judgment."

"I can handle it," Andrew replied. "My mom's family does the same thing. Every gathering turns into a test of who remembers which scandal, or who slighted which cousin at a funeral. The trick is to let them feel like they're teaching you something."

Olivia nodded, admiring his confidence. "Just be careful. Carmen doesn't give out secrets without taking some in return."

The house was five miles out of town, a low-slung adobe painted the blue of a bruise, set back from the road and ringed with wind-warped mesquite. Carmen was waiting on the porch, hands folded over the handle of her cane, her hair pulled back in a severe bun that made her look like a retired matador.

She eyed them both as they walked up, then addressed Andrew in Spanish, rapid and clipped.

Olivia answered for him, the words coming easier than she expected. "He's here to honor the stonework. He wants to know about the men who left their marks on the courthouse."

Carmen's gaze flicked to Olivia, then to Andrew, then back again. "Does he care, or does he just want a story for his report?"

Andrew looked the old woman square in the eye. "I care," he said in English, but with the gravity of someone who'd learned to make words count. "I want the names to survive."

For a long moment, Carmen said nothing. Then she motioned them inside.

The house smelled of garlic and dust, the walls lined with photos of weddings, funerals, and a single framed diploma from a university Olivia had never heard of. Carmen led them to the kitchen, where she poured bitter coffee into mismatched mugs and set out a plate of sweet bread.

She quizzed Andrew for a full ten minutes—about his family, his credentials, his plans for the courthouse—before finally relaxing enough to talk. The stories came in a flood, each more detailed than the last: the names of masons who carved their initials into the keystones, the rivalries between crews, the nights when half the town gathered to watch the dome go up.

Olivia listened, amazed at how much she hadn't known—how much the official histories left out. Andrew took notes, asking gentle, precise questions, never pushing but never missing a beat. By the time they stood to leave, Carmen seemed almost pleased, even as she warned them not to "make a circus" out of the secrets she'd shared.

Outside, the wind had picked up, carrying the dry scent of mesquite and far-off rain. Olivia turned to Andrew, expecting him to dive right into logistics, but he just stood there, watching the sky.

"What are you thinking?" she asked.

"That I wish every town took this seriously," he said. "The people, the stories. The marks they leave behind."

She looked at him, really looked, and saw not just the preservationist, but the grandson who'd grown up searching for hidden signatures in the backs of cabinets.

She smiled. "You might actually fit in here, you know. If you learn to dodge the land mines."

He grinned. "I have an excellent guide."

They stood for a moment, neither in a hurry to break the silence. Then Andrew said, "Next stop is the courthouse. Want to help me look for the marks?"

She considered. There was still a stack of bills waiting at the inn, a day's worth of petty grievances and low-level emergencies that no one else would ever handle. But there was also the sense, rare and heady, that she could actually change something. Leave a mark of her own, maybe.

"Sure," she said. "Lead the way."

As they drove back toward town, Olivia glanced at the old courthouse dome, shining dull gold against the clouds. It looked less like a ruin and more like a secret, waiting to be discovered.

For the first time in months, she felt almost at home.

Chapter Six

The interior of Andrew's truck—an ancient white Ford, cab redolent of sun-baked vinyl and chemical coffee—was a climate unto itself. Olivia climbed in, bracing for the low-level concussion of the door slam, and immediately regretted her choice of skirt over jeans. The seat creaked; the stick shift jutted between them like a provocation. There was a torn composition notebook on the dash, a forest of receipts bristling from the sun visor, and a quartered ruler rattling in the footwell. The only thing that looked new was Andrew, sleeves rolled, eyes locked on the parking lot as if he expected the asphalt to dissolve beneath them.

He glanced over as she buckled up. "Sorry about the mess."

She offered a brittle smile, hoping he wouldn't clock the sweat on her upper lip. "At least it's not bricks."

He grinned, not taking the bait. "Give it time."

As they pulled onto the main drag, Olivia studied the line of his jaw, the set of his mouth—how even in silence, he seemed to process five things at once, prioritizing which crisis to address first. She wondered if the same was true of his home life, if the neatness stopped at his shirt cuffs or extended all the way to the inside of his refrigerator.

"You hate this truck, don't you?" he said, eyes fixed on the road.

She started, then laughed—real, surprised, a snort that cracked the spell of tension. "I don't hate it. I just... I grew up with a dad who collected pickups the way some people collect whiskey. Most of them were 'works in progress.' This is giving me flashbacks."

He nodded, seeming to file this away. "It's my uncle's old ranch truck. He says it's the only thing in the family that'll outlast us."

Olivia let the road noise fill the space. The highway out of town was a stitched-together patchwork of repairs, dips and rises designed to test the will of anyone foolish enough to drive it at speed. Andrew took the curves with metronome precision, two hands on the wheel. She waited until they were past the first cattle guard to speak again.

"About Carmen," she said. "You should know she hates me. Or at least, she hated my abuela, and then by extension everyone who came after. It's genetic."

Andrew shrugged. "I've worked with worse. My first job out of grad school, the contractor tried to sabotage my drawings every week. Once, he filled the stairwell with pig shit."

Olivia laughed again, sharper this time. "That's not how we do it here. If Carmen wants to sabotage you, she'll just feed you until you're too full to move."

He smiled, a twitch at the corner of his mouth. "Noted. I'm not here to start a fight. I just need her to tell me what her father saw during the original build. Half the records from that time are lost, and the rest are..." He trailed off, flexing his fingers on the wheel.

"Lies?" Olivia supplied.

He shot her a look, impressed. "Optimistic projections."

She felt the old reflex to apologize on behalf of her town, or maybe her species. "It's not that people here want to lie. It's that they want to point at something and say, 'We built that.' Even if it means glossing over who actually laid the stones."

Andrew exhaled, the sound almost a sigh. "That's the part that matters to me. The hands that did the work. The hidden marks." He gestured as if the thought had physical heft. "I've spent two months on this courthouse, and already I know the official story is a fantasy. For one thing, the limestone's wrong. The south side is already starting to spall, which only happens if the job was rushed—or if someone substituted caliche for half the base layer."

"Caliche," she repeated. "That's... bad?"

"Caliche's like limestone's trash cousin," he said. "It's full of clay and sand, holds water, and breaks down twice as fast. But it's cheap. And if you're under pressure to finish on time—"

"You cut corners," she said, finishing the thought.

He nodded. "I've found at least three signatures embedded in the grout lines. Not the supervisors, not the architect. The laborers. And they're all code-switching between English and Spanish. Sometimes both on the same stone."

There was a raw pride in his voice, but also something wounded, as if he hated himself for caring so much.

"You sound like a detective," she said.

He didn't smile, but the line of his jaw relaxed. "I am, sort of. Architectural forensics. I want to know what really happened. Not just what the blueprints claim."

They hit a stretch of highway where the trees thickened and the air went cool even through the rolled-up windows. Olivia looked out at the dense stands of oak, the shadows tangled in the underbrush. For a moment, it felt like passing through a tunnel between two realities—the world she'd left, and the one she was still trying to claim as hers.

"Can I ask you something?" she said, before she could talk herself out of it.

"Sure."

"Why do you care? You're not from here. You could just turn in your report, collect your per diem, and go home."

He considered this, then said, "My grandfather wasn't allowed to sign his work—regulations, racism, whatever. But he'd carve a little star inside every drawer, somewhere no one would look. My dad found them all after he died." Andrew's voice got quieter, as if the story embarrassed him. "I guess I think every building deserves a record of who made it. Even if no one wants to admit it."

Olivia felt the words settle in her chest, heavy and comforting at the same time. "If it helps, I think that's the best reason I've heard in a long time."

He let the compliment hang, then flicked the blinker and took the next turnoff. The road narrowed, shoulders pressed in by weeds and sunflowers, the horizon blocked by low, weathered outbuildings and a distant line of fencing. Olivia felt her heart rate climb—not from fear, but from the excitement of a problem about to be solved.

"We're close," Andrew said. "You want to call, or just knock?"

"Carmen would appreciate the drama," Olivia said. "Let's knock."

The truck lurched to a stop on the rutted drive. They sat for a moment, listening to the engine ping and settle, neither one eager to be the first out the door.

Together, they climbed out and started up the path.

❧

Their second visit to Carmen's house went slightly better than the first. Carmen stood in the doorway, arms crossed over her black dress like she expected to deflect a firing squad with the force of her scowl alone. Her hair, white as road salt, drawn back so tight it left her eyes wide and wet-looking, two chips of obsidian scanning Olivia and Andrew from boots to brow. The porch swept clean, every plank polished to a matte shine, the only decoration a battered wind chime that had lost its voice to the seasons.

Olivia felt herself shrink under Carmen's gaze, though she tried to hide it. Andrew did not shrink. He offered a small bow, hands clasped, the gesture oddly formal and, for a moment, disarming.

"Señora Maldonado," he said, careful with the pronunciation.

Carmen's lips thinned, then she spat into the gravel. "I see you have more questions, Señor Kim."

"I am. And it's just 'Andrew'."

Carmen's attention flicked to Olivia, a beat of calculation, then back. "And why do you insist on bringing this one?"

Olivia braced herself for the blow, but Andrew took it instead.

"She is the owner of the Limestone Inn," he said, as if that explained everything. "We work together on the committee."

Carmen sniffed. "The committee. There's always a committee."

Andrew waited, unblinking. After a moment, Carmen sighed and stepped aside, leaving the door open but her body blocking most of the frame. "You come in, but you leave your shoes at the door this time. I don't allow city dirt on my floor."

They complied, the two of them hopping awkwardly on the stoop, Olivia's feet instantly chilled by the tile. Carmen led them to the kitchen, where the air was thick with the smell of boiled chilies and old coffee. The table was already set for three, as if she'd expected their arrival even while pretending not to.

"You drink coffee?" She said, already pouring. She didn't ask how they took it.

Andrew waited until Carmen was seated before speaking. "I've been reviewing the courthouse structure. There's more damage than the city will admit. And more... history, maybe, than anyone realizes."

Carmen's hand hovered over the sugar bowl. "What kind of damage?"

Andrew leaned in, voice low and direct. "Water intrusion from the south wall. Spalling from cheap infill. And most importantly, hidden signatures—maker's marks—left by the original masons. Spanish, sometimes code-switching with English. But all of them are buried beneath layers of repairs."

Carmen regarded him with fresh interest. "You read the marks?"

"Some. Not all. I was hoping you could help me."

She made a noncommittal noise, then turned to Olivia. "And you? What do you want with my family's story? You think it makes a good headline for your B&B?"

Olivia felt the words like a slap but forced herself to meet Carmen's eyes. "I just want to know the truth," she said. "The actual story. Not the one in the tourist guide."

Carmen stared at her, measuring something. "My father built half the town. He was paid less than a white man, sometimes paid nothing at all. They promised him a plaque, a statue. He died waiting for it." Her voice was rough but steady.

Andrew nodded, serious. "My grandfather was the same. Different war, different city, but they erased his name too. He started hiding stars in the backs of cabinets—just to prove he was there."

Carmen's face softened, but only a shade. "I've heard this before. Promises." She switched to Spanish, fast and pointed, addressing Andrew. "Y tú, joven, por qué te importa? No tienes nada aquí. Nadie te va a recordar."

He answered her in Spanish, slower, deliberate. "Lo sé. Pero me importa. Porque todos merecen ser recordados."

For the first time, Carmen's mouth twitched at the edges, almost a smile. "Your Spanish is terrible," she said, but it wasn't an insult.

They drank coffee in silence for a few minutes, the only sound the pop and hum of the refrigerator. Then Carmen rose and motioned them to follow.

They trailed her down a narrow hallway, walls lined with framed photos: weddings, graduations, a single, faded picture of a young man in work-stained overalls, staring straight into the lens. Carmen ran a thumb across the glass as she passed.

Carmen hovered behind him, pointing out names and dates, correcting his pronunciation when he fumbled a word. Olivia stood off to the side, feeling both included and invisible, like a child at a grown-up party.

She let her gaze drift over the shelves—canning jars full of spent seeds, a battered tape measure, and a shoebox labeled "evidence." Inside, a jumble of metal tags and crumbling coins, each one tagged with a name and date. Some were stamped with a single letter; others had elaborate, almost calligraphic designs. A bolt of recognition hit Olivia. She'd seen these before, but in the past she'd never paid them any mind.

Andrew looked up, eyes wide. "These... these are from the keystones. He took them before the bosses could toss them out."

Carmen nodded. "He said they were the only proof he existed."

The gravity of it landed hard on Olivia. "I know another place where someone recorded them." My grandfather's notebooks." The others stared at her in shock. She reached out, touching one tag, feeling its rough edge. "Can we show these? In the restoration? In the report?"

Carmen considered. "Maybe. If you don't let the county take them away."

Andrew looked at Olivia, then at Carmen. "We won't let them."

For the first time, Carmen's sternness cracked. She sat, suddenly tired, and rested her hands on the table. "You take what you need," she said. "But you do it right. No shortcuts. No more lies."

"We promise," Olivia said, the words coming out with more force than she'd intended.

They left an hour later, ledger and tags carefully packed. On the porch, Carmen watched them go, not waving, just standing sentinel as they climbed into the truck.

As they drove away, Andrew let out a slow breath. "She scares the shit out of me," he said, voice almost reverent.

Olivia smiled, watching the old woman recede in the side mirror. "She scares everyone. But you did good."

They were silent for a long time, the truck's engine filling the space where words weren't needed. The day was already sliding toward dusk, with the first streaks of gold and violet pooling in the sky.

Andrew sat, his desire for her to speak weighing on her. Olivia spoke before her mind could put the pieces together. "My grandfather made notes of the work. He even made sketches of the same designs. I thought he was being artistic and whimsical."

"He was helping us record history. And every bit goes into the report to the state." His jaw was set, but she saw the determination in his eyes.

For the first time, Olivia felt like they were on the right side of something.

❧

THE NEXT DAY, after a morning of wrestling with the inn's booking software and a silent lunch spent watching dust motes swirl in the parlor's light, Olivia found herself back in the courthouse rotunda with Andrew and, unexpectedly, Carmen. The older woman had arrived at the inn just after sunrise, ledger tucked under one arm and a paper sack of pan dulce under the other. She said nothing about her change of heart, only nodded to Andrew and barked at Olivia to fetch decent coffee.

They settled in the basement archives, a low-ceilinged warren of concrete and fluorescent hum. Olivia's heart pounded from the climb down the slick, unfinished steps, but Andrew navigated by instinct, flipping on work lamps and clearing a space at the nearest table.

Carmen set the ledger on the scratched laminate, flattening the creased pages with the care of a surgeon prepping for the first incision. The paper smelled of smoke and lard, every line crowded with inked script so tight it seemed to compress time itself.

"You read this?" Carmen asked Andrew, her voice gentle for once.

"I can try," he said, "but if I'm lost, please translate."

She nodded, and together they bent over the book.

For a while, the only sound was the flipping of pages and the halting rhythm of translation—Carmen reading aloud in Spanish, Andrew asking for clarification, Olivia scanning for words she recognized from her grandfather's blueprints. The entries started simple: lists of stone shipments, the names of workers grouped by crew, daily weather notes, the odd joke about city officials and their oversized hats. But as the months passed, a new tone crept in: bitterness, frustration, warnings in capital letters about "limestone swapped for clay" or "mixing crews to hide mistakes." Several times, a day's work was simply marked "cancelled—no pay."

Andrew traced a finger along the edge of a drawing pinned inside the book: a cross-section of the south wall, annotated with arrows and small, angry exclamation points. "This matches the cracks in the exterior," he said. "They must've known it was failing even as they built it."

Carmen nodded, a tightness at her mouth. "They knew. But the bosses only cared about the ribbon-cutting."

Olivia leaned in, inhaling the ghost of her grandfather's aftershave that lingered in the margins. She turned the page and saw a column of initials, each entry accompanied by a tiny, unique glyph—circle, triangle, star, spiral—next to the names. "What are these marks?" she asked.

"Code," Carmen said. "Each crew leader used a symbol instead of a signature. That way, if the city docked their pay, they could prove who'd done which section."

Andrew's eyes lit up. "This is brilliant. We can use these to match the marks in the actual building."

Olivia's mind drifted back to her grandfather's workshop, and the gritty smell of sawdust that blanketed every surface. To the whimsical marks that dotted the lines of his notebooks. For all the world, he looked like he was doodling, searching for a way to pass the time. To fill up his hours. He'd been recording, carefully cataloging what he'd witnessed all those decades ago.

Carmen arched an eyebrow, "The old man made notes of those? He was more anal retentive than I thought." She caught herself before a laugh erupted from her lips. She looked at Olivia, searching for a reproach to mirror the one she'd given Olivia after Mass. Finding none, her shoulders sunk down and she settled for a discreet throat clearing.

"Can you find, them? Do they still exist, of did you throw them out?"

Olivia pursed her lips. The town really did see her as a mix of philistine and ungrateful daughter. No amount of turning a profit from a molding relic would change that.

"I'll go through the boxes I have from his workshop. If I have enough notebooks to cross-reference if we get stuck. With these three sources as evidence, can we complete the record?"

Andrew fished his own battered notebook from his messenger bag, flipping to a page lined with sketches of stone joints, some circled or starred with the same glyphs. "Look. I found this one yesterday," he said, tapping a tight spiral. "And this—" he traced a double triangle—"is all over the north arch."

Carmen's hand hovered near his, her fingers trembling. "That's my father's," she said. "He taught the others how to do it."

There was a hush then, the three of them staring at the page, a silent communion of pride, grief, and vindication.

They pressed on, page by page, the air growing close and heavy as the hours blurred together. Sometimes Olivia and Andrew's hands would brush, fingers grazing as they reached for the same photograph or ruler; each time, Olivia felt a jolt up her arm, a charge that lingered even as she drew back. Carmen noticed, her gaze sharp but not unkind.

At one point, Olivia reached for a stub of pencil, only to find her hand covering Andrew's. She froze, but he didn't move, and for a moment their hands rested together on the table, the pulse in her wrist matched by his steady warmth. Carmen coughed, and the spell broke, but not entirely.

They came at last to a section near the back of the ledger. The entries had grown erratic; the handwriting slanting with fatigue. Olivia read aloud as Carmen translated, the words barely above a whisper:

"They say we are not worth the extra dollar. They say we

are slow, or lazy, or not able to work the way the Americans do. But we finish every day. We build the walls higher than they ask. They do not write our names in the papers, but we leave them in the stone. When they tear down this building, we will still be here."

Andrew's hand closed around the edge of the ledger. "This is everything," he whispered. "They wanted to be found."

Olivia swallowed, the lump in her throat sudden and fierce. She locked eyes with Carmen, daring her to contradict her. "We have to tell this story. The whole thing. Not just for the grant, but for the record."

Carmen nodded, eyes shining in the stark light. "You tell it right. With all the names. All the marks."

They worked into the night, cross-referencing every mark with every section of the courthouse, Andrew annotating, Olivia copying names onto a legal pad, Carmen supplying details that only the daughter of a master mason would know: which joints to check, which stones would bear the best evidence, where to look for "ghost marks" made with coal dust or pencil. Their energy built on itself, three separate pulses converging into a single, urgent drive.

At one point, Olivia's vision blurred, and she rubbed her eyes, only to find Andrew watching her with a tenderness she hadn't expected. "Are you okay?" he said, the question loaded.

She nodded, unable to trust her voice. Instead, she reached for another tag from the box, tracing the carved letter with her thumb.

In the silence, Carmen's chair scraped back. She stood, rolling her shoulders. "I'll make food," she said. "You keep going."

Upon her return, tortillas, beans, and a lively steaming casserole covered the table. She pressed plates into their hands, then sat across from them, watching as they ate. For a long time, no one spoke.

Finally, Andrew broke the silence. "Thank you for trusting us," he said.

Carmen shrugged, but her face was softer. "My father said, 'They can take your money. But if you leave your name, they can't take that.'"

They ate, and then they worked, until they fully mapped the ledger, the connections drawn, the story emerging with a clarity that left Olivia breathless.

Late that night, after Carmen had gone upstairs to sleep and Andrew had packed away his notes, Olivia lingered in the rotunda, staring at the dome overhead. The light was blue and hollow, the echo of their voices fading into the stone.

Andrew stood beside her, arms folded, his head tilted back. "What are you thinking?" he asked.

"That I wish my abuela could see this," she said. "The actual story. All of it."

He nodded, understanding with no need for more words. After a moment, he reached for her hand, their fingers intertwining as if it was the most natural thing in the world.

For a while, they just stood, hand in hand, looking up into the heart of the building that had, for so long, tried to erase them.

Tomorrow, there would be another committee meeting, more skeptics, more fights about budgets and timelines and whose version of history would win. But tonight, the three of them had built something of their own.

And Olivia knew, as surely as she'd ever known anything, that it would last.

The walk from the courthouse to the Limestone felt shorter than usual, as if the night air had thinned out the town's resistance and let Olivia glide through untouched. Andrew kept pace beside her, hands buried in the pockets of his jacket, his voice low and unhurried. They spoke in fragments—about Carmen's father, about the tags and sketches, about whether anyone else had ever tried to piece the story together.

By the time they reached the inn, most of the block had shuttered and darkened, except for the faint pink glow from the bakery two doors down, where the Rodriguez family's night-shift dough crew had already started rolling tomorrow's conchas. Olivia lingered on the bottom step of the porch, the old wood warm from the sun even at this hour. Andrew stood beside her, silent, then sat, arms resting on his knees.

"So what happens next?" she said.

He considered. "We finish the report. Submit the photos, the ledger, the tags. The state will have to recognize the real builders, not just the names on the county seal."

"And you think the town will be okay with that?" she asked. "That the history they've told for a hundred years gets torn up and replaced with something that... what? Makes them look like cheats?"

He shrugged. "Some people won't like it. Some will say it doesn't matter. But the ones who care—the ones who lost their names—they'll finally get them back."

She watched the bakery lights pulse, two soft rectangles on the sidewalk. "You know this will make you a villain, right? You and me both."

Andrew smiled. "I'm used to it."

"I'm not." Olivia hugged her knees, feeling a childish urge to disappear. "I wanted to come back and fix things. But I keep making it worse."

He shook his head. "You're the only one doing it right. Most people just want the credit. You want the truth."

She let the compliment sit for a minute, unsure whether to accept it or deflect. In the end, she split the difference. "You're not so bad yourself."

Quiet settled between them, dense and companionable. Olivia tried to remember the last time she'd felt so at ease on this porch. She couldn't.

She looked at him, taking in the lines of fatigue around his eyes, the way his hair curled stubbornly at the crown no matter how often he flattened it. There was something comforting in his steadiness, the sense that he would keep showing up, no matter how ugly the work became.

"Promise me something," she said.

He looked over, waiting.

"If the county tries to bury the story again—if they try to erase the marks—promise you'll fight them. Even if it means you lose the contract."

Andrew nodded, no hesitation. "I promise."

He stood, stretching, and extended a hand to her. She took it, letting herself be pulled to her feet, her hand lingering in his for just a moment longer than necessary.

"I should go," he said, voice gentle. "Early call with Austin tomorrow."

She nodded, then watched him walk to the curb, the tail-lights of his truck blinking red as he pulled away.

Inside, the inn was dark and cool. Olivia moved by feel, climbing the stairs to her office, where the ledger and the tags waited on the desk. The spreadsheets and constant fretting would have to wait for one evening. She had an inheritance to honor.

❧

FORTY MINUTES INTO HER HUNT, Olivia's hopes of finding her grandfather's notes were in danger of being dashed. She'd systematically searched every cardboard box that she'd sorted after her grandmother's funeral and had dutifully lugged from Madison to Houston and back to Madison once again. A year ago, in a wins- fueled moment, she'd considered Marie Kondo-ing up her place and donating as much as she could to Goodwill. A chill raced up her arms as the realization dawned that maybe he had, in fact, loaded up her car at some point and forgotten all about doing so.

"Dear God, no. Please don't tell me I'm exactly the disgrace that they say I am." Tears clouded her vision as the familiar blanket of failure settled on her once again. Indulging in the sensation, she sat in the box-strewn closet of the inn's tiny apartment. Curled into a fetal position, the idea of staying there until someone found her corpse had a certain appeal. Maybe they can spin it into some kind of tragedy—"She searched until her very last moment, dying of shame."

Her eyes lighted on a small box, one that she had dismissed in her earlier frantic search. The size and labeling were all wrong for the box she'd put his possessions in, so she had waved it off and refused to take it down from the corner she'd wedged it in over a year earlier. Still, what the hell? She'd failed to find them so far, and at least if she opened the stupid thing and didn't die of shame and failure on the floor tonight, she could at least know that she'd searched everywhere.

The box took some pulling to get it out of the corner where the cardboard had settled, and she considered giving up the effort. Eventually, it jerked out, and the edge of the soft cardboard tore as she pulled. Angry at the resistance, she jerked the box open.

As she'd thought, there was no sign of the notebooks, but using her hand as a makeshift shovel, she wedged under the bottom and pushed up with her wrist. The remaining items in the box spilled out, including several leather notebooks that spilled out like a waterfall. With a squeak of triumph, she fumbled after them as they slid away from her.

There they were, stuffed with thick homemade paper, yellowed with time but as strong as ever. She leafed through them, smiling at her grandfather's tight and regimented handwriting. Some notes would require Carmen's help to translate, but it took a few minutes to realize how little she'd remembered about the pages. Sketches crammed every margin and gutter, with initials clearly showing under each. Among the stylized roses and stars, she picked out several marks that Carmen had already identified at the courthouse earlier.

A slow exhale escaped her lips. She'd found what could be the missing piece in documenting the work crews' stories. As weariness finally took over her, she crawled into bed, buoyed by the feeling of triumph for finding her own contribution to their efforts.

Chapter Seven

The bang woke her before her phone alarm, a seismic clatter that shuddered through the guest wing and left Olivia tangled in the sheets, heart punching at her sternum. For a second, she thought maybe a pipe had burst—another casualty in the inn's slow-motion collapse—but then came the chorus: metallic clanging, a slur of voices, someone screaming her name like a four-alarm fire.

She was down the stairs in seconds, barefoot, pajama pants bunched at her knees and hair still wearing last night's argument with the pillow. The kitchen was a disaster zone: the ancient Vulcan oven belched clouds of black smoke, the pilot light clicked and re-clicked in an erratic light show, and the air was as hot and dense as a blast furnace. Over by the prep counter, Josefina, the head cook, wielded a spatula like a sword, batting at a tray of wedding cake layers now the color and consistency of roof shingles.

"¡Está muerta!" Josefina shouted, stabbing at the oven door. "Completely dead! All this for nothing!"

Behind her, the industrial mixer let out a morbid metallic

groan and then ground itself to silence, locking in place with half a batch of carrot batter clinging to the paddle. Next to it, the ancient reach-in fridge made a series of clicks that reminded Olivia of a dying grasshopper before the compressor fell quiet, the digital readout blinking a single, damning "H" for hazard.

Olivia tried to speak, but the smoke got there first, burning her throat and setting off a cough that sent her reeling against the tile. She staggered for the nearest window, wrenching the latch with numb fingers, and the chilly October air slammed into the kitchen, chasing out the smoke along with the fragile optimism she'd clung to last night.

Josefina let the spatula drop and crossed herself. "The cake, the tarta... ruined. For the Johnson wedding. Three days, mija! What do we do?"

Olivia fumbled for the spray bottle and attacked the smoke like it was a weed, squeezing out empty spurts as she tried to control her own panic. "It's okay. It's just—something electrical, maybe a fuse. We can fix it. Don't panic." But even as she said it, her eyes landed on the rusted breaker box, the patchwork of mismatched labels and half-stripped wires like the world's ugliest family tree. She grabbed the phone off the wall and dialed the repair service, thumbing in the number by heart.

On the fourth ring, a voice answered—bored, nasal, and already aggrieved. "Rivard's Appliance. No walk-ins today, only scheduled calls. If it's an emergency, press one."

She pressed one.

An even more disinterested voice, possibly a recording: "If you are calling about commercial food equipment, we are currently booking three days out. If this is life-threatening, please hang up and dial 9-1-1."

Olivia hung up, considered, then dialed again, this time

using the back number for the owner, a guy named Troy who had once fixed her ice machine for a case of Dos Equis and a promise never to call him at home. She called anyway.

He answered with a groggy, "You know what time it is?"

"Please, Troy," she said, not bothering with preamble. "Oven's down, mixer's shot, fridge is dying. I have three weddings in two weeks and every appliance just died in unison."

A pause, then the sound of a bedspring groaning and a dog barking in the distance. "You blow the main? Did you check the surge board?"

"Breaker's intact," she said, "but the pilot light is toast and the fridge is throwing hazard codes."

A sigh. "You're a historic property, right? I have to order parts from Houston. If it's compressor failure, you're looking at three days minimum. Oven's probably has an igniter. Maybe I can patch it by tomorrow, but only if you pay for rush."

"I'll pay. Just—please come as soon as you can."

She heard the scribble of a pen, the faintest grunt, then: "Fine. First slot tomorrow. Don't bake anything. You could start a fire."

She hung up, hands shaking. Josefina had already started scraping the charred cake layers into the compost, muttering under her breath in Spanish too fast and too expletive-rich for Olivia to keep up. The assistant, a culinary student from Blinn named Carla, was eyeing the mixer like it might wake up and finish the job itself.

"It's okay," Olivia repeated, even as the weight settled in her gut. "It's just a hiccup. We'll sub out the cakes to Bauer's for this week, and I'll call in a favor for a rental fridge if I have to."

Josefina snorted. "You think Bauer has time? Caleb is

swamped with the festival order. I know this because his wife told me so at the grocery last night."

Olivia winced, remembering the secondhand look of pity Elena had given her at the library meeting. "I'll figure it out," she said, grabbing a notepad and writing the triage list: fridge, oven, mixer, guest breakfast, wedding cake. And at the bottom, circled twice: "Fix by Friday or else."

The rest of the staff trickled in, the younger servers eyeing the mess with the polite horror of people who only understood disaster as content for TikTok. Olivia snapped at them to open windows, clear the prep, and call guests about the temporary breakfast change. She tried to sound in control, but her voice kept buckling, thin as tissue.

When the chaos ebbed, she crept back upstairs, collapsed on the edge of her bed, and let her mind cycle through the list of disasters: the appliance failures, the reservation book, the balance on the Stirling loan, and the freight-train approach of three wedding weekends that now threatened to bankrupt her in public and spectacular fashion.

She showered, dressed, and made her way to the antique desk in the foyer. She pulled out the battered MacBook, the reservation book, and, with trembling fingers, her grandmother's old ledger. It was a physical thing, bound in cracked red vinyl and dog-eared from decades of abuse, every page a battleground of blue ink and eraser scars. She thumbed to the current week, cross-referencing the digital and the analog with a desperation that bordered on superstition.

Friday: The Johnson wedding, 42 guests, full reception, cake and plated dinner.

Next Saturday: Ramirez y Gomez, 30 guests, buffet, custom cocktail hour.

The following weekend: Chen-Williams, 74 guests, vegan menu, three-layer cake.

She did the math in her head, then on paper, just to make sure: $12,000 in projected gross. But when she ran the expenses, accounting for the bakery outsourcing, the rush appliance repair, and the fact that she'd need to pay temp waitstaff at double time for the last event, the margin shrank to almost nothing. Stirling's $2,500 payment was due in five days, and her personal account had $310 to its name.

The euphoria from finding the notebooks, and the sense of belonging—it all evaporated under the raw, pitiless numbers. The page trembled in her hands as she ran the calculation again. No matter how she sliced it, the best-case scenario was "barely solvent," and the worst was "default with a side of public humiliation."

She considered texting Elena, or even Andrew—he'd be polite, maybe even helpful, but there was a part of Olivia that recoiled at yet another sign of her failure. Not when she'd just begun to feel like she was more than the sum of her mistakes.

She stared at the reservation book, the neat columns of names and dates and promises she wasn't sure she could keep. Her grandmother's voice surfaced, harsh but familiar: "You finish what you start, Liv. Even if it kills you."

She closed the book and pressed her palms to her eyes, willing herself to come up with a plan, any plan. The smell of smoke still lingered in her hair, the taste of panic sharp on her tongue.

For a moment, she let herself imagine just driving away—walking out the door, getting in the car, and leaving the whole mess for the next desperate soul with a love of old buildings and a talent for self-destruction.

But she didn't. She squared her shoulders, set the ledger aside, and started making calls.

First, she called Caleb, who picked up on the first ring and promised to fit her in after bakery hours, even if it meant pulling an all-nighter with his apprentice. Moments later, she called the rental company and begged for a floor fridge, promising a five-star review and lifetime access to her WiFi. She called every temp agency in the county, leaving voicemails that bordered on hysterical.

And then she called Stirling's office, just to confirm the payment date, as if there was a chance it had changed. It hadn't.

At noon, she brewed a fresh pot of coffee and returned to the kitchen, where the smell of bleach had almost, but not quite, managed to drown out the memory of disaster. Josefina was frosting a tray of salvageable scones, face set in a mask of resignation.

"Will you fire me?" Josefina asked, not looking up.

Olivia shook her head, voice ragged but sure. "No one's getting fired. We just have to survive the week."

Josefina grunted. "That's what I always said, too."

Olivia watched her work for a moment, then went to the prep table and started rolling out dough. The task was familiar; the motion anchoring. She let her mind drift back to last night's sense of purpose, the hope that maybe, just maybe, things could be better if she held on long enough.

But as she kneaded the dough, Olivia felt the cracks forming in her resolve. She wanted to believe, but the weight of reality pressed harder with every failed repair, every overdrawn account.

She shaped the rolls, lined them on the tray, and tried to remember what it felt like to win.

AT 6:30, Hahn's Ice House was already two decibels above comfortable, the air thick with the scorched-sugar tang of caramelizing onions and the blue haze of cigarette smoke that

clung to every thread of the upholstery. The walls pulsed with the light of vintage beer signs—Schlitz, Lone Star, Shiner—casting Olivia and her companions in a perpetual half-dusk as they huddled around the corner booth.

She'd ordered a burger and a side of onion rings, but both sat cooling in front of her, a testament to her inability to swallow anything that wasn't pure stress. Elena and Caleb split a pitcher, the condensation pooling beneath it like a threat. Caleb, still in his chef's coat (though he'd tried to dress it down with rolled sleeves and a faded Ragers cap), ate with the same stoic determination he reserved for meetings with county health inspectors. Elena nursed a pint and picked at her own food, pausing every few minutes to search Olivia's face for signs of life.

"You look like death, Liv," Elena said, voice low to avoid being overheard. "Did you sleep at all?"

Olivia poked a limp onion ring, watching it ooze grease onto the plate. "I didn't have time to sleep. Every appliance in my kitchen staged a coordinated revolt at six a.m. I spent the morning putting out literal fires and the afternoon on the phone with every repairman in three counties. I think I now owe half of Madison free rooms for a year, assuming I still have a business to run by then."

Caleb smiled, but it was the wry, close-mouthed variety. "Could be worse. You could be like the guy in El Campo who tried to fix his own walk-in freezer and got trapped inside for seven hours. They found him curled up in the meat locker, muttering about the cold cuts."

Olivia managed a weak laugh, then let her head drop into her hands. "It's not funny. I'm out twelve thousand if I can't deliver these weddings, and Stirling's payment is due in five days. After the repairs, I'll be lucky to break even."

Elena reached across the sticky table and caught Olivia's hand in both of hers. Her fingers were warm, nails short and bitten from years of archival work. "Liv. You can't give up now. We're just getting started."

"Started what?" Olivia said, not bothering to disguise the bitterness. "Started my next failure? Started disappointing the only people who thought I could make something of myself?"

Caleb shifted in his seat. "You know, I've burned down three kitchens in my life. The first time, I was sixteen, working in my uncle's bratwurst shop. He fired me on the spot. Next morning, he handed me the keys and said, 'You want to make it right, you come in at five and start cleaning.'"

Elena grinned. "Was that before or after you tried to make your own schnapps in the basement?"

"During," Caleb said. "Point is, it's not failure unless you stop showing up."

Olivia wanted to argue, but the words wouldn't line up. She settled for draining her glass, the cold beer biting at the back of her throat. "I'm thinking of slinking back to Houston. Selling the place to Stirling and pretending this was all just a fever dream."

"Don't you dare," Elena said, eyes narrowed. "This isn't about you. Not anymore. You've got staff who rely on you, families who booked those weddings months ago. You have a chance to do something that matters, Liv. Don't just chuck that away when things get rough."

"Yeah," Caleb chimed in, "plus, if you bail now, everyone will say you never had the guts to finish."

That landed harder than Olivia wanted to admit. She chewed her lip, feeling the old ache behind her eyes. "Fine. But unless you can teach me how to make a five-tier cake using an Easy-Bake oven, I'm still screwed."

Caleb brightened. "Actually, I have a workaround. You remember the convection unit from the bakery expansion last year? We never installed it, because it didn't fit in the new layout. It's collecting dust in my garage."

Olivia frowned. "You're saying I should just haul it over to the inn and set up a makeshift bakery?"

"Why not?" Caleb said. "It's certified, it runs on 220, and if you plug it into a different circuit, you won't fry your main panel. I'll help you set it up tomorrow morning. Between that and my apprentice, you'll have all the cake you need."

Elena clapped her hands. "See? Problem solved. Sort of."

"Sort of," Olivia echoed. She felt the tension slide away, fraction by fraction.

Elena squeezed her hand, then said, "And I'll keep digging at the library. We have uncatalogued city records in the annex —contracts, payroll, maybe even old construction rosters. They dumped them with us for free storage. This may be the first time that their doing so actually benefits somebody. If Andrew is right about the signatures, there's got to be paperwork backing it up. I'll scan whatever I find and drop it at the inn before dinner."

Caleb nodded. "And if you need muscle, I'll lend you the delivery van. Just promise not to let Olivia drive it, because she can't parallel park."

Olivia rolled her eyes, but the affection in the teasing was a lifeline. For the first time in days, she felt less alone.

They finished the meal in companionable silence, the only drama coming from the next booth, where a group of construction workers debated the finer points of the Astros bullpen. When the server brought the check, Caleb snatched it up and paid in cash, winking at Olivia when she protested.

"Consider it a loan," he said. "One you'll pay back when you're famous and writing memoirs about your time in exile."

She almost smiled at that.

As they slid out of the booth, Elena lingered behind. "You know, my mother called today," she said, lowering her voice. "Apparently word is out that you and Andrew spent a few hours at Carmen's house yesterday."

Olivia's face went hot. "It wasn't like that."

"I know," Elena said. "But the church ladies are already planning your wedding. I give it a week before they start taking bets on how many kids you'll have."

Olivia groaned. "Please shoot me before that happens."

"Not a chance," Elena said, hugging her. "I want a front-row seat."

They walked out into the evening, the parking lot lit up by the fluorescent glow of the icehouse sign. Olivia breathed deep, taking in the cool air and the faint smell of mesquite from the smoker out back. The world felt lighter, or maybe just a little less determined to crush her.

"Thanks," she said, turning to face them both. "For showing up. For not letting me run."

Caleb pulled the van keys from his pocket. "What else are friends for?"

Elena grinned. "Besides, we have too much history to let you bail now. Come on, let's get you back to the inn before you turn into a pumpkin."

They piled into the battered van, laughter echoing as they navigated the potholes and speed bumps on the way home.

Olivia found Josefina still cataloging what she could salvage from the walk-in, at the kitchen table. The oven was dark, the mixer silent, but the place felt different: the panic replaced by a stubborn, defiant hope.

She grabbed a pen and wrote out a new plan on the back of a menu: "Caleb's oven. Elena and city records. Wedding cakes by any means necessary." Then she underlined it twice and posted it on the fridge, where everyone could see.

For the first time since the morning's catastrophe, Olivia let herself believe they just might survive this week.

❧

They lingered after the meal, drifting to the edge of the patio where a string of fairy lights fought gamely against the gloom. A busboy cleared their plates with the brisk efficiency of someone already dreaming of closing time, leaving behind only the water glasses, a pool of ketchup, and a half-sketched map of the inn's main floor on a napkin.

Elena waited until the last plate disappeared, then leaned forward, her smile the dangerous kind Olivia remembered from their teenage double-dates and post-prom sleepovers.

"So," Elena said, voice pitched low. "Carmen Alvarez called my mother today. Said you and that handsome architect spent quite a while at her place yesterday."

Olivia's cheeks went hot, and she traced a line through the condensation on her glass, suddenly more interested in the pattern than the conversation. "It wasn't like that. Andrew just needed someone who understands Spanish for his report for the Master Plan that goes to the state. Carmen had her father's ledger, and she wanted to show us. Plus, her Spanish is way better than mine." Doubt crept at her, but she squashed it down, unwilling to admit that his interest was indeed only professional.

Elena's eyebrows shot up. "Us, huh? Was this a private tutorial, or did you invite the whole courthouse committee?"

"Hilarious," Olivia said, but she could hear the tremor of something like hope beneath the sarcasm. "We spent most of the time in her kitchen, drinking coffee and arguing over the difference between caliche and real limestone."

Caleb snorted. "Sounds romantic."

Olivia rolled her eyes. "If your idea of romance is debating construction defects in Spanish, then sure."

Elena didn't let go. "You know, word travels fast. By noon, half the church ladies had already decided you two were—how did my mom put it? 'Destined for partnership, if not in the courthouse, then in life.'"

"Jesus," Olivia muttered. "I'm going to be the subject of next week's prayer circle, aren't I?"

"Only if you're lucky," Elena said, laughter in her eyes. "You have to admit, he's a step up from the last guy. Plus, he is handsome... for a guy from Dallas." She added the last bit in a singsong and fluttered her fingers, her engagement ring from Caleb winking in the overhead lighting.

Olivia smiled, more at the memory of how quickly Andrew had disarmed Carmen than anything else. "He's... different," she said at last. "He sees things nobody else does. He doesn't care about the politics or the optics. He just wants to get it right."

Caleb nodded, tapping his finger on the table. "He's not afraid of pissing people off. That's rare around here."

Olivia hesitated, then let herself say it. "He makes me feel like I'm not crazy for wanting to save something. Like maybe it's okay to care, even if you look stupid doing it."

Elena squeezed her hand again. "That's not stupid. That's what you do best."

For a moment, Olivia let herself believe it. She watched the lights flicker above, the shadows cast by Caleb's hands as he traced lines on the napkin, and she imagined a world where she could just exist without the constant background hum of impending disaster.

Elena broke the silence. "You know what you need? A community dinner. Something big. Invite the wedding couples, the families, the committee. You show them the renovations, share the ledger, maybe even let Andrew do a demo of his maker's mark detective work."

Caleb grinned. "I'll cook. We'll do it buffet-style—three courses, plenty of booze, everyone leaves happy and stuffed."

Olivia blinked. "You think people would actually come?"

"Liv," Elena said, "half this town is just waiting for an

excuse to gossip about you in person. The other half is curious. Why not give them something to talk about?"

Caleb shrugged. "If it bombs, at least you get a free meal out of it. And maybe you win over a few doubters."

Olivia felt a rush of nerves, then excitement. "We'd need a theme. Something that makes it about the courthouse, the history. Not just me."

Elena laughed. "Easy. 'Building Madison, One Stone at a Time.' I'll MC, we'll project photos from the archives, and you and Andrew can give the official tour."

Caleb's grin widened. "You might even get the church ladies on your side. Especially if you bribe them with kolaches."

Olivia shook her head, but the idea was already catching. "Let's do it," she said, surprising herself with the conviction in her voice. "Friday night. Open house, dinner, and—" she glanced at Elena "—story hour. If we're going down, we're going down swinging."

They clinked glasses, sealing the pact.

After they'd parted ways—Elena heading home, Caleb promising to email a shopping list—Olivia lingered on the empty patio, hands tucked into her jacket, face tilted toward the faint distant shimmer of stars. The world was quiet, except for the hum of traffic and the rhythmic squeak of the icehouse's front door.

Chewing her lip, she thought about the ledger, the tags, the generations of names hidden in the courthouse stone. She thought about Andrew, earnest and awkward, the way he'd listened to Carmen's stories as if they were the only thing that mattered. More than that, she thought about her own hands, the work ahead, and the possibility—however slim—that she could change the story, not just for herself but for everyone who'd been written out before.

The cold cut through her, but she let it linger, a sharp reminder that she was still here. Still trying.

She texted Andrew, brief and directly: "Community dinner Friday. You in?"

The reply came a minute later. "Wouldn't miss it. I'll bring the chalk."

She smiled at the screen, then turned and walked back to the inn, ready to make good on her promise.

Chapter Eight

The courthouse records room always smelled like a hangover: stale air thick with the aftertaste of dust, paper, and the sharp undercurrent of bleach from generations of half-successful janitors. Olivia stood in the doorway a moment, letting the reek of bureaucracy wash over her, before stepping inside and letting the heavy door click shut behind her. The space was smaller than she remembered—cinderblock walls sweating condensation, narrow windows letting in a sliver of morning sun that painted the stacks with the watery light of a bad aquarium. Few would believe that any history worth keeping had survived in here.

Andrew was already at the central table, sleeves rolled, wire-rimmed glasses balanced on the tip of his nose, a row of legal pads and manila folders fanned out in front of him with the geometric precision of a man who found order more comforting than warmth. He looked up at her arrival, expression neutral as always, but the way his eyes flicked to the door, then back to her, told her he'd been waiting.

"Morning," he said, voice lower than usual, like he didn't want to disturb the ghosts.

Olivia set her bag on the nearest chair and pulled out her own notepad, willing herself not to look intimidated. "You beat me here. Figured you'd still be doing recon at the hardware store, or wherever it is you go at dawn."

He smiled, almost. "I wanted to make sure the city didn't lock the archives after last week's 'incident.'" He didn't elaborate, but Olivia caught the edge in his tone—the same way he'd said it at the last committee meeting, when the new city manager had tried to 'streamline' access by packing the public records into a windowless closet on the far side of the courthouse.

Elena was next, arriving in a swirl of denim and wind, hair up and wild, arms loaded with a precarious stack of photocopies and yellowed manila envelopes. She nudged the door open with her hip, deposited her quarry on the table, and exhaled like she'd just run a hundred yards in heels. "Remind me again why we can't just digitize this shit?" she said, addressing no one and everyone at once.

Andrew shot her a look that was both skeptical and amused. "Because then we'd have to trust the city's Wi-Fi, which is three firewalls and a ransomware attack away from being held for Bitcoin ransom."

Elena grinned, and for a moment the room felt lighter.

Olivia glanced at the pile. "Is that the original construction archive?"

"Plus all the payroll records Carmen could dig up," Elena said, thumbing through the folders with a practiced flick. "She called half the church directory last night—her kitchen was like a telethon for bitter old ladies. There's at least two names in here that never made it onto the county rolls."

Andrew reached for the first batch, careful not to smudge the photos. He wore latex gloves, a habit Olivia found both endearing and slightly paranoid, but she supposed it beat the alternative: city councilmen with Cheeto-stained fingers using public records as coasters. She wondered how many times he'd done practically the same thing, just in another county, another building. Was his behavior just a learned habit brought on by years of repeating the process, or was Madison special? The idea that he'd done something similar to just this didn't sit well with her. She shoved the bit of jealousy down, determined that he wouldn't see it registered on her face.

The three of them set to work, elbow to elbow around the battered table. Olivia read aloud from the oldest ledger—a ledger Carmen's father had kept, its entries a tense fusion of schoolboy print and day-labor urgency—while Elena sorted photos by decade and Andrew meticulously cross-referenced the marks with the building's floor plans. It was the kind of brute-force research that could only happen in person, the digital age defeated by illegible cursive and a thousand unscanned pages.

Every so often, Andrew would freeze mid-note, his attention caught by some detail in the margins. He tapped a faded snapshot: a line of men, stripped to undershirts, brick dust ghosting their hair and forearms. "That's the northeast wall," he said, tracing the background. "If you look at the sequence, they're going west to east."

Elena peered over his shoulder. "That's Carmen's dad on the end. He's the one with the bandana, see?" She tapped the face, which was all jaw and stubborn eyes, the features warped but unmistakable.

Olivia leaned in. "I remember this story. He got fired twice in the same week for back-talking the boss, but they kept rehiring him because he was the only one who could patch the limestone without it spalling in summer."

Andrew nodded, the technical term rolling off his tongue like a blessing. "That would explain the repair notes from '38. There's a different mortar signature—here." He flipped to a photo of the wall in question, the joints rougher, the tooling deeper than the surrounding stone. "That's deliberate. Meant to flex with the heat, so it doesn't crack."

Olivia translated the Spanish in the ledger's margin: "He writes, 'Today I put my name in the wall for when they forget.'" She let the words hang, their weight settling over the table like a shroud.

For a while, they worked in silence, the only sounds being the scratch of pencils and the slow hum of the ancient radiator. The city had cut the heat two years back, so every breath fogged a little in the chill. Olivia rubbed her hands, partly for warmth, partly to ground herself at the moment.

Elena started the next round. "Okay, so we have three more group photos, two from the dome work, one from the finish crew. I can't ID everyone, but Carmen's neighbor thinks the guy in the cap was her uncle."

Andrew squinted. "Let's scan the faces, match them to the signature marks. Sometimes the crews would leave a pattern—like a symbol, not just initials."

He flipped through his sketches and pointed to a tiny, almost invisible spiral carved in the keystone of the west portico. "This. It's not an error. In Spanish masonry, the spiral was a mark of the senior stonemason. Means they owned the wall, or at least claimed it for their lineage."

Olivia stared at the page, goosebumps prickling her forearms. "So they left their real names, but also a secret code. In case the records got erased." Thank God for her grandfather and his "anal retentive" determination to record everything. Thank God she'd never gotten around to driving those boxes to Goodwill.

Elena was already texting a photo of the spiral to Carmen. "She's going to lose her mind."

They kept going, the pile of evidence growing until the table itself seemed to buckle under the weight. Every page brought a new piece of the story—payroll logs showing the switch from German crews to Tejano laborers during the second summer, letters from wives to the city pleading for extra hours, even a scrap of newspaper wedged between ledgers, its headline reporting a “rowdy labor dispute” that never made it into the town’s official history.

At one point, Andrew paused, hands hovering above the ledger like he was about to say a prayer. “You ever think about what it means?” he asked, not quite meeting Olivia’s eye. “All this effort to avoid being forgotten?”

Olivia chewed the inside of her cheek. “I think it means you survive by leaving a mark, even if you know no one’s ever going to say your name out loud.”

He nodded. “My grandfather used to say the same thing, but he made cabinets. He thought buildings were too big—too easy to bulldoze when the next generation wanted a parking lot.”

The clock on the far wall ticked into the next hour, and the room grew cold enough that Elena wrapped her scarf around her neck, leaving the ends to dangle in front of her like streamers at a party. She looked at Olivia, then at Andrew. “So what now? We have the proof. But what do we do with it?”

Andrew set down his pencil. “We write it up. We add it to the restoration plan. And we—” He hesitated, uncharacteristically. “We tell them at the dinner.”

Olivia felt her pulse jump. “You mean present it to the entire room? Live?”

He shrugged, but there was a flicker of nerves in the motion. “If we don’t, it gets buried again. Might as well get it over with.”

Elena grinned. “You’re braver than I thought.”

Andrew smiled, just a little. “No. I’m just tired of ‘politely ignoring’ coverups.”

Olivia packed up the files, stacking them in order and double-checking the photos. She glanced out the window, catching a slice of blue sky through the grimy pane. It looked almost warm, almost promising.

She thought about the coming dinner, the room full of skeptics and old friends, the chance—however slim—that they could change the story for good. She let herself imagine, just for a second, the names they'd say out loud, the faces that would finally have a place in the open.

For the first time in a week, the courthouse didn't feel like a fortress or a tomb. It felt like a story waiting to be told.

BY NOON, the courthouse had woken fully, its hallways clattering with the footfalls of jurors and the arrhythmic ballet of county employees hustling between floors. The rotunda's echo doubled every sound, so even a muffled laugh from the clerk's office seemed to bounce three times before fading. Andrew led the way, always a half step ahead of Olivia and Elena, as if propelled by some private logic the rest of them could only hope to follow.

"Start with the attic," Andrew said. "It's the oldest part. Nobody ever touches it, so the evidence will be cleanest." He didn't look back to see if they were following; he just assumed they would, and they did.

The staircase to the attic was narrower than Olivia remembered, the last few steps warped and feathered with old paint. The place you learned to avoid as a child, convinced that if you lingered, something would reach through the banister and pull you into the dark. But Andrew navigated by instinct, hand tracing the curve of the rail, boots landing in the exact center of each tread.

At the landing, he paused and handed Olivia a flashlight, his fingers warm around hers for a moment longer than necessary. "There's no overhead up there. Just follow my lead."

She nodded, heart thumping, and tucked the light into her jacket pocket.

The attic was a study in filtered light and silence, every rafter hung with dust like the pelt of some extinct animal. The air was chilly, but it felt alive, similar to a library undisturbed for decades. Andrew moved straight to the east wall, where the original limestone met a patch of concrete from a later retrofit.

"Here," he said, rapping the stone with his knuckle. "Look at the base layer. See the tool marks?"

Olivia crouched, squinting at the seam. At first, she saw nothing but stone, the color of old teeth, lined with the faintest grooves. Then, as her eyes adjusted, she made out the faintest spiral, almost lost to time but unmistakable once seen.

"Same as in the photo," she whispered.

Andrew smiled, real this time. "They're everywhere if you know where to look."

Elena snapped a picture with her phone, the flash lighting up the whole crawlspace. "This is going in the slideshow," she said, already composing her next message to Carmen.

They moved along the wall, stopping at every joint that looked out of place. Andrew explained each one, sometimes referencing the ledger and Roberto Cuellar's notebooks, sometimes just tracing the lines with reverence. "This joint is off because they had to make up time after the north wall shifted. See how the stones don't quite line up? They patched on the fly."

Elena knelt beside him. "Why didn't they just tear it out and start over?"

Andrew shrugged. "Money. They couldn't afford the labor, and the schedule was everything. But the patch crew signed it with a diamond. It's a protest, if you know the code."

Olivia felt a sudden, irrational urge to touch the mark, as if it would transmit something through her skin—a fragment of stubbornness or hope. She let her hand rest on the stone a moment before moving on.

They finished the attic tour and descended back into the main hall, where the noise of the courthouse seemed louder now, more insistent. A group of maintenance men in coveralls waited at the bottom of the stairs, arms crossed, faces set in the lines of men who'd had to explain themselves one too many times.

"Morning, boss," one of them called to Andrew, with the friendliness that doubled as a challenge. "Find any buried treasure up there?"

Andrew smiled, but Olivia could see his jaw tighten. "Just history," he said. "Turns out, the building's got more signatures than the dedication plaque lets on."

The men laughed, but it wasn't cruel—just tired. "You mean all those graffiti marks? My granddad used to say half of 'em were just union jokes. Guys bored out of their minds, leaving their names for the next sucker to find."

Andrew shook his head. "Not these. These are different. If you ever want to see it , I'll show you."

One man, older than the rest, eyed Olivia and Elena. "You're the innkeeper, right? Heard you're planning some shindig for the whole town."

Olivia forced a smile. "We're just trying to tell the actual story. Not the ones that usually make it into the brochures."

He shrugged. "Doesn't matter. Folks around here already know what happened. They just don't care to make a big deal out of it." He made a point of turning away, dismissing the entire project with a wave of his hand.

Elena's eyes narrowed. "You'd think people would want to know who actually built this place."

The man grunted. "Maybe once. But these days, all it gets you is a lecture from the city about 'diversity' and 'heritage.' Some things are better left in the past."

Olivia felt her cheeks flush. "It's not about lectures. It's about respect. About remembering the people who got left out."

The man leveled his gaze at her, unsmiling. "Tell you what, Miss Cuellar. You put a plaque up for every forgotten name, and pretty soon there's no wall left for the living." He shuffled off, the other men following.

Andrew watched them go, then turned to Olivia. "That's the hardest part. Some people think there's only so much history to go around."

She nodded, the conversation ringing in her ears long after the men had disappeared down the hall. "I just didn't expect it to hurt this much."

He put a hand on her shoulder, light but steady. "That means you're doing it right."

They finished the tour with the basement—a warren of storage rooms, each with its own weird microclimate and smell. The main archive was at the end of a corridor lined with boxes of unused county forms and twenty years' worth of abandoned case files. Andrew led the way, stopping at a narrow door marked "Records—Authorized Only." He picked the lock with a smile and waved them in.

Inside, the light was fluorescent and ugly, but the walls were original. The stone here was untouched, cold to the point of dampness. Andrew ran his flashlight along the seam, illuminating a string of initials carved at knee height, each one dated and underlined.

"See these?" he said, pointing to a cluster of marks. "They're from different years, different crews. Some of them even overlapped—they didn't care about credit, just about surviving the job."

Elena knelt, running her finger over the marks. "There's more Spanish than English here," she said, amazed. "I thought the county only hired Anglo crews after the '20s."

Andrew shook his head. "Not in Madison. The records show the switch on paper, but in reality, the same guys kept working—just under someone else's name. Subcontractors. Laborers. Nobody ever promoted them, but they kept coming back."

Olivia read one signature aloud: "L. Maldonado, 1924. Same as the ledger." She felt a sting of pride, but also something darker—a sense that the building had been holding its breath all these years, waiting for someone to see it for what it was.

As they traced the line of signatures around the room, a knot of voices drifted down from upstairs. More courthouse workers, maybe even some early arrivals for the evening's open house. The sound made Olivia's stomach flip.

"Are we ready for this?" she whispered to Elena.

Elena grinned, but her hands shook a little. "Not even close. But we're not backing out now."

Andrew packed up his notes, the motions slower now, more deliberate. "We'll do one last pass after lunch," he said. "Then we set up the displays and hope someone cares enough to look."

They left the archive, the silence behind them replaced by the hum of courthouse business as usual. Olivia felt lighter and heavier all at once, every mark and story they'd uncovered crowding her mind.

As they stepped into the sunlit square, Elena nudged her in the ribs. "You see the look on that guy's face when you talked back to him?"

Olivia shrugged. "I don't know if it made a difference."

"It did," Elena said. "You made him think. Even if he pretended not to."

They walked the rest of the way in silence, but Olivia knew the words would keep echoing. The real history was messy, half-hidden and full of ghosts, but at least now it had a voice.

And as they approached the inn, she hoped—just a little—that the world was finally ready to listen.

The Bluebonnet Cafe was in full bellow, every booth occupied, servers running a tight choreography between tables and counter. The glass doors did nothing to muffle the din of traffic from the square, and every time someone came or went, the draft carried with it a punch of diesel and cigarette smoke, just enough to cut the sweetness of the meringue pies spinning under the counter dome. Olivia let herself get swept into the noise, using the chaos as a buffer against the slow creep of nerves. If she sat perfectly still and looked down at the chipped Formica, she could almost pretend this was just another Thursday lunch.

Elena had snagged them a booth near the back, the kind where the seats had been patched so many times the vinyl made a herringbone of electrical tape. Andrew slid in beside her, already scanning the room with an anthropologist's squint, absorbing the lunch crowd in one sweep.

"You ever seen it this packed?" he asked, tone admiring.

Olivia snorted. "Bluebonnet's the only game in town for the courthouse crowd unless you want to eat off a church basement folding table."

A server appeared, hair scraped into a bun so tight it looked like a threat. "What'll it be?"

"Coffee," Andrew said, before Olivia could answer, then, almost as an afterthought: "Pie, please. Whatever's left."

Elena raised an eyebrow at Olivia; the gesture sly and unspoken. "Just water for me. We're on the clock," she said, tapping the file folder she'd brought.

The server made a note and vanished. For a moment, the only sound was the ambient argument from the next booth over, two insurance agents bickering about appraisal fees.

Andrew leaned in, lowering his voice. "You want to go over tonight's agenda, or should I let you two interrogate me first?"

Olivia blinked. "What would we be interrogating you for?"

He shrugged. "Usually it's about my 'real reasons' for being here. Or what the state's actually trying to do with the courthouse."

Elena grinned. "You know us too well. But in our defense, the last out-of-town architect left town owing half the vendors in Madison and a trail of broken relationships that still gets brought up at Thanksgiving."

Olivia remembered the scandal. The guy had left with a married city councilwoman and the better part of the art déco light fixtures from the auditorium. "That's a low bar," she said.

Andrew sipped his water, eyes thoughtful. "I promise I'm not here to loot your courthouse. I just want to see it stand another hundred years."

Elena softened a little. "You're not like the others. The way you talked to Carmen—most people just try to out-stubborn her, but you actually listened."

Andrew looked down suddenly shy. "My grandmother used to say, 'Every problem is just a story waiting to be told right.' I figure, why not try to get it right the first time?"

The food arrived—three plates of blue-plate special and a wobbling slice of coconut creme pie. The pie looked like it would collapse under its own weight, but Andrew dug in like it was the first solid food he'd had all week.

Elena let him eat a few bites before launching the next round. "What's the worst job you've ever had?"

He smiled, a little wary. "Randolph County. They tried to put an elevator shaft through the original staircase. The developer told us to fudge the drawings, say the old stairs were 'unrecoverable.' We found signatures in the risers—dates, names, even a love letter chiseled under the landing. The elevator still went in, but we kept the stairs."

Olivia caught the edge in his voice. "But it bothered you. That they will lie about it."

Andrew nodded, his fork slowing. "Yeah. I kept thinking about the people who built it, who thought maybe their names would last. All it took was one guy with a Sharpie and a demolition order, and poof—gone."

Elena nodded, chewing this over. "Do you think that's what'll happen here?"

Andrew glanced at Olivia, then away. "Honestly? I think if we don't make the story loud enough, someone will find a way to bury it. That's why tonight matters."

The words landed harder than Olivia expected. She stared at her coffee, watching the swirl of cream as she stirred, and thought about all the times people with more power, better connections, or just a longer memory for grudges had rewritten her own history. She wondered if that was happening again, right under her nose.

She tried to shake the thought, but it stuck. "What about the other towns?" she asked. "Did any of them actually care about the actual history?"

Andrew set down his fork. "Some. Sharp County—they went all-in. Restored every inch, turned the old jail into a museum for the chain gang. The developer hated it, but the town got a grant from the Historical Commission and doubled their tourism. It worked, but only because enough people wanted it to."

"And the others?" Elena prompted.

He hesitated. "Most just want it fixed and done. The

names get painted over. The stories, if they don't fit the tourist pitch, get dropped."

The table went silent. Olivia felt the icy knot in her stomach tighten. She thought about Stirling's money, how her deal was presented to the county, and the unsaid expectation that she would be grateful and not ask too many questions.

She stared at Andrew, trying to read his face. Was he in on it, too? Or was he just another player, getting used like she was?

Elena finished her plate and wiped her hands on a napkin. "You know, you never told us why you got into this. The whole courthouse obsession."

Andrew's smile was tired, but honest. "My family lost everything after the war. My dad used to drive us to old buildings on Sundays, just to see what was still standing. He'd say, 'We may not have a house, but the town will always be there.' I guess I wanted to make that true for someone else."

Olivia felt a pang of recognition—different trauma, same logic. She looked at Elena, who raised her eyebrows in a way that meant, "See, not so different after all."

The check came, and Andrew insisted on paying, leaving a tip that would make Marta proud. As they gathered their things, Elena touched Olivia's arm.

"You okay?" she said, voice soft so only Olivia could hear.

Olivia nodded, but the doubt lingered. "Yeah. Just thinking."

"You think too much," Elena said. "Just do the thing. The rest will sort itself out."

Olivia smiled, then followed Andrew and Elena out into the midday sun, the bells from the courthouse clock ringing a few seconds slow.

They walked together, three abreast, toward the square. Andrew talked about the logistics for the open house, but Olivia only half-listened, her mind cycling through every conversation, every warning from home, every look from the men in the courthouse who didn't want their version of the story disturbed.

She wasn't sure what the night would bring—vindication, disaster, or just another chapter in a saga of disappointments. But as she watched Elena and Andrew argue over the best route to the annex, she felt something close to resolve.

It didn't matter what happened after tonight. The truth was out; the marks were there, and for once, she had a hand in ensuring they wouldn't be left behind..

She squared her shoulders, tucked her hands in her jacket, and kept moving forward.

Chapter Nine

By the time Caleb arrived, the kitchen had the raw, fluorescent glare of a postmortem. Olivia waited at the prep counter, a legal pad and three pens lined up with military precision, the air still carrying an aftertaste of ozone from the morning's oven trauma. She'd called him in desperation and now fought the urge to apologize for the state of everything: the failed equipment, the spray of scorched batter on the backsplash, even the way her own hands trembled when she tried to look busy.

Caleb entered with a toolbox slung from his shoulder, his chef's coat exchanged for a navy henley and work jeans. He surveyed the room the way a seasoned paramedic might assess a five-car pileup, eyes narrowing only at the most egregious damage before flicking to the next point of triage. There was a steadiness about him—a refusal to let the chaos infect his own rhythm.

"Show me the patient," he said, setting his kit on the tile with a thunk.

Olivia led him to the Vulcan, its battered surface reflecting the ceiling light in dull, streaked bands. She felt suddenly exposed, like she'd brought a child to the ER and was bracing for the verdict.

Caleb crouched, opened the oven's lower panel, and began a silent inspection: removing screws, running his fingers along wire harnesses, breathing in through his nose as if he could diagnose by scent alone. "Pilot's cold. That's a good sign—it means the thermal cutoff is doing its job. The bad sign is, you've got carbon scoring here and here." He pointed, and Olivia tried to track his movements, but his hands moved with a speed and certainty she couldn't match.

She hovered, pen ready. "What do I need to do?"

"Short-term? Nothing. Long-term? Pray for a new ignition switch and hope the county doesn't do another power surge." He straightened, dusting his hands on a rag. "You're lucky it didn't blow the whole burner manifold. Or set off the fire suppression."

She wrote it down anyway: "IGNITION SWITCH. BURNER MANIFOLD. FIRE SUPPRESSION." Each word in all caps, as if by inscribing them she could gain some measure of control.

Caleb moved to the fridge, giving it a slow, appraising look. "This is a dinosaur, Liv. It'll keep working until the compressor shits the bed, but when it goes, it'll go big." He popped the panel, checked the lines, then closed it with a sigh. "If you hear a grinding noise, call me before you panic."

She wrote: "GRINDING = CALEB. PANIC LATER."

He moved around the kitchen in a slow circuit, testing the mixer, flicking switches on the hood, gently repositioning knives in the block so the edges didn't clang. It was like watching a musician tune an entire orchestra, each adjustment small but necessary.

"Did Stirling's people give you grief over the breakdown?" he asked, not looking up.

"Not yet," Olivia said, "but I expect a call. Or a strongly worded email, followed by a surprise inspection."

Caleb snorted. "Classic Alex. The man runs his trust like a mafia front—tough but always with plausible deniability. He ever threaten to pull your funding?"

"Once. During the last heatwave, the A/C fried. Said if I couldn't maintain 'a minimum threshold of guest comfort,' he'd have to recommend a replacement operator."

Caleb's hands paused on the counter, then resumed their gentle alignment of the salt shakers. "Alex plays both sides. But I don't think he'd sabotage you on purpose. If he wanted you gone, he'd do it through the back channels. More likely, the appliances are just old, and the state's power grid is held together by nostalgia and coat hangers."

Olivia felt the tension in her neck loosen by a fraction. "So I'm not cursed?"

He grinned, lines creasing his face in a way that suggested he'd smiled through worse. "If you are, it's a very polite curse. One that breaks down at regular intervals and always gives you just enough warning to fix things."

She managed a genuine laugh, then pressed her hand over her mouth, surprised by the sound. "Thank you, Caleb."

He shrugged, then wiped his hands and started packing up. "You're not alone, Liv. You never were."

She looked at the kitchen—its battle scars, its persistent warmth, the ghosts of a hundred family feasts—and wondered if that was true.

He lingered, one hand on his toolbox. "This place reminds me of Dallas, you know. My first proper restaurant was three times the size of this, but it never felt as alive. Maybe because I was always too busy worrying about the next inspection, or whether I'd make payroll. Here, even with the chaos, it feels like someone actually cares."

Olivia eyed the list she'd made: all the crises, all the quick fixes, all the borrowed time she was living on. She wondered if "caring" was enough.

Caleb gestured to the mixer. "Next time it stalls, let it rest for ten minutes before trying again. The gear's stripped, but it can still work if you're gentle. Don't push it."

She wrote: "MIXER = GENTLE. REST 10 MINS. DO NOT PUSH."

He grabbed a wooden spoon from the drying rack, twirled it in his fingers. "You know, I miss this. Not the breakdowns, or the customers, or the endless city paperwork. Just the cooking. The way a kitchen smells in the morning. The weight of the bread dough when it's proofed just right. You ever get that?"

"All the time," Olivia admitted, her hand unconsciously tracing the edge of the counter.

He tossed her the spoon. "Good. Don't lose it. The tech stuff is simple—the parts are just money and time. But if you lose the rest... that's when you need to worry."

She caught the spoon, surprised by how steady her grip was. "I'll try."

Caleb smiled again, this time softer. "You're going to be fine. The town just needs to get used to having someone who doesn't quit."

With that, he headed out, toolbox in hand, the door swinging shut on a current of warm, yeasty air.

Olivia stood in the center of the kitchen, looking at the scars and patches, the hand-me-down equipment and the memories baked into every tile. She gripped the wooden spoon, then set it in the holder by the stove, as if to promise she'd be back to use it.

She flipped the switch on the coffeepot, watched the thin stream pour into the carafe, and let herself breathe for the first time that day.

On the counter, her list of crises seemed smaller, almost manageable.

Outside, the afternoon light shifted, and Olivia turned her thoughts to the dinner service ahead, her hands already moving in practiced, determined lines.

❧

EVENING CREPT up on the Limestone the way a tide does a flat beach, slow and inexorable until suddenly every surface wore a glaze of lavender dusk. The dining nook, narrow as a ship's galley, caught the last of the day through a single window overlooking the herb beds. Olivia moved with the methodical calm of someone who'd already spent all her anxiety for the week: she ladled soup—leek and potato, flecked with black pepper—into bowls the color of raw clay, and tore hunks of bread from a still-warm boule Josephina had baked off after lunch.

She had just set the bowls on the table, more out of habit than hunger, when she heard the front door rattle and Andrew's distinct shuffle over the threshold. She thought about ducking into the kitchen, pretending to be busy, but something in his gait sounded off: the weight of a bad day, or maybe just the exhaustion of having to explain himself one too many times.

He appeared in the doorway, hair flattened by a day's worth of hard hats, sleeves rolled and splattered with chalk and something darker—mud, maybe, or the oil from old elevator gears. There was a stripe of dust across his cheek that made him look improbably younger.

"Oh," he said, catching sight of her, then the food. "Sorry, I didn't realize you'd be—"

"It's fine," Olivia said, and meant it. "I made too much. Sit, if you want."

He hesitated just long enough to make her regret the offer, then nodded and slid into one of the mismatched chairs. The seat let out a creak of protest, and Olivia almost laughed, but caught herself.

She poured water into jelly glasses, then sat opposite, the bowls steaming quietly between them.

They ate in silence at first, the way people do when they are hungry in a way that isn't quite about food. The only sound the scrape of spoons and the occasional rustle of bread crust tearing.

Andrew was the first to break. "I read your memo," he said, not quite meeting her gaze. "About the bricks and the front walkway."

Olivia tensed, bracing for a bureaucratic reprimand.

He shook his head. "You were right to be pissed. The city dropped the ball. I tried to get them to route the salvage to the county yard, but..." He gestured, helpless. His kindness, instead of a bureaucratic reflex to make excuses, softened her anger from earlier.

"I'm used to being the afterthought," Olivia said, dipping bread into her soup. "Comes with the territory."

He gave a dry laugh. "Same."

She looked at him, really looked, and saw the fatigue in the slump of his shoulders, the way his right hand trembled slightly before it settled on the glass. "Rough day?" she asked, softer.

He shrugged, weighing whether to answer. "I spent two hours on a video call with the state commission. The county is debating doing a full demo on the north wing before we can even talk about restoration. It's like they're hoping we'll find an excuse to tear it all down and start over."

She grimaced. "It's cheaper, isn't it?"

"Infinitely. But wrong." He stared into his soup. "It's not just stone. It's stories. Every time I walk the scaffold, I find something the record doesn't mention. It's like the building is trying to leave clues for anyone who bothers to look."

Olivia smiled at that—unexpected, but true. "Like the initials you found last week?"

He perked up. "Exactly. Most people think those are just vandalism, but if you line them up with the ledgers, you can see which crew did each section. It's a code. A way to prove you were here."

They lapsed into quiet again, but it wasn't awkward. Olivia felt something loosen in her chest.

After a while, she said, "Can I ask you something personal?"

He looked up, wary but open. "Sure."

"Do you think Stirling—Alex—knows what he's doing? I mean, with the trust and the grant. Or is he just playing the angles like everyone else?"

Andrew considered. "Developers like Stirling operate in the gray. In Dallas, I saw a dozen guys like him: they talk preservation, but only so long as the permits go through. The minute it gets hard, they pivot to 'economic development' and call it progress." He paused. "You're right to be cautious. But I don't think he's out to ruin you specifically. He just doesn't see you unless you're in his way."

Olivia nodded, feeling the truth of it in her bones. "I just —" She stopped, not sure she wanted to finish.

He waited.

She started again, quieter. "I don't want to be that person. The one who gets used up and then replaced because she's too easy to overlook."

"You're not," Andrew said, voice steady. "You're the only one fighting for this place. If you weren't, no one would even remember the old crews. Or care what happened to the bricks."

She looked at her hands, the faint lines of flour and pen

ink on her knuckles. She thought of the ledger, the hidden marks, the endless, grinding work of making a dent in the world.

"Can I tell you something?" she said, surprising herself with the urgency.

He nodded.

"In Houston, I went all in on a partnership. Woman named Muriel. We bought a brownstone, renovated it from the ground up, and ran the guest house together. It was the happiest I'd ever been." She paused, gathering herself. "Turns out she was bleeding us dry. Skimming, padding invoices, slowly making me the sole owner on paper so she could bail with the money and leave me holding the debt."

Andrew whistled low. "That's—brutal."

Olivia's lips twisted. "Yeah. It made the news. I was a punchline for months. When I left, I promised myself I'd never let anyone else have that kind of power over me. But now I'm here, and it feels like I'm just waiting for the next Muriel. Or Stirling. Or even the city. To pull the rug out."

Andrew was quiet for a long moment. "You're not her," he said. "And you're not alone."

She wanted to believe him. She really did.

He set his spoon down; the metal rang softly against the bowl. "Since we're sharing," he said, "I'll tell you mine."

She met his eyes, startled.

"My wife left me because I was more married to historic buildings than to her," he said, a wry twist to his smile. "I'd spend nights mapping load paths, weekends hunting for original blueprints. One day, she just packed up and said she couldn't be second place to dead architects anymore."

Olivia blinked. "That's—actually, I get it."

He laughed, for real this time. "Not my proudest moment, but at least now I know what not to do."

They both looked out the window, where the garden

lights flickered on against the dark. In the glass, their reflections sat side by side, not quite touching but closer than before.

Andrew stood, gathering their empty bowls. "Thanks for the meal. It helped."

She surprised herself by saying, "Anytime."

He carried the bowls to the kitchen, pausing at the door. "If you ever need to talk—about Stirling, or Muriel, or just about how much the city sucks—my line's always open."

She nodded, her throat tight.

He left, the sound of his steps fading into the creak of the old house.

Olivia lingered by the window, watching the steam curl from her half-empty glass. She replayed the conversation in her head, the confessions and the silences, the things said and unsaid.

For the first time since arriving in Madison, someone truly saw her.

She cleared the table, then went to the kitchen, where the scent of soup and bread hung heavy in the air. She washed the dishes slowly, letting the hot water scald her hands, and let herself believe that maybe, just maybe, things would be different this time.

Chapter Ten

Olivia woke to a stillness so complete it rang in her ears. No hiss from the radiator, no creak from the old oak above the window, not even the distant whirr of Josefina prepping in the kitchen. Just the faint, pulsing pain behind her left eyebrow and the sense that something essential had gone missing overnight.

She lay there for a moment, inventorying the silence, then rolled out of bed. The floor was cold enough to make her gasp. She pulled on her robe, a navy wrap with a coffee stain over one pocket, and padded to the bathroom. The light switch stuck, then flicked on with a vindictive snap. She turned the faucet, expecting the rattle of pipes and the sputter of last night's sediment.

Nothing.

She jiggled the handle, leaned closer, and tried again. The faucet coughed a single spit of air, then nothing. No water. Not even a drop.

For a split second, her mind went blank—blank in the way that only comes when disaster skips its warning shot and lands a direct hit. Then: adrenaline, as if the lack of water had detonated a charge in her spinal cord. She yanked open the medicine cabinet, slammed it, and yanked it again. She flushed the toilet (empty gurgle), tore off the shower curtain (dry as fresh paper), then sprinted barefoot down the hall, the hem of her robe flapping behind.

Down the main staircase, the air shifted from silence to a kind of pulsing dread. She stopped at the front door, where a bright-orange rectangle fluttered in the morning breeze, duct-taped over the glass like a quarantine notice.

CITY OF MADISON—EMERGENCY WATER MAIN REPLACEMENT. 48-72 HOUR OUTAGE. IMPACTED BLOCKS: ALL OF TRAVIS, FANNIN, AND Lamar.

At the bottom: IF YOU HAVE QUESTIONS, CALL 1-800-881-0401. DO NOT ATTEMPT TO ACCESS THE WORKSITE.

A handwritten line had been added in blue Sharpie: "SORRY!—Public Works"

Her hands shook. She pressed her palm flat against the glass, as if she could will the notice out of existence. But it remained defiant and vivid. The sky outside was already the wrong color, too bright and too blue for the disaster now rising in her chest.

She spun on her heel, headed straight for the kitchen, and found it dark—no hum from the espresso machine, no scent of bleach or coffee or yeast. Josefina was absent, her usual trail of flour footprints missing from the tile.

Olivia checked the digital clock above the range: 6:23. Her first guests would expect breakfast by eight. With no water.

She darted back to the office, fumbled the guest ledger open, and scanned the reservation column. Five rooms, all occupied. Two more parties arriving tomorrow: one the Johnson wedding, forty-two guests, a three-layer cake and a rehearsal dinner, every ounce dependent on running water.

She checked her email, then her phone—nothing but two

spam messages and a text from Elena ("library Wi-Fi down again, send help or caffeine"). Her hands trembled so badly she had to sit, the chair digging into her hipbones as she dialed the emergency number.

The phone rang six times, then a flat, unmoved voice: "Madison Public Works."

Olivia spoke in a rush. "I'm calling from the Limestone Inn—Travis and Fannin. I have a full house and no water. The notice says three days? Is that real?"

A slow exhale on the other end. "Yup, that's real. Got an old main, goes back to the forties. Section collapsed overnight. We got crews on it, but earliest you're looking at is Thursday."

"Thursday?" She heard the octave of her own voice spike. "I have a wedding here in forty-eight hours. People have paid—"

"Ma'am, there's nothing I can do. It's an emergency repair. If you need potable water, the county is setting up a distribution point at the fire station. "

She pressed her free hand to her sternum, willing her heart to slow. "Is there—could I get a tanker or a—" She ran out of words, mind skipping like a scratched CD.

A beat, then: "That's a question for the city manager. I can transfer—"

"No." Olivia felt herself floating above the situation, watching as she scribbled down the number anyway, the pen nearly tearing through the paper. "Thank you."

The call disconnected, leaving a dead space so deep she almost screamed.

She set the phone down, then gripped the edge of the desk so hard her knuckles bleached white. Her thoughts fanned out: the guests, the wedding, the health inspector who could show up at any moment, the half-dozen negative Yelp reviews that would follow the moment anyone found out about the outage. Worst of all, the loan payment to Alex

—$2,500—circled in red on the paper calendar tacked above her monitor. Due in eight days, no exceptions, no extensions.

Her skin prickled as if someone had doused her in ice. She reached for the wall calendar and traced the date with a shaking finger, the red circle bleeding through to the next page. If she lost the wedding, if guests demanded refunds, she would default on the payment. The penalty clause alone would wipe out her profit for the rest of the year.

She forced herself to breathe, counting to four on the inhale, six on the exhale. Her left hand wouldn't stop trembling. She balled it into a fist, let go, then balled it again. She had a sudden, vivid image of herself as a marionette, arms jerking in panic, while the real Olivia hovered somewhere far above, unable to cut the strings.

She made herself stand. She walked to the kitchen, surveyed the disaster, then opened the utility closet and retrieved the emergency case of bottled water. Six bottles. Not even enough for one round of morning coffee.

She thought of her grandmother, who would have made a joke about using the tequila from the pantry as a backup. The line almost made her laugh, but the sound withered in her throat.

She forced herself upstairs, stripped off her robe, and changed into jeans and a plain black shirt—no time for the usual uniform, no time to iron or even button the cuffs. She twisted her hair into a bun and looked at herself in the mirror: dark circles, jaw clenched, eyes two black holes.

By the time she returned to the kitchen, Josefina had arrived, face drawn and skeptical, arms crossed as if bracing for battle.

"No water?" Josefina asked, not even pretending to hope.

"No water," Olivia confirmed.

They stood in silence for a moment, then Josefina

shrugged and said, "I have a cousin who runs a taco truck. Maybe he'll let us use his sink."

It was absurd, but it was also the best idea she had heard all morning.

She smiled, fierce and thin, and reached for her phone.

She would not let this be the straw that broke her. Not today.

THE RACKET STARTED at 7:01 sharp. Jackhammers, three in stereo, shuddered through the windows and vibrated the cups on the breakfast table. Olivia had known it was coming —the city notice had said, "Crews may begin work as early as 7 AM"—but she hadn't expected the way it would ricochet through every floor, every pipe, every nerve ending.

She propped open the front door, hoping to head off the first wave of guest complaints, but the path outside was a gauntlet: caution tape, orange water-filled barriers, and a single wobbly plywood ramp bridging the trench that now bisected the entire block. The air was sharp with the chemical reek of asphalt and the fine mist of pulverized concrete.

The first guest found her at the desk before she could even finish her emergency pot of lobby coffee. He was the kind of business traveler Olivia recognized instantly—pressed slacks, angry Bluetooth in one ear, face set to "I want the manager and I want her now." He strode up, damp from the neck down, and dropped his keycard on the counter with a wet thunk.

"I need a refund," he said, voice clipped. "No shower. No water. I have a meeting in an hour, and I smell like a construction site."

Olivia summoned her best "dealing with a telecom rep" voice. "I'm very sorry, sir. The county is working on the water main. We're providing bottled water and have partnered with a local gym—just down the street—where you can shower free of charge. We're also offering a fifty percent discount on your room, and—"

He snorted. "You think I have time to jog to a gym before my meeting? I have to Zoom in with a European office at 8:15."

"I understand, and I apologize for the inconvenience. If you'd like, I can call the gym and have them hold a shower stall—"

"I want the full refund. Today. Or I'm leaving a review on every travel site in existence."

She made herself nod. "Let me process that for you." She'd learned not to fight these battles. The bad reviews cost more than the lost room rate.

He watched her type, jaw flexing. "You should tell guests up front when you're going to cut the water off. Some of us actually have jobs."

She smiled, showing teeth. "It was not my decision, but I agree with you." She handed him the refund receipt and a business card for the gym. "Have a great day, sir."

He took it and left without another word, but she watched through the front windows as he navigated the plywood ramp—only to catch his loafer on the edge and stagger, arms windmilling, into a patch of construction mud. He swore loudly enough for her to hear, then stomped off, trailing brown streaks in his wake.

The second round arrived in tandem: a couple in coordinated tennis gear, both tanned to the point of parody, rolling matching suitcases behind them like prize pigs at the county fair. Her sunglasses were the size of salad plates, while the man wore a UT visor at a rakish angle.

The woman started in before she'd even crossed the threshold. "Our car is covered in dust. We just washed it yesterday, and now it's ruined. Also, the noise—this is supposed to be a historic district, not a war zone."

Olivia pasted on her customer-service smile. "I'm so sorry about the dust. We're providing complimentary car washes at the Exxon on Main. I can give you a voucher. The construction should pause after five, and in the meantime, we have earplugs available—"

"We were told this was a quiet property," the man said, voice thick with Houston suburbia. "We paid for premium. This is not premium."

"We're offering a thirty percent rebate for all affected guests," Olivia said, opening the drawer with the pre-printed refund forms. "And if you'd like, I can move you to a room at the back of the building, away from the street."

The woman gave a little huff. "We're only here for one night. Might as well leave now."

Olivia nodded, keeping her smile just on the right side of unhinged. "I completely understand. I'll issue your rebate and provide a car wash voucher on your way out."

They left in a flurry of annoyed murmurs, tennis bags thumping the walls as they navigated the obstacle course back to their SUV.

For a brief interval, the lobby was empty except for the echo of jackhammers and the faint, desperate gurgle of the espresso machine in its death throes. Olivia poured herself a shot, black as sin, and drank it standing up, eyes squeezed shut against the morning's onslaught.

But before she could breathe, the phone started. First a local number—probably one of the walk-in regulars, cancelling on account of the chaos. Then an unfamiliar out-of-state number, the kind that always belonged to an angry parent or an event planner with a newly discovered allergy to "unforeseen circumstances."

She answered on the third ring. “Limestone Inn, Olivia speaking.”

A woman's voice, brittle and cold as hotel ice: “Is this the owner?”

“Yes, ma’am, how can I help?”

“This is Mrs. Shepherd. My son is checking in for the Johnson wedding this weekend. He just texted me a video of the mess outside your building. Is the wedding even still on?”

Olivia choked down the urge to scream. “Yes, ma’am. The county expects to have the water restored by Thursday. We’re working around the clock to ensure all amenities are available. We have alternative facilities for showers, and—”

The woman cut in, voice climbing the octave ladder. “I have three granddaughters in that party. Are you telling me they have to walk through mud and construction tape to get to their rooms?”

“No, ma’am. We’ve set up a safe walkway, and we’re offering all guests help with luggage. We're sweeping the path hourly. I can assure you—”

“Unacceptable. I will call the bride’s mother. You can expect to hear from her lawyer.”

The line went dead.

Olivia set the receiver down, careful not to let it slam. She noticed her right hand was shaking again, the tremor worse than before. She looked at her to-do list: check wedding cake order, call temp staff, print new menus. Each item now felt like a practical joke.

She tried to breathe. One, two, three, four. The air tasted like burnt rubber.

She glanced out the front window, where the construction crews were now swinging massive iron claws into the trench, pulling out clumps of ancient pipe like it was wet spaghetti. The men worked with cheerful indifference, shouting over the din, occasionally waving at passing cars.

A silver sedan slowed, signaled, then hesitated at the entrance. Olivia watched as the driver took in the barriers, the clouds of dust, and the battered plywood ramp. The car idled for a moment, the driver's face barely visible through the windshield. Then, with a final shake of the head, the sedan pulled away, tires spinning a little in the loose gravel.

She watched it until it disappeared around the corner.

Another sale gone before it even started.

Her phone buzzed again: a text from Elena. "Saw the construction. Need lunch? I'll bring tacos."

Olivia typed back with numb fingers: "Yes, please. And beer if they have it."

She set the phone down and wiped her palms on her jeans, leaving two wet, anxious prints. She was supposed to be the calm at the center of the storm—the reliable one, the fixer, the woman who could face down a kitchen fire and still serve breakfast by eight.

But this was different. This was relentless. This was death by a thousand county-sanctioned cuts.

She squared her shoulders, steeled her jaw, and started drafting an email to the Johnson wedding planner. She would get ahead of the disaster, or at least learn how to make it look intentional.

But her hands trembled so much it took three tries to spell "amenities" correctly.

Outside, the jackhammers doubled down, as if they'd sensed her weakness.

Inside, Olivia bared her teeth, the smile now feral.

Let them try, she thought.

She'd survived worse.

❧

BY TWO, the sky was the color of a nicotine stain and the street out front looked like the world's worst slip-and-slide. Melissa Harrington—maid of honor, project manager for a Houston law firm, and self-appointed guardian of bridal standards everywhere—arrived exactly when she said she would, her black Suburban nosing up to the construction barrier with predatory grace.

Olivia watched from the parlor as Melissa stepped out, heels piercing the plywood ramp with pitiless precision. She wore business black, hair scraped into a bun so tight it made her cheekbones look engineered. She carried a manila folder and a tablet, and navigated the obstacle course with the air of someone conducting a hostile takeover.

Olivia smoothed her shirt, drew a deep breath, and moved to intercept.

"Melissa?" she called, voice bright as the safety vest on the flagger at the corner.

Melissa glanced at the chaos, then at Olivia. Her gaze was cool and measuring, like a jeweler appraising a cubic zirconia. "I'm here to do a walk-through for the Johnson event," she said, not quite a question.

"Of course." Olivia gestured past the barricades. "Sorry about the mess. The county's on a strict timeline, but they say it'll be finished before Saturday. We have staff standing by to assist your guests—"

Melissa stepped closer, frown lines deepening. "This is not what we discussed. You said the venue was 'undergoing minor improvements.' I wasn't told the entry would look like a demolition site."

"It's a temporary inconvenience," Olivia said, injecting what she hoped was just the right note of regret. "Once inside, everything's as planned. The dining room is prepped, the kitchen is fully operational—"

Melissa sniffed, as if she could detect the aroma of substandard service in the air. "What about the bathrooms?"

Olivia hesitated a split second too long. "We have portable facilities in the rear garden. They're high-end units, with fresh flowers and hand sanitizer—"

"Portable?" The word hung between them, toxic. "Are you telling me the bridal party will use a trailer?"

"They're really nice trailers," Olivia said, hating herself for the desperation in her tone.

Melissa opened her folder, tapped on her tablet, then peered through the front windows. "And the noise?"

"The crews stop work at five. We've spoken to the foreman —they're very respectful about event times."

Melissa looked unimpressed. "And if they don't finish?"

Olivia forced a smile. "They will."

Melissa took a lap around the foyer, her heels leaving angry punctuation marks on the polished wood. She checked the parlor, the breakfast room, even the staging area where the cake table waited under its muslin shroud. Her face didn't soften once. At last, she returned to the front desk.

"Olivia," she said, folding her hands, "I'm going to be frank. The bride's mother is in tears over this. She doesn't want her daughter photographed against a backdrop of caution tape and port-a-potties. If it were just a brunch or a corporate event, maybe. But this is a wedding. There are standards."

Olivia felt the floor tilt beneath her. "We can offer a significant discount—seventy-five percent, if that helps. I'll throw in free suite upgrades, extra staff—whatever you need. The kitchen can prepare a specialty menu, and—"

Melissa cut her off, voice flat. "We're canceling. The family wants the deposit returned. All four thousand by close of business tomorrow. If it's not, we'll be forced to pursue a chargeback."

The words landed like a sucker punch. Olivia grasped the edge of the counter, willing herself not to fold.

"Melissa, please. We're a small operation. That deposit is—"

"I understand it's hard," Melissa said, but her voice said the opposite. "But the bride deserves better than dust and jackhammer noise and bathrooms in the backyard."

Olivia's vision went blurry at the edges. She tried to marshal another argument, but the words stuck in her throat.

Melissa relented, just a hair. "If the county finishes early, call me. Maybe we can work something out for the brunch. But the wedding is off."

She turned, heels clicking a staccato on the wood, and braved the plywood gauntlet back to her car.

Olivia watched the Suburban reverse, then disappear in a rooster-tail of muddy spray.

For a minute she just stood, hands numb, chest hollowed out. Then she made her way to the office, moving in a slow-motion daze.

She closed the door behind her, the noise outside barely muffled by the old insulation. She sat at her desk, opened her laptop, and logged in to her business account.

The numbers made her stomach clench: $3,116.77. barely enough to make payroll, much less pay Stirling his next installment. She pulled up the event ledger, scrolled through the months ahead, and did the math—how many room nights, how many weekend brunches, how many desperate "specials" she would need to survive without the wedding money.

Three months, tops. Maybe less if the other events fell through. Maybe even less if she started losing walk-ins, which she would, because the construction was scheduled to last through winter.

She scrolled to the next tab: her calendar, every week a new blood-red circle. The next payment due to Alex was in six days, and the one after that less than a month out. If she defaulted, the "grace period" was a joke—a onetime-only extension, after which she'd be in default and likely lose the inn itself.

Her hands trembled, not with anger but with the sharp, almost electric clarity of defeat. She ran the numbers again, as if repetition might conjure a miracle.

Nothing changed.

She stared at the screen until her vision blurred, and the numbers swam. At some point she heard herself laugh, the sound jagged and small in the empty office.

She thought of Andrew, of the courthouse project that had started this whole chain reaction—his brisk, efficient optimism, the way he talked about "preserving stories," as if stories could pay for new pipes or make the weddings come back.

She let the resentment build, slow and hot, until it filled the hollow inside her.

She considered calling Elena, or maybe even Alex, to beg for help. But something stubborn in her snapped shut, hard as brick.

She shut the laptop, sat back, and listened to the steady, relentless thump of jackhammers through the walls.

She wondered how many more days she could keep this up.

Then, with deliberate slowness, she opened the ledger and started planning.

❧

THE SUN WAS ALREADY DIPPING behind the courthouse dome when Andrew's truck pulled up to the curb, two wheels in the mud and the back heavy with blue water tanks. He cut the engine, climbed out, and in five seconds flat was waving a crew of county workers into position. They moved with the crisp, choreographed rhythm of people who knew they had exactly one hour of daylight left and three hours' work to do.

From her office window, Olivia watched as the crew unloaded the tanks, rolled them up the makeshift plywood ramp, and snaked bright-green hoses through the garden gate. Andrew supervised with one hand and made calls with the other, his face tight and voice low. Even from this distance, she could see the tension in his jaw, the way he kept glancing at the inn as if expecting a sniper to take the shot.

She felt a prick of guilt, or maybe it was just that same old anger, repackaged with a bow of gratitude. Either way, she couldn't bear to watch another second from behind glass.

She pulled on her jacket, ran a hand through her hair, and stepped out onto the porch.

The evening air was sharp, the smell of gasoline and damp earth swirling around her like bad perfume. Orange construction barriers looked even more grotesque in the half-light, their plastic skin slicked with condensation. Beside them, the crew worked on, oblivious.

Andrew caught sight of her and walked over, hands shoved deep in his pockets, eyes tired.

"I'm sorry," he said, before she could speak. "I pulled some strings with a contractor friend—these tanks should get you through until the main's back up. It's not perfect, but it's potable."

She nodded, arms folded tight over her chest. "Thanks," she said, trying to make it sound neither grateful nor sarcastic. "You didn't have to."

He shrugged, then stared down at the churned-up lawn. "I did actually."

For a moment, neither spoke. The only sound the slap of

boots on plywood and the low whine of a generator as it kicked to life.

Olivia broke first. "The Johnson wedding canceled. Four grand deposit, gone. The rest of the season might follow if this keeps up."

Andrew winced, raking a hand through his dust-blond hair. "I heard. The city manager called me, said the mother of the bride was threatening legal action."

"She's not bluffing," Olivia said. "They'll drag the inn's name through every review site in Texas."

"I know," Andrew said. "If it helps, I'm getting the same treatment from the county. There's a rumor going around that I planned the outage to push through my project faster." He gave a bleak half-smile. "If I were that smart, I'd be out of a job by now."

She looked at him, really looked. He wasn't the picture of smug efficiency she'd painted in her head. The lines around his eyes had deepened; his nails were ragged, rimmed with the blue-black of hard work. He seemed smaller, or maybe just more real.

"I'm trying to do the right thing," he said, voice dropping. "For the courthouse. For the town. But it feels like every time I move, I screw something up for you."

The words caught her off guard. She'd expected deflection or defense—maybe even a bureaucratic apology. Not this.

She felt the anger drain a little, replaced by something more complicated. "You're not the problem," she said, surprising herself. "Or at least not all of it. The county's been gutting infrastructure for years. They just needed a scapegoat."

He nodded, shoulders slumping. "Doesn't make it easier."

"No," she agreed. "It doesn't."

They stood like that for a long minute, not quite facing each other, both watching the crew work.

The crew boss shouted over, "We'll have the first tank live in ten!"

Andrew raised a hand in acknowledgment, then turned back to her.

"For what it's worth," he said, "I'm rooting for you."

She gave him a look. "You know that doesn't actually pay the bills, right?"

He smiled, small and tired. "I know."

She watched as he walked back to the crew, issuing instructions in a low, steady voice. There was an awkward grace to it —an engineer playing at being a general, or maybe just a man trying to solve a problem that didn't want to be solved.

When the last tank was installed, Andrew came over to show her the hookups. He explained the valves, the backup filters, and the schedule for refilling. His hands moved with precision, but his eyes darted to her every few seconds, as if waiting for the final verdict.

She nodded along, taking it in. At one point their hands brushed, just for a second, and she felt the jolt, a static spark that lingered even after she stepped back.

As the crew packed up, Andrew lingered by the porch, boots planted in the mud.

"You know," he said, "I used to think enough math would solve problems like this. Enough planning."

"Let me guess," Olivia said. "You've reconsidered."

He laughed, and this time it sounded genuine. "A little. Turns out, people are messier than blueprints."

She smiled, not entirely without warmth. "That's what keeps it interesting."

The last light faded from the sky, leaving only the harsh glare of work lamps and the soft blue glow of the inn's sign.

Andrew looked at her, a question hovering in the space between them. But then he just nodded, gave a small wave, and headed for his truck.

Olivia watched him go, feeling the weight in her chest shift —not gone, but lighter. The tanks were ugly as hell, but they'd keep the inn alive for another day.

She went back inside, locked the door, and leaned against it, the cold wood grounding her.

Maybe she thought, that's all anyone could hope for.

One more day.

❧

Night came in with a hush, the only sound inside the Limestone a slow, distant thrum—the water pump doing its best impression of a heartbeat. Olivia moved through the darkened halls with practiced care, not wanting to jostle the delicate peace she'd bought herself for a few hours. The lobby was silent; the phones had stopped ringing, and even the rowdy construction crew down the block had packed it in for the day.

In the office, she dropped into the battered chair, rolled her shoulders, and snapped on the desk lamp. The pale light washed out everything except her ledger, her laptop, and the calendar where the next loan payment to Alex loomed in block letters. She could hear the numbers ticking in her head, the days trickling away like sand through a busted hourglass.

She pulled up her bank portal and the event spreadsheet, cross-referencing every dollar, every "maybe" booking, every wild possibility. Her fingers flew over the keyboard as if speed alone could conjure extra income, or bend time enough to make next week's disaster someone else's problem.

The reality stared back: she was eight days out. Maybe less, if the county's "timeline" slipped the way it always did.

The urge to call Alex surged within her—felt it like an itch in the back of her throat. She imagined the conversation: him listening, silent and shark-eyed, then offering the extension with a note of paternal disappointment, his posture confirming that she was indeed a total failure. She could almost hear his voice, calm and unimpressed: "You sure this is the business for you, Liv?"

No, she wouldn't give him or anyone else the satisfaction.

She stared at the phone anyway, jaw tight, hand trembling until she balled it into a fist. Her pride was all she had left, and she'd be damned if she traded it for a few extra days of oxygen.

She squared her shoulders, closed the ledger with a violent snap, and opened her browser. If the weddings were dead, she'd fill the rooms with business travelers, locals, visiting professors, anyone desperate enough to take a gamble on her battered old inn. She drafted email after email—"Travis Street Construction Special!" "Short-term Corporate Rates!" "Quiet Retreat Just Blocks from Downtown (Earplugs Included)"—and hit send on every one.

Each time she closed a window, the silence deepened, punctuated only by the steady mechanical pulse of the temporary water tanks outside.

She thought of Andrew, of the way he'd looked at her in the fading light—not with pity, but with something close to respect. Maybe he understood how it felt to be the last line of defense, to hold a crumbling relic together with nothing but stubbornness and tape.

She sat back, let her eyes close for a second, and listened. She could still hear the city outside—sirens, the rumble of a far-off truck, a single barking dog—but the loudest sound was her own breath, sharp and deliberate.

She wasn't beaten. Not yet.

Tomorrow, she'd wake before sunrise. She'd put on her best face, field the next wave of complaints, and—if she had to—she'd move every metaphorical brick herself to keep the doors open.

She'd come this far, farther than anyone had bet she would.

And if the world wanted to take the rest, it was going to have to fight her for it.

She shut the laptop, turned off the lamp, and let the night settle in.

The water pumped on, steady as resolve.

Chapter Eleven

The next morning came in on a knife-edge—thin, bright, and sharp enough to open every old wound Olivia thought she'd bandaged. She parked three blocks from the county courthouse, left the engine idling for the last shudder of AC, and watched as the square filled with trucks, battered Subarus, and the odd, gleaming Cadillac. Every parking spot taken; on the steps, clusters of people buzzed, their faces set with the same expectation she'd seen on parents about to meet the principal.

Inside, the Verde County Commissioners Court had turned the basement hearing room into a pressure cooker. The benches were already overfull, so people packed the aisle and braced themselves against the walls—contractors in monogrammed shirts, business owners in faded polos, elderly couples clutching property tax statements like grim invitations. Olivia moved toward the back, scanned for an empty seat, and slid in next to a man she dimly recognized from Rotary breakfasts. He smelled of sweat and fertilizer, and his boot tapped a relentless Morse code on the scuffed tile.

The judge's bench loomed over the room, flanked by four

commissioners, each with a nameplate and a stack of manila folders. At the center, County Judge Patti Williams banged the gavel with the force of someone who needed the world to know she was in charge.

"Order, please. This is a special emergency session. Let's keep comments to two minutes per speaker, and I will gavel anyone who interrupts. Is that clear?"

A ripple of sarcastic "Yes, Ma'ams" moved through the crowd, but it was all bark. The room was electric with the knowledge that, for once, the people in the back actually had more power than the ones up front.

Olivia's pulse quickened. She recognized three faces from her own disaster week alone—a laundromat owner whose grand opening had been ruined by the water main, a realtor who'd called her at midnight to ask if the block was "still under siege," and Mrs. Krantz from the dry cleaner, whose only crime was existing in the blast radius.

At the front, an easel held a foam-core presentation board: "Verde County Courthouse Renovation, Projected vs. Actuals." The numbers were already in red.

Judge Williams started in, her voice a practiced mix of brisk and folksy: "First agenda item—budget review. We're six weeks into restoration, and already over budget by nearly twenty percent. Second, community impact: I understand there's been disruption to business and home life. That's why we're here. Third—" She looked pointedly at the wall clock, "—I want solutions, not just complaints. Let's proceed."

The first speaker—a hardware store owner—practically sprinted to the microphone.

"This is a joke," he barked. "You told us at the Chamber meeting it'd be done piecemeal, not this all-at-once apocalypse! I've lost twenty-five percent of walk-in business, and my regulars can't even get to my shop without crossing a damn moat."

Scattered applause. The next speaker, a petite woman in a

neon-bright dress, followed before the judge could even call her name.

"I own the daycare on Jefferson. My families are parking a quarter mile away and dragging kids across construction tape! You all said, 'minimal disruption.' This is not minimal."

From the benches, shouts and side-chatter: "Tell 'em, Cindy!" and "They don't care about us, just the damn courthouse!" Someone booed.

Judge Williams banged her gavel. "Let's keep it civil. You're being heard, but please respect the process."

Olivia watched the judges, but her eyes kept sliding to the front row—where Andrew stood, half-shadowed, beside the presentation board. He wore a pressed oxford, the sleeves rolled just so, and his hair looked like he'd fought with it on the drive over. He held a sheaf of blueprints in one hand, his thumb tracing the edges in a nervous loop, and the other hand drummed a silent tattoo on his thigh.

The public comment devolved fast. Every speaker tried to outdo the last—each with a story of lost business, missed deadlines, children terrified by the jackhammers, elderly parents trapped indoors because of the "deathtrap" plywood ramps. The litany built, wave after wave.

Then the attacks got personal.

"Why's this taking so long anyway?" a man in a reflective vest called. "You bring in these guys from Dallas, and they milk us for every hour!"

"My taxes pay your salary!" yelled another. "You treat us like we're just some obstacle to building your personal legacy!"

Someone else pointed directly at Andrew: "He's not even from around here! You think he cares what happens when the money runs out?"

The room turned, and for a moment the entire scene focused on him—a single, pale spot of calm amid the storm.

Andrew didn't shrink, but Olivia saw the way his jaw tightened, the measured way he set his shoulders.

Her fingers curled around the strap of her purse. She hated the reflex, the urge to leap in and shield him, but it flared up anyway. He was outnumbered, and she knew better than most what that felt like.

She scanned the dais. Judge Williams looked tired already, eyes flicking from the crowd to her phone. The other commissioners wrote notes, whispered among themselves, or just stared into space. The architecture of county government: built for endurance, not heat.

"Next on the list," the clerk said, voice shaky, "is—uh—Ms. Teresa Alvarez."

A hush, then a ripple of whispers. Olivia felt her breath catch. Teresa rose in the third row, papers in hand, her gaze laser-bright as she took the mic.

"We all know what this is about," Teresa said, not bothering with pleasantries. "It's not just about money. It's about who gets to decide how Madison remembers itself."

The words landed heavily. Olivia's heart ticked up a notch. She recognized the rhetoric—it was the same speech she'd written, line by line, in the back of her mind every night since the project started.

Teresa kept going. "We've got people from out-of-town making decisions, re-writing our history, acting like they know better than the folks who actually live here. I grew up in this square. My father worked on the courthouse crew in the eighties. He never once got credit for it—not in the paper, not on any plaque. Now we're supposed to be grateful when an outsider comes in and tells us how to fix our own building?"

There it was. The punch. The line that would end up in the next day's paper, the one that would echo around church suppers and school board meetings for the next decade.

Olivia felt her cheeks burn. Not just for Andrew, but for herself.

The next speaker, a man in a bolo tie and a suit two decades out of date, went even further. "This is the same damn thing they tried in Blanco County—turn the courthouse into a museum and force all the real people out. You want to know where the money went? Consultants. Fancy plans. Meetings at the Mexican restaurant." He paused, to a swell of laughter. "Y'all are eating better than the rest of us combined!"

Judge Williams called for order, but it was a lost cause. The crowd had a taste of blood.

Andrew shifted, glanced at his notes, then up at the room. Olivia saw the moment he decided to just take the hit. He waited for the microphone, stepped up, and spoke with the same measured calm she'd seen in him that night in her kitchen.

"My name is Andrew Kim. I'm the lead preservation architect for the Madison Courthouse project. I'm here because the state historical commission requires it and the county hired me. Not because I wanted to disrupt anyone's life, or because I think I know better." He looked around the room, met as many eyes as he could. "But I know this: if we do nothing, this building falls apart in five years. If we do it cheap, we're back here in two. Every dollar we spend now saves three down the line."

A silence. Not quite respectful, but not hostile, either.

He turned to Judge Williams. "The cost overrun is real, but it's because we found more structural problems than anyone predicted. The foundation's worse than the records showed. If you want to see the files, I'll stay after and show you every page."

Olivia's chest loosened, just a little. She could see the room shift—some people rolling their eyes, but more just sitting, listening, waiting to be convinced.

He finished: "I know it's hard. I know it sucks. But if we do it right, this building outlasts all of us."

He stepped back. The hardware store guy grunted, but didn't challenge him. Teresa looked away, biting her lip.

The judge banged her gavel again, voice clipped now. "Thank you, Mr. Kim. We'll open the floor to written suggestions and review the budget with the committee after this meeting. This public meeting is adjourned."

It was over in a blur. People filed out in muttering packs. The man next to Olivia leaned over. "He's not so bad, that Kim. Better than the last one, at least."

She smiled, brittle. "He tries."

In the lobby, Andrew stood by the doors, face unreadable, hands in his pockets. A few people stopped to talk, quieter now—some with proper questions, some just to say their piece. He answered every one, never once checking his phone or glancing at the clock.

Olivia hung back, letting the room thin out. She watched him, trying to see the cracks—did he regret coming? Was he angry at her, at the town, at the whole charade?

She thought of the water tanks, the ruined wedding, the $4,000 deposit she'd never see again. Then she thought of his steady hands, his refusal to flinch, the way he'd stood in front of a mob and explained himself instead of hiding behind a title.

She was still there, watching, when the room finally emptied. He looked up, saw her, and smiled—small, tired, but real.

"Thanks for not running out the back," she said, surprising herself with the softness in her voice.

He shrugged. "If I did, they'd chase me down, anyway."

They walked out together, not talking, just matching strides through the sun-bleached courthouse square. The fight wasn't over, not by a long shot, but for now they'd both survived.

And tomorrow, the work would start again.

❧

THEY'D BARELY MADE it to the sidewalk before the aftershocks started: clumps of townsfolk clustering on the courthouse steps, lit cigarettes and terrible coffee passing hands, everyone replaying the hearing like a high school football game. Olivia tried to slip by unnoticed, but the old man from the Rotary bench caught her with a tap on the elbow.

"You doing okay?" he asked, voice softer now, almost kind.

She nodded. "It's not my first rodeo."

He smiled. "You ever want the actual story on this town, you come by my shop. We've got plenty of tape if you need to patch any more disasters."

She promised she would, though she doubted she'd ever actually go. Not when the to-do list back at the inn was multiplying by the hour, not when the bank account was bleeding out in real time.

Back home, she made it to her office before the adrenaline wore off. She closed the door, braced herself against the desk, and counted her breaths until her hands stopped shaking.

She should've gone for a walk, or called Elena, or at least thrown something, but she logged on to the reservation portal and stared at the dashboard. Five new cancellations, three "pending," and two more negative reviews—both of which cited "ongoing construction," "lack of amenities," and, her favorite, "proprietor did not appear to care about guests' well-being."

She tried to reply, to compose the right words, but nothing came that didn't sound like a plea. Or worse, an excuse.

Her phone buzzed. Unknown number.

She hesitated, then answered. "Olivia."

A voice she didn't recognize, thick with local vowels: "You the woman who runs the Limestone?"

"That's me."

"This is Carl at the water company. We got your note. You want the tank refilled, you've gotta call ahead. The crew's on split shifts this week. Also, your pressure's running low—you got a leak?"

She closed her eyes. "Not unless you count the entire town's infrastructure."

A bark of laughter. "You're all right, Ms. Cuellar. Just giving you a heads up. Don't want your guests in the lurch."

She thanked him, hung up, and resisted the urge to scream into the phone.

When the next call came, she almost didn't answer. But the number was local, and the voice on the other end was Elena's, clipped and fast.

"Liv, did you see the local Facebook page? People are losing it. They're saying the wedding fallout was your fault. That you called in a favor to sabotage the pipes and get a payout from the county."

Olivia felt her mouth go dry. "What?"

"It's everywhere. Even my mom heard it, and she hasn't been online since the pandemic. They're coming for you, Liv."

Olivia said nothing for a long time, then: "Let them. I can't stop them, anyway."

Elena's tone softened. "That's not you. You always fought back."

"I'm tired, El."

A pause, then: "If you need backup, I'll be at the next meeting. We'll sit together. Show them we're not scared."

Olivia almost laughed. "You think that helps?"

"It helps me," Elena said. "And maybe it helps them remember who you are."

Olivia promised she'd think about it, then hung up, feeling the exhaustion crack through her bones.

She stared at the ceiling, listening to the whir of the water pump. She wondered, not for the first time, if it would be easier to just fold. To walk away and leave the town to its ghosts, its endless cycle of rebuild and rot.

That night, she barely slept. She lay in bed listening to the distant thunder of trucks, the occasional whoop from the bar down the block, the clink and sigh of the inn settling in for the night. Every sound felt like a dare.

Morning came gray and close. The air already tasted of rain. She dressed in the dark, pulled on her best jacket, and left the house before sunrise.

The courthouse was already awake—a crowd gathering on the square, the promise of another public spectacle drawing everyone out of their routines. She walked the perimeter, keeping to the shadows, then ducked into the side door and slipped into the hearing room as Judge Williams hammered the meeting into order.

Today, they planned to focus on "public solutions," but the list contained names Olivia recognized from every angry Yelp review and whispered complaint.

The first half hour passed in a blur—more arguments over the water, more accusations about the "outsider architect," more dire warnings about the town's future. But then, in the third row, Teresa Alvarez stood up, her hair perfect, her folder of notes even thicker than before.

She took the mic and didn't wait for permission.

"This isn't just about money," she said. "It's about outsiders coming in and changing Madison without our say-so."

A wave of agreement rippled through the room. Heads bobbed; fists clenched.

Teresa pressed on. "First, Alexander Stirling buys up half the square. Now we've got people turning our history into a commodity. Tourist traps, overpriced B&Bs, phony preservation efforts." She let the words hang, then zeroed in on Olivia with a point so deliberate it was almost cruel. "Like the Limestone Inn—another outsider using Stirling's money to profit off our heritage."

The room snapped to attention. Every head swiveled toward Olivia, its collective gaze burning through her skin. She wanted to shrink, to disappear, but she forced herself to sit up straighter.

She felt the numbers flash behind her eyes: the overdue payment to Stirling, the looming default, the knowledge that her entire shot at redemption was hanging by a thread.

Teresa was still talking. "I know the grants help, but who gets the benefit? Not the families who built this town. Not the people who stuck it out through drought and fire and every damn recession. It goes to consultants, to out-of-towners, to anyone with the right handshake or a fancy degree." She looked at the dais, then back at Olivia. "We can't just let them erase us."

A smattering of applause, not much, but enough to count.

Judge Williams banged her gavel, her patience clearly at a breaking point. "That's enough. Ms. Alvarez, please stick to budget proposals, not personal attacks."

But the damage was done. Olivia felt her cheeks burn hot. She stared at the table, wishing she'd brought a scarf or sunglasses—anything to hide.

For a moment, she wondered if it was worth it. If she could walk away now, let the inn go, maybe find a job that didn't involve waking up every day to another small, relentless humiliation.

But when she looked up, she saw Andrew at the front. He was watching her, not with pity, but with the same calm, measured look he'd worn the day before. Not quite a smile, but something that said, You're not alone.

The moment steadied her, just enough.

When the clerk called her name—"Ms. Cuellar, you're next on the docket"—she stood, knees trembling, and crossed to the microphone.

She was going to fight back. Even if she lost.

SHE STOOD AT THE MICROPHONE, hands knotted, heart banging against her ribs. For a second, all she could see were the blank faces of the commissioners, the slow-turning heads of neighbors and old classmates, every eye drilling into her. In the sea of them, Andrew's gaze stood out—a steady line in the fog, the one face that didn't want her to disappear.

But before she could gather her voice, Andrew stepped forward and placed a gentle hand on her elbow. He spoke softly to the bench, but his words cut the air clean.

"If I may," he said, and Judge Williams—relieved for the interruption—nodded.

Andrew didn't bother with the microphone. He just spoke, his voice rising above the room with no amplification.

"I understand your concerns about outsiders and change," he said, looking not at the judges, but at the crowd. "But what Ms. Cuellar is doing at the Limestone Inn isn't exploitation—it's preservation. She's investing in Madison's future while honoring its past."

He paused, let it land.

"Look. My team could finish this courthouse in half the time if we ignored the original stonework and just slapped on new siding. The state would call it good, the money would get spent, and in ten years, we'd be back here doing it all over again. But we're not doing that. We're rebuilding the way it was built, using the hands and the hearts that made it the first time."

He gestured to Olivia, then to the bench. "That's what Ms. Cuellar is doing with the inn. She's not turning it into a theme park—she's trying to keep the story alive. That's what real preservation means."

The room was dead quiet.

He turned back to the dais, his tone softer now. "The courthouse renovation isn't just about fixing a building. It's about acknowledging all the hands that built it—past and present. That's what makes it worth saving."

A few people in the crowd nodded; few, but enough.

Andrew drew a slow breath. "Through our efforts, Madison heals old divisions and creates a more inclusive future for Verde County. That's what I came here to do. That's what Ms. Cuellar's doing, too."

He stepped back, hands folded, expression patient and open. For a moment, the commissioners looked stunned—maybe by the bluntness, maybe because it was the first time in years anyone had made them sound like part of the solution.

Olivia sat, the feeling that Roberto Cuellar had dutifully documented not to prove himself, but in order to ensure that his community's story survived. Here, decades later and for all the talk about progress, she was witnessing the same urge to subdue that history. Was she the person to expose their story to the light? Was she worthy enough, or would she fail at doing that, took repeating the pattern of her life.

She'd turned her back on Madison, fleeing to a "fresh start" by disappearing among the crowds of Houston, but in doing so, she'd made the choice to turn her back on her grandfather's community. She may not have known what she was turning her back on back then but didn't her rejection of them make it that much easier to cover up his story? In her own way, wasn't she as guilty as the intransigent voices currently ringing around the room?

Judge Williams cleared her throat, softened. "Thank you, Mr. Kim. That was well put."

He nodded, then turned to Olivia and said, "Would you like to add anything?"

She found her voice. It came out steadier than she expected.

"I just want to say," she said, "that I chose Madison because it was a place that didn't give up, even when things got hard. I'm trying to do my part to keep that spirit alive. That's all."

She looked at Teresa, at the laundromat owner, at the retired teachers who'd watched her grow up. No one called her a liar. No one shouted her down. For once, that felt like a win.

The meeting rolled on, but the mood had changed. The tension thinned, the angry speeches lost their venom, and by the time the session ended, people were talking in normal tones again. There was even laughter.

Olivia left with Andrew, their steps matching on the courthouse stairs.

"Thank you," she said, quiet but fierce.

He shrugged. "You would've done the same for me."

"Maybe," she said, then smiled. "But you did it first."

They walked the rest of the way in silence, the courthouse dome catching the early light, the town slowly waking up around them. She felt lighter, more solid, like she belonged in her own skin again.

She looked at Andrew, then at the square, and realized the fight wasn't over. But now, for the first time, it didn't feel like she was fighting alone.

Chapter Twelve

As she emerged from the courthouse, Olivia kept her eyes on the scorched sidewalk. The heat rolling up in invisible waves from the concrete, amplifying the hive-buzz of bad news and neighborly venom still ricocheting through her skull. Most of the crowd had already dispersed, the cluster of picketers and rubberneckers thinning to a few diehards chain-smoking beside the accessible parking. She didn't recognize them—not as guests, not as adversaries—but that was the nature of small towns: sometimes the threat wasn't a person but the way an entire block could bend to watch you break.

She flinched at the sudden metallic clang behind her, then realized it was just Andrew, wrestling with a stuck hinge on the courthouse's west door. He stepped out, shoulders set, a portfolio of blueprints clamped under one arm. He wore the same pale Oxford from the meeting, but dust and lime mortar streaked his boots to the ankle, as if he'd just waded through the bones of the building itself.

For a second, she considered making a break for it—slipping down the side street, avoiding the awkward dance of

"What happens now?"—but it was already too late. He'd seen her. Worse, he'd started toward her, stride half a beat too fast, as if propelled by some unfinished thought.

"Hey," he said, then stopped, as if the word itself was a hand grenade he had to check for pins.

She nodded, wiped her palm on her jeans, and tried to keep her voice even. "You survived."

He grinned, but it was the closed-mouth kind, the one she'd learned to recognize as code for "Barely." He looked at her, then at the last few stragglers, then back at the courthouse, as if unsure which building might collapse first.

"You got plans tonight?" he asked, and immediately winced, like the sentence had escaped before he could properly vet it. "I mean—I was going to get a drink. You want to join? Unless you need to—" he gestured, vague, "—regroup."

She blinked. The idea of sharing a beer—let alone with the architect whose entire presence in Madison had upended her life—felt like a dare. Or a test. Or maybe just the only thing she wanted that didn't come with a bill or a warning label.

"Is this a work thing?" She said, voice flat.

He shrugged, awkward. "Does it have to be?"

She weighed him: the way he held his portfolio, knuckles gone pale; the nervous shuffle as he rocked heel to toe; the faint sweat darkening his collar, even though he seemed otherwise immune to the heat.

She said, "Fine. One drink."

He nodded, then added, "You okay to ride with me? I'm parked just up on Lamar."

It was a simple offer, but she felt herself bristle. For months, Andrew's truck had been a harbinger—whenever it appeared outside the inn, it meant some new regulation, some fresh disaster, some last-minute inspection or demand. She'd learned its sound before she'd learned his name, and the memory of that reflex still prickled in her blood.

But now, after the way he'd stood up for her in the meeting, after the way he'd spoken about preserving things for the people who actually built them—she wasn't sure what the truck meant anymore.

"Lead the way," she said, and followed him.

❧

The truck was exactly as she remembered: a vintage Ford, two shades darker than county-issued, the interior scrubbed clean except for a layer of limestone dust that seemed impossible to defeat. The dash was a war zone of Post-Its, reference books, and a few carefully stacked manila envelopes labeled with dates and terms only another bureaucrat would care about.

He opened the passenger door for her, then moved around to the driver's side, as if suddenly unsure what the protocol was for civilian passengers. As she climbed in, she caught the scent of motor oil and coffee—strong, bitter, almost grounding. She settled into the seat, aware of the way her legs looked against the stained vinyl, the way her hands hovered uncertainly before she folded them in her lap.

He started the engine, then paused. "I should warn you, the AC's dead. Window okay?"

She nodded, and he rolled hers down first, then his own. The breeze was wet with humidity, but at least it was movement. He put the truck in gear, checked his mirrors with methodical precision, and eased it into the light.

For a block, they drove in silence.

Olivia forced herself to look out the window, to count the telephone poles, to pretend she didn't notice the way his hands gripped the wheel—tight, then loose, then tight again. She'd spent most of her life learning how to read the room, how to gauge threat level from posture, tone, the angle of a smile. She was used to people who performed their confidence in loud, messy gestures. Andrew wasn't that. He kept everything close, like a pocket of air beneath a sheet of ice.

At the stoplight by the old Dairy Queen, he said, "You did good in there."

She almost laughed. "You mean I didn't get lynched."

His lips twitched. "They wanted someone's head. You made sure it wasn't yours."

She let the silence stretch, then said, "You didn't have to speak up. You could've let me tank. It probably would've made your life easier."

He shook his head. "That's not how it works. You can't do this job and not get blood on your boots. I knew what I was signing up for." He glanced at her, quick. "You're not what they say. I can see that."

She snorted. "They say a lot of things. None of them are true."

"Doesn't matter," he said. "What matters is what you do next."

She let that hang. The words were almost comforting, but there was a challenge in them too.

After a minute, she said, "Where are we going?"

"Hahn's," he said. "Unless you have a better idea."

She shook her head. "Hahn's is fine. You'll be the only person in there who orders anything other than domestic beer, though."

He grinned, and for a moment the tension broke. "That's okay. I'm trying to fit in."

They drove the rest of the way with the windows down and the radio playing low. It was an oldies station—nothing post-Nixon, and the volume just low enough that the wind and the road noise could drown it out if you wanted. Olivia relaxed, bit by bit, the way you do when you're finally far enough from disaster to convince yourself it can't still be following.

At the edge of downtown, he pulled the truck into the crushed-gravel lot behind Hahn's. The place hadn't changed since she was a kid—same neon beer signs in the windows, same lopsided deck out back, same hand-lettered "CASH ONLY" sign taped crookedly to the door. She remembered the first time she'd snuck in as a teenager, the taste of watered-down Shiner and the sense that, for a few hours, nothing outside the bar could touch her.

She stepped out and waited for him to lock up. He did, then met her by the front steps, hands jammed into his pockets, portfolio left behind in the truck.

Inside, the bar was three-quarters full—mostly regulars, a few out-of-towners in khakis, a group of construction workers nursing buckets of longnecks at the far end. The lighting was bad and the music worse, but it was familiar, and for the first time all day, Olivia felt her shoulders drop.

They found a table near the back, under a framed jersey from some long-defunct softball team. He waited for her to sit, then slid into the booth opposite.

The waitress appeared in seconds, pad at the ready. "What'll it be?"

"Two Lone Stars," Andrew said, glancing at Olivia for confirmation.

She nodded, grateful he hadn't tried to order something fancy.

The waitress was gone before she could thank her. Across the table, Andrew picked at a salt shaker, then stopped and folded his hands, as if determined not to fidget.

"I'm not great at this," he said, voice low. "Just so you know."

She arched an eyebrow. "At what? Socializing with Public Enemy Number Two?"

He smirked, then shook his head. "At talking, when it's not about work. Or buildings. Or stuff I can draw a diagram for."

She laughed, and to her own surprise, it felt real. "Same. Except I usually just say the wrong thing and wait for people to leave."

The beers arrived, bottles sweating, two shot glasses of well tequila delivered with a wink from the waitress. "On the house," she said, then disappeared.

Andrew lifted his glass, clinked it against hers, and said, "To making it through the day."

She drank, felt the burn settle behind her teeth. "To survival," she echoed.

They talked, but not about the project. For a while it was small stuff: the best breakfast tacos in town ("Lupita's, no contest"), the old game of trying to guess which oil company had funded which downtown renovation ("If it has a mural, it's Conoco; if it has fake copper awnings, Exxon"). She learned he'd grown up in Dallas, that his dad was a second-generation carpenter, that he'd flunked out of high school calculus but got into Rice anyway because he built a scale model of the Alamo that won a state competition.

"Is that a true story?" she said, lips numb with beer and laughter.

He nodded. "There's a plaque in the school library. Still has my name, last I checked."

"So, what about your parents?" His question was light.

"You know the caution light over on 90?"

"Yeah, drove through it on my way to town."

"My parents are the reason it's there." Her voice was so small, he almost thought he'd misheard her. But a glance at her face told him he hadn't.

"I'm sorry. So your grandparents?"

"I moved in with them that night."

They drifted back to the courthouse. This time the talk was lighter, edged with the humor of people who knew the worst had already happened.

"At least I didn't get a pie in the face," she said.

He grinned. "There's always the next meeting."

She watched his hands—the careful way he lined up the beer bottles, the way he tapped the label with his thumb, the brief nervous twitch when he pushed up his glasses. It was like watching a time-lapse of a man trying to get comfortable in his own skin.

They finished the beers, then ordered another round. The bar thinned as the sun dipped behind the water tower, and the jukebox shifted from outlaw country to '80s pop.

She realized she'd stopped checking her phone, stopped thinking about the next disaster. For the first time in weeks, she felt almost okay.

Andrew paid the tab, cash from a crisp stack he kept in a binder clip. As they stepped outside, the air was cooler; the sky turning navy.

He walked her back to the truck. At the door, he paused.

"I meant what I said," he said, quieter now. "You're not alone in this. I know it feels like you are, but you're not."

She nodded, words caught in her throat. She wanted to say something—to thank him, or to tell him how much she needed to hear it—but the language of gratitude felt foreign, like a suit tailored for someone else.

Instead, she climbed into the truck and waited for him to start the engine.

He did, and they drove in silence, but this time it was the comfortable kind.

❧

WHEN THEY REACHED THE INN, the windows glowed gold against the twilight. He parked and killed the lights, but didn't move to get out.

She looked at him, waiting.

He said, "I'll see you tomorrow?"

She hesitated, then smiled. "Yeah. I'll be here."

He nodded, then watched as she walked to the porch, keys in hand, head high.

Only when she'd closed the door behind her did he start the truck again, the sound fading into the night.

Inside, Olivia leaned against the door, heart thumping.

She wasn't sure what came next.

But for the first time, she hoped it was something good.

THE NEXT MORNING, Madison was slow to wake—a town hungover on its own drama, the air thick with last night's humidity and the aftershocks of everything that had passed between dusk and dawn. Olivia woke to the muffled sounds of Josefina humming in the kitchen, the aroma of coffee brewing somewhere on the first floor, and the faint vibration of her own nerves, still tuned to the frequency of the night before.

She dressed in the dark, pulled her hair into a quick twist, and padded barefoot to the office to find Andrew already there, shoulders hunched over a sheaf of paperwork. He'd changed into clean clothes—navy button-down, jeans with no rips—but there was a smear of ink on his jawline, evidence of a hand run too hastily across his face. She lingered in the doorway, watching him for a second, the way the early light caught in his hair, the calm patience in his movements.

He looked up, caught her, and smiled. "Morning."

She smiled back, unable to stop herself. "Did you get any sleep?"

He considered it. "Some. I spent an hour rewriting the oral history interview questions. I think I was trying to impress you."

She rolled her eyes, but the warmth in her chest surprised her. "You didn't have to."

He gestured to the papers. "I know. But I wanted to." He hesitated. "We're supposed to meet Carmen Alvarez at the annex at nine. You still in?"

She nodded, and the two fell into a simple rhythm of shared work. She made coffee—real coffee, strong and dark, none of the guest blend—and he spread maps and blueprints across the lobby table. For a while, their conversation was all logistics and names, a relay race of facts and corrections and the occasional inside joke. But under it all, there was a current, a new willingness to linger in each other's presence, to let the small touches and shared glances mean more than the sum of their words.

As nine approached, she pulled on her shoes and grabbed her bag, turning to find Andrew standing at the base of the staircase. He held the door open, and when she passed, he placed his hand gently—almost accidentally—at the small of her back.

The touch was electric, as if every nerve ending she had tuned to the same radio frequency as his. She froze, unsure whether to lean into it or laugh it off, but then he let his hand drop and flashed her an apologetic smile.

"Ready?" he said.

"Yeah," she replied, though her voice was breathier than she intended.

They walked to the annex together, trading stories about their worst job interviews (hers: a stint at a haunted Victorian in Galveston; his: a three-day contract in Waco that ended with a fistfight over a parking spot). By the time they reached the records office, the tension was more anticipation than anxiety—a promise, not a threat.

Carmen was waiting, her arms full of battered boxes and her smile wide enough to disarm even the surliest bureaucrat. She greeted Olivia with a hug, Andrew with a brisk handshake, and then set them to work cataloguing a mountain of brittle photographs and half-legible census reports.

For the next two hours, they lost themselves in the labor—reading names aloud, matching faces to lists, arguing gently about whether a particular stone wall had been patched in 1921 or 1932. Andrew deferred to Olivia's instincts, quick to cede any point where her memory of the town trumped his own research. Carmen, seeing the dance, simply smiled and took notes.

At noon, they called it quits. Carmen promised to email the scans by the end of the week, so Elena could eventually keep them at the library for safekeeping. Olivia agreed, knowing Elena would carefully catalog the scans and make them available for future researchers.

They sat at a window booth, side by side this time, sharing a basket of chips and two Tecates poured over ice. The conversation drifted, lighter now—music, travel, the best places to see the Perseid meteor shower (his: Big Bend; hers: any church roof, if you could talk the sexton into letting you up there). They laughed over childhood injuries, over family secrets, over the time Olivia's mother tried to bribe her into attending Mass by promising to adopt the town's ugliest dog.

Somewhere between the second round of beers and the arrival of their tacos, Olivia realized she was happy. Not the adrenaline high of victory or the brittle relief of disaster averted, but something steadier, something that felt like it might actually last.

Andrew noticed the change, of course. "You seem lighter,"

he said, reaching for her hand under the table, the gesture so natural it was as if they'd been doing this for years.

She looked at their intertwined fingers, then at him. "I am."

He squeezed her hand, then said, "I know we're both a little..." He trailed off, searching for the right word.

She grinned. "Damaged?"

He laughed. "I was going to say complicated. But yeah. That too."

She let the silence stretch, then said, "I don't mind."

He looked at her, searching for any sign of doubt, but she held his gaze, steady and sure.

"I don't either," he said.

After lunch, they wandered the square, neither of them wanting to head back to real life just yet. They visited the old bakery, then the antique shop where Olivia's grandmother used to trade preserves for thrifted tablecloths. He bought her a tin sign shaped like a rooster, declaring it a "housewarming present for your next kitchen emergency."

When they finally made it back to the inn, it was late afternoon and the sun had begun its slow descent behind the courthouse dome. The porch was empty, the air humming with the promise of summer thunderstorms.

They paused at the front door, both unwilling to break the spell.

Andrew leaned in first, his hand gentle on her shoulder. "I had a good time," he said, voice low.

She met his eyes, saw the question there, and this time she didn't hesitate.

She closed the distance between them, pressing her mouth to his. The kiss was soft at first, then hungry, years of caution melting away in the heat of it. She felt his arms around her, anchoring her to the world, and she let herself believe—for one rare, golden moment—that the worst was behind her.

When they finally broke apart, both were laughing, a little giddy.

He kissed her forehead, then whispered, "See you tomorrow."

She watched him walk away, hands in his pockets, head down but smiling.

Inside, she climbed the stairs to her room, shoes in hand, the taste of him still on her lips. She dropped onto her bed, stared at the ceiling, and let herself daydream—just for a minute—about what it might be like to build something new, together.

The next day, there would be more meetings, more arguments, more impossible budgets and stubborn townsfolk.

But for now, she let herself hope.

She was done building alone.

Chapter Thirteen

Andrew walked into the inn with blueprints curled under one arm and a face that had only two settings: taut or more taut. He parked his truck at the far end of the gravel lot as if distance might buffer what he was carrying, then strode up the walk in slow, deliberate steps, the gait of a man sentenced to deliver his own eulogy.

Olivia heard the old door's hinges protest, then the staccato thump of his boots crossing the foyer. She was at the reception desk, organizing the afternoon's mountain of invoices into neat stacks—urgent, past due, and lost cause—when he appeared in the doorway.

He nodded hello. "Got a minute?"

It was never just a minute. She swept the ledgers aside, dusted flour from her shirt (last night's desperation bake-a-thon still lingering on her shirt), and gestured at the desk's cleared surface. "For you? Always."

He didn't smile. He set the blueprints down with a care that bordered on reverence, then reached into his bag for a second set of documents: a battered legal pad and a thumb drive, the latter of which he held up like a prop in a magic trick. "You want PDF or old-school?"

She didn't answer. He plugged the drive into the lobby computer anyway and pulled up a rendering of the courthouse cross-section. The monitor was too small to show the detail, but the blue and white lines glowed sharply in the gloom of the overcast afternoon.

He pointed with a capped pen. "See this? All the visible limestone—the good stuff on the façade—it's just a veneer. The core is caliche."

Olivia leaned in, blinking at the screen as if the name might resolve into something less menacing. "Is that...bad?"

Andrew nodded, slow. "It's a sedimentary fill. Sand, silt, and clay, bound by calcium carbonate. The old crews used it because it was local, easy to cut. But it's soft. Porous as hell. And in this climate, it soaks up water like a paper towel."

He zoomed in on a striated gray section. "I cored three test holes. All of them came back high in moisture content. Some spots are basically mud with a crust."

Olivia tried to make herself care about the chemistry, but her mind was already fast-forwarding to the cost. She chewed her thumbnail, a nervous habit she'd resurrected from junior high. "Can it be stabilized?"

"In theory." Andrew tapped the screen, then flipped open his notebook to a page dense with equations and bullet points. "But the load paths are compromised. That's why the west wall is bowing out. The 1960s addition is pulling away—the concrete pilings under it are stable, but they're moving at a different rate than the caliche. So now you've got a stress shear along the join."

He hesitated, then glanced up. "Sorry. I'm boring you."

"You're not." She said it too quickly, then softened. "I want to know. All of it."

Andrew's lips pressed into a line. "All right. Next issue—" he brought out a folder labeled ENVIRONMENTAL, its tab already thumbed soft "—asbestos. In the dropped ceilings, everywhere they did a 'modernization' in the eighties. It's not airborne now, but if we demo any of it, we have to do full abatement. Same with the lead paint on the window frames."

Olivia exhaled, the sound sharp in the hush of the lobby. "How much does that add?"

"Minimum? Half a mil. That's with state-approved crews, disposal, the whole nine." He glanced away. "But if you want it certified for kids' field trips or public tours, there's no way around it."

The words were clinical, but the effect was personal. Olivia felt the cost slide under her ribs, a cold splinter. She looked at the antique clock on the wall, watched the second hand tick, then met his gaze. "What about the roof?"

Andrew ruffled through another stack. "Worse than we thought. The subroof is okay, but the drainage design is... historically accurate. Water pools up top, finds the cracks, and then follows the rebar down into the masonry. It's why you see all the efflorescence here and here." He pointed to the white blooms spidering across the east elevation. "That's salt. It means water's moving through the wall. Which means so is everything else—heat, cold, whatever's in the air."

He clicked to another screen. "Bottom line, it's a systemic issue. Every fix compounds with the others. You can't just patch and run."

Olivia listened, face blank, hands knotted beneath the desk. Every detail was another line in the ledger of her failure, another reason she would never get ahead. But she was past the point of flinching. She let him keep going.

Andrew cleared his throat. "Last thing. The original wiring is still active behind the breaker box. Two generations of it, some cloth-insulated, some just bare copper. It's a fire waiting to happen. The state fire marshal saw my notes and said if it's not addressed, they'll shut down occupancy."

That did sting, but Olivia only nodded. "How long would a full rewire take?"

He did a quick calculation. "Two months, best case. But you can do it in phases if you want to keep offices open."

She stared at the screen, at the lines and shaded blocks that had become the blueprint for her own personal apocalypse. "How much?" she said, and her voice sounded alien—like she'd already stepped outside herself and was just reading from a script.

Andrew tapped the notepad. "We're at five point one million. That's up from the original three." He said it flat, no apology, but his thumb drummed the table in a staccato that betrayed him.

She didn't trust herself to speak. Instead, she stood, circled to the other side of the desk, and braced her hands on the cool marble edge. The room spun a little, the dust motes in the air suddenly magnified by the sting in her eyes.

He waited.

She steadied herself, dug her nails into the stone. "How are you going to sell that to the county?"

Andrew's brow furrowed. "If I don't, it's malpractice. Someone will find out, and then they'll blame me for hiding the ball. I could lose my license."

She almost laughed, but the sound died before it made it out. "You think they'll thank you for being honest? They'll run us both out of town."

He shrugged, a small, helpless gesture. "I didn't come here to lie for anyone."

"Neither did I." She turned away, blinking hard at the west-facing window, where the sky was already bruising with the promise of another storm. "But we can't save this place if no one wants to pay for it."

Andrew watched her for a long time. Then, with a gentleness she didn't expect, he gathered the blueprints and folded them into his satchel. "You're not the villain here, Olivia."

She let that hang, then said, "Tell that to the people with pitchforks at the next meeting."

He almost smiled. "I'll be right there with you."

She swallowed, then made herself look at him, really look, the way she had in the bar when the world felt less lethal. "What's the worst that could happen?" She said, and it was half a joke, half a plea.

He met her eyes, and for the first time all afternoon, she saw the tiredness crack into something warmer. "Worst? They fire us both, and we start our own preservation firm. Better lunch breaks, fewer angry mobs."

She laughed, low and shaky, then wiped at her eyes with the heel of her hand. "You're a terrible liar," she said.

He bowed his head in mock deference. "That's why they pay me the big bucks."

The computer screen faded into screensaver; the courthouse reduced to a slow dissolve of sepia and blue. Olivia exhaled, felt her lungs sting with the effort. "We have to tell them," she said, voice barely above a whisper.

"We do."

"And then?"

He slung the satchel over his shoulder. "Then we fight for it. Or we let it fall. But at least we know."

She reached for the invoice stack, the papers now feeling weightless compared to the number in her head. "Thank you," she said, though she wasn't sure who she was thanking—Andrew, or herself, or just the indifferent universe for sending someone who cared enough to bring her the bad news straight.

He nodded once, then left the way he'd come, boots quieter this time, like the old building had absorbed some of his burden.

For a while, Olivia stood in the empty lobby, watching the dust motes spiral in the late light, listening for the sound of something—anything—that would tell her which way the world was about to turn.

Outside, thunder rolled, low and steady.

Inside, she set her jaw and started typing the email that would set everything in motion.

Five million, she thought, and let the number echo in the empty room.

Might as well be a hundred.

But she'd built things out of less before.

THE NEXT MORNING, the basement hearing room of the courthouse vibrated with a fury more potent than any jackhammer. The air was heavy with sweat and the tang of institutional coffee, every bench packed shoulder-to-shoulder with a cross-section of Verde County's finest: angry business owners, retired engineers, ranchers in their battered Carhartts, and at least one bored child flicking spitballs at the AV equipment. Olivia hovered near the back, blinking at the fluorescent haze, her nerves frayed down to the quick.

Elena slipped in beside her, hair pinned in a severe twist and a legal pad clutched to her chest like a shield. "You ready?" she whispered, though from the look in her eyes she already knew the answer.

"Not even close," Olivia muttered, then traced the curve of the room. Up front, the Commissioners Court sat elevated at a battered laminate dais—Judge Patti Williams at the center, two commissioners to each side, the county clerk already looking like she regretted every life choice that led her to this moment.

Behind the dais, the Texas flag drooped halfheartedly, the only splash of color in a room otherwise painted a shade Olivia had come to think of as "budget gray." The folding tables in front of the dais were draped with poster boards and binders, each one bristling with sticky notes and the anger of a thousand man-hours wasted.

Andrew was already there, seated at a table marked PROJECT TEAM. He had a tie on, which meant things were even more dire than Olivia had guessed. He caught her eye, gave a quick nod, then buried himself in the papers. She could tell from the set of his jaw that he hadn't slept.

At precisely 8:30, Judge Williams banged her gavel so hard it left a divot in the pressboard. "Order, please. This is a continuation of our emergency session regarding the courthouse stabilization project. We'll hear from the project architect, then open the floor for public comment."

She nodded to Andrew. He stood, rolled his shoulders, and walked to the front like a man facing a firing squad.

He began with the facts—just the facts. "The original project scope, approved at $3 million, was based on preliminary, non-invasive surveys and existing records. During phase one, we encountered significant structural issues not in those records." He glanced at the judges, then at the audience. "Core sampling revealed that the interior masonry is caliche, not limestone. It's absorbing moisture, which means the walls are moving. Substantially. If we don't reinforce the superstructure before this winter, there's a high probability of catastrophic failure on the west wall."

A murmur swept the room—disbelief, anger, a few high-pitched "I told you so"s from the corner where the property tax activists had gathered.

Andrew pressed on, his voice never wavering. "We also

identified active asbestos above the drop ceilings, lead paint in all the window casements, and non-compliant wiring behind every panel we've opened. If we attempt patch repairs, we'll be cited by state inspectors and risk loss of occupancy."

He clicked the remote; the screen behind him displayed a color-coded diagram of the courthouse, with bright red shading on every trouble spot. It looked less like a building and more like a crime scene.

"Estimated cost to remedy all critical issues is now $5.1 million, with a contingency of plus or minus 12 percent depending on what's behind the remaining closed walls."

That's when the room erupted.

A man in a seed company baseball cap leaped to his feet. "We voted for restoration, not a blank check!" he shouted, voice ricocheting off the low ceiling.

A chorus of "Damn right!"s and "Tell it!" s rose in response, the entire room suddenly a single angry organism. Two women in the second row began yelling over each other, one waving a rolled-up newspaper, the other jabbing her finger at Andrew like she hoped it might draw blood.

Judge Williams pounded the gavel again, but the sound was lost in the cacophony. "Order!" she barked. "We will hear from the architect—then you'll all get your turn."

Andrew waited, stone-faced. Olivia felt the urge to rush the dais, to shield him from the onslaught, but Elena gripped her arm, eyes sharp. "Wait," she hissed. "He knows what he's doing."

A familiar voice cut through the melee. "This is exactly what we feared—outsiders spending our money!" It was Teresa Alvarez, standing in the aisle, her smile thin as paper and twice as sharp. She didn't look at Andrew. She looked straight at Olivia, and the message was clear: You did this. This is on you.

The next volley came from a red-faced man in the third

row, veins bulging at the temple. "I don't give a damn about building codes—I want that money spent fixing Main Street, not lining the pockets of consultants!"

Laughter and boos, all at once.

Andrew raised his hand, waited for the wave to pass, then spoke directly into the storm. "I understand. But if we ignore these issues, the building fails. Not in twenty years—in two. You'll have a demolition order, not a renovation."

He let the words settle, then added, "The previous studies missed this because no one wanted to fund destructive testing. We did the work. Now we know."

Judge Williams seized the lull. "Let's keep this constructive. We'll take questions from the committee first. Ms. Cuellar?"

Olivia felt every eye in the room turn to her, the heat of their collective suspicion a physical force. She stood, smoothed her skirt, and walked to the table beside Andrew. His hand brushed hers as she sat, a fitting anchor in the turbulence.

She addressed the bench. "I've reviewed the findings. There's no way to do this within the original budget without cutting corners. The cost increases are not waste—they're what it takes to save the building."

The judge cocked an eyebrow. "And if the voters say no?"

Olivia let the silence stretch. "Then the building will fail. Maybe not this year, maybe not next, but soon. And the cost to the county then will be even higher."

From the back, a woman's voice—raspy, older: "So we're hostages, is what you're saying."

More laughter, but it was hollow now, the room's energy shifting from outrage to dread.

Elena stood up, without waiting to be called. "Would you rather the courthouse fall down?" she asked, loud enough to cut through the grumbling.

It landed. The noise ebbed, a tide receding, replaced by an uneasy quiet.

Andrew moved to the whiteboard, uncapped a marker, and in neat print wrote three options:

A) Full remediation: $5.1M

B) Partial patch: $2.8M (No guarantee of success, non-compliant)

C) Abandon project: Estimated $1.2M in demolition/temporary relocation

He turned back to the room. "Those are your choices. I don't benefit from any of them. I'm just here to tell you the truth."

The judge looked at the chart, then at the silent commissioners. "Thank you, Mr. Kim. Public comment is now open."

The first ten speakers repeated the same chorus of anger, betrayal, and budget anxiety. But as they cycled through, a pattern emerged: the insults grew less pointed, the arguments more technical. The man in the seed cap pressed for a line-item breakdown; a retired contractor quizzed Andrew on the specific core sampling protocol. Andrew fielded each question with mechanical precision, never defensive, never flinching.

At one point, a heavyset man in the back—one of the old-timers, a relic from the Cavanaugh era—stood up and called out: "Why didn't we know about the caliche before?" His voice was loud, but behind it was a whiff of fear.

Andrew answered. "Because the earlier assessments were surface-only. To do a core sample, you need permission to drill, and no one wanted to risk opening up a new can of worms. They were hoping the building would hold just long enough."

Several of the older men at the bench shifted in their seats. Olivia recognized the look; it was the same one her grandmother wore when forced to admit a recipe had failed.

The session stretched for hours, the temperature in the

basement rising as tempers slowly cooled. By noon, Judge Williams called a recess, her own voice hoarse. "We'll resume at one. Bring your proposals."

In the corridor outside, Elena hugged Olivia, then hurried to the restroom, her own composure cracking at last.

Andrew found Olivia near the vending machines, hands jammed deep in his pockets. "You okay?" he asked.

She shook her head, but then shrugged. "You?"

He almost smiled. "I've had worse."

They leaned against the wall, silent, listening to the echo of voices from the meeting room.

"You pissed off half the town," Olivia said, not quite a joke.

He nodded. "They'll get over it."

"Will they?"

Andrew looked at her, eyes raw but steady. "They'll have to."

The bell rang, summoning them back. As Olivia took her seat, she saw Teresa Alvarez in the aisle, jotting furious notes. Teresa didn't meet her gaze this time; her job was done.

Back at the table, Andrew presented three detailed paths forward. Each was ugly, but the numbers were inescapable.

The judge polled the bench. Two of the four commissioners, both younger, both newer to office, voted to recommend the full remediation—"Painful but necessary," as one put it. The others abstained, "pending further public comment." Williams herself split the difference, motioning to appoint a task force to review the proposal.

It was a punt, but a punt that kept the building (and Olivia's livelihood) alive for another week.

As the crowd filed out, quieter now, Olivia sagged against the table, energy spent.

Andrew gathered his papers. "Let's get lunch," he said. "You look like you need carbs."

She nodded, unable to muster a joke.

On the way out, she caught sight of the Cavanaugh loyalist, now deep in conversation with a woman in an acid-wash denim vest. He wasn't angry anymore; just tired, like a man watching the world he'd built finally succumb to gravity.

Outside, the heat hit them like a wall.

Elena waited at the top of the stairs, sunglasses on, jaw set. "It'll get worse before it gets better," she said, but her arm linked through Olivia's as they walked to the square.

Andrew trailed them, his tie loosened, eyes on the sidewalk.

For the first time, Olivia felt a flicker of hope. Not that the town would forgive her, or that the money would magically appear, but that sometimes just telling the truth—even when it was a disaster—could be its own kind of victory.

She squeezed Elena's arm. "You coming to Hahn's later?"

"Wouldn't miss it," Elena said, and her laughter sounded more real than it had in weeks.

They reached the inn. Andrew peeled off toward his truck, but turned at the curb. "You did good," he said.

"You too," Olivia replied.

As she let herself into the cool, dark lobby, she was almost surprised to find the building still standing.

They'd won nothing. But the fight was theirs now.

It would have to be enough.

AT HALF PAST EIGHT, Hahn's Ice House was already full of people who'd rather drown their troubles than sit alone at home and count them. The Friday crowd was rowdier than usual—half the room packed with construction crews and city staffers blowing off steam, the other half a shifting menagerie of townies, campaign hangers-on, and the occasional lost tourist lured by the promise of "coldest beer in Texas" and the blue-neon glow that bled out onto the street.

Olivia claimed a booth in the back, its fake-leather bench already splitting at the seams. Elena and Carmen slid in beside her, the former with a tequila sunrise, the latter with a Diet Coke that would spend the night untouched. Andrew arrived last, his tie gone, shirt untucked, hair still damp from a post-meeting shower. He set a six-pack of Shiner on the table and collapsed into the seat across from Olivia, their knees knocking under the Formica.

No one spoke for a minute. They just sat in the jukebox din and bar chatter, letting the reverb shake the last dregs of courthouse rage out of their skulls.

It was Carmen who finally broke the spell. She took one look at Andrew's face, then jabbed a finger at the six-pack. "You bring enough, or do we need to mug the off-duty oilfield boys for their bucket?"

Andrew shrugged, then twisted the cap off a bottle and handed it to her. "I can always get another round. If they don't ban me first."

Elena snorted. "You could set this place on fire and they'd just tell you to close your tab. Not like you're a county judge."

Carmen took a long pull, then leveled her gaze at Andrew. "So. How's it feel to be the least popular man in Verde County?"

He didn't flinch. "I'm not here to win friends."

Olivia laughed, but it came out tight. "That's good, because you've already pissed off everyone in a ten-mile radius."

Andrew tipped his bottle in acknowledgment. "If it's any consolation, I've done worse. Once got chased out of West Texas by a county commissioner in a John Deere combine."

Elena perked up. "Did you run, or did you stand your ground?"

"I ran." He smiled, a ghost of it. "But not before I gave them a five-point memo about their septic tanks."

The table cracked up, the first genuine laugh of the night.

Olivia leaned back, her shoulders finally unknotting. She watched the way the neon sign behind the bar threw a corona around Carmen's silver-streaked hair, the way Elena's laughter punched the air in sharp bursts. She watched Andrew, too—how he sipped his beer slowly, how his eyes kept flicking to her, like he was checking for a pulse.

The nachos arrived, and for five minutes the only sounds at the table were crunch and gulp and the wet slap of salsa on wax paper. The conversation drifted—bad dates, old school rivalries, the time Elena's mother tried to poison the principal with an undercooked tamale. But eventually, the centrifugal force of disaster pulled them back in.

"So," Carmen said, lowering her voice. "What's the real reason they're so mad at you?"

Andrew wiped his mouth, considered. "Because I told the truth about how bad it is. And because I wrote it down. No one wants a record of failure, even if it's not their fault."

Elena nodded. "They'd rather blame a stranger than own the mess. Makes them feel in control."

Carmen grunted, a sound that carried more wisdom than a dozen lectures. "It's not just that. You embarrassed the old guard. This town runs on memory, and you called out every person who ever signed off on a shortcut."

Olivia let the words marinate. She looked past the table, to the bar itself, where three generations of "gatekeepers" were lined up—each watching her and Andrew with the same thinly veiled suspicion. She thought about her own grandmother, the way she'd fight to the death over a recipe but never admit she got it from someone else.

She turned to Andrew, who was already watching her. Their eyes locked, and for a split second she saw the exhaustion, the shame, and something else—relief. Like a man who'd finally thrown off a weight he didn't know he was carrying.

"They can yell all they want," Olivia said, her voice steady. "But the building doesn't care who's to blame. If it's going to stand, someone has to tell the truth."

He smiled, this time for real. "I'm glad you're on my side."

Carmen pointed at both of them, then at Elena. "The three of you are dangerous together. The town won't know what hit it."

Elena raised her glass. "To troublemakers."

Olivia clinked bottles with Andrew, then with Carmen, who rolled her eyes but joined in anyway.

The next hour passed in a haze of beer, stories, and the laughter that leaves your ribs sore for days. Every so often, a patron would shout something in their direction—"Hey, are you the demolition guy?" or "When's the next surprise inspection?"—but it was never more than a half-hearted jab. The actual heat had burned off in the hearing room.

Near midnight, as the crowd thinned, and the jukebox cycled back to Merle Haggard, Carmen leaned in close, her voice low. "You know what you're really up against, don't you?"

Andrew shrugged. "Stubbornness? Tradition?"

"Pride," Carmen said. "If you want them to let go, give them something better to be proud of."

He nodded, filed it away.

Carmen squeezed his hand, then Olivia's. "You'll do it. Or you'll die trying. Either way, I'll make sure your story's the one that sticks."

They all laughed, but there was an edge to it.

Elena stood first, stretching her arms over her head. "If I don't get sleep tonight, I'll fall asleep at the library and end up catalogued under 'local disasters.'"

Olivia hugged her, then watched as Carmen herded her to

the door. The older woman lingered, gave Andrew a long, measuring look, then said, "Don't let them get to you. And if they do, come find me."

He promised he would.

When they were gone, Olivia and Andrew lingered at the booth, a field of empty bottles arrayed before them. The air was quieter now; the tension dissolved. She toyed with a tortilla chip, then set it down.

"Do you regret taking the job?" She asked, not quite meeting his eyes.

"No," he said. "Not for a second." He reached across the table, his hand warm on hers. "Especially not after today."

She squeezed back, the pressure quick and sure.

They said nothing for a while, just sat and watched the world outside the windows—cars flashing past, the flicker of lightning on the horizon, the slow-motion ballet of people closing down a night that had outlasted all their better judgments.

When the bartender announced last call, Andrew stood, gathered the bottles into the recycling bin, and helped Olivia into her jacket. They walked out together, shoulders brushing, boots in sync.

Outside, the air was warm; the storm moving off to the east.

He walked her to her car, lingered at the driver's side, and said, "I meant what I said. You did good."

She smiled wide and real. "You did, too."

He opened the door for her, waited as she slid in, then closed it gently. "See you at the next disaster?"

She laughed, the sound ringing out into the empty street. "Wouldn't miss it."

He watched as she started the engine, then turned and headed for his truck.

For a moment, Olivia just sat there, watching him walk

away. She felt light, almost buoyant—like maybe the truth, once told, could hold its own.

She drove home with the windows down, neon and starlight tangled in her hair.

Whatever came next, she was ready.

Chapter Fourteen

At 1:41 a.m., the parlor of the Limestone Inn looked less like a Victorian-era relic and more like the war room of a failing startup. Olivia sat cross-legged on the carpet, laptop heat pooling against her thighs, the low glass coffee table lost beneath a landfill's worth of color-printed flyers, Post-Its, and conference swag from hotel management expos. The only illumination was the blue-white slab of her MacBook, the recessed ceiling lights above long since extinguished to keep guest rooms on the second floor in darkness. The rest of the house was silent, broken only by the faint, arrhythmic whir of the overnight water pump in the basement.

She highlighted the last bullet of her new deck—slide number twenty-seven—and scanned it with a tired but critical eye. "Leveraging Heritage: Sustainable Tourism Through Authentic Preservation." It sounded like a grant proposal, not a battle cry, but she was too exhausted to punch it up any further. She checked the next slide, then the next, eyes flicking between pie charts, case-study pull-quotes, and the mockups of her own face pasted onto hypothetical promotional mailers. The deck was good. Maybe the best work she'd produced since college. But in Madison, good didn't mean safe.

She checked her phone again. 1:42. No new emails from the Chamber, no emergency calls from the night desk. She allowed herself one minute to rest her chin on her knees, close her eyes, and try to remember what it had felt like to be a "rising star" in her University of Houston days—when confidence was currency, and she had spent it like she'd never run dry.

A voice cracked the silence, muffled by the closed double doors: "If you're dead, I'm telling them you overdosed on boxed wine and regret."

Olivia blinked, checked the lock, and called back, "Come in. I have not been dead for at least thirty minutes."

The door opened to reveal Elena, in pajamas and a battered UT hoodie, carrying a tray with two mugs of coffee and a stack of half-burned pop tarts. Her hair was a sleep-pounded mess, her eyeliner ghosted onto her cheekbones, but her eyes were sharp as ever.

"You are not seriously still working on that," Elena said, toeing aside a pile of printer debris to clear a landing zone for the tray.

"Do you want me to go in front of the Chamber with a half-assed deck?" Olivia snapped, though it was mostly reflex. She closed her laptop but left her hand on the lid, a hostage negotiation with herself.

"Liv," Elena said, "they're the Chamber of Commerce, not a congressional subcommittee. If you have three working PowerPoint slides and a tray of gas station donuts, they'll name you Small Business Hero of the Year."

Olivia snorted, but the compliment landed with a soft thud somewhere in her chest. She reached for the coffee, burning her tongue on the first sip, and let the bitterness suture her back to the moment. "I can't let them take me apart. Not again."

"Who's 'them'?" Elena asked. "Most of the old guard is gone. It's a bunch of lawyers and, like, one guy who does landscaping and is on parole."

Olivia shoved a stack of tear-off guest surveys into a folder, her hands shaking just enough that she had to steady the pages with her forearm. "It's not the Chamber. It's the town. The myth of me, the myth of the quitter, the myth of the girl who couldn't hack it in Houston."

Elena rolled her eyes. "You're the only one who still cares about that. Everyone else is just trying to get through the week without getting audited."

"They care," Olivia whispered. She remembered the way the crowd's words had cut at the hearing, the way people could turn a rumor into a gospel with three sentences and a nod. "They care about keeping things the same. I'm the exception."

Elena stared at her, then leaned in and dropped her voice. "You know what your grandma would say about this, right?"

Olivia tried to laugh, but her throat caught. "'Don't bring Houston drama into my house'?"

"Close. She'd say, 'If the haters have time to talk, you're not working them hard enough.'" Elena grinned. "Seriously, Liv. You're doing this town a favor. You've trained for this, and you're more than capable of kicking ass on this."

"Tell that to the committee tomorrow when they ask why the project manager is a single, thirty-something woman with a hotel degree and a foreclosure on her record." She tried to smile but couldn't quite sell it.

Elena's eyes softened. "Madison needs you more than you need Madison. If you want to nuke the deck and go full improv, I'll back you. But you have to show up. Otherwise, the assholes win."

Olivia looked at her best friend—the one person who'd never once called her a sellout or a lost cause, even when she'd slept on Elena's couch for three months after Houston went up in flames. She tried to believe the words. "Yeah. Okay."

"Atta girl," Elena said, and passed her the pop tarts.

They worked in silence for a bit, Olivia marking up the handouts while Elena circled any slide that looked "too academic" with a pink Sharpie. Every so often, Elena would pause to lecture her on "tone" or "vibe," and Olivia would bite back the urge to defend her choices, knowing the criticisms were half joke, half shield.

When they'd made it through the entire deck, Elena set down her pen and leaned back, arms folded. "You should pick an outfit tonight. Nothing with shoulder pads. Don't go full Houston, but don't let them catch you in a fucking cowgirl shirt, either."

Olivia rolled her eyes, but the advice had merit. She left the parlor in Elena's hands and headed upstairs; her phone light guiding her through the creaky darkness. In her closet, she weighed the options: blazers in shades of eggplant and navy, three "power" dresses purchased on clearance at the Galleria, the one suit she'd worn to her bankruptcy hearing. In the end, she built her armor piece by piece—dark denim slacks, a crisp white blouse with French cuffs, a moss green blazer that struck the right balance between authority and approachability. She skipped the heels, opting for sensible flats with just enough shine to say "I have my shit together, thank you very much."

She did a dry run in the mirror, checked her posture, forced herself to smile with her eyes and her mouth. The woman looking back at her was...almost believable. Maybe even a little dangerous.

She returned to the parlor, where Elena was already curled up on the sofa with her own laptop, headphones blasting an indie playlist. Olivia tiptoed past her, gathered the deck, the flyers, the pop-tart wrappers, and stacked them into a single, coherent bundle.

As she moved to turn out the lights, she heard Elena's voice—soft this time, not a joke. "You're going to crush them."

Olivia didn't answer. Instead, she let the darkness settle, the only light now the promise of morning outside the frosted glass.

She was ready. Or at least, she was done pretending she wasn't.

Tomorrow, she would face them all.

And this time, she'd do it as herself.

❧

THE COUNCIL CHAMBER was built to intimidate. Every detail—heavy walnut trim, leaded glass, the iron clock above the dais—communicated the authority of the institution and the futility of argument. The rows of mismatched chairs, borrowed from other eras of city government, were packed with the same faces who'd showed up to every budget fight and zoning brawl since the Reagan administration. Olivia sat dead center in the front row, the glow of her slide deck seeping through the manila folder in her lap. She tried to look casual, but every muscle below her jaw locked in spasm.

Elena had claimed a seat to her left, next to the a councilman's daughter, whose chief contribution to the local economy was a semi-legal dog grooming side hustle. Three rows back, Alex Stirling sat alone, thumb-skimming a legal pad and ignoring the woman next to him, who was loudly describing the "unholy gentrification" of Travis Street. At the far right, half the faces belonged to men who wore county-branded polos or golf shirts with dead startup logos on the breast—guys who would never admit to googling "how to get rid of mold smell in a historic building" but would still blame the odor on a woman.

The meeting started five minutes late, as always. The Chamber president—a cheery, barrel-chested contractor who resembled a more sunburned Fred Flintstone—banged his novelty gavel on the aluminum podium and called everyone to order. He read off a list of the previous month's business, mostly small victories: a new dry cleaner, an ice cream shop that would survive one summer, a liquor license renewal that the local Daughters of the Republic had bitterly contested.

Olivia barely heard it. Internally, she ran the opening line of her pitch in her head on repeat: "Heritage is Madison's greatest asset, and it's the only one that a developer can't replicate with a blank check." She pictured herself saying it without the telltale warble in her voice, the way she'd practiced in front of the guestroom mirror at least seventeen times. Lost in her thoughts, she didn't notice her left hand drumming a Morse code of panic against her knee until Elena covered it with her own.

When the "Community Presentations" segment arrived, the president called her up with a smile that was both encouraging and predatory. "Let's give a warm welcome to Olivia Cuellar, who'll tell us about the new Heritage Tourism initiative. I hope it's cheaper than the last one!"

Laughter, too loud and too long, rang out.

Olivia uncapped her water bottle, approached the dais, and squared her notes. The only person who seemed not to expect her to fail was Andrew Kim, who sat near the end of the fourth row, notebook open, gaze steady. He wore a powder-blue dress shirt with the sleeves rolled to the elbows, and his eyes flicked from her to the screen behind her and back, as if he alone understood that her entire future hinged on this hour.

She cleared her throat. "Thank you, Mr. President. I'll try to make it worth your while."

A few polite titters from the side. She clicked to the first slide: a full-screen photo of the Madison Courthouse in sepia; the dome rising above a crowd of marching suffragettes.

"Madison has never been about monuments. It's about people, and about the stories we tell with the buildings we keep. The restoration of the courthouse is just one piece. If we want to make Madison a destination—not just a waypoint—we have to invest in the town's narrative, not just the paint job."

Slide two: a collage of other towns that had made the pivot from "drive-through" to "stay over"—Lockhart, Nacogdoches, Fredericksburg. The chart beneath showed a spike in small business openings, bed and breakfast occupancy, and a figure Olivia had highlighted in bold: a 15.6% year-over-year increase in taxable tourism revenue.

She continued, voice stronger now. "The number one predictor of successful heritage tourism is authenticity. That means honoring what's here, not importing a prefab 'historic' experience from outside. It also means marketing our heritage without selling out the people who built it."

She saw Andrew nod almost imperceptibly. She clicked again.

"Here's what I propose—" She walked them through her plan: weekend heritage tours led by locals, seasonal food and craft festivals staged on the courthouse lawn, partnerships with the library's oral history project, a micro-grant fund for family-run businesses to upgrade facades without losing their identity. Each slide was a combination of aspiration and practicality, the incremental steps that wouldn't scare the old-timers but might actually move the needle.

Then, inevitably, the questions came.

A realtor in a red pantsuit stood up without waiting to be

recognized. "I notice you reference a lot of outside consultants. Are we just paying other people to tell us how to fix our own town?"

Olivia forced a smile. "I understand the concern. But each proposal is built around local leadership—local voices at the center. The outside expertise is there to supplement, not dictate. Every dollar spent has to be matched by local input, or it doesn't get spent."

A man in a camo vest, voice like crushed gravel: "Who's funding all this? Is this more of Alex Stirling's big-city scam?"

She turned to face him. "Most startup costs come from preservation grants already awarded to the city. I hope to leverage those funds to generate self-sustaining revenue through tourism and events, so we're not dependent on anyone's charity—including Mr. Stirling's." She glanced at Alex, who looked amused but stayed silent.

A woman from the historical society: "Last time we tried this, the antique shops on Main went under. You think it'll be different this time?"

Olivia nodded. "We've already partnered with several business owners to coordinate opening hours, cross-promote events, and create bundled experiences for visitors. The data from other towns shows that coordinated marketing—when done right—keeps visitors downtown longer and increases retail sales by up to thirty percent in the first year."

A beat, then another salvo: "Aren't you just setting up Madison to be another tourist trap? What about the people who actually live here?"

The question stung, because she'd asked it herself in the dark, so many times.

"I don't want Madison to lose its soul," Olivia said, letting the words hang. "That's why I came back. My job isn't to turn us into a theme park. It's keeping what matters intact, so that people can come here and see the real thing. And so our kids can grow up with a town that hasn't been bulldozed into a strip mall."

She caught Andrew's eye—he was leaning forward now, elbows on knees, a small smile curving his lips. She felt the old adrenaline surge, the same one that used to fuel her through six-hour shifts in front of the toughest guests in the city.

She ended on a slide with the Limestone Inn front and center, not as a self-promo but as a case study: how careful restoration and smart management could create something new out of what they nearly lost.

She took a breath. "I'm not here to argue that Madison needs to change. Madison is already changing, whether or not we want it to. I'd rather we have a say in where it goes than just watch it happen to us."

For a moment, silence. The president nodded, lips pursed, then opened the floor for a straw vote: "Who's in favor of exploring a heritage-tourism subcommittee, with Olivia as interim chair?"

The hands didn't shoot up at once, but they rose—five, then seven, then a slim majority. Even Alex Stirling, whose hand was slow and deliberate, voted yes.

Olivia didn't hear the applause at first. It was polite, not raucous, but it was still applause.

She left the dais on shaky legs, notes clutched to her chest, and made it back to her seat before her knees buckled.

Elena squeezed her hand. "You nailed it," she whispered.

Olivia didn't trust herself to reply. Instead, she took one last look at Andrew, who was now standing at the back, arms folded, smile unguarded.

It wasn't a home run. But it was a win.

And for the first time since coming back to Madison, Olivia believed she might actually keep it.

THE EXODUS from the council chamber had the choreography of a church potluck: paper plates, plastic forks, a little too much small talk and not quite enough appetite for any of it. Chamber members and hangers-on shuffled out in clusters of two and three, the men in golf shirts muttering to each other, the women from the historical society already plotting a calendar of subcommittee meetings. For every stiff handshake and perfunctory "well done," Olivia received three skeptical looks and at least one dismissive "Houston style, huh?" But she recognized the code-switching now. These people only respected you after you'd made them uncomfortable at least once.

She gathered her deck, laptop, and the rogue handouts scattered across the front row. Elena had vanished—probably out the side door to update her mom and the Rodriguez phone tree—but Olivia felt okay on her own for once. The room was empty except for the janitor breaking down the folding chairs and Andrew Kim, who lingered at the back, face softened from its usual tight lines.

He waited until she'd packed her things before approaching. "You made the case better than I ever could," he said, not quite looking at her. "Thank you."

The compliment hit harder than she expected. "You set it up. I just ran with it."

He shook his head, a brief smile curving his mouth. "I couldn't have convinced them. They don't trust experts. They trust people who look them in the eye and tell them what it's going to cost."

Olivia tucked a stray lock of hair behind her ear. "I got that from you. And from Elena, if we're being honest."

He moved a little closer, close enough for her to catch the scent of his aftershave—something faintly woodsy and expensive, out of step with his rumpled shirt. "You were right about authenticity," he said. "Most people just want to be seen. The rest follows."

They exited together, the slow clang of the janitor's mop bucket echoing behind them. Outside, the courthouse square was washed in orange sodium light, every shadow thrown long and thin against the parched grass. It was late enough that only two cars remained in the lot, and the walk back to the Limestone Inn was silent except for the occasional creak of a porch swing or the distant coyote yipping at the moon.

Andrew carried her stack of presentation boards, balanced against his hip with the same care he'd shown the courthouse blueprints. The streets were so empty that every footstep seemed to ring. Olivia found herself hyperaware of the rhythm of their stride, the way their arms nearly touched at every corner, the weird gravity that seemed to pull their steps into sync.

Halfway down Travis Street, he said, "I never asked why you left Houston."

Olivia hesitated, then answered honestly. "It left me first. Lost the inn, lost the partner, almost lost my credit rating for life."

He nodded, as if he'd expected as much. "You landed on your feet."

She laughed, dry and low. "More like, I landed and then crawled a few blocks on my elbows."

He stopped in front of the gate to the Limestone, shifting the boards so he could look at her fully. "It suits you. This place. The fight."

She felt the heat in her face, unsure if it was the compliment or just the closeness. "Sometimes I think I'm just inventing reasons not to leave again."

He set the boards on the porch bench, straightened, and looked at her in the streetlight's hush. "There's nothing wrong with making a place your own. Or with needing someone to help."

The implication hovered, fragile and heavy.

She opened the door, let them both in, and flicked on the foyer lights. The inn was silent except for the clock in the parlor and the low hum of the night staff's radio in the kitchen. Olivia set her laptop bag down, then turned to find Andrew standing at the foot of the stairs, his expression uncertain for the first time she could remember.

She heard herself say, "You want to come up for a minute? I still have beer in the fridge, if you don't mind Shiner."

He considered, then nodded. "I'd like that."

She led the way up the stairs, pausing at the top to make sure he was following. He was, hands tucked in his pockets, eyes fixed on her in a way that made her skin tingle under the thin blouse.

They stepped into her apartment over the garage, a space that still smelled faintly of drywall and fresh paint. She waved him toward the couch, then pulled two Shiners from the mini-fridge and popped the tops with the back of a butter knife. She handed him one, sat at the far end of the couch, and for a moment they drank in parallel, the silence more companionable than awkward.

Andrew set his bottle on the coffee table and turned to her. "I'm not great at talking about things that aren't buildings."

She grinned. "That's fine. I'm not great at talking about things that are."

He laughed, the sound softer than his usual clipped sentences. "You ever wonder what you'd be doing if you hadn't come back?"

"All the time," she said. "Usually I'm rich, with a perfect credit score and a penthouse in Dallas. In reality, probably bartending. Or teaching high school English in a district no one's ever heard of."

He shifted closer. "I like this better."

"Me too," she admitted, and felt a tremor in her hands that had nothing to do with the caffeine crash.

He saw it, of course. He always did.

"Are you okay?" he said, voice lower.

She bit her lip, then nodded. "I just—" She broke off, unsure how to say it. "I didn't expect tonight to matter so much. Or for you to be the one who gets it."

He moved his hand, hesitated, then set it gently over hers. "You're not the only one trying to build something new."

The words sat between them, brittle and bright.

She closed the distance, pressed her lips to his before she could lose her nerve. The kiss was soft at first, cautious, the kind that tests whether the bridge will hold before stepping all the way across. He tasted like beer and mint, and his hand cupped the back of her head, anchoring her even as the rest of her wanted to fly apart.

She deepened the kiss, fingers threading into his hair, and felt him pull her closer until she was half in his lap, blouse wrinkling beneath his palm. He was gentle—so much so that she almost wanted to scream at him to stop handling her like something precious. But she realized, as his mouth moved to her jaw and her neck, that she didn't want to be handled any other way.

They broke for air, foreheads pressed together. She laughed, this time for real, and felt his smile against her cheek.

"Should we slow down?" he said, but there was no conviction behind it.

She shook her head. "We've waited long enough."

He carried her to the bed, setting her down with a care that made her feel weightless. He unbuttoned her blouse one snap at a time, kissing every new inch of skin revealed. She fumbled with his shirt, desperate and clumsy, but he let her have the lead, let her learn the shape of him at her own pace.

When they came together, it was as if every wall she'd built had never existed. His hands mapped the scars—both old and new—with a reverence that made her ache in places she'd forgotten she possessed. She touched the hollow of his collarbone, the ridge of muscle at his hip, and felt something inside her rearrange to make space for the possibility of this being real.

They moved together in the dark, bodies slick and urgent, the silence filled with whispered confessions and the laughter that only comes when you've survived something nearly impossible. He said her name the way no one else ever had—deliberate, savoring every syllable, as if to prove to her she belonged here.

Afterward, she lay against his chest, listening to the slow return of his heartbeat to normal. He ran his fingers through her hair, tracing circles at the nape of her neck.

She almost didn't notice the tears at first—silent, then shaking, then spilling out in a flood.

He didn't ask why. He just held her, arms steady around her shoulders, and let her finish the work of putting herself back together.

When the worst of it had passed, she propped herself on his chest, wiped her face, and laughed again. "Sorry. That wasn't very sexy."

He looked at her as if she were the only person in the world. "It was perfect."

They lay like that for a long time, listening to the night beyond the window, the occasional car passing, the rustle of wind in the oak outside.

Eventually, she found the words she'd been reaching for. "I was never enough for anyone in Houston. Not smart enough, not tough enough, not—"

He silenced her with a kiss, then said, "You're enough. For me."

She believed him.

In the morning, they'd face the next set of crises, the next round of suspicion and envy and small-town politics. But for now, Olivia let herself drift, anchored by the weight of his arm and the slow, sure rhythm of hope beating in her chest.

For the first time since she'd lost everything, she felt not just capable, but whole.

She slept through sunrise, the world outside unspooling as it always had.

But inside the Limestone, Olivia was building something brand new.

Chapter Fifteen

The morning was pale gold and old coffee. Olivia padded through the limestone foyer barefoot, the chill from the marble tiles rising through her heels, her mind still half-sunk in the residue of a restless night. The air held a thin, necessary quiet unique to the hour before guests started their slow parade down the stairs—just the purr of the basement water pump and the faint ticking of the grandfather clock anchoring her to the here and now. The front door, never quite straight on its hinges, was wedged shut by a rolled copy of the Verde County Gazette, its headline font screaming two points larger than standard. She stooped, fished the paper from the gap, and read:

ARCHITECT UNCOVERS LOST HISTORY OF COURTHOUSE—VERDE COUNTY'S HIDDEN MAKERS MARKS

It was always strange seeing your own war played out in the columns of the local press. She hesitated on the threshold, paper limp in her hand, the door left ajar to let in the dust-mote sunlight. It hadn't been two months since she'd presented her ideas to the Chamber of Commerce. Still, a new script was printing itself right here on her front step, and she had to remind herself: This time, it wasn't an obituary.

She moved to the entryway bench, sat with her knees pressed together and the Gazette spread across her lap like a body waiting to be autopsied. There were photos—full color, this time. One of the courthouse dome, sunlit and noble, and another, smaller and grainier, of Andrew perched on a steel scaffold, peering into the belly of the old cupola like a man searching for his own future. The byline belonged to a freelancer, but the words—meticulous, a little mournful, surprisingly kind—felt like they belonged to someone who understood the weight of inheritance.

Olivia ran her thumb along the edge of the first column, reading slowly, savoring the tactile drag of cheap newsprint against her skin. The article began with a recap of the project's public drama, the budget overages, the emergency meeting, but quickly pivoted to what it called "the most significant historical discovery in a generation." According to the Gazette, Andrew's structural survey of the courthouse walls had turned up more than just structural headaches. Beneath a patch of crumbling plaster—exposed only after the building's west wall threatened to shear loose—he'd found a line of chiselled initials, dates, and a cryptic symbol that matched none of the standard mason's marks.

She held her breath.

The piece cited Andrew by name—Andrew Kim, Preservation Architect—but what followed made her sit up taller on the bench.

The real hero of the story, the Gazette declared, was not Andrew, but the late Teodoro Alvarez: local stonemason, amateur poet, and father of Carmen Alvarez, Madison's own custodian of local history The article reprinted a section of Teodoro's 1978 field notebook—meticulously catalogued and, until now, ignored by every prior architect on the project—

where he described the practice of "leaving a piece of your life in the wall." Not just a signature, but a story. A hope that when the limestone finally gave way, someone would care enough to read what was hidden.

The Gazette made it clear that without Carmen's dogged cataloguing and Andrew's willingness to listen, the names would have crumbled to dust. The hidden maker's marks were not just the code of the local Mexican labor crews, but a running ledger of who had built and rebuilt the courthouse through every fire, every repair, every change of regime. Names that had never made it onto any plaque or commemorative display, now permanently attached to the public memory.

The effect was immediate and electric. Olivia's pulse did a quick, surprised stutter. It was the recognition she had dreamed of, but never dared put into words: the possibility that someone might look at this town, look at her, and see more than just a replacement part in a worn-out machine.

She scanned further. The article quoted Carmen at length, then—unexpectedly—Olivia herself. There was a photo she didn't remember being taken: her in the side yard of the Limestone, garden shears in hand, hair pulled back with a paint-splattered bandana, a streak of dirt across her cheek like the mark of a half-remembered ancestor. The caption called her "innkeeper and local historian," and she had to bite back a laugh at how official it sounded.

But it was the next paragraph that stopped her cold.

The reporter detailed how, after the courthouse's instability threatened to derail the entire project—and possibly force the eviction of every business on the square—it was a coalition of local women who'd pushed for the hard fix instead of the quick patch. "In a town built by the hands of the overlooked," the article read, "it is perhaps fitting that its future now rests with those same hands." The story gave a nod to Olivia's "leadership in crisis" and "foresight in envisioning

Madison's future." It credited her with "restoring faith in Madison's ability to rescue itself."

There was no mention of her Houston failures, or the foreclosure, or even the bankruptcy. Just her name attached to a fight that mattered.

She felt a hot, complicated thing rise in her chest. She let it sit there.

The rest of the front page was a kind of coda: an aside about Alexander Stirling's historic preservation and revitalization fund, a summary of his role in local community revitalization despite his checkered past, and a careful, almost deferential mention of his "faith in local talent." There was a line about Olivia's "resilience" and her "creative vision for heritage tourism," the phrase that, if you squinted, almost sounded like a compliment instead of a warning.

She finished the article, then read it again, slower this time, savoring every sentence that felt like a correction to the old narrative—the one where her family was only ever an afterthought, the one where nothing she did would ever quite be enough.

The phone rang in the office, startling her back to the present. She let it ring once, twice, before setting the Gazette carefully on the bench and moving to answer. Even as she crossed the tiled floor, she kept her hand pressed to her chest, holding in the heat of the victory.

"Limestone Inn, Olivia speaking," she said, voice steady for the first time in days.

The caller was a woman from Austin, asking if they still had rooms available for the "Stonemasons of Madison" walking tour next month. "I read about you in the paper," the woman said, excitement leaking through the receiver. "My daughter's doing her thesis on women in rural preservation. Do you give tours yourself, or is that just for guests?"

Olivia smiled, felt her feet root to the floor, a tree suddenly aware it was in the center of the whole damn forest. "I'll be happy to show you

❧

BY EIGHT-THIRTY THE NEXT MORNING, the phone at the Limestone was ringing with a frequency that suggested a wiring fault or, possibly, the onset of the apocalypse. Olivia had not planned this. She'd made three pots of coffee, scheduled Josefina and two housekeepers for extra shifts, and even tidied her own desk—but nothing in her resume, not the Houston years nor the bitter lessons of small-town Texas, had prepared her for the rate at which the outside world was now discovering the inn.

She perched behind the front desk, headset pressing her ears, fingers flying over the keyboard as she tried to keep pace with the digital hailstorm of reservation requests. Her other hand scribbled notes—names, dates, dietary restrictions, one party requesting "the exact guest room where the stonemason used to sleep"—into a spiral-bound ledger already sprouting Post-its like fungus on a tree. The lobby bell chimed every six minutes, as if to remind her that, oh yes, the internet was not the only force capable of moving bodies through a door.

"Limestone Inn, this is Olivia—" she said, breathless, as the next call punched through. The voice on the line wanted to know if they could book the "courthouse history package," and also if there would be a tour featuring "the actual masonry." She put them on hold, flipped to the next call, and repeated her greeting before the previous "hello" had even faded. The voices blurred together: retirees from Oklahoma, bloggers from Austin, one elderly woman who insisted that she had "blood ties" to the original masons and would arrive "with evidence and an appetite."

She hung up, then immediately dialed out to a supplier for

more cinnamon rolls and extra linens, then dashed a note to the kitchen to "double the eggs, triple the salsa, warn about the gluten people." At some point, she needed to bring in a ringer to conduct the "Stonemason Tours" in her stead, but for now the guests demanded she do them personally. Plus, she didn't know how long Andrew could guarantee her inside access to the building while work was going on.

The front desk was already a battlefield: folders spread wide, two phones engaged in dueling hold music, a line of check-ins stretching toward the door. Behind her, the morning sunlight threw a warm rectangle onto the polished tile, but Olivia ignored it. Her eyes flicked from laptop to ledger to the line at the counter, then back to the blinking notification that told her the next call was already waiting.

A new couple checked in, each holding a battered copy of the previous Sunday's Austin- American Statesman, the front page folded out to the feature on "Rediscovering the Hands That Built Texas." Even the larger papers were picking up the story. The woman glanced up at Olivia with a conspiratorial smile. "Is it true?" she whispered. "About the stonemason's mark under the windowsill?"

Olivia grinned, the reflex so old and well-practiced it had survived even Houston. "It's true. If you check in before noon, I'll show you myself. There's a story about every lintel and tile in that place."

The woman's eyes went glossy. "That's all I've ever wanted from a vacation. Heritage you can actually touch." She handed over her credit card, as reverent as if she were passing an heirloom.

Within the hour, three more parties arrived, all requesting "a courthouse view." Two of the men wore T-shirts with courthouse blueprints silkscreened onto the chest; a third, who looked like he'd done time as a docent at some graveyard, asked whether the "preservation architect" from the article might make any public appearances. Olivia's fingers ached from the typing, her voice felt like sandpaper, and still the requests rolled in: gluten-free pancakes, personal histories, a family reunion that wanted a stonemason theme for their Saturday breakfast.

At one point, Olivia set down the phone long enough to press the heel of her palm against her eye. She was proud, yes, but also dizzy—like she'd been spun around three times and asked to pin a tail on the future. She checked the ledger, then the online system, then the kitchen prep list, and realized for the first time in weeks that every single room was booked solid for the next two weekends.

A voice broke through the blur. "Liv," Josefina said, peering around the edge of the door. "Front walk is full. Do you want me to bring out more of the lemonade or just start handing them beers?"

Olivia blinked. "Is it that bad?"

Josefina grinned. "They're all smiling, but yes."

Olivia was about to respond when she noticed a familiar figure standing at the end of the front desk line. At first, she thought she'd hallucinated it—a product of exhaustion or maybe wishful thinking—but there was no mistaking the severe bob of Teresa Alvarez, or the way she held herself, arms crossed, posture crisp as an ironed sheet.

Teresa wore her usual: black blazer, pressed jeans, and a necklace that looked both understated and threatening. She was not holding a newspaper, nor was she tapping her phone. She just stood there, watching Olivia work, eyes narrowed in a way that made even the most veteran teachers wilt. Retired or not, the woman was downright terrifying.

Olivia cycled through two more guests—one with a lost dog, another with a demand for "real coffee, none of this pod stuff"—before Teresa advanced to the counter.

"Ms. Cuellar," Teresa said, voice pitched low, "I see you've found your calling."

Olivia forced a smile, not sure which weapon to reach for —humor, humility, or just the basic civility of customer service. "Welcome to the Limestone. How can I help you?"

Teresa didn't answer right away. Instead, she let her gaze travel the full length of the reception area: the guests leafing through local guidebooks; the housekeeper ferrying luggage up the stairs; the thicket of checked-in cards on the wall behind the desk. At last, she spoke. "I'm not here as a guest. I'm just...observing."

"Observing what?" Olivia said before she could remind herself to be gracious.

Teresa's mouth twitched. "How fast the world turns when it finally notices you."

Olivia set down her pen; the click was loud in the stillness. "I'm not trying to make anyone look bad. I just... I want people to know."

Teresa's expression softened, but only a fraction. "And now they do. So what's next, Liv? You give them a tour, feed them a story, then send them home with a souvenir?"

"If they want the truth, yes," Olivia said, a little too sharp.

Teresa looked at her, really looked, and for a second Olivia wondered if she'd overplayed her hand. But then Teresa leaned in, elbows on the counter, her voice dropping to a private register. "You're actually helping the community, not just using it," she said.

It landed like a verdict, but not a sentence.

Olivia stared momentarily thrown. "You think so?"

Teresa shrugged. "I think it's rare, is all. To see someone win that isn't supposed to."

She pushed a card across the counter. "If you need help managing the press, call me. I've done this before." She turned, then paused. "And if you see Elena, tell her to bring back my punch bowl. She knows which one."

Olivia almost laughed, the relief blooming in her chest like a slow sunrise. She watched Teresa walk out—shoulders squared, hair shining in the lobby's morning light—and then, only then, let herself exhale.

By noon, the front desk was a scene of triage: calls queued, keys handed out in rapid succession, a waiting list for breakfast reservations. Guests milled about the lobby, some swapping stories about the courthouse, others admiring the stonemason's mark under the windowsill, as promised. One little girl, clutching a coloring book with the Limestone's façade on the cover, asked Olivia if she could become a stonemason when she grew up.

"Of course," Olivia said, kneeling to the girl's level. "All you need are firm hands and a good eye for detail."

The girl nodded, serious. "And shoes that don't slip."

Olivia grinned. "Definitely shoes that don't slip."

She straightened, smoothed her blazer, and glanced at the reservation book. For the first time, every slot was full, the neat columns of names and dates a testament to the fact that she'd actually done it: built something, and kept it, and filled it with people who wanted to be here.

She returned to the front desk, flipped the phone off hold, and said, "Limestone Inn, this is Olivia—how can I help you?"

The voice on the other end was familiar. "It's Andrew," he said, and she felt the old, fluttery panic, now reframed by the knowledge that she could handle whatever came next. "Looks like you're the only show in town, Liv. You ready for the big leagues?"

She laughed loud enough that the couple with the blueprints turned to look. "Always."

And as the phone lines blinked, the lobby hummed, and the old bones of the house creaked under the weight of its newfound fame, Olivia let herself believe, for once, that this was the way it was always supposed to be.

❧

AT THE END of the month, Olivia took the stairs two at a time and retreated into the quiet sanctum of her office, shutting out the echo of guest laughter and the steady traffic of housekeepers up and down the hall. For the first time in living memory, the inn was between crises. She sat at the antique rolltop desk, smoothed the faded blotter, and opened her laptop—every movement deliberate, reverent, as if the machine might vanish if she startled it.

The spreadsheet waited, glinting in the warm pool of her brass reading lamp. She scrolled through the columns: reservation codes, nightly rates, incidental charges that had once been shameful but now seemed almost respectable in their volume. At the bottom, under the thick black line where the formula used to spit out a sickly red deficit, a new number glowed in stubborn, defiant green.

She checked it again, then ran the calculation by hand. Still green. Still hers.

For a moment, Olivia did nothing but stare, the click of her own pulse louder than any sound in the office. She traced her finger along the rows as if the numbers were Braille for a language she'd never dared hope to read again. Then she reached for the battered ledger that held her grandmother's handwriting—pages fat with decades of guest tallies, grocery lists, penciled-in corrections from lean years and flush ones. She added a new entry, her pen stuttering for a second before she wrote the word "profit" in blue ink.

The air in the office tasted different after that.

She could have called Andrew. She could have texted Elena or even Alex, who would have responded with a three-word email and an emoji that was both congratulatory and smug. Instead, she closed her eyes and let herself feel the victory in private: the heat in her cheeks, the sudden ache in her knuckles, the relief that vibrated in her sternum like the aftermath of a hard sob.

She thought about Andrew, about how he'd said the building could outlast them all if someone just told the truth and did the hard work. He'd believed in the process, even when everyone else had wanted an easier fix. She thought of Alex, who'd wagered good money and his reputation on her, never doubting that she'd eventually find the way through.

But at this moment, Olivia realized, was not for them. This was for herself. For the woman who'd limped back from Houston with nothing but a duffel bag and a stack of overdue bills. For the girl who used to hide in the dry goods pantry with a flashlight and dream up new ways to keep the inn alive. For every failure, and every inch of ground clawed back since.

She logged into the online banking portal, entered the payment to Alex's trust, and watched as the balance shifted—modest, but enough. She printed out the confirmation, folded it into an envelope, and weighed it in her hand before setting it atop the outgoing mail stack. It felt heavier than its contents warranted, as if it contained not just money but the first solid proof she could do this.

She leaned back in the chair, let her head tip against the wood, and drew a breath so deep her ribs popped. The world outside was blue twilight, the last edge of sun bleeding into the courthouse dome across the square. The construction lights cast long shadows against the limestone, illuminating the scaffolding and the slow, steady work of making something broken hold together for another century.

Olivia walked to the window, pressed her palm against the cool glass, and watched as a crew of workers—most of them local, a few with family names she'd seen in her own reservation book—hauled equipment into the belly of the building. They looked small from this distance, but she could see how sure-footed they were on the stone, how unhurried and deliberate.

She thought of all the guests who'd come through this month, the ones who wanted to touch history, to run their fingers along the cracks and find themselves in the courthouse's story. She'd told them the truth—sometimes blunt, sometimes dressed up in a little marketing, but always honest about how nothing lasted unless someone kept the fight going.

She wasn't building alone anymore. But the thing she was building—this stubborn, patched-together future—felt like hers.

She watched the courthouse crew for a long time; the window dimming until only the hard outlines of people and stone remained. Then she returned to her desk, set her pen down, and allowed herself one silent moment of pride before the next wave of work rolled in.

There would be more problems tomorrow, and the day after, and the month after that.

But tonight, the ledger balanced.

And that, Olivia thought, was enough.

Chapter Sixteen

Olivia prided herself on reading the morning mail with a steady hand, but the official envelope from the County Appraisal District—logo embossed, windowed, never friendly—had a weight that made her thumb sweat. She slit it open at the Limestone's front desk, already bracing for the number inside. The inn was between guests, the air in the lobby bright and lemony with the aftermath of breakfast, the only witness being the battered reproduction of "Madison at Dawn" hung lopsided over the key rack.

She scanned the page. The new property tax assessment had come in at a number that would have broken her two years ago. Now, after the best quarter on record and a waiting list for the first time in living memory, she could almost—almost—take the hit without thinking about which vendor she would have to dodge for thirty days. Forty percent increase, neat and ruthless, right there in the second column.

"Forty percent?" She said, half laughing, half threatening. She'd been expecting thirty tops.

She read on. The explanation was boilerplate, but someone at the County Office had underlined the phrase "due to revised Heritage Tourism District status" in green marker, like it was a congratulatory note.

She let the page flutter onto the desk and leaned back in the creaky chair, a tired smile unspooling across her face. It was insane, sure, but it was also a kind of victory lap. A few years ago, no one in Madison would have bet that the old inn—which had languished as a decaying relic under the previous owner—would ever break even. Now, it was an asset, a rising tide. She pictured Alex Stirling reading the same letter and muttering, "You're welcome," into his single-origin espresso.

The front door rattled and swung open without a knock, the bell clanging so hard it threatened to come off the bracket. Teresa Alvarez entered at a stride, a reusable grocery tote over one shoulder and a face set in lines that had nothing to do with age.

"Morning," Olivia said, folding the assessment and sliding it under a pile of invoices.

Teresa didn't bother with pleasantries. She set the tote on the reception desk and pulled out a battered manila envelope, sliding it across like a dealer in a backroom game. "You got yours?"

Olivia hesitated. "Just now."

"My mother's went up seventy percent," Teresa said. She was not angry, not exactly. Her voice was too flat for that. "That's a record."

"Seventy?" Olivia echoed, as if the number might shrink if she said it out loud.

"Yep." Teresa drummed her nails on the desk. "Same story for half the block. Mrs. Martinez down the street? She's been here since the 1950s. Pension hasn't gone up since Reagan." She took a breath, forced a smile. "But the assessor says it's all fair market value. And that it's because of 'rising property values because of heritage tourism district designation'." She looked at Olivia, gaze sharp as a file. "That's your doing, isn't it?"

The question was not a challenge, but it hurt anyway. Olivia felt her pride collapse into a small, dense core of something sour. "I never asked for—" She stopped, then tried again, softer. "This wasn't the goal."

Teresa watched her, unblinking. "I know. You wanted to save your place. Maybe the courthouse, too." She made a face, a brief flash of her old humor. "But now my mother gets to choose between groceries and her own damn house."

Olivia shifted in her seat, heat rising in her neck. "Is there any appeal process? For seniors?"

"Of course," Teresa said, but there was no hope in it. "She can file and pray someone cares. Or she can sell and get out of the way for the next boutique Airbnb." She grabbed the envelope back, tucking it under her arm. "I told her it's not your fault, but you know how people talk."

Olivia wanted to apologize, but the words got stuck behind a wall of defensiveness. "The town was dying, Teresa. We both know it. If nobody did anything—"

"I get it," Teresa said, cutting her off. "I do. But sometimes the cure is as bad as the disease." She softened finally. "Just... don't forget who lives here, okay? We're not all flipping houses for the weekenders."

The words landed like a cold compress. Olivia nodded, fighting the urge to defend herself again.

A sharp ping from the computer broke the moment. Olivia glanced at the screen: a new email, flagged "Urgent" from Mayor Johnson's office. The subject line was "Tourism Board Invitation—Mandatory Attendance."

She read it out loud; the words turning to dust as she spoke. "They want me at the board meeting. Tomorrow. 'To celebrate recent successes and discuss the future of the heritage district.'" She made a noise somewhere between a snort and a groan. "Like it's a party."

Teresa rolled her eyes. "If you ask me, it's a firing squad."

Olivia almost smiled. "You coming?"

Teresa hesitated, then shook her head. "I'll be at home. Mom needs me to fill out paperwork. She's not good with the Internet."

A silence stretched between them, not quite awkward but heavy with all the things they couldn't fix.

"If you want me to say something..." Olivia started.

"Don't," Teresa said, soft but sure. "Just be ready. The more you succeed, the more they'll blame you for the fallout. Even the people you help."

Olivia stood, hands flat on the desk. "You think I should quit?"

Teresa shook her head. "No. I think you should remember whose story you're telling." She nodded at the pile of mail. "For some of us, the past is all we have. Don't let them turn it into a souvenir."

She turned to go, then paused at the door. "Tell your abuela's ghost I said hi."

Olivia watched her leave, the bell's echo fading into a hush that felt both triumphant and funereal. She looked down at the property tax bill, then at the mayor's email, and wondered how it was possible to win and lose at the same time.

She sat in the emptiest inn she'd ever run, waiting for the next guest to arrive.

❧

THE OLD COUNTY annex had never seen so much glass or daylight. Someone had swapped out the war-era fluorescent fixtures for sleek LEDs, and the faint smell of recently laid carpet fought a losing battle against the ghosts of copy toner and burned coffee. Olivia paused outside the conference room, checked her reflection in the narrow glass sidelight, and steeled herself. The business-casual blazer was a size too tight at the shoulders, but it read "competent" at a glance and that was all she could ask.

She opened the door to a scene straight out of a municipal TED Talk. A half-moon of conference tables lined the far wall, flanked by freestanding easels bearing glossy renderings of the future downtown: wide sidewalks, restored facades, smiling tourists in sun hats, a cartoon bat as unofficial mascot. At the head of the room, a projector cycled through slides with bold, sans-serif numbers: 82% INCREASE IN FOOT TRAFFIC, 46% JUMP IN SALES TAX, 112% SOCIAL MEDIA ENGAGEMENT.

Olivia blinked, caught off-guard by the volume . Only half the board had shown up in person; the rest dialing in on a big screen by the window. The live members included Randy Morrison, a former Chamber president who looked exactly as Olivia remembered him—comb-over, a blue blazer with his lapel pin, and the smile of a man who believed in his own agenda as a secular gospel. To his right, Mrs. Patterson from the elementary school board, nose already buried in a notebook. On the screen, the mayor's face loomed in grainy HD, slightly out of sync with the room's energy.

"Olivia!" Randy boomed, waving her in like a returning champion. "Just the woman of the hour. Grab a seat—coffee's fresh, donuts on the sideboard."

He gestured to the padded chair at the end of the table, which Olivia occupied with the slight reluctance of someone stepping into an unmarked trap. The board members looked at her with undisguised delight, as though she were a lottery ticket they'd all bought and just watched hit the jackpot.

Randy started with the numbers, never his strong suit, but delivered with enough gusto to make them sound like gospel.

"This is all you, Ms. Cuellar. We tracked the spike in visitor reviews back to the week after your historic preservation feature ran in the Statesman. We're getting incredible interest from out of town guests looking for Hill Country beauty and forgotten history. Our main street hotel revenue's doubled, and bookings at the Limestone? Through the roof. No, really —look at the chart!"

He stabbed at the screen. Olivia watched a red line—her inn's line—jump skyward, followed by smaller upticks for every other lodging in town. "We're calling it the Cuellar Effect," Randy said, grinning with all teeth. "And it's only going up."

She forced a smile, feeling a pulse of misplaced pride. It was one thing to keep her own business alive; it was another to be the nucleus of an entire town's fiscal redemption. The thrill was undeniable, even as she braced for the catch. Smart growth was one thing; blindly reeling towards gentrification was another. Dear God, don't let us be heading towards the latter.

Mrs. Patterson chimed in, voice brisk and faintly breathless: "Our research says people come for the courthouse, but they're staying for the 'authentic' experience. That means the shops, the walking tours, the food." She ticked each off with a manicured finger. "We're even getting field trip requests from Dallas now."

Randy nodded, satisfied. "Which brings us to the big reason we're here today. Branding!"

With a flourish of motion and one assistant—an undergrad intern in a bowtie—wheeled in a triptych of poster boards, each more lurid than the last. The first showed the courthouse mid-restoration, the dome lit up like an Italian wedding cake, but foregrounded by a cartoon stonemason, sombrero askew, winking at the viewer. The second showed a family of four at a Tex-Mex buffet, margaritas looming in exaggerated scale. The third was a jumble of souvenir concepts:

bats on mugs, "Authentic Texas-Mexican Experience!" banners, and what appeared to be a limestone snow globe.

Olivia's face went hot, a flush that started at her collar and burned all the way up. "What… is this?"

"It's what sells," said Randy, with the confidence of someone who'd just landed on the moon. "The Mexican stonemason angle is really bringing people in. Did you know the historic district's property values are up 35% since we started leaning in?" He spread his hands, basking in the magic of his own spreadsheet. "You were right, Olivia. People want a story. They want the grit."

She tried to swallow, but her mouth was dry. "That's not — I mean, it wasn't supposed to be—" She searched for Elena, who hunched in the far corner, legal pad in hand, eyes locked on Olivia's with an intensity that said, I told you this would happen.

She turned to the branding boards again. The cartoon stonemason's features were exaggerated into a broad smile, his brown skin a few shades darker than the photo reference Olivia had submitted months earlier as part of the oral history project. The name tag read "Teodoro," though the real Teodoro Alvarez had never worn a hat like that, never set foot in a Tex-Mex cantina except to repair the back wall after a hurricane.

Randy leaned forward, voice softening as if he'd sensed her hesitation. "Listen, I know it feels a little on the nose. But this gets the grants. The historic commission loves an underdog story." He glanced at Mrs. Patterson, who nodded, her hands folded in satisfaction. "And let's be honest, it's good for everyone. Even the locals—Teresa Alvarez is getting walk-ins at her brokerage. Little League signups are up. Main Street's at ninety percent occupancy."

Olivia pressed her palms to the edge of the table, knuckles whitening. "What about the people who actually built this place? Their families?" She said it softer than she meant to, but it cut through the room's cheer like a broken glass.

The intern blinked, a little lost. "They're part of the story, too?" he offered, uncertain.

Mrs. Patterson jumped in, tone chirpy. "We're adding a stonemason unit to the Texas history curriculum!" She beamed as if bestowing sainthood. "All the kids will learn about Teodoro and the others. It's empowering."

Randy shrugged, smiling like a man who'd just been paid in cash. "This is an economic revitalization success story, Olivia. And you're the face of it."

A sharp metallic click from the back of the room broke the moment. Teresa Alvarez had appeared, unseen until now, and leaned against the wall with arms folded tight, the lines around her mouth set in stone. She said nothing, but her presence changed the chemistry in the air.

Randy, undeterred, pushed on: "We want you to lead the next phase. Public tours, media interviews, maybe a cookbook —your recipes are all the rage." He shot her a look that was both pleading and triumphant. "Will you do it?"

Olivia couldn't find her voice. She looked at the branding boards, at the manufactured smiles and the fake bat wings and the story of her family's legacy, compressed into a marketing slogan and a snow globe. She thought of her grandmother, who'd once told her that history was for remembering, not for selling. Or for profiting.

A single bead of sweat tracked down her back, cold and humiliating.

She glanced at Elena, who mouthed, "Say no," but the words jammed in her throat. She could see Teresa's expression, unreadable but far from forgiving.

"Can I... can I have a minute?" Olivia said, standing so fast the chair nearly toppled.

Randy gestured magnanimously. "Of course! This is a lot

to take in. But we're all so proud of you. Don't ever forget that."

She made her way out, not sure whether she was walking or fleeing. In the hallway, she braced herself against the cool plaster, counting slow until the pins-and-needles in her arms faded.

It wasn't the taxes or the workload or the weird fame that hurt the most. It was the realization that she had been right about Madison all along: it could change, but only into the thing it hated most. A copy of a copy, with a fresh coat of marketing to hide the cracks.

She stood there, listening to the muffled cheer from the conference room as they moved on to the next agenda item—gift shop proposals and a "Cinco de Mayo Weekend Package" even though the courthouse hadn't been built in May—and tried to remember what she'd ever wanted to save in the first place.

After a while, Elena joined her, notes clutched to her chest.

"They're idiots," Elena said, without preamble. "But it's better than letting the town die, isn't it?"

Olivia wasn't so sure. But she nodded anyway, and together they listened to the echo of the future—tinny, a little off-key—ringing down the hall.

❧

When Olivia and Elena drifted back into the conference room, the board had moved on to "action items," but the enthusiasm was undimmed. Mrs. Patterson, still beaming, was up first: "We're already drafting the curriculum supplement. The kids are going to write their own stonemason stories—diaries, maybe even a skit. The district's never had a more relevant local history unit!"

Mr. Henderson from the hardware store chimed in via speakerphone, his voice a gravelly echo: "I'm getting a whole shipment of specialty limestone hand tools. Going to give a set to the school for display. Maybe even sell a few 'junior stonemason' kits to the tourists!" He laughed at his own cleverness, then detailed how he'd sourced the tools—never mind that they were made in a factory in Ohio and shipped overnight. "It's a legacy thing," he added, as though the point were self-evident.

Olivia tried to speak, to find some diplomatic objection, but her mouth just opened and closed. These people weren't monsters or even cynics. They were genuinely thrilled to be "doing the right thing." Every gesture laced with sincerity, every decision fortified by data and anecdote. How could she say no to a curriculum about forgotten workers? How could she fight a community so eager to honor its own diversity—so long as it came in a branded box, with a side of chips and queso?

She caught Elena's eye. Her best friend, for all her quiet, wore the expression of a woman who had just watched someone paint over a Rembrandt with finger paints. Elena set down her pen, waited for the tiniest lull, and raised her hand. "I have a concern," she said, voice clear but gentle. "The way you're framing the stonemason story—don't you think it maybe, um, simplifies things? The real Teodoro Alvarez wasn't a cartoon. Neither were the other masons. I just... I worry we're turning their history into a costume and a gift shop."

The silence after was heavy, not with hostility but with a kind of blank confusion. Randy Morrison fielded it with practiced ease. "I totally get what you're saying, Elena. But this isn't about costumes—it's about pride! We're celebrating their heritage. Isn't that what you wanted?"

A few board members nodded, murmuring agreement. Mrs. Patterson said, "If anything, it's making them into heroes!" The intern scribbled something onto his legal pad, face pink with effort.

Elena tried again, more pointed now. "But is it really honoring them if we're just... selling souvenirs? None of these families wanted to be mascots. I don't think they'd want their faces on mugs, or their stories retold as cartoons."

Teresa Alvarez, still at the back wall, let out a soft snort, but said nothing.

Randy smiled wider, not missing a beat. "You're raising a great point, and we'll make sure the educational materials have input from the community. But the feedback we're getting is overwhelmingly positive. People want to be a part of the story. It's what's making Madison different from every other small town in Texas right now."

He pressed a button on the projector, and the next slide was a montage of social media posts: tourists snapping selfies under the new "Historic Limestone Inn" banner, a family from Tulsa holding up bat-shaped cookies, the mayor posing with a sombrero-wearing cutout of Teodoro, mid-wink. The captions were all hashtags and exclamation points; the comments were universally delighted.

Olivia's stomach turned. She remembered her first trip to the courthouse as a child, the hush of its echoing stairwell and the way her father's hands lingered on the carved stone as if he could still feel the men who'd built it. She'd wanted to make history visible, to carve the names back into the story. Instead, she'd paved the way for a parade of knockoff merchandise and Instagrammable "heritage" with the real people quietly swept aside.

She barely registered the rest of the agenda—plans for a mascot costume at Founder's Day, a partnership with a national fast-casual chain for a "Stonemason Special," a limited-edition series of Teodoro bobbleheads. The board was unanimous in its excitement, the momentum impossible to stop. It was all theatrics, no careful scholarship or meaning to their plans. Nothing but crass shallowness.

At the end, Randy stood and gathered up the branding boards with a flourish. "This is exactly what we needed," he said, voice ringing with missionary zeal. "Finally, we're putting Madison on the map!"

The board members erupted in polite applause, as if they'd just wrapped a historic peace accord.

Olivia stood, her hands cold and bloodless at her sides. Her eyes drifted toward the easels and stared at the cardboard Teodoro, at the merry-eyed bat, at the neon "Authentic Texas-Mexican Experience!" banner that would soon festoon her own street. She thought of Teresa's mother, tallying grocery bills against a tax increase engineered in the name of heritage. She thought of Carmen's father, handwriting his story in a notebook, never dreaming that one day his legacy would be a logo on a margarita glass.

Behind her, the room emptied, everyone eager to call the press or order more coffee. Even Elena slipped away, shoulders hunched, too demoralized for comfort.

Olivia stayed, staring until the cartoon faces blurred, then backed away from the table, her hand creeping up to cover her mouth. It was a reflex—shock, or shame, or both.

She had done this. She had wanted them to see. But not like this, never like this.

She lingered as the lights went out, the only sounds being the whir of the air conditioning and the faint echo of applause from the hallway.

She left the branding boards behind, a silent army of smiling ghosts, and stepped out into the corridor, alone with her victory and its cost.

Chapter Seventeen

The first time Olivia walked into the annex conference room, she had been sixteen, delivering a tray of party rolls and off-brand soda to the PTA. Now, nearly twenty years later, the same scuffed Formica table waited for her, but this time, the room was thick with the feral energy of adults playing at governance. Someone—probably Randy Morrison, who never met a cliché he couldn't laminate—had draped a runner of faux-linen bunting down the center of the table, studded with commemorative pins, printed agendas, and a few strategically placed "Heritage District" coffee mugs. At every seat, a county-issue tablet flickered, each device locked to the same slideshow: a mural of the courthouse, a smiling family in mid-laugh, and, sandwiched between them, a freeze-frame of Olivia herself, arms folded, standing in front of the Limestone.

She hesitated in the doorway, unsure whether she should sit or stand. Johnson, always the showman, saw her and waved with the exaggerated vigor of someone expecting applause. "Olivia! We were just talking about you."

She moved to a seat near the midpoint, ignoring the name

placard—her name, in all caps, spelled wrong, but at least close enough for government work. To her left, Randy Morrison peered over his tablet with undisguised glee, pen tapping a nervous tattoo against the tabletop. Across from her, Mrs. Patterson hunched over a banker's box of curriculum binders, clutching them to her chest with the reverence of a minister cradling the Book.

And at the end of the table, the only other Latina in the room: Teresa Alvarez, hair pulled back so tight it looked like it hurt, face blank except for the set of her jaw, which telegraphed nothing but the urge to be anywhere else.

Johnson cleared his throat and dove in. "We're here today to discuss the final rollout of the Heritage District expansion. Thanks, everyone, for coming on short notice. Olivia, this wouldn't be possible without you." He beamed, and a ripple of polite laughter followed, as though it might soften the impact.

Olivia managed a diplomatic smile, but let her eyes travel the length of the table. On one side, the old guard: Randy, two realtors, a financial advisor who never stopped talking about the "big picture." On the other, the "community stakeholders"—which, today, seemed to mean whoever will show up and sit through a morning of self-congratulation. She caught Teresa's gaze, but Teresa just raised an eyebrow, as if to say, Good luck, querida.

The entire enterprise was built around their community, but not once had the community been solicited for their input. Just run through some marketing consultants. Consultants who were probably in Dallas and Houston.

Johnson fired up the projector, and the mural snapped onto the wall, three times life size. "As you can see, the numbers speak for themselves. Tourism revenue is up, vacancy is down, and the press has never been more interested in Madison."

Randy jumped in, tapping a slide that showed a series of upward-trending arrows. "We've modeled the property tax implications, too. The new zoning means more incentive for heritage-appropriate businesses, which means higher values, which means—"

"Which means more taxes," said Teresa, dry as old mortar.

Randy blinked, then recovered. "Well, yes, but also more opportunity. We're already seeing the trickle-down."

"Flood," said Teresa. "It's a flood. My mother's taxes doubled."

A moment's hush, then Mrs. Patterson piped up. "But think of the children, Teresa! The new curriculum—" she brandished a spiral-bound manual, color-coded tabs bristling "—will help them see themselves in history for the first time."

Olivia bit back a comment, but Randy wasn't finished. "We need your voice, Olivia. The Limestone is at the heart of the campaign. If we can get you to sign on to the expansion, we'll have the credibility to apply for more grant funding. And —" he paused, lowering his voice to something conspiratorial "—we'd like you to chair the Heritage Board. Officially."

Olivia blinked. "I thought this was about promoting the town, not crowning a queen."

That drew a genuine laugh from the financial advisor, who wore his cynicism like a custom suit. "It's both, honestly."

Johnson cut in. "The chamber needs a face. The tourists love the authenticity, but they want a story. You're the story, Olivia."

Mrs. Patterson pushed the binders toward her, the weight nearly bowling over the complimentary mug. "We're launching 'Stonemasons of Madison' week in the schools. The kids will make paper replicas of the courthouse and do oral history interviews. You could come in, talk to them—tell them what it means to preserve a legacy."

Olivia leafed through the top binder, fingers tracing the laminated worksheet inside. The stonemason's face on the cover was a clip art mashup, brown skin, cartoon hammer, the name "Teodoro" in Comic Sans underneath. The air in her throat went tight.

She closed the binder and looked at Teresa, who had not moved except to draw her arms tighter across her ribcage.

"Are there any programs to offset the tax hike?" Olivia said, voice steady. "The families who've been here for generations—are we just pricing them out so we can serve pie and wear hats for the tourists?" There it was, the insidious side of gentrification, successes dark twin.

Randy gave a quick, not-quite-reassuring shake of his head. "The city council is looking into it. There's talk of a homestead freeze for certain age brackets, but it's not in this year's budget."

Johnson shrugged, palms up, the universal gesture for out of my hands.

The conversation tumbled on, mostly numbers and policy, until Olivia realized she was no longer a participant but an exhibit. Every statement was a referendum on her value—not as a business owner, or even as a citizen, but as a proof that Madison could change without actually changing.

She tried to listen, but her mind drifted. Thoughts of her grandmother's stories, the way the old woman had refused to let go of her house even as the neighborhood collapsed, how she'd once told Olivia, "If you don't hold your ground, someone else will build on your bones." She remembered the men who'd worked on the courthouse, how their names were purposefully left off the plaque, and how, now, they were being resurrected as the face of a campaign to make the town more "welcoming."

At the end of the table, a real estate agent rattled off a list of vacant lots that could "benefit from the cultural branding."

On the screen, the digital map showed every house, every shop, reduced to a dot—red for pending acquisition, green for "heritage aligned," yellow for "potential."

She felt a kind of vertigo, as if she could see the town's future mapped in the same colors. She looked again at Teresa, who was still and silent, but whose eyes had never once left the map.

Randy tapped his pen, bringing her back to the table. "This is exactly what we needed—finally putting Madison on the map."

The room nodded, the idea settling like concrete. Only Teresa shook her head, and even then, only just.

For a moment, Olivia wanted to laugh. Not because any of it was funny, but because the inevitability of it was so perfect. She had spent her whole life running away from being defined by other people, only to find herself immortalized as a brand.

She wondered if she could even say no, or if the machinery had already rolled too far. She wondered how many people would lose their houses before the tourists lost interest.

She wondered if this was what legacy really meant.

"Is there a vote?" she asked.

Johnson smiled, teeth gleaming under the LEDs. "Not today. We just wanted you to see what you started."

The implication was clear: whether she agreed or not, the train was leaving the station, and she'd better decide if she was going to ride it or end up under it.

The meeting adjourned with a flurry of handshakes and cheap ballpoint pens. Mrs. Patterson pressed the binder into Olivia's hands, beaming like she'd just handed over the keys to the city. Randy gave her an extra-long handshake, promising to email her the "latest projections." Johnson just winked.

As she left the room, Olivia looked over her shoulder. Teresa still sat, hands flat on the table, eyes fixed on the map.

Somewhere in a room just like this, another town was

probably having the same meeting. Maybe Olivia thought, they even had the same brand of coffee.

She held the binder to her chest, feeling its weight, and walked out into the hallway, no more certain than when she'd come in.

But she knew one thing: This time, she'd be the one writing the report.

❧

THE ANNEX LET out onto a windswept patch of concrete masquerading as a courtyard. Olivia found Carmen seated on the edge of a low planter, the kind filled with underperforming perennials and the skeletal remains of last year's Christmas lights. The old woman's purse lay on her lap like a shield; her hands, liver-spotted and gnarled, gripped the strap with the patience of someone waiting for the next inevitable disappointment.

Olivia tried a smile. "You didn't have to wait for me," she said.

Carmen met her gaze, then shrugged. "Better than going home. At home, the phone is waiting." The words held no bitterness—just a familiar fatigue.

Before Olivia could reply, the glass doors snapped open and Mrs. Patterson hustled out, box of binders pressed tight against her ribs. "There you are!" she said, voice pitched bright with optimism. "Carmen, I'm so glad you're here. I wanted you to see what we're planning for Heritage Week." She rifled through the top of the box and produced a stack of colored flyers. "The elementary school is having all the children make stonemason tools out of clay, and we're going to have a mariachi band at the end-of-year picnic. Isn't that wonderful?"

Carmen's jaw tensed. "So. You want to make us into a theme park."

Mrs. Patterson's smile did a little hiccup but survived. "No, no, we're trying to celebrate your culture! Isn't that what you want?"

"My culture is not a costume for your children to try on," Carmen said. The words were soft, almost a whisper, but Olivia saw how Mrs. Patterson recoiled.

Mrs. Patterson dug in, voice defensive but quivering at the edges. "But we're honoring the stonemasons! We're teaching their names! I spent three nights researching Teodoro and the others. I made sure the kids will pronounce every name right."

Teresa's voice cut through the chill: "My mother just got her tax bill. She can't afford to keep her house. The one her father built." She stood just inside the doorway, arms folded, face unreadable.

Mrs. Patterson's brow furrowed. "But—property values going up is good! Your family's investment is worth more than ever before!"

Teresa stared at her, the silence that would survive a tornado. "She doesn't want to sell. She wants to live there. Where will she go when she can't afford the taxes?"

Mrs. Patterson shifted her grip on the binders, eyes darting from Olivia to Carmen, then back to Teresa. "Well, surely there are programs. We can help. This is about celebrating Mexican-American heritage."

Carmen's hands tightened on her purse. "My niece cleans houses for a living. Same house her grandfather built after working on the courthouse. She can't afford to keep it because tourists want to take pictures of it." Her voice was brittle, dangerous. "If you want to celebrate us, stop pricing us out."

Mrs. Patterson blinked, confusion sliding into something like offense. "We're trying to do the right thing!" Her voice wavered. "You're being ungrateful."

After a long beat, Elena appeared, sliding between Teresa and Mrs. Patterson with the ease of a practiced referee. "You are trying," she whispered, but the words landed with the force of a slap. "But celebration without protection is just... performance."

The words settled over the courtyard like a fresh coat of frost. For a moment, no one moved.

Carmen looked at Olivia, eyes gone soft at the corners. "Mija," she said, "they always told us to be proud. But they never told us what it would cost."

Teresa took Carmen's arm and steered her toward the parking lot, their shadows stretched long across the pitted concrete.

Mrs. Patterson stood frozen, knuckles white on the binders. Olivia thought about offering comfort, but walked away instead.

Behind her, she heard Mrs. Patterson's voice, thin and wounded: "We just want the kids to remember. We want them to know who built this place."

Olivia didn't answer. She walked to her car, keys tight in her fist, feeling the shape of the old world pressed sharp against the new.

She had wanted to put the names back into the story.

She just hadn't expected the story to end this way.

THE PARKING LOT was half full but somehow felt abandoned, the blue midsummer sky drained of color by the haze of asphalt. Olivia leaned against her car, binder pressed to her chest, and watched as Mrs. Patterson wept openly, surrounded by the board members who had, moments ago, been floating on the pure helium of a good deed.

Randy hovered at her shoulder, offering a handkerchief with all the delicacy of a man lowering a flag to half-mast. "You did nothing wrong, Gail," he said, voice just loud enough for Olivia to catch. "People are so sensitive now. Everything you do just offends them. You bend over backwards and it's never enough."

The financial advisor—Anderson, she thought, or maybe Andersen—shook his head, looking for a place to pin the blame. "We finally include them, and they're still upset. If they want to be part of the future, they have to accept that change is hard."

Mrs. Patterson dabbed her eyes, mascara streaking, and muttered, "I just wanted them to feel seen."

From the far side of the lot, a fresh voice: "Maybe see them without raising their rent first." It was Stuart Morrison, sleeves rolled, hands pocketed, his smile sharp as a shovel. He'd brought a cooler with him—cold drinks for the board, a legacy of his mother's PTA dominance—but he had offered none to the others.

He spotted Elena and drifted over, cracking a Dr. Pepper and sipping it slow. "It's a no-win," he said. "Ignore the Mexicans, you're racist. Even if you make them the center of the entire campaign, you're still racist." He said it loud, like a dare.

Elena gave him a look that could freeze a thunderstorm. "Maybe stop trying to win," she said, her voice the only soft thing in a hundred yards. "Maybe just listen."

He snorted. "Do you ever listen to yourself? You can't be happy unless you're angry about something."

She took a step closer, lowering her voice. "You think we want to be angry, Caleb? We want to belong. But you keep moving the finish line." She left him there, can in hand, and went to where Carmen and Teresa were waiting by the curb.

Olivia hung in the middle, unsure which gravity to obey. The board members gathered near the doors, rehashing the meeting, each casting themselves as the hero or, at worst, the innocent bystander. The other group—a splinter of three, now four—stood apart, the only heat between them coming from old pain and a fresh sense of betrayal.

She tried to imagine how it would feel to see her grandfather's story on a flyer, to hear children sing a song about her own bloodline, only to come home to a letter telling her it was time to leave. She tried to picture her grandmother's face, stoic but so easily wounded, in the lens of someone else's nostalgia.

In the far corner of the lot, Anderson—or maybe Andersen—said, "We're trying to honor their heritage. That's all. They act as if we're stealing something."

From the curb, Carmen's voice: "You're not stealing. You're just selling it back to us at twice the price."

The phrase hung in the air, undeniable.

Olivia's mind wandered, as it did when the world grew too sharp to look at directly. She saw a future where the only brown faces left in Madison were smiling out from laminated menus, or waving from parade floats in borrowed costumes. She saw tourists posing in front of houses no one could afford to live in, holding up fake hammers, squinting in the sun.

She wondered if legacy always required a sacrifice, or if she'd just been too naïve to see what it would cost.

She closed her eyes, listening to the two halves of her world talk past each other, and realized she was alone on her little island, the last unclaimed dot on the map.

Maybe it had been a ghost town all along. Maybe she'd just been the first to haunt it.

❧

SHE FOUND herself on the steps of Our Lady of Guadalupe before she realized where she was headed. The parking lot behind the church was empty, the night leaching color from the world in wide, slow bands. She sat, elbows on knees, tracing the pitted grooves in the limestone with her fingertip, the dust collecting under her nail, until the skin stung and the urge to cry passed.

The limestone was the same as the courthouse, the same as her inn. It was the town's true inheritance, dug from the same vein, laid by the same hands. The cold seeped through her jeans, up her spine, settling like regret behind her ribs.

A shuffle of gravel, then the slow approach of boots across the lot. She knew it was Andrew from the pattern of his steps —deliberate, careful not to startle.

He said nothing at first, just sat beside her, arms draped over his knees, eyes fixed on the darkening horizon. They sat like that for a while, breathing the same chill air, watching the sky turn from bruise to ink.

"I thought I was correcting history," Olivia said, voice hoarse. "Instead, I made us into a tourist attraction."

Andrew's face was unreadable in the blue half-light. "You made people see what was always there."

She shook her head, laughed bitterly. "I weaponized my family tree. My community. Gave them the story, the faces, the whole heritage package—then stood by while they priced out everyone left who remembered the real thing."

She looked at her hands, the fine dust tracing her cuticles. "Teresa's aunt is losing the house her grandfather built. Mrs. Patterson thinks she's helping. There's a waiting list for the tour, but nobody wants to stay in the actual town." Her voice broke, a fine fissure that spread before she could contain it. "At least before, they erased us. That was honest. Now it's erasure with mariachis and hashtags and piñata-shaped business plans."

Andrew was silent, but not in a way that felt absent. She wondered if he was measuring his words, or if he simply knew there was nothing to say.

"I don't know what to do," she said. "If I go along with them, I'm their pet Mexican—smiling in the brochure, telling cute stories about how we built the place. If I fight it, I'm the angry brown girl who hates progress." She spat the last word as if it were a mouthful of stones. "Maybe Doña Carmen was right all along. Maybe I'm just exploiting it, too."

Andrew exhaled. "You can't fix everything at once."

She almost laughed. "You ever try holding back a flood with your bare hands?"

"Every day," he said, and she believed him.

The wind shifted, rustling the branches overhead, a scatter of old leaves across the concrete. Olivia felt the ache of it in her chest, the sense of something ancient slipping away, replaced by a copy that looked right in photos but felt hollow when you touched it.

She leaned against Andrew's shoulder, just enough for warmth, not comfort. They sat like that until her fingers stopped shaking and the last vestige of light slipped below the courthouse dome.

She thought about the invisible builders—her people, their names now on mugs and lesson plans—and wondered if it was better to be a ghost or a mascot. Her grandfather really would be ashamed of her now.

She pressed her palm against the cool stone, as if she could siphon up what was left of the real thing.

When they finally stood, she wiped the dust from her hands and said, "Let's go home."

Andrew nodded, offering his arm.

They walked down the steps together, not saying another word, leaving only a pair of fine, white handprints on the limestone behind them.

Chapter Eighteen

The Inn's office was a shoebox crammed with ghosts, illuminated by the sallow flicker of a desk lamp and the red LED of a clock that had refused to show the right hour since her renovations first kicked off. Olivia sat behind the battered hotel ledger, her left heel hooked on the rung of a rolling chair that spun when she fidgeted. The room's original wainscoting was partially buried behind two years' worth of half-unpacked moving boxes, old guest registers, and a mass grave of marketing mailers that multiplied every time she turned her back.

Tonight's debris had a theme: the future, gift-wrapped and weaponized.

Her desk was a battlefield. On one side, the freshly unsealed county tax notice—bold black numbers, three crisp columns, and a neat summary that told her she owed forty percent more than last year "due to revised Heritage Tourism District status." Whoever had typed the letter had underlined the key phrase in yellow, the bureaucratic brashness that made her teeth hurt.

On the other side, the "Heritage Tourism Board"

marketing kit, a crisp folder that had arrived via certified mail, no return address but unmistakable: the handiwork of the Chamber's new PR firm, rumored to charge by the exclamation point. The top sheet was a mockup for the summer campaign: a cartoon stonemason in a sombrero, teeth bared in a grin, hoisting a Christmas ornament next, the courthouse retouched to look cleaner, whiter, shinier than the real thing ever could. The banner at the bottom read: "Build Your Memories in Madison!"

Next to it, a fat stack of gift shop proposals. Bats on mugs, bats on T-shirts, bats in ponchos. "Authentic Tejano Flavor!" read one, the typeface a bastardization of vintage vaquero hand embroidery. Olivia ran a palm over the top of the pile, feeling the glossy finish, the waxy confidence of a design meant for instant mass production.

And between these two, sandwiched like a confession between lawyer's letters, was the Heritage Board's "Community Endorsement," with a place for her signature. A sticky note protruded from the top, inked in that forced-casual handwriting only seen in committee minutes: "Olivia, please return signed by Friday! Your story is the heart of this campaign."

She stared at the signature page, a blank line, the only place left for her to leave her own mark.

For a moment, Olivia imagined signing it. How simple it would be to surrender: endorse the circus, take the Chamber's grant, turn the Limestone into a carnival ride for the Austin weekenders. Maybe even run for the board herself, play mascot for the kids with their "junior stonemason" plastic helmets and the tourists who wanted a selfie with the "face of Madison." Forty percent tax hike, handled. Payroll for her people, handled. Reputation, handled, for whatever that was worth now.

She set the pen down. Her hand left a faint sweat-shadow

on the endorsement form, the only honest watermark she'd produced all month.

On the corner of the desk, a half-empty mug of cold coffee propped up a stack of folders labeled: "Grand Reopen Plan." The edges of a construction permit curled out from beneath a legal pad, frayed and yellowed by a year of hard use. She spotted a loose post-it: "CALL ELENA," with a phone number and an apology about not making it to the fundraiser. A dusting of drywall powder implicitly attached itself to every surface, a reminder that even here, in her supposed sanctuary, the work never stopped.

Her gaze drifted over the edge of the desk, to where a slip of paper had slid half out of a folder during the day's bureaucratic triage. She recognized the pattern immediately—a pencil sketch, years old, the lines gone faint but sharp with meaning: her grandfather's sketch of a maker's mark, a looping signature that someone had carved into the base of the courthouse's east parapet. She'd copied it out herself, aged twelve, not long after her grandparents had taken her in. It had survived every move, every spreadsheet migration, every attempt at growing up and away. Now, it looked out from under a pile of cartoon bats and tax bills, and it made her eyes sting with the certainty that nothing lasted except the stuff you never meant to keep.

She thought about the story in the newspaper, the one that had called her "Madison's Living Legacy" and credited her for "restoring pride and financial stability to a town on the brink." Seconds later, she thought about Teresa Alvarez, who'd once said that pride was nice but didn't pay for insulin or air conditioning. The unwelcome thought followed an image of the parade of "heritage experts" who'd emailed her, most of them with zip codes nowhere near Texas, all wanting to license her "brand" for their next conference keynote.

She leaned on her elbows, digging into the desk, and let her forehead sink down until the skin went cold. The office was dead quiet, save for the distant rumble of a train and the tick of the antique wall clock, which had once belonged to her grandmother and let no one forget who was in charge of the hours.

After a while, Olivia picked up the endorsement form again, pen between her fingers. She held it poised, the way she might have done for a check or a guest-book entry. For a second, she could almost see herself signing. The motion would be graceful, definitive, an act of surrender so complete it might pass for bravery.

Instead, she let her shoulders slump; the pen rolling to a stop against the keyboard. She pushed the folder aside, slow and deliberately, as if the weight of it might otherwise crush her knuckles.

She reached for the phone, the screen's blue light harsh in the dark. The inbox was a graveyard—payment receipts, grant rejections, a reservation cancellation from a corporate client she'd spent six months aggressively courting. At the top was a text from Elena: "You alive? You don't have to show up tonight, but I'm making you dinner, anyway. xoxo."

She typed, then deleted, then typed again: "Sorry, late with paperwork. Don't wait for me.

❧

SHE DIALED the number from memory. It had been four years since she'd heard Maria Evans's voice, but the digits were tattooed into her brain, the recall that came from months of begging for work, first as a matter of principle, then as a matter of survival.

The line picked up on the second ring. "Houston Placement, this is Maria. "

"Hey, stranger," Olivia said, aiming for breezy, landing just north of excruciatingly casual.

A beat of surprise, then a low, predatory laugh. "Liv! I thought you'd sworn off the industry. Did you tire of your rural adventure already?"

"Something like that," Olivia said, tapping the endorsement form with her index finger. "Things are good. Better than they were. Just... testing the market, you know. Seeing if there's any blood in the water."

Maria barked out a laugh. "Always with the metaphors. The market's wild. And you're still a commodity, believe it or not. Half the hotels in Houston would shoot their own sales team to get you running their desk."

A wave of pride and disgust washed over Olivia, the way it always had. "What's the going rate for a washed-up innkeeper with a local media scandal and a lot of opinions about authenticity?"

Maria didn't miss a beat. "You're more famous than half the GMs on the Gulf Coast. And listen—this is strictly off the record, but there's a new build going up on Memorial. They want a manager who knows how to open, train, and stabilize. Six figures minimum. They want 'diverse leadership experience.' I said I'd float some names. You want a meet-and-greet?"

The number. The words. It was all theoretical until now, a soft-focus fantasy she'd used to put herself to quiet sleep. "Just send me the contact. If it's a fit, I'll come down for a weekend."

Maria's tone softened, just for a second. "You okay, Liv? You sound..." She left the adjective dangling, the way only a genuine friend or a predator could.

"Alive," Olivia said, and meant it. "That's the important part."

"Always was," Maria said. "Text me if you want to talk more. My number changed."

She hung up. Olivia set the phone down slowly, as if the table were made of ice. She scribbled Maria's number on a legal pad her handwriting unsteady for the first time since the worst day in Houston.

"You tried, Olivia," she mumbled, the words sour on her tongue. "Sometimes authentic visions don't survive contact with reality."

She looked again at the endorsement form, then the stack of cartoon mockups, then the tax notice, each one a distinct flavor of surrender. If she signed, she'd be the face of Madison for a decade—maybe enough money to buy out half the block, if the property values kept climbing. If they stayed the same, she could be back in Houston in a month, with a salary and an expense slate, and nobody would know she quit until the brochures came out with someone else's face on them.

Her eye caught the edge of her grandfather's sketches of the maker's mark, half-obscured paperwork. It looked up at her patiently, immortal, waiting for her to decide the future it would inhabit.

She picked up her phone, thumbed the screen, and stared at the message chain with Maria: old emojis, in-jokes, a thousand reminders of who she'd been before.

She didn't text. She just let the phone sit in her palm, heavy as a debt.

The night pressed closer; the office collapsing inward like a lung gone flat.

Outside, the courthouse dome stayed lit, and Olivia waited for herself to make the next move.

❧

THE KNOCK WAS SO light it almost didn't register. Olivia looked startled to see Andrew Kim in the doorway, his architect's folio clutched tightly to his chest, the black nylon strap digging a groove into his palm. His shirt was rolled to the elbows, collar open one button beyond professional, hair damp from the evening drizzle that had crept in off the river.

He didn't step in immediately, just stood there, assessing. She knew the look: forensic, the way he scanned a facade for signs of decay. His gaze moved from her face—drawn, she realized—to the desk, where the marketing barrage lay in lurid detail.

Andrew's mouth twitched, but his eyes didn't leave the desk. "You're not answering your phone," he said.

She shrugged, then tried for a joke. "I'm transitioning to snail mail. Slower but more dignified."

He took a step in, closed the door gently behind him, and set his portfolio on the edge of the desk, keeping one hand anchored on it like a tether. "You're not actually going to sign off on this, are you?"

Olivia didn't look up. She shuffled the endorsement form under the stack of papers; but she knew he'd already seen it. "I'm considering all the options," she said. "That's what grown-ups do."

He let out a breath. "This isn't you, Liv. You hate this shit."

She rolled her eyes. "I hate not paying my bills. The town hates me if I win, hates me if I lose. Maybe it's better to just let them have what I want."

Andrew's hand lifted from the portfolio. "Let who have it? The people who never built a damn thing, or the ones who'd be erased again by this?" He tapped the top sheet, the cartoon mason with the mustache and the exaggerated grin.

She felt the heat rising. "I'm already profiting from the story, Andrew. This is just scaling up. At least this way, the money stays here. They're talking about job training, business grants, a real after-school program for the kids. It's not all evil."

He shook his head, bitter. "That's how it goes sometimes.

But this?" He picked up the flyer and jabbed it at her. "They're making us into mascots. They're commodifying the one honest thing you ever did."

Olivia pushed back from the desk, chair rolling to the wall. "I don't have the luxury of idealism anymore," she snapped. "You can afford to walk away from projects. I don't get to walk away from myself."

Andrew's jaw flexed. "You think I wanted to stay?" He let the question hover. "You think I wasn't tempted to take the Dallas offer?"

She blinked, thrown off. "You turned it down?"

He exhaled, setting the flyer back down with precision. "I turned it down. Because I thought—" He stopped, then started again. She thought he was about to say Because I want to stay here with you. Would his saying those words out loud make any difference, though? Was he a big enough part of her life for her to selfishly expect him to uproot his life in favor of staying with her? "Because I thought it was worth fighting for something real. I thought you did too."

The room was so quiet she could practically hear her own pulse.

He added, softer: "The difference is, you were making invisible builders visible. Now they're just cartoons."

She couldn't look at him. "Maybe that's what they always were, Andrew. Maybe I'm just the last to admit it."

He didn't reply. The clock on the wall ticked, slow as a funeral dirge. Outside, a train horn keened in the distance.

They stood on opposite sides of the desk, the paperwork and the past a trench neither wanted to cross.

For a moment, Olivia thought he would reach for her, maybe bridge the distance with an apology or a plea. But Andrew only collected his portfolio, fingers clenched so hard the nylon strap whitened beneath his knuckles.

He said nothing else before letting himself out, the click of the office door precise and absolute.

Olivia stayed where she was, heart racing as the clock ticked down the minutes.

❧

It wasn't more than a minute before the door cracked open again. Andrew stepped inside, this time less architect than contrite trespasser. He crossed the room in two strides, reached for the slip of paper—the one with her grandfather's looping, almost calligraphic, signature—and held the paper up to the light, the motion executed with clinical delicacy.

"What would your grandfather do?" he said. Not accusatory, just curious. Maybe even hopeful.

Olivia squared her shoulders. "He made a record, never knowing if anyone ...

Andrew shook his head. "He didn't want recognition for it. He wanted his brothers to know they'd done something worth remembering." His thumb traced the penciled curve, a gesture so gentle it almost rewrote the past.

"He didn't sign his work for the tourists," Andrew said. "He signed it for the ones who came after, so they remember they had a part in it." He set the sketch down, careful not to crease the edge.

Olivia met his eyes. She tried to hold on to her defensiveness, but the grip wasn't as tight anymore. Andrew leaned in, not menacing but intent, the weight of the desk suddenly not a barrier but a bridge.

For a heartbeat, she could almost see the town the way he did: the courthouse stones each stamped by a secret lineage, the hotel led by hands that never expected a plaque or a parade, just the knowledge they'd done good work.

"Maybe I'm not a builder," she said, softer than before. "Maybe I'm just the cleanup crew."

Andrew smiled, thin and real. "You build more than you think."

He lingered a second, then retreated, this time for real. The door shut with a softness that was almost kind.

Olivia looked down at the sketch, the lines dark where her child self had pressed the pencil too hard. She touched the page, felt the drag of the old graphite, and tried to picture what her grandfather would say to her now.

She didn't know. But she knew it wouldn't be to quit.

The clock on the wall ticked, and the town beyond the office window held its shape, waiting for her decision.

❧

ANDREW RETURNED JUST BEFORE MIDNIGHT. This time he knocked, waited, then hovered at the threshold until she gave a nod.

He'd changed shirts, the new one less formal, a t-shirt so worn that it might fall apart if he touched it. The portfolio was gone, replaced by a folder she recognized instantly: the black-and-gold logo of Stirling Heritage.

"Couldn't sleep," he said. "Wanted to clear the air."

Olivia watched him cross the room, the way his steps slowed as he got closer to the desk, as if the gravity in the room had shifted.

He set the folder down, then stood with hands on the back of the chair, looking not at her, but just over her shoulder. "I got another offer. From Alex Stirling."

She arched an eyebrow, waiting.

"Full time," Andrew went on, "running projects, documenting overlooked histories, real fieldwork." His eyes glinted, his passion barely contained. "They want me to focus on multiethnic architecture in the region. The forgotten artisans. The actual hands that built half this town."

He waited for her to react. When she didn't, he pressed: "This means I'm staying. For real. I want to do the work right."

The words hit, but not in the way Andrew meant them to. Something in Olivia recoiled, but whether it was from the threat of creating a life with Andrew, or the guilt of the idea of him staying for her, she couldn't say.

Olivia felt her jaw tighten. "You think I'm going to melt because you're staying?" The sentence was out before she could throttle it.

Andrew recoiled, blinking. "That's not what—"

"I'm not the kind of woman who sticks around just for a man," she cut in. "If you need a girlfriend who'll drop everything and follow your job, call someone who never left."

He opened his mouth, then closed it again.

Olivia hated herself for the way the next words sounded: cold, sharp, nothing like the voice she wanted to use. "I don't owe you anything, Andrew. I'm not your legacy project."

He flinched, genuinely hurt. "That's not—"

But Olivia was already locking her jaw, the panic and the anger fusing into a hard, professional calm. She kept her expression blank, every gesture telegraphing: I will not be saved. I will not let you anchor me here.

Andrew lingered, lips pawing for the right comeback. When he found it, it was a soft, embarrassed, "Sorry. I thought you'd be happy."

He left, careful to close the door behind him, quieter than before.

Olivia listened to the silence for a long time, the apology echoing off the walls, mixing with the memory of every old argument and betrayal she'd ever cataloged in the back rooms of her mind.

She glanced at the phone, Maria's number still scrawled on the legal pad, and wondered which one of them she hated more: Andrew, for believing she was worth staying for, or perhaps for showing her what it felt like for the ones she left behind.

❧

THE SILENCE after Andrew left wasn't clean. It stuck to the walls, filled every fissure in the old plaster, crawled under Olivia's skin until she could breathe without dragging it in with every inhale.

She didn't move. Just sat at the desk, spine stiff, palms flat on the blotter, the world beyond the office a nullity. No guests checking in, no phones ringing, just the slow, arthritic tick of the clock on the wall and the tap of condensation from the A/C onto the radiator.

She let her eyes wander over the desk.

Tourism Board materials: bright, cartoonish, promising "authentic" experience in size-14 font. She imagined the whole town papered in those colors, every story ironed flat for the tourists and the board members and the grant reviewers.

Next to them, the maker's mark sketch. The lines looked bolder than before; the graphite smudged by years and by the pressure of memory. She traced it with a finger; the page rippling beneath the touch.

The phone sat silent, Maria's number still in the memory, each digit a rung on a ladder out of here. Six figures. A city that didn't care about legacy. A town that wouldn't ask for her autograph, wouldn't even remember her name.

Her hand hovered above the desk, caught midair between the sketch, the phone, and the endorsement form. It trembled, not from indecision, but from the effort of holding all the futures at once.

The clock ticked. The lamp threw shadows across the paperwork, warping the cartoons into something monstrous, making the graphite mark stretch across the whole blotter like a crack in the foundation.

Olivia stayed like that for a long time, the air dense with unchosen options.

Outside, the courthouse dome glowed. Inside, she was the only ghost left awake.

❧

She picked up the phone. Dialing slow, each number an absolution.

Maria answered after one ring. "Liv. " I didn't expect to hear from you so soon."

"I'm ready," Olivia said, voice level. "Let's set up the interview."

"Tomorrow at nine?" Maria's tone was all business, but underneath it a thrill of victory. "You want the address?"

"I know the place," Olivia said. She let the silence sit for a second, then added: "Thanks. For remembering."

Maria laughed, not unkindly. "Hard to forget someone who gets things done. See you then."

Olivia hung up. She looked at the endorsement form one last time. She read the blank line, the sticky note, the whole sad parade of exclamation points.

Then she slid it into the drawer, shut it gently, and put her hand on top until she was certain it was staying closed.

She stood, rolled her shoulders, and started sorting the desk. Heritage tourism files to the left, hotel invoices to the right. Vendor contracts, payroll spreadsheets, a pile of grant rejection letters—each in its own neat stack. She found a dented can of La Croix from last week, poured it out in the trash, and wiped the ring from the blotter with a tissue.

She gathered her personal stuff: the dog-eared copy of Garcia Marquez her grandmother had pressed into her hands before college, a mug that had survived three bankruptcies and a hurricane.

The last thing was Roberto's maker's mark sketch.

She hesitated. Then she folded it, careful not to crease the line of the signature, and slid it into her purse. Not because she thought she'd need it, but because it was the only thing that still felt true.

The front desk bell chimed, a polite punctuation to the evening.

Olivia glanced at the clock, saw it was nearly midnight, and let the sound go unanswered.

She turned the lamp switch, locked the drawer, and left the office as neat and silent as a courtroom after hours.

Outside, the courthouse dome glowed in the dark, waiting for someone else to carry the story forward.

Chapter Nineteen

Houston's freeways ran like fevered arteries, each ramp and merge pumping fresh waves of commuters into the city's gridlocked heart. Olivia's Mazda rattled at seventy miles an hour, then slammed into the familiar stall-out just past the Beltway, where lanes funneled into a sluggish, sullen clot of steel. She eased off the accelerator and let the car coast, her eyes skimming the ring road for openings that would never come. A hanging threat of rain pressed the sky to a flat, unnatural gray.

She checked the dashboard: 8:32 a.m., ninety minutes to spare, and yet her pulse scudded along like she was already late. The air conditioning groaned against the humid onslaught, failing to do more than swirl the inside of the car with refrigerated dampness and the scorched-mildew smell of a recent urban downpour. She wiped her palm on her slacks, checked the rearview—only her own face, blurred by the condensation creeping over the back glass.

The concrete here felt heavier, more intentional than anywhere else in Texas. Every overpass was shored up with extra columns, each billboard stacked with a surplus of grinning realtors and healthcare warnings. Olivia's years in the city did nothing to ease her navigation: she hit every abrupt lane closure, every poorly marked exit, as if magnetized toward inconvenience.

She merged left with a sharp jerk of the wheel, catching the brief, wide-eyed glare of a bearded man in a black F-150 who shot her a single, declarative finger. The gesture rolled off her; she didn't have any spare bandwidth for road rage, not with the job interview's coordinates pinging every synapse in her skull. She pictured the office—a high-rise near downtown, all polished glass and brushed steel—and her stomach gave a tight, sour twist.

The rain started as a warning, a scattershot of fat drops that evaporated on contact with the windshield, then built into a greasy, insistent sheet. Wipers set to maximum, she strained to see the brake lights ahead, red beads smeared across the fogging glass. Olivia's hands whitened on the wheel, a habit from Madison that had calcified into reflex. She forced her shoulders down, tried to unclench, but every time she caught her reflection in the rearview—hair fighting its way out of the bun, dark circles winning against the concealer—her pulse doubled down.

She reached for her purse, one hand skimming the interior until it closed around a travel-sized deodorant. She rolled it on with blind efficiency at a stoplight, then smoothed her navy blazer over her shirt, tugging at the cuffs to fake crispness. The car's vent spat a ragged breath of cold air, not enough to chill the beads of sweat pooling at her collarbone.

In the slow-moving traffic, she rehearsed the pitch. "I led a complete turnaround—" — No, too vague. "After a multi-year revenue slump, I revitalized..." She trailed off, the phrase sounding fraudulent even in the vacuum of her car. She tried another: "My approach to management is adaptive, collaborative, and guest-focused." She imagined saying this to the man in the F-150 and almost laughed.

A sedan in the next lane honked, inching its nose in front of hers, and she let it through. All around her, the city bristled with tension, every driver desperate to be two car-lengths ahead of where fate had assigned them. The skyline loomed closer, glass towers sheared by mist and low-slung cloud. Houston always felt less like a city and more like a threat—an ultimatum delivered in the language of infrastructure.

With each mile marker, her certainty eroded a little more. She pictured Madison, its battered limestone and fresh coat of paint, the faces that still looked at her with skepticism or outright hostility, and wondered what she was doing hurtling back toward a life she'd already outgrown. Maybe she was only good at running away, and this was just the latest iteration.

She caught a green light at Chimney Rock, veered right onto a feeder, and was rewarded by another snarl of stopped traffic. The sky opened, rain pounding so hard she felt it in her molars, each drop a miniature hammer on the roof. Olivia switched off the radio. In, out. Easy, steady.

She ran a finger down the side of her nose, checking for shine, then twisted around to inspect her skirt in the back seat. There was a faint crease from the drive, but nothing she couldn't smooth out once she arrived. She reviewed the directions in her head, making sure there would be enough time to fix her face and her posture before walking into the lobby.

Another quarter mile, and she was spit out onto a frontage road lined with donut shops, auto loan offices, and the pale green bulk of a CVS. She made a left into the parking structure, found the guest section on three, and reversed into a spot by rote. Her hands shook as she let go of the wheel.

She sat for a long moment, letting the engine tick in the sudden silence. The rain hammered the car with a sound like frying eggs, slicking the windows so completely the outside world turned abstract. Olivia exhaled, then opened the visor mirror and took stock: hair slightly wild but presentable, eyes sharp despite the fatigue, lipstick intact. She flexed her jaw, rehearsed a neutral smile, then locked her gaze in the mirror.

"You're the only person who can do this," she whispered. The sentence hung there, half a mantra and half an accusation.

She gathered her bag, steadied her hands, and waited until the rain ebbed into something survivable. Then she stepped out, heels landing in a shallow, oily puddle, her lined blazer already damp at the shoulders. She squared her posture, leveled her breathing, and walked toward the elevator—toward a new future, or at least toward the best version of it.

The city's humidity swallowed her up, and her phone buzzed once with a calendar reminder: "Interview—30 minutes."

She didn't check it. She just kept moving, each step a dare to the universe to stop her.

❧

THE ELEVATOR SHOT up with the hush of serious engineering, stopping every third floor to swallow or spit out another business suit, another intern clutching a laptop, another consultant in a panic over their phone. Olivia pressed herself to the mirrored back wall, clutching her interview packet so tight it left indentations on her thumb. When the doors opened onto the lobby of Paragon Hospitality Group, a lobby desk staffed with a woman whose makeup was more permanent than cheerful met her.

The receptionist pronounced her name correctly, handed her a guest badge, and gestured with two fingers toward the executive floor. The corridors here were a study in money—blue carpet that looked hand-combed, chrome accents on every vertical surface, and the faint, persistent whiff of eucalyptus from the HVAC. Framed on the wall was a rotating display of "partner properties": Mediterranean villas, mountain spas, even a private island off Belize.

She waited in a glass box of a waiting area, flipping through the branded print materials (heavy paper, matte finish, three colorways), until a tall man in a suit the color of wet granite called her in by her last name. "Ms. Cuellar?" he said, and she followed, feeling for a moment like she was trailing a surgeon to an operating theater.

His office was all angles and glass, the desk a single slab of walnut, the skyline arrayed behind him like a threat. There were no personal photos, only two abstract prints—rectangles stacked on rectangles, in exactly the right proportions to match the window grid. The man's handshake was perfectly calibrated: assertive, but with a hint of deference that said, "I'm the boss, but I read books about empathy."

"Olivia, right?" he said, using her first name now, and she nodded. "You came highly recommended. I'm Brent, Senior Director of Acquisitions and Brand."

"Thank you for having me," she said, deploying her own handshake—firm, slightly slower, a power move she'd borrowed from her mother.

Brent offered her water, La Croix, espresso, all in rapid succession, and when she declined, settled back with a stillness that said he'd already begun the interview.

"We're expanding our portfolio," he began, leaning forward as if to pull her into the confidence. "Houston is a dynamic market, but we've struggled to find management talent that understands both the legacy brands and the lifestyle sector. You've done both."

She nodded, careful not to break eye contact. "It's a unique market. The guest profile changes every year."

"That's what we like about you," he said. "You bridge the old and the new. Our analytics team flagged your property's performance; the turnaround at Limestone Inn was... frankly, astonishing. Forty percent revenue growth in under two years, despite the pandemic's tailwinds."

He paused, and she gave the expected nod, but her eyes drifted to the window—downtown Houston in full panorama, every square foot of skyline monetized, leveraged, on the brink of either boom or extinction.

Brent walked her through the job, each bullet point polished to a high gloss: Base salary, plus incentive; relocation support, even though she was already local; the ability to staff her own team ("within reason," he added, eyebrows arched in HR candor). The hotel was a ground-up build, ten floors, a rooftop pool, a "Heritage Texas-Mex" restaurant to anchor the lobby. She'd be the first general manager, the face of the brand, responsible for everything from hiring to crisis PR.

"Your resume says you thrive on autonomy," Brent continued. "You'll have it. The only thing that matters is results. We're not married to any particular process, so long as the numbers come in."

She answered questions about leadership style ("collaborative but decisive"), preferred technology platforms ("anything cloud-based with a good support team"), and how she'd resolve a guest complaint with potential for viral escalation. She gave the answers they wanted, but felt her mind ping-pong between the words and the invisible math of her own life: payroll spreadsheets, vendor negotiations, the endless maintenance crises that defined her actual days.

Midway through the conversation, she realized she was speaking in the past tense about the Limestone—about Madison, the courthouse, the entire world she'd built and was now, apparently, ready to sell off. She wondered if that was a betrayal, or just the natural endpoint for people who knew how to move the numbers.

Brent must have seen her attention falter, because he recalibrated. "We're looking for someone who can set the tone for the property. Make it a destination, not just a room for the night. We want guests to remember the feeling of being here."

Olivia almost said, "Like a brand," but caught herself. Instead, she said: "It's all about the people. You can build a beautiful hotel, but if the guests aren't treated like neighbors, it's just another box on the highway."

Brent smiled, as if she'd passed a secret test. "That's exactly our philosophy. You understand legacy. That's why I think you'd be a great fit."

The conversation shifted to logistics. Start date. Benefits. Signing bonus. Olivia nodded in the right places, but every time her gaze drifted to the window, the skyline was a little more distorted; the clouds pushing lower and darker against the highrises.

He asked if she had questions. She did, but none that were appropriate: Will this job make me less lonely? Will the money be enough to fix what Madison broke? She settled for, "How hands-on is the regional team? I've always worked best with a long leash."

Brent assured her that the regional support was "minimal but impactful." "You'll be the boss," he said, a smile pulling at the edges of his face, "but you'll also have resources when you need them. That's the Paragon promise."

He paused, as if to let the phrase sink in, then said, "I won't beat around the bush. We want to move quickly. You'd have the rest of the month to transition, but we'd need a commitment by Friday. Do you think you could see yourself here?"

She should have said yes right then. It was what every prior version of herself had wanted—to be wanted, to be the rainmaker, the star. Instead, Olivia felt her tongue lock in place, her mouth going sandpaper dry.

"I'll need some time to consider," she said, surprising herself with the steadiness in her voice.

Brent's face shifted in the microsecond before the smile returned, the smallest flash of surprise. "Of course. I'll have HR send over the formal offer. It's a lot to take in."

He stood, extended a hand, and she shook it again, registering the faint roughness of a callus on his ring finger.

As she left, the receptionist handed her an envelope with the company logo embossed in blue. "They said you'd want a hard copy," she said, with a wink.

Olivia thanked her, then made her way back to the elevator. She stepped in alone this time, and watched as the lobby retreated, floors blurring together into a smear of neutral carpet and glass.

By the time she reached her car, the humidity had returned, coating everything in a skin of sweat and static. She sat behind the wheel, the offer letter on the passenger seat, and tried to imagine herself a year from now, ruling over this new domain. Instead, her mind snapped back to the parlor at the Limestone, the way the light hit the old wood, the way Josefina could defuse a guest's temper with a single raised eyebrow, the way her grandmother's ancient analog clock still kept better time than any digital system.

She thought of the "legacy" that Brent had admired so much, and how easily it could be rewritten by a single signed offer.

Olivia sat in the car for a long time, watching the clouds build up for another storm, feeling the weight of her own future pressing down like the thick, metallic air.

She didn't open the envelope. She just watched it, waiting for it to blink first.

❧

The coffee shop was two blocks from the parking garage, its windows fogged over with the communal breath of freelancers and postgrads grinding out the day's business. Olivia ducked in, shaking off the thin drizzle that had already streaked her blazer with dark, uneven patches. The interior was all polished concrete and burnt-orange chairs, a kind of place that wanted to be an institution but still reeked faintly of dry-erase markers and startup money.

She ordered a latte, half-caf, and claimed a corner table facing the window. The job offer sat on the laminate next to her laptop, unopened except for the embossed seal that had torn when she stuffed it into her bag. She stirred the coffee, never tasting it, letting the paper cup rotate in slow increments as she tried to will herself into a decision.

Outside, rain collected on the glass in rivulets, each droplet distorting her reflection into something barely recognizable—a face stretched by fatigue, eyes bright with the nervous energy that didn't have anywhere left to go.

She glanced at the offer, then at her phone, then back to the glass, where the city's silhouette loomed indistinct and spectral. For a while, she simply watched her own outline refracted and doubled by the storm.

A group of students commandeered the next table, their laptops open and already forming an ad hoc fort against the world. The nearest one—a young man with blue-dyed hair and a geology textbook as thick as a dictionary—caught her eye and offered a nervous smile before returning to his screen.

Olivia looked past them, through the running lines of water, and spotted a building across the street she'd never noticed before. It was two stories, cut from pale stone, with a balustrade above the door and a quartet of arched windows peering out over the traffic. Even through the veil of rain, it radiated an old, battered authority, the confidence that modern towers couldn't counterfeit.

She watched for a long minute, then flagged down the barista with a gesture. "Do you know what that building is?" she asked, nodding to the apparition outside.

He followed her gaze, then grinned. "That's the Houston Public Library—Frost Branch. Supposedly haunted, if you ask half the staff."

She laughed genuinely. "Haunted by what? Lost library cards?"

"Probably," he said, "but also, like, actual ghosts. The story is that some of the guys who built it never really left."

She sipped her coffee, savoring the bitterness. "When was it built?"

He shrugged. "Nineteen-twenties? My dad said they brought in stonemasons from San Antonio to do the front. Supposedly a bunch were Mexican immigrants, and they left their initials hidden in the stonework. Kind of cool, right?"

Olivia let the words settle, a familiar ache blooming at the base of her throat. "Yeah," she whispered. "That's pretty cool."

He left her with a smile, and she returned her attention to the street. The library looked both out of place and perfectly at home, as if it had been waiting for the city to rise around it and justify its stubborn existence.

She traced the rim of her cup, watching as the students next to her settled into their private universe of shared complaints and half-laughed jokes. She imagined herself as one of them, younger and less freighted by consequence, and the thought almost made her laugh.

Instead, she pulled the job offer closer, tearing the envelope open with a decisive rip. The numbers inside were better than she remembered, the benefits more generous, the bonus almost obscene. She read the words, then set the offer back on the table and folded her hands in her lap.

Outside, the rain intensified, obscuring the library almost completely. She could have turned away, buried herself in the warm churn of the coffee shop, let the storm pass and her doubts about it. Instead, she gathered her things, left her coffee half-finished, and walked out.

Her heels caught on the uneven concrete, but she kept her pace quick, purposeful. By the time she reached the curb, her blazer was soaked through, but she didn't care. She looked both ways, then jogged across the street, past a double line of honking cars, straight to the stone steps of the library.

She stood beneath the lintel, breathing hard, the air rich with petrichor and distant books. She felt the old limestone beneath her palm, rough and pitted with decades of weather. For a second, she wanted to find those initials, to run her fingers over the names of men who had built something and stayed behind to haunt it.

She laughed, wiped rain from her cheeks, and pushed open the door, already knowing what she needed to do.

THE INSIDE of the library was colder than she expected, the echo of the front doors booming down a corridor lined with battered marble. Olivia paused just past the entry, letting her eyes adjust to the softer light. Stained glass threw slow rainbows across the floor, and the smell of floor wax and paper mingled in a way that instantly recalibrated her nervous system. She let her pulse settle, counting the seconds as she oriented herself.

At the information desk, a young woman in a navy cardigan sorted a stack of returns. Her hair was dark and sharp-cut, her nametag a simple "Lucia." She glanced up, clocked Olivia's damp clothes and the slight wildness in her eyes, and smiled like she was used to people arriving from the storm.

"Hi there," Lucia said, voice pitched to the hush of the

reading room. "You need a card, or just looking for a dry spot?"

Olivia wiped her palm on her skirt. "I'm actually interested in the building itself. Someone told me there's—uh—stonemason marks? In the stonework?"

Lucia's smile broadened. "You heard right. Most people miss them, but the old architecture journals are obsessed with it. You want to see them?"

"Absolutely," Olivia said, surprised by her own urgency.

"You caught me at the perfect time," Lucia said, swinging out from behind the desk with a practiced grace. "I was just about to re-shelve these." She gestured to a cart stacked with faded hardbacks and a few slick modern volumes. "Follow me."

They walked through a colonnade of white-painted pillars, past the quiet chuff of an ancient radiator. The floors creaked, not with age but with authority. A pair of massive limestone columns anchored the far corner of the main hall, each one adorned with subtle, swirling patterns that could easily be mistaken for the natural whorls of the rock.

"This is my favorite spot," Lucia said. She ran her hand along the base, fingers hunting for something. "They used local stone, but the builders had a tradition—they left their mark, but not on the face. You have to get in close."

Olivia knelt, peering at the join between the column and the plinth. There, just above eye level, was a set of initials—T.A., crisply carved and perfectly straight. She reached out, letting her fingers hover over the surface.

"Some say it's for the foreman," Lucia said. "Others think it's a kind of code. But the coolest thing is, there's like twenty of these, all different, all hidden away."

Olivia laughed quietly and breathlessly. "My grandfather did this. Not this building, but back home. He'd leave a coin, or his initials, in the frame before the drywall went up." She hadn't realized how much she missed the feeling of stone under her skin, the proof of someone's hand in the work.

Lucia crouched down beside her, voice lower. "There's more too. Some guys from the Mexican crews—they'd put in little messages. You can see them if the light's right." She angled her phone flashlight along the edge, and another symbol popped out: a tiny sunburst, almost erased by time.

Olivia felt the words catch in her throat. She traced the symbol with her thumb, felt the precise ridges left by the chisel. The sensation was electric, a pulse that shot up her arm and settled behind her breastbone.

"It's so cool," Lucia said, genuine and unguarded. "The city wants to sandblast the columns for some restoration thing, but a bunch of us are trying to stop them."

"They should," Olivia said, the words coming out sharper than she meant. "It's history. Genuine history."

Lucia nodded. "You get it. Most people don't."

They spent another minute there, Lucia pointing out more signatures, Olivia cataloging the differences in style and depth, as if by reading them she could reconstruct the lives of the men who left them.

When they finished, Olivia straightened, her knees aching from the cold marble. Lucia offered a gentle smile and a handshake.

"Thanks for showing me," Olivia said. "It means a lot."

"Anytime," Lucia said, then hesitated. "You should come back for the architectural tour. First Sunday of every month. We get a lot of people whose grandparents worked on these buildings."

Olivia smiled, meaning it. "I will."

She left the library lighter than when she had entered. The rain had let up, leaving a shine on the sidewalks and a clarity to the air. She strolled back toward her car, turning the conversation over in her mind, the memory of the stone still tingling in her fingertips.

For the first time in days, she felt sure of her next move.

❧

BY THE TIME Olivia turned the last corner, the storm had returned with a vengeance, water sluicing from the library's gutters in heavy, vertical sheets. She jogged the final yards to her car, breath fogging in the chill, hair already a lost cause. The parking lot glimmered with new puddles, each one deep enough to reflect the dim sky.

She threw open the door, slid into the driver's seat, and let the wetness soak straight through her skirt to the upholstery. For a minute she just sat, hands braced on the steering wheel, watching the rain batter the windshield until the world outside lost all hard edges.

The offer letter was still there, its embossed logo now blurred at the corners from the earlier rain. Without ceremony, she grabbed it, crumpled it, and tossed it onto the passenger seat. The decision was made. She didn't need to talk herself into it anymore.

She started the car and let the engine idle, watching as the defroster cleared a small, circular portal in the fogged glass. Through it, the street was transformed: traffic slowed to a crawl, brake lights painting the slick asphalt with streaks of red. The gutters had already overflowed, water swirling around the tires of a stalled truck halfway up the block.

For the first time all week, Olivia felt calm. There were still a thousand things to do, calls to make, people to face, but the next move was clear. She keyed Madison, TX into the GPS, not bothering to check the estimated arrival time.

The wipers fought to keep up as she eased out of the lot, swinging right onto the feeder road and merging into the thick, sluggish artery of westbound traffic. The city seemed to close in behind her, glass towers disappearing into the gloom as the rain blurred everything into a wash of gray and silver.

At a stoplight, she looked into the rearview and saw nothing of the skyline—just her own face, resolute, eyebrows knitted against the storm. She tightened her grip on the wheel, feeling the curve of bone beneath the skin, the steadiness in her knuckles.

When the light changed, she pressed the accelerator. The car leapt forward, splashing through the pooled water with a sound like applause.

She didn't look back. Not once.

For the next three hours, she chased the tail of the storm all the way home.

Chapter Twenty

The rain's residue still ghosted Olivia's shoulders when she entered the lobby of the inn. The world outside had gone sullen and blue, thick with the hush that always followed a real Texas deluge. Every light in the inn flickered; but the public rooms lay empty, the ghosts on the old ledger undisturbed. She set her tote and the soaked blazer by the hall tree, then settled at the parlor desk, ignoring the way the wetness had seeped through her skirt to leave a cold band across her hips.

The first thing her hands reached for was the pencil sketch. The page had curled at the edges, gone thin as an onion's skin, but the mark—her grandfather's mark—remained. Three looping letters, the capital C with the flourish, underlined twice for defiance. She braced her palm over the page and traced the lines, remembering how he'd drawn it for her in this very room, laughing at the waste of "fancy art paper" when scrap would do. "It's only a secret if someone remembers to look," he'd said, and she'd wanted so badly to be the kind of person who remembered.

She stared at it now, letting the graphite ghost onto the

pad of the specially ordered Heritage District stationery. She pressed her thumb hard, then harder, until the pulp of her thumb blanched. Above the desk, the antique clock ticked time in uneven measure, each swing a nudge closer to the next, inevitable confrontation.

Doña Carmen's voice, unbidden, surfaced: He signed his work in stone so it wouldn't be forgotten.

The idea cut through her like a bracing slap. Her Carmen's father didn't leave his mark for the county or the mayor, or even for the generations of Cuellars who would work the same limestone for wages that never quite reached par. He left it for the people who would need to know someday that this place was theirs too—that they had built it, named it, held it in place even as history tried to rinse their fingerprints away.

The truth landed hard and clear: He hadn't left it to later be replaced or rebranded with a cartoon sombrero. He'd left it so the story would be too heavy to lift, too real to sandblast away.

Olivia's jaw clenched. She remembered the Tourism Board's meeting, the cartoon characters layered over her grandfather's photo, the callous pride in Randy's voice as he sold the town's soul one hashtag at a time. She pictured the mugs and t-shirts, the "authentic heritage" keychains, the lesson plans that would turn Teodoro and Carmen and every Alvarez into a mascot for tourists from Tulsa.

She wanted to scream. Instead, she dug through the desk drawer, found a spiral notebook still in its packaging, and cracked the spine. The tip of her pencil snapped on the first press—she didn't care. She sharpened another, and this time, the lead held.

On page one, she scrawled the word: "Alt Plan." Underline. "Heritage Tourism, but not for the Board. For us."

She started a list, quick and brutal:

- Community-led heritage tours. All profits to local families, not the Chamber.

- Oral history program—real interviews, not stories polished for outsiders.

- Museum space in the old jail, curated by Mexican-American elders, not the county.

- Kids' workshops taught by retired masons. Spanish-language versions mandatory.

- Stonemason's Day as a memorial, not a spectacle. No costumes, no charades.

- Legal fund for property tax appeals. Help the old families stay in their houses.

She pressed the point so hard that the next page tore, a jagged lightning strike through the margin. It felt good. Her hand ached with the motion, each letter less legible than the last, but she kept writing, not stopping for sense or style or legibility. She wrote until the shiver in her wrist steadied, until the ideas smoothed out and made something like a shape.

She paused only to catch her breath, then flipped back a page and started again: "Mexican-American Heritage, by and for Madison." Underlined and with three stars.

She wrote up a script, loose and fast, for how she'd present it: "We're not an exhibit. We are the history. We're not selling the past—we're keeping it from being sold off."

The clock tolled the hour, and in the brief silence that followed, she heard the distant rumble of the courthouse bells, maybe two minutes behind, the way they always were. It felt like a signal.

She went back to the sketch, set it next to her own scribbles, and stared at the two marks together. The old one, dignified and precise; the new, frantic and smudged but just as desperate to last.

The familiar urge to run, to go back to Houston and let someone else take the hit, nudged up her spine—but she set her palm flat on the desk, steadied it. She remembered how the city had looked through the rain, ghosted and blurry, and how solid the library's limestone had、 felt under her hand.

She looked at her hands: the graphite tattoos, the half-moons of sweat and grit under her fingernails, the swollen bone at her knuckle from the day she punched the inn's ancient, creaky dumbwaiter back to life. She thought: This is a stonemason's inheritance too.

She drew a deep breath and wrote the last note of the night, the one she knew she'd have to recite to herself over and over:

"Legacy doesn't mean profit. It means proof."

She shut the notebook with a clap, straightened her shoulders, and looked around the empty room.

In the silence, the clock kept ticking, as if the next move was already overdue.

❧

Olivia parked the car on a yellow curb, hazard lights blinking their own lopsided melody, and hurried up the cracked walkway to Our Lady of Guadalupe. It was near dusk, that hour when the heat of the air but leaves a sticky residue, and the insects chirred in the shrubbery like a bad dial-up connection. She barely slowed, just grabbed the battered spiral from the passenger seat, and dashed for the side entrance.

Inside, the church was refrigeration-cool and dim, a limestone vault pressed shut against the world's noise. The hush wasn't just spiritual; it was a sound that pressed back, the way a down comforter can smother the loudest grief. Olivia's shoes —still damp from the earlier rain—squelched, a sharp report against the marble, and she wondered if the entire church could hear her coming.

She found Father Reyes in the transept, laboring over a

battered wooden folding table. Across from him, Doña Carmen, hair in its usual net, reading glasses perched on the tip of her nose. The table was a thicket of paperwork: summer camp applications, fundraiser flyers, a half-empty box of home-printed offertory envelopes. In the candlelight glow, the priest and the abuela looked conspiratorial, heads together in a small rebellion against entropy.

They looked up at once, alarm turning to recognition as Olivia's silhouette cut against the glass-paned doors.

"Livita," Carmen said, voice sharp. "You look like you robbed a bank."

Father Reyes smiled with the calmness of a man who saw confessions in every human drama. "You found us," he said, and gestured her in. "Please—sit."

She sat. The pews behind them seemed to listen in, the old wood groaning just enough to remind her that even sanctuaries had ears.

She set the notebook on the table, opened it, and pressed both palms to the paper to even out the shivering in her wrists.

"I can't do it," she said too loud. "I can't sign off on their plan. It's a lie."

Neither interrupted, so she plunged on, breathless. "They want a mascot, not a history. I saw the cartoon, Carmen. The hat, the mustache, the little 'Teodoro' label. They're making you a meme. They're making all of us a meme. And they'll make money off it—money that never gets back to the people who built the damn town."

She looked at Carmen, then at the priest, her eyes adjusting to the deep jewel tones that stained the floor. Light slanted in through the rose window, polka-dotting their faces in madonna blue, martyr red.

She flipped open the notebook, thrusting the page forward. "There's a better way. We make the tours ourselves. We teach the kids ourselves. We put our own names on the plaques, and we open the museum in the old jail, not the stupid Main Street visitor center with its slot machines and bath bombs." The page trembled, her words streaking up the margin where her hand had slipped. "We can do it. We can make it so that nobody forgets, and nobody gets erased again."

Father Reyes nodded, slow, contemplatively. "You want to take on the Establishment," he said, voice soft. "That's a tall mountain, Olivia."

"Is it more impossible than my abuela paying her taxes on time?" Olivia shot back. "Is it more impossible than you keeping the lights on in here without another bake sale?" The words buzzed through, fierce and feral.

Carmen eyed the notebook, suspicious but curious. "And who will do the work? You?"

"Me," Olivia said. "And anyone who wants to remember. And anyone who's tired of being the punching bag for someone else's narrative."

The silence that followed was slow and somber as a funeral hymn. It was Carmen who broke it: "You are talking about giving up the money," she said, a warning, not an accusation. "There is no profit in being real."

Olivia felt the heat rise, but she breathed it down. "Maybe not now. But the profit from a lie doesn't last. If it did, I'd still be in Houston, running a hotel that looked like a prison on the inside."

Father Reyes reached across, set his hand on Olivia's. His palm was cool, the skin gone papery with years of holy water and hospital visits. "If you do, they will try to break you. They will say you are not loyal or not grateful. Are you ready for that?"

She looked at her hands, the graphite still streaked across her knuckles, the shadow of her grandfather's signature ground into the cuticle. "I don't care," she said, and meant it.

"I won't be a mascot. And I will not sell our people for a grant check and a poster."

Carmen stared at Olivia, face unreadable. Her jaw was set, the lips a thin line, but in her eyes, a gleam that was almost... proud. "This is a lot of work for a girl with no money and no army," Carmen said.

Olivia cracked a proper smile. "You're the first recruit, Doña. The army starts with you."

Father Reyes grinned and folded his hands in front of him. "Then we will do this together." He pointed at the notebook. "Write the plan. Not in pencil. In ink. I'll call the bishop—he owes me. And Carmen can call every woman in town with a bone to pick."

Carmen leaned forward, her forearms muscled from a life of rolling tortillas and carrying grandbabies. "We will need to be loud, mija. And we will need to make them look foolish."

Olivia nodded, feeling the wild relief of a diver hitting cold water. "I'll make it so even the mayor has to tell the truth. Even if it ruins me."

For a minute, none of them spoke. The sanctuary was full of possibility, and the slow, kind rhythm of the night pushed in from outside.

A bell rang in the hallway, a wind-up timer from the kitchen, and Carmen shot to her feet. "Time to eat," she said, a command and a blessing.

Olivia closed the notebook, fingers lingering on the front cover. She looked at the two elders across the table, their faces aglow in the cut glass and candlelight. She thought: This is the true story.

They walked together down the nave, their shadows stretched long and dark behind them. At the door, Olivia paused, looked back at the altar, the candle flame steady and unshaken.

This is what she had chosen. Not to win, but to belong.

Not to profit, but to prove. She felt the peace of it, as deep and cold as the limestone, and it held her up all the way to the parking lot, where the car was waiting, hazard lights still blinking in solidarity.

Father Reyes's office was a confessional in miniature: icons on every flat surface, a rosary tangled on the lamp pull, and a portrait of Our Lady glaring benevolently from above the door. The walls were the same stone as the nave, but here it looked softer, worn smooth by decades of whispered schemes and unpaid bills. The furniture mismatched—one good chair behind the desk, two penitential folding ones for guests. Carmen chose the one with the least wobble, then sat and pulled Olivia's notebook into the light.

The priest busied himself at a battered percolator, pouring grounds by the palmful and adding water from a chipped pitcher. The thing groaned to life, bubbling and hissing, turning the office's chill into a warm, bitter cloud.

Olivia perched on the edge of her chair, fingers tight on her knee, watching Carmen flip through the pages. The old woman's lips were pursed in concentration, her thumb tracing each line. She'd pause, go back, and reread certain sections, then jot in the notebook with a pen from her purse, crossing out "kids' crafts" and replacing it with "apprenticeship."

After a few minutes, Carmen set the notebook down. "It's good," she said, surprising herself. "But you need proof. You need Andrew's diagrams, his reports. Without it, the men downtown will say it's just a story."

Olivia nodded, relief and dread mixing in her stomach. "He's already mapped the marks. He has the oral histories. If the Texas Historical Commission wants verification, we'll bury it in evidence."

Father Reyes poured the coffee into three mismatched mugs, then set them on the desk with priestly precision. "We should form a committee," he said, "not just the three of us. Every family with skin in the game should have a voice. Elders only, no board members, no Chamber shills."

"Except Andrew," Carmen said, half-joking. "He's not old, but he's stubborn enough."

They all laughed, the kind that comes when you realize your army is three strong but ready to riot.

Father Reyes' expression sobered. "They'll come after you, Olivia. The mayor, the Chamber—they'll say you're a traitor, or ungrateful, or making trouble for no reason."

Olivia held the coffee mug with both hands, the heat biting into her skin. "Let them. If they want a fight, they can have it. I'd rather lose the inn than sell it out."

She said the words and meant them. She thought of the hotel in Houston, the empty pride of being "the face of a brand," and realized she'd never felt less real than in that moment.

Carmen reached across the desk and took Olivia's hand in both of hers. The skin was thin, but the grip was iron. "You will lose things," she said, soft. "But you will gain something too. Respect. And maybe, if we are lucky, a place for the kids that is not just a memory."

Olivia smiled, then blinked against the sudden sting in her eyes. "I'm not scared," she lied.

Father Reyes grinned, ancient and mischievous. "You're terrified. That's good. All the best revolutions start with someone scared out of their mind."

They drank the coffee, bracing and sour. Carmen scribbled a few more notes in the margin, then set the pen down with a click. "We meet tomorrow, here, with Andrew. And the others you trust."

Olivia nodded, the resolve settling in her bones. “We’ll do it. And we’ll do it right. No mascots. No erasure.”

Carmen squeezed her hand again, then let them “Your grandfather would be proud.”

The priest raised his cup. “To stubbornness,” he said, and they drank, the three of them, in the company of saints and ghosts and the faint, sweet promise of belonging.

Outside, the church was dark, but inside the little office, the lamp threw a halo around the table, and the hands joined across it glowed with their own holy light.

Chapter Twenty-One

The room buzzed like a hornet's nest. Even before Olivia entered the meeting room, she could hear the voices: sharp, overlapping, hungry for blood. The folding doors had been pushed back, the air conditioner going full tilt, but it still smelled like metal chairs and sweat and the promise of a fight. She caught her reflection in the brass kick plate—hair tight, blazer defiant, shoulders squared for a battle she'd already lost in her head a dozen times. Behind her, Carmen and Father Reyes walked in step, their silence an armor. Teresa Alvarez followed, a half step behind, scanning the crowd as if for snipers. Elena fell into place at Olivia's side, lips moving in silent rehearsal.

The meeting room was a fishbowl: windows on three sides, every seat filled, the overflow standing hip-to-hip along the back wall. The town's old guard dominated the center rows—Randy Morrison, Mrs. Patterson, the entire Economic Development Committee, and enough local business owners to fill a Chamber mixer. Along the far side was a wall of unknown faces: Main Street shopkeepers, out-of-town consultants in sport coats, even the guy who ran the vape shop and always tried to get meetings adjourned early. At the head table sat Mayor Johnson, heavy in his chair, fingers spread wide on the Formica, presiding like a judge with both verdict and sentence already written.

Olivia had planned to enter quietly, maybe take a seat at the perimeter, but a voice from the front announced her with surgical volume. "Ms. Cuellar! Over here, please." It was the Tourism Board director, a smile fixed so tight it threatened to bisect his jaw. Olivia walked to the appointed table, Carmen and Father Reyes in her wake, and set down her battered accordion folder. Her hands shook so badly she almost fumbled the zipper, but she snapped it open and spread the contents with clinical precision: annotated diagrams, bullet-pointed agendas, a stack of color-copied handouts she'd killed two printers to produce.

Mayor Johnson gave her a nod—just short of polite—then called the room to order with a series of hammerless gavel raps. "Let's settle in, folks. The next agenda item is the Community Heritage Initiative, proposed by Olivia Cuellar and, uh, partners." He didn't bother hiding the skepticism; the word "partners" landed with the same weight as "co-conspirators."

Olivia stood. For a second, her knees threatened to buckle, but she locked them tight and forced her breath out slow. "Thank you, Mayor. I appreciate the chance to present." She let her eyes sweep the room, met each stare for a half-second, trying to sort hostility from curiosity. The balance was not promising.

She cleared her throat, clicked on the projector, and brought up the first slide—a photograph of the courthouse, sunrise striking the limestone a deep gold. "We all know why we're here," she began. "Madison is at a crossroads. We can sell our history to the highest bidder, or we can be the ones who tell it." She clicked to the next slide: a grid of archival photos, stonemasons frozen mid-swing, their faces resolute and dusted with sweat. "The people who built this place were never invited to the table. I'm asking that this time, we let them sit at the head."

The room shifted, a restless animal. Someone near the back muttered, "Here we go," but Olivia pressed on. She outlined the five pillars of the Community Heritage Initiative—each point punctuated with a new slide, each slide calculated to undercut the Chamber's campaign with equal parts data and guilt.

"First: Mexican-American-led storytelling. All tours, all programs, all official narratives to be managed by a committee made up of descendants from the original stonemasons and community elders. Not outsiders, not consultants." She flicked her wrist, slide two. "Second: profit-sharing. Every dollar from guided tours and educational events splits fifty-fifty between the town and the families whose stories built this place." Slide three. "Third: real educational programming, not mascot day or craft fairs. We will create an apprenticeship for local youth—real training, actual skills, taught by retired masons and tradespeople from our community." Slide four. "Fourth: authentic artifacts, not merchandise. No more cartoon mugs, no snow globes. We open a micro-museum in the old jail, and every display has to be approved by the families it represents." Fifth and final slide—a photograph of the inn's parlor, filled with children listening to Doña Carmen read from a spiral notebook. "Last: community approval for all interpretive displays. If you want to use our names and faces, you ask us first. That's non-negotiable."

She let the words hang. The silence that followed was not polite. It was dense, prickly, the air so tight that even the A/C seemed to pause for effect.

Olivia exhaled and braced for the backlash.

Mayor Johnson found his voice first. "So your solution is to turn economic revitalization into a private club?" His fingers drummed the table, sharp and deliberate. "You're going to kill the one shot this town has to get on the map."

Olivia didn't blink. "With respect, sir, this town was already on the map. You just never looked past Main Street."

Laughter, thin and mean, rippled from a knot of business owners by the window. The Tourism Board director leaned forward, voice syrupy and condescending. "Ms. Cuellar, this is very... passionate. But it's not realistic. People want simple. They want fun. They want to buy something with a bat or a funny stonemason on it and post it to Instagram."

Stuart Morrison from the back stood up. His arms were folded, eyes narrowed in a way that made his words land like a slap. "So, what—you want us to ask permission to celebrate our own town? You want us to have to run every T-shirt slogan by a committee?"

"That's not what she's saying," said Carmen, voice carrying over the hum. "She's saying, "Don't celebrate us while you erase us. Or price us out."

A man from the Chamber—Olivia didn't remember his name, but his face was the kind that had haunted every local politics meeting since the Reagan era—spoke up. "This is too complicated. Our plan is simple. We sell the story, we use the revenue, everyone wins."

"Everyone except the people who actually built it," said Elena, sharp as a tack.

The business owners lined up behind the simpler, shinier plan. "People want souvenirs, not lectures," said one. "The mascot is cute. The history is a bonus, but nobody's going to pay extra for a lecture about labor rights in the 1900s," said another.

Olivia saw the split in the room—some faces frozen in outrage, some lit with the shock of seeing the game called by its real name. On the far side, Mrs. Patterson sat quietly, her hands folded in her lap, watching the volleys with an expression Olivia couldn't read.

Mayor Johnson held up his hands. "Let's call it. All in favor of the Tourism Board plan—raise your hand."

Half the room went up, not in unison but in nervous bursts, as if checking to see who else had committed.

He lowered his arms. "Opposed?"

Fewer hands, but the ones that rose did so with fists, not open palms.

The mayor nodded; the matter settled. "We'll bring the proposal to the next council meeting. But for now, we're sticking with what works."

The room erupted—not with applause, but with a noise like a stadium boo, half of it relief, the other half rage. Olivia felt a rush of adrenaline, her own pulse so loud it nearly drowned out the exit shuffle. She caught Carmen's eye. The old woman gave her a tight, knowing smile.

"We're not done," Carmen whispered, just for Olivia. "They think it's over. They think we'll sit down."

Olivia smiled back, the expression brittle but unbroken.

"We make them remember," she said. "Even if it's the last thing we do."

The meeting broke up in a storm of muttering and pointed looks, but Olivia didn't move. She gathered her papers, hands steadier now, and walked out with her people, head high. Outside, the storm clouds had gathered over the courthouse dome, dark and sharp against the horizon, waiting for someone to call down the lightning.

It was only after the crowd thinned that Mrs. Patterson made her move. She waited until the anger had decanted, until the mayor's supporters had drifted out to the parking lot, their voices fading behind the hush of a town that had run out of things to say.

Mrs. Patterson walked up the aisle with all the hesitation of a first-grader called to the principal's office. Her hands trembled, not with age but with something closer to shame. When she stopped in front of Olivia, it took her a full five seconds to find her voice.

"I don't understand," she said. "We're trying to honor the stonemasons. Why is that wrong?"

Every conversation in the room blinked out, the silence going deep and sudden. Even the mayor, already halfway out the door, paused at the threshold.

Doña Carmen turned to face Mrs. Patterson. The lines around her mouth softened; her eyes, which had been all steel and vinegar, went unexpectedly gentle. "You want to honor them," Carmen said. "I believe that. But honor without asking costs us our homes." She held Mrs. Patterson's gaze, voice unhurried. "That's not honor. That's harm in honor's costume."

The effect was immediate. Mrs. Patterson's chin dropped, her shoulders caving inward, the set of her jaw dissolving into confusion. "I didn't know about the property taxes," she said, her voice cracking in the middle. "I just wanted the children to learn the truth." She looked at Olivia, and in her expression was the full, unfiltered ache of someone who'd made a mess with the best of intentions.

Teresa stepped forward, hands folded tight. "Then let us teach the truth," she said. "Not clay tools and mariachi songs. My grandfather laid bricks for the courthouse. Let me tell his story. Not a tourist board version."

Mrs. Patterson's eyes filled with tears, not the dramatic kind, just the slow overflow of an old reservoir she hadn't checked in years. "I'm sorry. I thought — I thought finally including you was enough."

Father Reyes (who, Olivia realized, no one called Miguel outside of a confessional) rested a hand on the back of a chair.

"Inclusion isn't enough if it destroys what you're including," he said, his tone soft as a benediction.

Mrs. Patterson looked adrift. "So what should I do? Just... ignore the history? Pretend it didn't matter?"

Olivia drew in a long, deliberate breath, weighing her words. "Partner with us," she said. "Let Teresa approve the curriculum. Let Doña Carmen speak to the students. And support the property tax relief fund. That's how you honor them—let them stay."

Mrs. Patterson stood quietly, every nerve in her face turned inward. Then, after a long moment, she lifted her head and wiped her eyes with the flat of her palm. "I'll vote for it," she said, voice wobbling but certain. "And I'll talk to the other board members. If you write the curriculum, Teresa, I'll make sure the school uses it. I promise."

Teresa's mouth opened, then closed. She nodded slowly, the nod that meant she was still deciding whether to believe it. Carmen put a hand on Teresa's shoulder, her touch both grounding and proud.

"Thank you, Gail," Carmen said, and the use of her first name broke something in the tension, like a hairline crack releasing all the pressure.

The room relaxed, the collective exhale almost visible.

Mrs. Patterson stepped away, but not before squeezing Olivia's hand. "I'm sorry," she repeated, then walked out into the fading daylight, her posture uncertain but her steps heavier with purpose.

The mayor had long since vanished. The Chamber folks regrouped on the sidewalk, not plotting so much as sulking, their power suddenly less absolute. Olivia caught the Tourism Board director watching from the window, arms crossed, face unreadable. She gave him a nod. He didn't nod back.

As the last of the crowd bled out, Elena drifted close. "You did it," she whispered, low enough for no one else to hear.

Olivia shook her head. "We just bought ourselves time."

"Time is all we need," said Carmen, and Teresa echoed the sentiment with a determined little half-smile.

They walked out together, a vanguard of three, their shadows stretched long across the municipal lawn. The air was thick with storm, but for the first time in months, Olivia felt the weight shift, the future—however uncertain—tilting ever so slightly in their direction.

❧

By the time the next morning rolled around, the courthouse lawn looked like a protest was about to break out. Lawn chairs, umbrellas, parents corralling strollers and sticky-faced children. Word had gotten out: if you cared about the future of Madison, this was where you'd show up, even if you never planned to vote for anyone in your life.

The meeting wasn't in session yet, but you'd never know from the roar inside the community room. The board sat behind a plastic folding table, fanned out like a tribunal, nameplates at the ready. At the other end, the public took up every seat, with Elena, Teresa, and Carmen up front, Olivia parked in the row behind with Father Reyes and a rotating cast of local troublemakers.

Mayor Johnson opened with the usual pro forma, but within five minutes, the debate was back on. The room wasn't just divided—it was frayed, splitting at every seam.

Elena stood first; despite her diminutive height, she was impossible to ignore. "Some of us want an authentic celebration," she said. "Not performance." The hush was almost reverent. "If you're going to call it heritage, at least ask us what it's worth."

A few heads nodded, mostly from the left side of the room. On the right, someone muttered, "Nobody's stopping you," but Elena ignored it, pressing forward. "The fact is we don't need another festival with piñatas and face paint. We need a library with our names on it. We need our grandparents' stories told before there's nobody left to tell them. If you want to build a legacy, start with respect."

Teresa rose, her voice so quiet at first Olivia worried it would be lost. "My grandfather laid brick for the courthouse," she said, eyes on the Board. "You want to put his name on margarita specials, or do you want to make sure his granddaughter can keep the house he built?" The line cut through the noise like a wire.

The room shifted again—this time, even some of the Chamber set couldn't pretend to look away.

Father Reyes cleared his throat. "If we profit from their sacrifice without honoring their truth, we dishonor them twice." He said it calmly, hands folded. "If we celebrate them while displacing them, we erase them again—just more slowly."

Doña Carmen had the last word, her voice pitched to the back row. "You can make money. Nobody's saying you can't. But you don't get to make it our story unless we agree. And you don't get to celebrate us while making us homeless." She said it with the gravity of a woman who had seen her entire world priced out from under her, then lived long enough to see it sold back at retail.

The Board shifted uncomfortably. A few members nodded—Mrs. Patterson chief among them. Others looked ready to bolt for the parking lot. The Tourism Board director tried to regain the floor, voice desperate. "That's not what we're doing," he protested. "We're honoring your legacy—"

Olivia cut in, not bothering to stand. "No, you're branding it. There's a difference."

The business owners were visibly split. Some glowered, arms folded; others looked at the floor, picking at their cuticles. A woman in the front row—Olivia recognized her from the local bakery—leaned into the aisle, face fierce. "Let them have the museum. If the tours are good, people will come for them. Nobody needs another bobblehead."

An older man—white hair, face like a bruised apple—raised his hand. "I just want to keep my hardware store," he said. "But if Teresa says this helps her family, that's enough for me."

Murmurs of assent from the left; sullen quiet from the right.

Mayor Johnson pounded his gavel, but the sound was less thunder, more petulant woodpecker. A voice rang out from the back: "This is political correctness gone mad!" "You want to kill our primary industry for the sake of a few hurt feelings?"

Carmen rose, slow as a sunrise. "You want to kill our families for the sake of a few dollars." She let it hang there. The mayor's face flushed, but he had nothing to offer.

The meeting adjourned in chaos; the room breaking into knots of argument, but Olivia could see the lines had shifted: the usual voting blocs had fissured, a whole new axis of loyalty etched into the old limestone of the courthouse walls.

Outside, the air had turned electric. Storm clouds boiled overhead, thunder rolling in on a timeline no one could predict. Olivia and her crew made for the steps, but a knot of teachers blocked their path. Mrs. Patterson was there, purse clutched to her chest like a life preserver.

She stopped Teresa with a gentle hand. "I really didn't understand," she said, voice raw. "I thought making your grandfather's name known was enough."

Teresa softened, the fight draining out of her. "My mother cried when she got the tax bill. That house is all she has of him. All I want is to make sure it doesn't end with us."

Mrs. Patterson's eyes welled again, but she blinked it away.

"I'll help with the tax relief fund. And... I'm sorry. I was so focused on celebrating, I didn't ask what you needed."

A tentative smile from Teresa. "You still want to teach the kids about the stonemasons?"

Mrs. Patterson nodded, a little shy. "If you'll help me do it right."

Elena caught Olivia's eye, a smile spreading slowly and fiercely across her face. "That's what I'm talking about," she said.

Olivia almost laughed. For the first time in months, she saw a future where the past wasn't just an exhibit. Where it was alive, fighting, stubborn as a weed.

She left the courthouse lawn behind, the echoes of the day's debate swirling in the charged air, and walked home through a town that was, for the first time in memory, changing on its own terms.

BY THE TIME Olivia reached the Limestone, the sun had already surrendered. Thunder rolled down the cross streets, bouncing off the inn's broad porch, rattling the gingerbread trim. She unlocked the front door with numb fingers and stepped into the entryway, fighting the urge to strip off her blazer and torch it for warmth. The familiar smell—coffee, old books, a hint of wax from the battered church candle she kept at the registration desk—nearly undid her.

Andrew Kim was in the parlor, on hands and knees. He'd lined up a parade of measuring tools along the rug: laser level, tape, a battered engineering clipboard. She watched for a second, unobserved, as he squinted at the baseboard and scribbled notes. He had that look again, the one that said he was already reconstructing the building from the inside out. She didn't know whether to laugh or to throw something at him.

He glanced up, caught her watching, and straightened. "You look like hell," he said, but the warmth was real.

"Thanks." Olivia dropped her bag and slid into the nearest armchair, the motion leaking every ounce of adrenaline she had left. She let her head fall back and closed her eyes. "If I don't make it, donate my skeleton to the museum. They'll want to put it in the gift shop."

She heard him set the clipboard on the table. "That took courage. What you did at the meeting."

She snorted. "It might have killed my business. You think anybody's going to book a stay at the inn that tanked their souvenir gravy train?"

He shrugged, rolling the level between his palms. "People who want the real thing will." He hesitated, then added, "Not everyone likes the cartoon version. And you'd be surprised about Mrs. Patterson. Some people actually listen when you explain the harm."

Olivia opened one eye, watching him cross the room. "You sound optimistic."

He handed her a sheaf of paper, dense with blue ink. "I'm realistic. That's the difference."

She scanned the first page, picking out phrases: 'localized settling,' 'normal subsidence for region,' 'no critical compromise.' She flipped to the diagram and saw the outline of the courthouse, every wall annotated, her grandfather's original layout still ghosted under Andrew's neat overlay. At the base of the stairs, the sketch showed a tiny, looping C—the maker's mark her grandfather had left, still visible under the plaster if you knew where to look.

Andrew pointed. "You see? That's old-school craftsmanship. None of this prefab stuff. It holds up."

Olivia traced the C, fingertip tingling. "He didn't believe in shortcuts," she said.

Andrew nodded. "Neither should you."

She looked up, caught the flicker in his expression. For a second, she saw the exhaustion behind the careful posture. "You okay?" she asked.

He considered, then sat on the ottoman, just far enough away to be polite. "This is why I turned down the job in Dallas," he said, voice soft. "I didn't want to leave this one unfinished."

She let that settle. The quiet between them was not empty —it hummed, all the words that didn't need to be said filling up the space.

"Thank you," she managed.

Andrew looked at the blueprints, then at her. "I think you're wrong about killing your business," he said. "But if I am, there's always room for another architect in Houston."

She smiled, the exhaustion bleeding into something more like gratitude. "Do you ever think about running a bed-and-breakfast?"

He laughed. "With these hours?"

She shrugged. "Maybe we'll start our own revolution. No cartoons. No mascots. Just the truth, one busted water heater at a time."

They both reached for the sheaf of diagrams at the same moment. Their hands collided, then paused—knuckles grazing, neither of them in a hurry to pull away.

"I'm sorry," he said, but the apology was for more than the touch.

"Don't be," Olivia said. "It's fine."

He didn't move. "You know," he said, "not all of them are like Johnson. Some of the Chamber folks. Patterson, even the old hardware guy. They just... they're used to things being simple."

She nodded, thinking of the crowd, the lines shifting. "I get it. Not everyone wants to hurt you. Some people just don't see it until you show them the harm."

He exhaled long and evenly. "You did that. Today. You showed them."

For a long moment, neither of them spoke. Lightning flashed, illuminating the window glass, a perfect inverted reflection of the inn's parlor. Olivia saw herself there, seated with Andrew, both of them holding the blueprints as if cradling some delicate, irreplaceable thing.

She turned the page, scanning the next diagram. "You said there was settling around the courthouse?"

He nodded. "Normal for buildings this age, on clay soil. But the pattern's... interesting. Looks like the stone settled into the foundation, rather than away from it. The masons must have compensated as they built."

She could see it, imagined the men in sun-bleached shirts, hands scarred and steady, coaxing the stone into place so it would last. "They knew what they were doing," she said.

Andrew tapped the paper. "So do you."

She didn't argue. For the first time in months, she didn't want to.

Outside, the thunder moved on, leaving only a gentle drum of rain against the porch. Olivia watched the droplets chase each other down the glass, felt the fatigue lift, just a little.

She thought of the meeting, of Teresa and Mrs. Patterson, of Carmen's iron-willed smile. She thought of her grandfather's mark, hidden under layers of paint and time, and the truth that even if you couldn't see it, it was still holding up the world.

She closed the file, set it on the table, and let her hand rest atop Andrew's.

"I think we're going to be okay," she said.

He looked at their hands, then at her, a smile flickering to life. "I know we are."

They sat like that, sharing the silence, while the old inn held steady around them.

Eventually, Olivia got up and made coffee. The two of them drank it in the kitchen, talking about nothing and everything, and when the phone rang with a new reservation, she answered with a smile, her voice steady, sure, and ready for whatever came next.

Chapter Twenty-Two

The room stank of Pine-Sol and old grievances. Olivia sat at the long vinyl-topped table in the Madison Community Center, alone except for the stack of binders and the thrum in her chest. The overheads sizzled in their tubes, making every surface harsh and every face three degrees more haggard than in daylight.

She counted twenty-one chairs around the table, and a descendant of the courthouse stonemasons or someone who'd married into their bloodline filled all but hers. The rest of the folding chairs ringed the wall, packed with a surplus of spouses, a few adult children, and a handful of infants wrangled by over matched teens. She recognized nearly every face—many from the weekly grocery run, more from church—but here, gathered like this, they looked less like a family and more like a jury.

At the head, Teresa's aunt presided, severe in a black shawl despite the relentless HVAC. Flanking her were two retired masons who spoke little English but kept their hands, oversized and red from decades of labor, spread on the table as if daring anyone to challenge their right to be there. Farther down, Elena and Carmen, whispering behind their hands; opposite them, a man who'd once thrown Olivia off his porch for "city slicker" trespassing, now watching her with a mild, predatory curiosity. Every eye was on her, waiting for the sell.

She stood. The muscles above her knees fluttered, but she made her voice sound as bored and unbreakable as she could. "Thanks for coming out. I know most of you would rather be anywhere else, but if you want to keep what's left of this town, this is how it happens."

The response was a ripple of shrugs and throat-clears. Olivia flipped open her first binder. "I won't waste your time. We all know the Tourism Board's plan. Mascots, history walks, cultural 'celebration'—" She let the sarcasm do the work— "but zero say from the people who built any of it." She pulled a map from the binder and laid it flat, weighting the corners with plastic water bottles. "This is the expansion zone. You'll see every house is color-coded: green for 'heritage aligned,' yellow for 'redevelopment,' red for 'pending sale.'" She paused, letting them look. "If you don't have a dot, you're not in the next round of grant funding. In two years, every red house will be owned by someone who doesn't know the first thing about this place. That's not me being dramatic. That's what the realtors told the Chamber last week."

A snort from the far end, where a cousin of the Alvarezes sat arms folded. "Who's funding this, then? The county?"

Olivia shook her head. "The county's broke. They can't even patch the roads out past the river. But there are grants, and there are ways to keep property taxes from pushing people out—if we play it smart."

An older man, thin as baling wire and missing two fingers, lifted his chin. "Why should we trust you now? Your grandmother never sold us out, but you—" He left the rest unsaid, but the point landed.

A woman in a cherry-red cardigan—the same who, years

ago, had watched Olivia get bounced from a quinceañera for bringing a white friend—broke the silence. "At least she asked instead of assumed." There was a brittle humor in her voice. "We've had enough surprises."

Olivia took the lifeline. "Look, I know I haven't been here. But I've been reading up. There are places—San Antonio, El Paso, even Marfa—where they turned heritage into actual power for the community. Not just a parade and then back to minimum wage. If you want to keep the houses, the names, the families—" She let her hand hover over the map, landing on the yellow and red. "We have to set it up so you're not just being celebrated, but paid. And kept."

A man with a cane—Olivia recalled his brother had died in the last freeze—leaned forward. "All I hear is talk. Where's the money?"

"Here." She turned the binder, flipped to a tabbed section labeled 'Revenue Offsets.' "The idea is a Heritage District Property Tax Relief Fund. We make the museum an actual nonprofit, not a cash cow for the Chamber. Every tour, every ticket, every grant dollar—ten percent goes into the fund. When your property tax gets hiked, we pay the difference. If you're a descendant of a builder—" She scanned the faces, holding them. "Or if you've owned your house since before the last century, you qualify. Teresa's aunt would be first. The Alvarez place, the Rodriguez duplex, even the old Molina trailer out by the mill. This is how you keep your houses when the rates go up for the next round."

A woman in the front, hair dyed a brilliant silver, said, "That's nice, but they'll find a way to take it back." Her hands trembled slightly on the table. "They always do."

Olivia met her eyes, steady. "Not if we control the fund. Not if we are the board. I'm not interested in running it—I already have a full-time job keeping the inn afloat. But this—" She jabbed a finger at the binder—"is the only way to keep the next generation from getting priced out. If we do nothing, it'll be all Airbnbs and antique stores in three years."

The man with the cane gave a sardonic bark. "So, instead of charity, it's restitution. That what you're saying?"

A little too loud, Olivia answered, "Exactly." She felt her heart spike, knew the word was radioactive in this room. "Your grandfathers built the courthouse. They didn't get plaques or back pay. The only way to make it right is to let you stay, and benefit, from what's being marketed."

The crowd was silent, but not of the good kind. Olivia realized she was sweating through her blouse. She let the silence hang, then continued, softer. "If you have a better plan, I want to hear it. But I think the only way to fight the Board is with numbers and a plan that can't be torpedoed with one election."

The room's energy shifted, uncertain but no longer hostile.

A woman at the far end, with gray hair in a tight plait, asked, "Who does the museum belong to?"

Olivia thought of the contract on her desk, the clause that would give her sole operating control if she wanted. She took a breath and said, "It'll be community-owned. Even if I run it for a while, the profit split is hard wired. I want a board of elders to run it—people who remember when the town had more than one last name."

A rustle of cautious amusement. Someone—Teresa's aunt, Olivia thought—said, "This is more democracy than we ever got before."

The old man with the missing fingers tapped the table. "I'll sign up. But if you screw us, we'll bury you in the new heritage garden. Right next to Randy Morrison."

Laughter, sharp and real, cut the tension. Olivia smiled for the first time, meaning it. "Deal," she said.

She fielded the next hour's worth of questions—some

practical, some loaded, some designed to see if she'd crack. She answered each one. Sometimes she had numbers, sometimes just a promise. Either way, she kept standing, kept making her case.

When the clock struck nine, the eldest of the group called a halt. "We'll talk it over. If we agree, you get our signatures."

Olivia nodded, adrenaline running out at last. "I'll be here when you're ready."

She gathered her binders, fingers numb, and walked out into the parking lot, where the light was mercifully dim and the air smelled only of rain and cut grass. Her pulse slowed. She leaned against the hood of her car and let herself breathe.

Inside, the lights in the community center were still on, the jury still in session. Olivia stayed by her car, not ready to go home until she saw them leave, until she knew which way the vote would go.

The waiting didn't hurt as much as she expected. For the first time in a long while, she felt the ground beneath her was solid. The pitch had been hers, but the choice was theirs. That finally was the point.

❧

TWO WEEKS LATER, the proper fight began. Olivia stood behind the microphone at the Commissioners Court, the smell of floor polish and hot toner thick in the air. The wood-paneled chamber looked less like a seat of democracy than a high-end funeral home, and the only thing stiffer than the chairs were the faces of the five men who would decide her future.

The room was packed, standing room only, with the overflow crammed into the corridor outside. Reporters, local activists, three generations of the Alvarez family in matching church clothes. At the back, Elena, notebook in hand, eyes fixed on Olivia with the intent that could raise the dead. Olivia squared her shoulders, scanned the agenda, and waited for the chair's signal.

"Next on the docket," announced Commissioner Holt, who wore his boredom like a badge of honor, "is citizen comment regarding the Heritage District expansion and related funding measures." He looked up, eyebrows cocked. "Ms. Cuellar, you have the floor."

Olivia took a breath that didn't quite fill her lungs. She flipped her folder, stacked the pages for comfort, and read from the top sheet. "Thank you, Commissioners. I know you've all had time to review the written proposal, so I'll keep this brief. The Heritage District initiative is bringing additional money to Madison, but it's also bringing tax hikes that threaten to displace the families who made this town what it is. My proposal creates a relief fund for qualifying homeowners—descendants of the original builders, people over sixty-five, those who've lived in the district for over twenty years. The fund is entirely paid for by a ten percent levy on museum admissions, historic tour tickets, and special event fees. Not a single dime from county revenues."

She let that hang, then turned the next page. "I've also attached projections for years one through three. If attendance tracks the pilot programs in Fredericksburg and San Antonio, we'll cover all qualifying households with room to spare."

Commissioner Holt didn't bother hiding his skepticism. "Ms. Cuellar, you're asking us to create a protected class for people who happen to have been born here at the right time. Why should the county back a scheme that subsidizes private property owners with public money?"

Olivia didn't blink. "Because the economic boom you're chasing depends on those families being here. Nobody's coming to Madison to see a Disney version. They want the real thing." She tried to keep her tone flat, but the words stuck on her tongue. "You can't sell heritage if there's nobody left to remember it."

A ripple in the audience—half agreement, half a hiss.

Holt pressed on. "The Board's proposal doesn't use public funds either. If the Chamber wants to set up a scholarship or a grant, that's their business. Why tie the county to it?"

Olivia could feel her jaw clench. "Because the Chamber's proposal does nothing to stop displacement. It's window dressing. And once these families are gone, they're gone forever."

From the gallery, a voice cut through the murmur. "She's right." Elena, hair pulled back and face set hard, stood. "My research in the county archive shows that the original stonemasons not only built the courthouse, they built the school, the church, and the entire north side. Their names aren't on the plaques, but we know who they are. You're benefitting from their labor. This is restitution, not a handout."

The room went still, all eyes swinging to the commissioners. Olivia watched Holt's mouth purse, but before he could volley back, another voice rose—a slow, measured Texas drawl.

"We've been here since 1880." Randy Morrison, the old antagonist himself, stood in the aisle, his weathered hands on the pew in front of him. "If property taxes keep climbing, I'm out. My neighbors are out. It doesn't matter if you built the courthouse or not—it ain't right to run folks off the land they broke their backs to keep." He shot a sideways look at Olivia, with the faintest flicker of a grin. "Ms. Cuellar's proposal is the best shot we've got to stay put."

Holt looked ready to explode, but the senior commissioner—one who'd gone to high school with Olivia's father—raised a hand. "Let's hear her out. Nobody's asking for a blank check."

Olivia nodded, took the opening. "The other part of the proposal is the museum. Initially, the plan was for me to run it as an extension of the Limestone, but after talking to the elders and the families involved, we're changing course. The museum will be set up as a community nonprofit. The board will include direct descendants of the original builders, as well as local historians and, if the Court allows it, a rotating seat for a sitting commissioner."

She slid a revised chart onto the overhead, fingers only trembling a little. "Fifty percent of the net revenue goes to the relief fund. Thirty percent to a scholarship fund for descendants. Twenty percent to operating costs. Zero profit to me or the inn." She let the words land, then scanned the bench. "I don't want the money. I want the stories preserved. And I want the people who lived them to be here to tell them."

This time, the silence was heavier. Holt tapped his pen, drumming out a war march. The senior commissioner, whose name she always forgot, leaned forward. "And if it doesn't pencil out? If the tourism dries up, what happens?"

"Then the fund sunsets," Olivia answered. "And we can say we tried something better than what came before."

A few heads nodded. Elena, behind her, was scribbling furiously. Randy Morrison sat, arms folded, but his eyes on the commissioners said the decision was made, even if he'd never admit to siding with a Cuellar.

They called for public comment, and half the room lined up. Some, like the man from the car repair on Main, spoke against the proposal—too complicated, too "woke." But every time a descendant spoke, the words echoed: "We don't want a handout. We want to stay." "Don't erase us twice." "If you sell the past, at least pay us for the pieces."

Olivia stood through it all, the nerves never fully going away, but her back straightening with each speech. At the end, the Court recessed for deliberation.

She stepped out into the hall, where the air was a thousand

percent humidity and smelled of old paper and nerves. Elena caught up with her, eyes wide.

"You did it," Elena said. "Even Morrison."

Olivia let herself smile, just a little. "That's a first."

They stood together in the echoing corridor, the thrum of debate leaking through the closed doors. Olivia watched the old courthouse clock, its hands jerky but determined, and thought: Maybe history could be changed after all. Or at least, bought back piece by piece, if you kept the receipts.

She did not know if it would be enough. But for the first time, she felt like she might be in the right fight.

The courthouse was never truly empty, not even after hours. The air in the hallway was cool and still, echoing with the distant vacuum drone of the janitorial staff and the less distant click of Carmen's sensible shoes as she trailed Olivia down the marble corridor.

Carmen had not spoken since the hearing ended, not even to Elena or the others who crowded around with their nervous gratitude. She waited until the last of the crowd peeled off toward the parking lot, then caught up with Olivia at the landing of the grand staircase, where the courthouse's stained-glass dome turned the evening light into bruised stripes across the floor.

"You," Carmen said, with no preamble, "are too smart to give away this much for nothing." She fixed Olivia with a stare that could core an apple at thirty paces. "You don't need to prove yourself to these people. So why are you giving up control and profit both?"

Olivia slouched back against the railing, her spine a snapped string. "Because it was never mine to control," she said, voice low. "It's not charity if I keep the receipts. And I can't profit from keeping people here who built what I'm selling."

Carmen's mouth twisted. "You think you're the first one

who tried to do it right? There are always promises. Always someone who says, 'This time, we'll do better.'" She gestured at the windows, the stone, the whole courthouse. "They don't remember, Livita. Not unless you make them."

Olivia let her head tip back, eyes on the fading colors in the dome. "Maybe I can't make them remember. But I can make it cost more to forget."

Carmen leaned in. "You're still young. You could go back to Houston, make a life. Why chain yourself to this?"

A tired smile cracked Olivia's face. "Because I want to earn it. Not the building—anyone can buy a building. I want to earn belonging. And that means protecting the people who already belong."

Carmen's eyes narrowed, testing for weakness. "And if they don't want your protection? If they'd rather sell and run?"

"Then I'll help them pack," Olivia said, voice hardening. "But I won't let them get priced out by the same story that's supposed to celebrate them."

A long silence, broken only by the sweep of a mop somewhere on the floor above.

Carmen's posture softened, just a notch. "You are your grandfather's blood," she said. "But you should know, he would have hated all this paperwork."

Olivia laughed, then let the laugh fall into a long, relieved exhale.

Carmen's hand came to rest on Olivia's shoulder, the grip both maternal and unyielding. "I will tell the others. If you keep your word, they will back you. But if you start acting like the Chamber, I will come for you myself."

Olivia nodded, the weight of it almost pleasant. "I hope you do," she said.

They walked the length of the corridor together, past the shadowed portraits of mayors and judges who had never invited their kind to the table, until they reached the front doors. The night air outside was muggy, the streetlights buzzing. Carmen left without ceremony, but not before squeezing Olivia's hand, hard.

Olivia stayed on the steps for a while, watching the bugs spiral in the lights, thinking about how history only ever changed in increments.

❧

Later that evening, she met Andrew behind the Limestone. The carriage house—soon to be a temporary museum if she hadn't just tanked her own future—was an oblong shed with battered French doors and a roof line that listed toward the river. Andrew had come early, measuring tape hooked to his belt, blueprints rolled under one arm. He'd already marked the walls with sticky notes and lengths of blue masking tape.

"You get the verdict?" he asked, not looking up from his clipboard.

She nodded. "They didn't vote yet. But Carmen's on board."

Andrew grunted, approval embedded in the silence. He pressed a tape against the doorframe, made a note, then looked at her over the rim of his glasses. "Most people would just turn the parlor into a gift shop and call it done."

"Most people," Olivia replied, "aren't trying to keep the town from eating itself."

He smiled, thin but real. "You always this much fun at midnight?"

"Only after a public shaming," Olivia said.

They worked in tandem, Andrew calling out numbers, Olivia jotting them in the spiral. He asked about humidity, about drainage, about the likelihood of children swinging on the fire doors. She answered as best she could, but mostly, she tried to stay present. The work was soothing, honest—something she could see growing from nothing.

After the measurements were done, Andrew rolled up his plans and set them on the paint-scarred desk that would, in time, be the museum's admissions counter. "You know," he said, "in Dallas, they tried a similar program. Heritage fund, nonprofit museum, the whole deal. Lasted three years before the board sold it to a hotel developer."

Olivia let the fear flicker through her, but only for a second. "Then I'll last four."

He grinned. "You might."

He helped her close the French doors, then lingered on the porch. "You're making a lot of enemies, you know."

"I've got enough friends," she said. "Or at least one."

He left her with the blueprint tube, a silent offering. She watched him walk down the gravel drive, steady and unhurried, and felt, for the first time in a long time, that she was exactly where she needed to be.

Inside, the carriage house was shadowy and strange, but she could see the outline of the future in the bare studs and empty shelves. She pressed her palm against the wall, imagined her grandfather's mark hiding there, and promised herself that whatever else happened, she'd keep it safe.

She turned out the lights, locked the door, and walked home in the humid dark, the blueprint under her arm like a rolled-up flag.

❧

THEY SCHEDULED the vote for high noon, as if that would stop the inevitable drama. Olivia sat three rows back in the packed commission chamber, hands clenched in her lap, watching as every seat filled with faces she knew: business owners, school board retirees, teenagers in soccer jerseys, and at least six reporters with digital recorders rolling.

Mayor Johnson took his time with the preamble. He rehashed every controversy—tax rates, gentrification, "community character"—but mostly he wanted to be quoted. "This sets a dangerous precedent," he thundered, voice perfectly modulated for the live feed. "If we start picking winners and losers, if we start carving up the tax code for special interests, then I don't know what's left of Madison's future."

The air in the room was so tight, Olivia thought she might pass out. She stared at the scuffed wood of the chair in front of her, then at Teresa's aunt across the aisle, hands knotted around her purse. Next to her, Randy Morrison wore the bored expression of a man who'd already decided the outcome, but his foot tapped an anxious rhythm under the table.

The commission called the roll. One by one, the votes: "Yes." "No." "No." "Yes." It came down to the chair, whose hair was so white it caught the sunlight like a warning flare. He looked down the row at Olivia, at the crowd, at the old-timers pressed shoulder to shoulder in the back row. Then he voted: "Yes."

A beat of silence, then the room erupted—half with applause, half with angry, wounded noise. Johnson slammed his hand on the table, then stalked out, the tails of his jacket flapping behind him like he was trying to escape the building before the decision could stick to him.

Olivia didn't cheer. She just let her lungs fill for the first time in an hour. Elena found her in the chaos, squeezing her shoulder, eyes wet but bright. "They did it," Elena whispered. "You did it."

Teresa's aunt pressed a tissue to her face, laughing and

crying at the same time. "We stay," she said, to no one and everyone. "We stay."

Outside, the press crowded around for statements, but Olivia slipped away. She crossed the square, past the courthouse steps where the new plaque already glinted in the sun, past the cluster of kids playing tag around the fountain, and ducked into the alley that ran behind Main. The air was cooler there, the hum of the crowd fading behind her.

She walked home slowly, letting the heat and the quiet settle her nerves.

THAT NIGHT, she sat at her desk under a single lamp. The inn was silent; the only sound was the tick of the clock and the faint clatter of dishes from the kitchen. Her spreadsheet was a battleground: in column G, the projected museum costs; in column H, the extra donations she'd promised to the community fund if the proposal passed. The two columns bled red onto her balance sheet, and the total at the bottom made her stomach flip.

The numbers were brutal. She'd have to push the last loan payment to Alex Stirling by four months. The inn would run at a loss through the next winter. Even after that, she'd be lucky to break even before year three. She rubbed her temples, feeling the old familiar throb behind her eyes.

She could have played it safe. She could have run the museum as a vanity project, kept the money, paid off the loan by summer, taken her place in the Chamber and called it a win.

Instead, she had chosen the harder thing.

She stared at the spreadsheets, at the relentless logic of the numbers. She wondered what her grandfather would say—if he'd call her a fool, or if he'd just smile the way he always did when the world pushed back. She looked up at the sketch on the wall, the looping mark he'd carved, and let herself breathe.

In the end, she closed the spreadsheet. She opened a new document, labeled it "Implementation Plan," and started typing. Within minutes, she'd outlined the first three months, mapped out the board selection process, drafted talking points for the first museum committee. She wrote the names of the families who would get relief, and she wrote Teresa's aunt's name first.

When she finished, the sky was already turning a faint pale blue beyond the window. Olivia closed the laptop, leaned back in her chair, and felt the exhaustion give way to something quieter and steadier. It wasn't hope, exactly. It was more like the satisfaction of knowing she'd chosen the thing that mattered, even if it meant taking the hit.

She left the lamp on for a while longer, the light a small circle in the empty inn.

In the morning, she would call Elena and Carmen, maybe even Andrew. There was a lot of work to do.

But for tonight, it was enough to know that she had kept her promise, and that when she looked at the inn—her inn, their inn, the town's—she would know it belonged to more than just her name on a deed.

Chapter Twenty-Three

The nave of Our Lady of Guadalupe thrummed with the low electric current of anticipation. It was not a holy day, nor any particular feast, yet the pews were as full as at Christmas, every aisle packed with parishioners in their Sunday shirts and pressed pants, toddlers in princess costumes already sticky with frosting, and a haze of local dignitaries sweating quietly in the back row. The candles in the alcoves flickered nervously, their orange light stuttering over the faces of saints and ancestors. Near the altar, Father Miguel adjusted his vestments, then beckoned Olivia forward with the subtlety of a traffic cop.

Olivia's hands were a live wire. She pressed them to the smooth wood of the lectern, grounding herself in a palm print left tacky by whoever had spoken last. Above the altar, the Christ figure hung in extravagant agony, the painted blood on his knees bright as new berry jam. She stared at it, let the slight anchor her breath, and then looked down the nave to the waiting crowd.

The usual format would have called for a solo lecture: thirty minutes, bullet points, a few audience questions about historic paint colors. Instead, Olivia stood not alone, but with Carmen on one side and three elders from the parish on the other. Behind them, a row of folding chairs hosted the rest of the ad hoc heritage council, all with their feet flat on the floor and hands knotted in their laps or wrestling in their purses. There were no scripts, only the stack of spiral-bound notes Olivia had carried up the aisle, now as useless as a candle in a hurricane.

Father Miguel cleared throat into the microphone, his voice a surprising tenor. "Today, we honor those who built not just our beautiful courthouse, but the families and community that are the living stones of Madison." He turned to Olivia, the gesture broad but unhurried. "Miss Cuellar has prepared remarks. She also invited some of our own to share their memories. We thank her for remembering that history is not a solitary effort."

He stepped aside, leaving Olivia exposed in the warm light of the nave. It was, she supposed, the most public thing she'd done since junior year debate finals, and possibly the last public thing she would do if this crashed and burned.

She started slowly, letting the room settle. "Thank you, Father. And thanks to everyone who showed up tonight, and for the extra food, and for letting us meet in this place. My grandmother used to say the church was the only building in town where people would listen to a woman for longer than it took to say a Hail Mary."

A muted laugh from the front rows, nervous but present.

Olivia found her cadence, voice steadier with each word. "I'm supposed to talk about the courthouse, the architecture, the masons who built it. But I'm going to ask for a little patience and a little help from those who are here with me." She gestured to the row of elders. "If it's okay, I'd like to start with the voices that aren't in any of the history books."

She looked to Carmen, who nodded—once, sharply—and

then to the first elder, a man whose head was as bare as the marble floor, his cane clutched between both fists. He hesitated, then stood with a slow, ceremonial effort.

"My name is Eulogio Martinez," the man said, voice like a dry creek bed. "I was born behind the rail depot, same year they finished the courthouse. My father—" he looked down, as if consulting invisible notes on his shoes—"he laid the cornerstones. They didn't put his name on the plaque, but he showed me which ones were his. He said, 'If you see a brick that isn't straight, that's not me.'" Laughter again, louder, some of it laced with pride.

Eulogio gestured at the congregation. "The courthouse was the first place in town that let us work without a pass. The men wore ties to church on Sundays, but the dust from the week stuck to them always. It was a badge. Even if you wore your tie, they knew what you were." He shrugged, then sat, the act almost defiant.

Olivia caught Carmen's eye: approval, and perhaps a dare to keep going.

She continued, "Thank you, Mr. Martinez. I didn't know that story—most of us didn't. That's why I want to share the next few minutes with others who remember more than what the records say."

A woman in the second folding chair rose, her hair in two brachia-long implicates braided into a crown. "Some of you know me as Tía Lolita," she said, beaming at a knot of teenagers in the front row. "I was not allowed to visit the courthouse as a girl, but my brother cleaned the windows. He came at sunrise, before the offices opened. Afterwards, he would bring home scraps—bits of granite, sometimes a nail or a stamp with a date on it. He built me a toy house out of those scraps." She opened her palm, and in it sat a pebble-sized cube of pink granite, smoothed by decades of handling. "I keep this because he told me, 'Every stone matters. Even the ones nobody sees.'"

She sat, the granite tight in her fist.

Olivia felt the room tilt, the balance of silence and attention now entirely with the speakers. She caught her own breath, then gestured to the next elder, who shook his head with a laugh and waved the spotlight on to the next. A third man stood, his accent thick with the flavor of Mexico City, the vowels bright and proud.

"My English is not perfect," he said. "But I want to say: we are not ghosts. The people who built this are still here." He pointed at the pews, the walls, even the crucifix. "Every piece of this town, our hands are in it. If you want to remember the truth, remember this." He paused, then added, softer, "They tried to take our names away, but the work stayed."

His words landed. Olivia felt a sting in her chest, saw the ripple of resonance in the room.

She turned back to the lectern. "Thank you, all of you." Her hands were steady now, her words clear as the evening air. "When I started researching the courthouse, I thought I was collecting facts. But what I learned is that you can't separate the building from the people who made it, and you shouldn't try. The names missing from the plaque—those are not just lost; they were taken. And it's up to us to put them back."

She looked up, scanning the room, letting her gaze land on old rivals, new allies, and a few familiar faces from the Limestone. "This is not just my project. It's ours. It's not about preserving a building, but preserving a truth. A story that won't be erased just because someone thinks it looks nicer without us."

At the far end of the first pew, a hand rose, trembling in the air. An elderly man, beard so white it matched the communion cloth cleared his throat. "May I say something?"

Olivia nodded, then stepped aside so his words would ring out.

He stood with effort, his voice a little hoarse but bright enough to reach the back of the nave. "My name is Tomas Chavez. I remember your grandfather, Olivia. He was a hard man—sometimes too hard, maybe—but he always said, 'Don't sell out the truth, even if it costs you.'" He fixed Olivia with a look both gentle and devastating. "Tonight, your grandfather would be proud—not because you made money from our story, but you chose the right way over the easy way."

A murmur swept the congregation: agreement, pride, the shiver of recognition that comes when someone names a thing everyone has felt but never voiced. Olivia blinked, the tears sharp behind her eyes, then took another breath and let them sit there. The moment was heavy, but it held.

She looked back at Carmen, who gave a small, regal nod.

Olivia closed with words she hadn't planned, but felt appropriate. "My grandmother taught me that the best legacy is not what you build, but what you keep safe for the next person. I want to keep this story safe. For all of us."

She stepped back, letting the applause rise—not loud, but sustained, growing in the corners and the back rows until it filled the air, sacred and unpolished.

Father Miguel resumed the altar, but not before shaking Olivia's hand, his eyes bright with pride.

Afterward, the crowd lingered, breaking into knots of conversation: old men arguing about the best mortar mix, teenagers filming Carmen on their phones as she brandished the granite pebble, mothers and grandmothers swapping names and rumors that hadn't been spoken in fifty years. Olivia found herself surrounded by a small battalion of children, all wanting to know if she could show them the secret marks in the courthouse stone. She promised to set up a tour, and for the first time in years, she meant it.

In the vestibule, Carmen caught Olivia by the elbow. "You did well," she said, the words simple but carrying a century's worth of approval. "Now you are really one of us."

Olivia smiled a real smile, and let herself enjoy the lightness in her chest. She looked back at the nave, the candles still burning, the voices echoing under the arched ceiling, and thought: This is how history should be told.

Not in silence, but in chorus.

The last to leave were the elders, who shuffled out together, their steps slow but their backs unbowed. Outside, the night was warm, the church bells ringing over the rooftops, calling the story forward into whatever came next.

❧

By the time the season's second wedding party checked in, the Limestone Inn had gone from haunted relic to overbooked organism, each vein and nerve humming with purposeful activity. In the foyer, the grand staircase creaked with the weight of rented tuxedos and poly-blend bridesmaid dresses, the banister glossy from a recent, frantic re-varnish. The parlor gleamed, brass polished and dust banished, and the lobby's antique sideboard bore a sacrificial heap of overnight bags in every color of the HEB reusable spectrum.

Olivia ran the front desk like a general, but with the patience of a practiced parent. Josefina and Lucia tag-teamed the kitchen—one prepping the ceremonial "historic" breakfast, the other corralling the espresso machine through its biweekly breakdown. Outside, a team of local teens hung paper lanterns in the rose arbor, their sneakers painting temporary circles in the dew-soaked grass.

At nine sharp, Olivia completed her first tour of the guest rooms. The night's wedding couple—both in their thirties, both with the efficient, slightly nervous air of mid-level Austin professionals—had requested the Couthouse Suite. Olivia double-checked the towel pyramid and the personalized welcome card, then descended to the breakfast room, where a half-dozen early risers were already powering through fruit plates and oat bowls.

From the window, she watched the carriage house museum light up as the groom led a flock of groomsmen through its doors. The usual response to the space was to ogle the staged photo op—a Victorian loveseat, a wall of sepia-toned photos, the faux jail cell installed for "character." Instead, Olivia watched as the groomsmen actually read the interpretive plaques, peered over the stonemason's tools in the display cases, and asked her, upon her second round through the common areas, about the difference between limestone and granite.

The groom—Jon, if she remembered—caught her at the museum entrance, his hand on a length of chipped chisel under the glass. "You said the original builders made their own tools?" he asked, voice soft as if afraid to disturb the ghosts.

She nodded. "They forged them on site. The story goes that the town blacksmith—who wasn't actually a blacksmith, just the only man in town with a forge—let the workers use his fire after hours. The stonemasons traded him tamales and sometimes moonshine for the privilege."

The groomsmen nodded, murmuring, and one whipped out a small Moleskin notebook to jot down the detail. Olivia smiled; she'd never seen a bachelor party so seduced by local lore.

The bride, Clara, drifted in next, hair in curlers, eyes sharp above the tissue-laden veil. She ran her fingertips along the display and pointed at a photograph of a group of Mexican workers, shirts off in the summer heat, faces lit up in mid-laughter.

"My great-grandfather was on a crew like this,"pant said,

voice tight. “I used to think it was embarrassing—my mom always wanted us to be white collar.” She shrugged, blinked once. “But I think it’s kind of... badass, now.”

Olivia nodded, too choked to answer. For a second, she pictured her own grandfather, the myth of him made real by how often strangers claimed to remember his hands, his temper, his unwavering demand for the straight line and true edge.

She left them to their exploration, then circled the main floor, where the other guests were in various states of lounge. A couple from Chicago—first-time in Texas, according to the booking note—sat in the library, their tablets and phones dark, their attention fixed on a volume of oral histories she’d sourced from the local historical society. They flagged her as she passed.

“You run this place, right?” the woman asked.

Olivia braced herself, then nodded. “Yes, ma’am. Welcome.”

The woman grinned. “We read about the restoration. Saw it on some architecture blog. I love what you did with the colors—did you know the sage trim is the same as a house in Oak Park in Chicago?”

Olivia feigned surprise, then admitted, “That’s not a coincidence. We used a lot of reference photos from the Midwest. Turns out immigrant stonemasons left their mark everywhere.”

The man, silent until now, piped up: “You don’t get this vibe anywhere in the city. There, it’s all, you know, Instagram moments. Here, you can actually feel the story.”

Olivia let that praise soak in, then offered a list of walking routes through the old quarter, including which businesses were run by the stonemasons’ descendants. The couple nodded, and the woman scribbled the suggestions in her journal.

At noon, Olivia watched the guests converge in the dining room, where her staff had set up a "welcome table" laden with homemade tortillas, cinnamon-sprinkled fruit, and a towering punchbowl of lime agua fresca. She overheard a guest recommend Teresa's restaurant for dinner, explaining the genealogy of the cook staff with the pride of a local. Another guest countered, "But you have to try Esperanza's for breakfast—her tortillas are the size of your head, and she sells the local ceramics out the back."

The buzz of the inn was a web, each guest pulling another into the fabric of the town, the way Olivia had always hoped it could be. This wasn't a packaged experience, a weekend of "authenticity" curated for social media. It was instead a messy, ongoing negotiation between past and present, one you had to be present for to understand.

Later that afternoon, as the wedding party prepared for photos in the rose garden, a guest in a UT hoodie intercepted Olivia near the side door.

"Excuse me," the woman said, "but do you know where to buy authentic Mexican souvenirs? Not like airport stuff—something real."

Olivia almost laughed; the question was so old it had grown new teeth. "Esperanza's shop on Main," she said. "Descendants of the original masons make everything. Ask her about the Milagro pottery—she'll show you the maker's mark."

The guest scribbled down the address, then hesitated. "You're the owner, right? I just want to say I've stayed at a lot of B&Bs. Most of them are trying too hard, or they're frozen in time. This place..." She gestured at the inn, the town beyond. "This place is alive."

Olivia watched her go, the compliment warming her more than she would have admitted. She surveyed the parlor, the foyer, and the porch where the wedding party gathered for one last group photo before the ceremony. Every detail was sharp, real, a far cry from the brochure vision the Chamber had once pitched her.

By the end of the day, as the sunset burned orange through the porch lattice, Olivia allowed herself a few minutes of stillness at the kitchen table, a cup of bitter coffee cooling between her palms. She listened to the sound of laughter, the easy shuffle of feet on the floor, the distant lilt of a mariachi cover band setting out for the night's reception.

At that moment, Olivia realized the inn had become what she'd dreamed—a waystation for stories, a refuge for the people who wanted to matter. Every guest carried something forward: a detail, a rumor, a recipe, a name.

She looked out the window toward the carriage house museum and saw the lights still on, the silhouettes of the Austin couple pressed close against the glass. She smiled, took a deep breath, and let herself feel—for a moment, at base—the small, stubborn satisfaction of a thing done right.

Even if it never made a dime. Even if it never lasted more than a generation.

It was enough to see the truth keep moving, hand to hand, table to table, story to story.

And for the first time since she had returned to Madison, Olivia believed it might actually last.

Teresa arrived precisely on time, a legal pad and a sample box of sugar cookies clamped in her arms. Olivia caught her in the vestibule; the two of them nearly collided as Teresa bent to remove her shoes out of respect for the newly refinished hardwood. Once a teacher, always a teacher.

"You're fine," Olivia said, ushering her in with a wave. "If the floor survives wedding season, it can survive your boots."

The parlor was set for business: contracts, menus, feedback cards arrayed in order across the table that once hosted Olivia's childhood Thanksgiving. Beside them, Josefina perched on the edge of the chair, her gaze quick and measuring.

"Okay," Josefina began, opening the menu portfolio. "Today's couples want authenticity, but they don't know what that means. Last night, the groom's mom asked if we could do 'something more Mexican' than brisket." She rolled her eyes, but not unkindly. "I said, 'We can do cochinita pibil, but it might stain your teeth for a week.'"

Olivia barked a laugh, then passed over the latest stack of guest comment cards. "The Chicago party wants to franchise your breakfast tacos. And the Austin group left a five-star review just for the mole sampler."

Josefina fanned herself with the menu, pretending at flattery. "Tell them to leave a tip next time." Her fingers found a stray sugar cookie, which she broke in half. "You're doing it, you know," she said after a beat. "They're talking about this place in the city. I got three new bookings this week, all from word of mouth. Not the Chamber. Not the Board."

Olivia scanned the spreadsheet, not trusting herself to answer. The numbers weren't spectacular, but they were steady, and the column marked "community partners" had doubled in a month.

Teresa leaned in, voice lower. "You ever regret not going corporate? Signing on with one of those big chains?"

"Never," Olivia said, and meant it. "They wanted the marketing, the photo ops, the fake history. I wanted this." She gestured to the busy hum beyond the glass: guests, vendors, the smell of lemon cleaner and, distantly, freshly baked pan dulce.

Teresa nodded, her mouth tight. "My mom, she's doing better with the tax relief. First bill that came in under three digits since—" She shook her head. "She still doesn't believe it'll last."

"It'll last," Olivia said, with a confidence she had not earned but displayed, anyway.

They finished the referral review, then packed up and headed to Main Street. The morning was bright; the sidewalks pocked with puddles spring from the night's storm. As they passed the courthouse, Olivia watched a new group of tourists lining up for the heritage tour, the guidebook in the hand of a kid with a neon fanny FMG.

Esperanza's Mercantile sat just off the square, its window crowded with a rotation of painted Milagros, pressed-flower candles, and the newly trending "courthouse stone" coasters. Inside, the air was cool and sharp with sage and lavender.

A couple from Kansas City—Olivia recognized them from the inn's guest book—browsed the shelves, picking up each piece, turning it over, reading the story card before setting it down with careful hands.

Teresa drifted to the ceramics, tapping a mug with the thumbprint of the maker still visible in the glaze. "This one's my cousin's kid," she said, almost shy. "They're teaching the kids to make them after school."

Olivia let her fingers graze a textile, a table runner woven in a pattern she recognized from her abuela's kitchen. "I didn't know you had so many artists in the family."

"Everyone does, if you look hard enough," Teresa said.

Customers came and went, some buying, some just touching, always reading the cards: Made by Lucia M. of Madison. Glazed by Emilio Alvarez, 9th grade. Heritage from the hands that built the town.

Esperanza bustled in from the back room, a clipboard stacked with orders and receipts. "You two here for the audit?" She called out, eyes bright. "Or is this a social call?"

"A little of both," Olivia replied. "We wanted to check the numbers, maybe brainstorm a fall event."

Esperanza corralled them behind the counter, spreading out a printout of her online sales: museum tour bookings, special orders for reunion weekends, "heritage boxes" mailed to addresses as far as Seattle and Newark.

She tapped the page. "This is working. I don't know how you convinced the town to buy in, but they are. Even the Chamber sends people to my store now. Half the board has grandkids in the school arts program."

Teresa grinned, a rare, genuine thing. "You should see Caleb Bauer's bakery on Sunday. Last week, there was a line out the door, all wanting the 'authentic Madison' pastry. My uncle said it was the first time he didn't see a single kolache left at closing. Maybe he should set up a satellite location here like Esperanza did."

Esperanza snorted, "The power of scarcity marketing. I tell them every mug is an original, even if there's twenty in the back." Her smile softened. "It's more than marketing, though. People want something real."

Olivia nodded, feeling the weight and lightness of the moment. "This is the real thing. Not a mascot, not a brand. Just... us."

They ran through ideas—artisan pop- ups, a winter market, expanding the museum hours—and for every suggestion, Esperanza had a statistic, Teresa had a recipe, Olivia had a vendor list. It was all so brisk, so productive, that when the conversation turned to family, it caught them by surprise.

"Your grandmother would be proud," Teresa said to Olivia, her voice less than a whisper.

Esperanza leaned across the counter, conspiratorial. "She'd also say we're making a mess of her recipes. But she'd forgive us if it kept the story going."

They laughed, a laugh that is as much about grief as it is about joy.

As they parted at the corner, Teresa caught Olivia's hand and squeezed it. "This is how it should be," she said. "Our community telling our own story."

Olivia felt the echo of it all the way back to the office. The world outside was busier, louder, more itself than it had ever been.

And inside, at her desk, Olivia started sketching out a plan for a fall fair—one that would require no mascots, no board approval, and no apologies. Josephina and Eseperanza could duel it out for the breakfast taco crowd.

Just the truth, and the proof of hands on the work.

❧

The house had gone silent except for the whisper of the ancient radiator and the soft, relentless click of Olivia's laptop keys. The kitchen was dark, the only light in the inn coming from her desk lamp—a globe of golden calm in a sea of shadow.

Spreadsheets blank covered the desktop, lined up like soldiers awaiting inspection. Each cell, a pixel of risk or relief. Olivia clicked through the tabs: occupancy, payroll, supply costs, catering commissions. The charts moved slowly, but they moved up.

She reached for the legal pad, running her index finger down the newest column of numbers. September was behind projection, but October was over by a fraction. She drew a tight line under the sun, then cross-checked the bank app. The number there was not extravagant, but it was steady. Enough to cover next quarter's payroll, the utilities, and the balloon payment because of Alex. Enough that she didn't have to obsessively check the account every night before bed, or play out the thousand tiny disasters that had haunted her since Houston.

She compared the growth curve to the old Chamber proposal: no sudden spike, no "heritage festival" wind piazza, just a slow build of regulars and referrals. She tapped her pen against the desk, the sound echoing through the parlor.

Next to the laptop, the guest book lay open. Olivia thumbed through the pages, each one filled with the ballpoint scripts of strangers' gratitude.

Thank you for letting us see the real Madison.

We learned something about the history—never expected to cry at a museum, but we did.

The food! The beds! The stories! We'll be back next year.

Olivia let herself smile, the tiredness falling away for a moment. She closed the ledger, the clap of the cover as satisfying as a gavel. She leaned back, stretching the knots from her neck, and let her gaze drift to the window.

In the glass, her reflection hovered—hair a mess, eyes bright, mouth set with the stubbornness of the past year. For the first time since she'd moved home, she didn't flinch from the image. She met her eyes and nodded, the gesture small but certain.

The inn was quiet. The numbers were honest.

And Olivia was still here, still standing, with proof enough to last her through whatever came next.

THE INN'S conference room was Olivia's last domain of chaos before the day began in earnest. She moved the chairs into two neat rows, then adjusted them out of spite, leaving the center aisle a little off-kilter. The agenda for the business association was on the table, each copy weighted with a pen that clicked just once before she caught herself.

A few minutes early, the bell above the door gave its nervous jangle. Olivia looked up and saw three figures in the vestibule: Chamber suits, the same sharp creases and colder expressions she remembered from her first board hearing. Amongst them, the woman who had lobbied hardest for the Cinco de Mayo Weekend Package—a pitch that involved fake maracas, novelty margaritas, and a literal piñata drop at the courthouse.

The three entered with the caution of tourists in the wrong neighborhood. Their eyes swept the foyer, taking in the guests in the parlor—two women in matching hijabs, a young man explaining the "history wall" to his toddler, and a couple of men in hiking boots eating scones from Esperanza's mercantile. The visitor book on the stand was open to a page signed by a couple from Laredo and another from San Francisco.

Olivia stayed behind her reception desk, watching as the group hesitated, then approached.

"Ms. Cuellar," said the lead woman, her voice lower than usual, "we were hoping to speak with you before the meeting."

Olivia gestured to the lobby. "We can talk here if you like. It's quieter."

The three gathered close, awkward in their sudden proximity. The lead cleared her throat, glancing around to ensure the conversation wouldn't be overheard. "We just wanted to say... maybe we were too quick to judge your approach. The numbers from the pilot program—"

"Up by seventeen percent," said the man to her right, reading from his phone. "Even with the softer launch."

"People are staying longer," added the third, the novelty margarita enthusiast. "They're spending more. The local businesses... well, they're not complaining."

Olivia offered a professional smile, the kind with no edges and no room for gloating. "That's what we were hoping for."

The lead hesitated. "The, uh, museum tours? They're booked out through next month. Even the waitlist is... considerable."

"I'm happy to recommend a private tour," Olivia said. "If the Board wants a preview, I can arrange it."

The woman nodded, her cheeks coloring. "Thank you. That would be... helpful."

They stood in silence for a moment, then the group migrated toward the coffee urn, clearly relieved to have finished the errand.

Olivia watched them go, then turned to the lobby window, where the morning sun cut a stripe across the square. She caught sight of the three board members standing outside after the meeting, shoulder to shoulder as they glanced down at the new Verde County Historical Commission's historical marker by the front entrance.

The plaque was fresh, the lettering clean and sharp: "Madison Courthouse and Community—Built by the Hands of Many. Dedicated to the Stonemasons of Mexican Descent Who Raised Its Walls."

The woman in charge read it, then read it again. She said game thing to the others, and together they looked at the inn, the square, the bustling coffee shop across the way.

In the window's reflection, Olivia saw her own face, calm and unruffled.

Across the plaza, the lights of Teresa's restaurant and Esperanza's shop glowed against the morning, a pair of beacons testifying to a new order. The town was louder now, but it was the right noise: truth passed honestly, not sold in bulk.

Olivia let the scene sink in, then went back to arranging chairs, content to leave the center aisle a little crooked.

It was, after all, more authentic that way.

Chapter Twenty-Four

She managed to claim a seat at the very back, knees pressed so tight together they ached, her hands braided and whitening in her lap. The county renovation committee met in the basement of the annex, a room done up in every shade of beige known to office supply catalogs, lined on one side by a rack of spare folding chairs and on the other by a photo collage of previous Commissioners, all white men with parted hair and an allergy to smiling. Above her, the ceiling was a grid of acoustic tile, each rectangle a little darker than its neighbor, and the fluorescents overhead were so sharp they drew halos around every silhouette. The air smelled of copier toner, industrial coffee, and old newsprint.

In front of her, the regulars: business casual crowd from the Chamber, a smattering of local activists (three, by her count), two reporters, and at least a dozen people who'd shown up just to see who'd win this round of the town's eternal civil war. Olivia spotted Carmen near the middle, sitting with Tía Lola and a rotating cast of church women; on the opposite side, Randy Morrison's nephew slouched in a camo jacket, arms folded and face set to passive obstruction.

At the head of the room, on a makeshift dais, sat the five-member Committee, presided over by Judge Delacruz, who wore his golf tan like armor. Beside him, a court recorder with a steno pad the size of a legal textbook; on his other side, the county facilities director, a man who once threatened to ban Olivia from the building for "meddling with historic records." None of them looked excited to be there.

Andrew Kim waited at the edge of the dais, tablet in one hand, the other bracing a thick, battered portfolio against his hip. His suit was crisp, tie perfectly knotted, but the nerves showed in the way he shifted his weight from foot to foot, as if measuring every seam in the carpet. He caught Olivia's eye just once before the session started, and the look was not quite a plea but a kind of hope—willing her to believe he had it covered.

The committee called the meeting to order, read through the consent agenda, and then skipped ahead to the real reason anyone had bothered to show up.

"Next item is the review of the courthouse restoration master plan," intoned Judge Delacruz, his ancient voice stripped of warmth. In an earlier time, that same voice would have sent the fear of God into a defendant. "Mr. Kim, you have the floor."

Andrew stepped to the lectern, connected his tablet to the projector, and in three keystrokes filled the wall with a high-res scan of the courthouse's north facade. He cleared his throat. "Thank you, Judge. I'll try to keep this to thirty minutes."

A few chuckles—some genuine, some brittle.

He started, as all presenters must, with history: the original build date, the fire, the decades of "improvements" that had hollowed the bones of the place. But within two slides, it became clear this was not the usual cut-and-paste summary. Andrew zoomed in, not just on the stonework but on the stone. He showed images taken at sunrise, the light raking across the facade to reveal a scattering of shallow marks: some initials, a date, a spiral that looked like it belonged on an old church more than a county courthouse.

"These marks," Andrew said, the pointer steady on the screen, "were not visible in any of the original blueprints, nor are they documented in the construction archives. They only appear in low-angle sunlight, and many were plastered over during the 1948 interior refit."

A slide advanced, and now the screen showed a macro shot —Olivia's own, she realized, taken with the borrowed a camera from the historical society—of a chisel-inscribed "M" just beneath the third-story window. "Most of the marks correspond to signatures found in the old jail ledger, courtesy of the Cuellar family archives," Andrew said, voice gaining strength. "It's a vernacular tradition, common in European and Mexican construction, to leave a 'builder's mark'—a permanent record of who actually shaped the material."

The next slide was a lineup: photos of workers from the turn of the century, their faces sunburnt and grave, and next to each, a scan of their signature from pay stubs, marriage licenses, or, in two cases, parish birth records. Andrew pointed: "You can see that each mark on the stone aligns, not with the architect or the contractor, but with the stonemasons. Almost all are names traced back to the Mexican crews brought in for the project—documented by Carmen Rodriguez's father, and now cross-referenced in the current proposal."

Olivia's pulse was somewhere up in her throat, beating out a panicked Morse code. She scanned the room. Half the committee watched Andrew; half checked their phones, but a ripple had started in the audience—a shifting of posture, a new attention. She saw Carmen's hand squeeze Lola's. Even Randy's nephew was sitting up straighter.

Andrew clicked to a page of the master plan, lines of red

ink showing corrections to the existing county narrative. "The previous assessment, funded by the Chamber, credited the construction to the primary contractor, who never laid a stone himself. Our revised plan," he said, "not only restores the physical fabric of the courthouse but also restores the historical record. The actual work—the real heritage—is in the hands that built it."

A pause, just long enough for the point to land.

He outlined the preservation plan: strip back the plaster, expose the marks, create interpretive panels using Carmen's father's original notes. "There's precedent," Andrew said, flipping to a case study from San Antonio. "It's more expensive. It's also the truth."

Committee member number two, the facilities director, cleared his throat. "Is it necessary? Does it add value to the grant application?"

Andrew didn't miss a beat. "The Texas Historical Commission prioritizes authenticity and underrepresented narratives. By making the stonemasons' contributions visible, we're not just preserving stone. We're preserving the story. It's the strongest argument we can make for the full grant."

Murmurs from the table. The court recorder, who had never spoken in a meeting before, leaned in: "It's the first time anyone's mentioned the builder's marks since I started here."

Andrew wrapped up with a slide that said, in bold type, "Documentation courtesy of Olivia Cuellar and the Madison Heritage Collective." He turned from the screen and said, "This work would not exist without the field notes and archival research of Ms. Cuellar. She and her network did the heavy lifting; I just put it into the plan."

For a second, the room was so quiet the lights buzzed louder.

Olivia didn't know what to do with her hands, so she kept

them knotted in her lap, fighting a sudden, prickly heat at the back of her neck.

The Committee asked the expected questions—budget, labor pool, compliance with state historic codes. Andrew answered every one with a precision that bordered on the surgical. When they ran out of questions, Judge Delacruz polled the room: "Anyone else wish to speak?"

Carmen stood. "It's not about plaques or names. It's about the truth lasting longer than the people who made it."

No one else stood.

The Judge nodded, a gesture of both exhaustion and approval. "Thank you, Ms. Rodriguez."

They took the vote. Three hands for yes, two abstentions. It passed.

Olivia watched Andrew's face as the vote was called. He didn't smile—he did little of anything—but there was a slow exhale, a softening, as if the tension in his shoulders had unspooled all the way to his shoes.

The room began to clear, the usual trickle of business cards and handshake promises. Committee members clustered near the coffee urn, discussing the cost overages and the "optics" of giving credit to the undocumented. The crowd thinned, leaving Olivia and Carmen and a few other diehards at the back.

She stood, knees shaky, and made her way to the front, where Andrew was already repacking his portfolio.

He looked up, voice low enough for only her to hear. "You did it."

Olivia shook her head. "We did it."

He shrugged, conceding the point. "The old story was easier to sell. You made the new one impossible to ignore."

Olivia couldn't help herself. She smiled wide and recklessly.

Carmen found her, pulled her into a quick, fierce hug.

"Your grandfather would have said you did the right thing," she whispered. "Even if he'd pretend he hated all this drama."

Olivia nodded, not trusting herself to speak.

They walked out together—Andrew with his blueprints, Olivia with the battered folder of evidence, Carmen with her memory. Outside, the evening sun made the courthouse dome glow gold and pink, the marks invisible from here but now, for the first time, impossible to erase.

As they crossed the lot, Andrew paused, almost as an afterthought. "The next part's harder," he said. "They'll try to take credit for the work. Or water it down."

"I know," Olivia said. "But now we have the record. And the stone."

He nodded, satisfied.

They walked on, each step making the past a little heavier, but also a little more real.

At the end of the block, Olivia looked back. She imagined the marks, the hidden signatures, the proof of hands on the work. She imagined, for a moment, that history could hold more than one truth at a time.

And she promised herself, as the sun dropped behind the hill, that she'd keep fighting for the version that mattered.

❧

AFTER THE LAST HANDSHAKE, after Carmen and the others had drifted into the dusk, Olivia waited in the corridor outside the hearing room, bracing herself against the marble rail. The courthouse was emptying, the rush of adrenaline giving way to a hollow, restless fatigue. She could hear the after-meeting conversations ricocheting down the hallway: "Smart move, backing the new plan," "Never thought I'd see the day," "You think the grant will actually come through?"

She kept her head low, pretending to scroll her phone, but her ears caught every syllable.

Committee members filed out in pairs or singles. Some glanced her way with a nod, a few offered stiff congratulations —"Nice work, Ms. Cuellar," "Glad to see the young blood stepping up"—but most just looked straight ahead, as if passing the scene of a minor accident. Judge Delacruz strolled by, whistling tunelessly, never breaking stride.

Behind her, the lights in the meeting room went dark, leaving the hall illuminated by only a single strip of fluorescent and the watery evening sunlight that bled in through the transom windows. The contrast made everything look unfinished, or maybe just stripped to the bone.

She was about to leave, already planning how she'd recount this to Elena and the rest, when Andrew appeared at the far end of the corridor. He walked with deliberate, measured steps of someone who'd been carrying tension for hours and had finally set it down. Portfolio under one arm, tie loosened, the top button of his shirt undone.

He saw her and offered a genuine smile—not the public one, but the off-duty, worn-at-the-edges version she liked best.

"Hey," he said, voice low. The word echoed in the empty hall.

She straightened. "You survived the gauntlet."

He rolled his eyes, glancing over his shoulder. "You'd think we were rolling out a moon landing, not a building code revision."

They stood a few feet apart, the air between them crowded with unspoken things.

He tapped his portfolio. "You know," he said, "I came here thinking I'd just make a prettier version of what already existed. Add a couple of ramps, restore the clock tower, maybe tweak the landscaping so people could Instagram it from the street."

She laughed, a short, involuntary bark. “You hate Instagram.”

He shrugged sheepishly. “It’s a disease. But you—” he gestured at the now-empty hearing room, at the air itself—“you flipped the script. You made it so that the building couldn’t be separated from the people who made it.”

The words hit harder than she expected. For a second, she looked away, letting her gaze drift to the window. The sky was a flat, washed-out gray, the dusk that promised a thunderstorm but probably wouldn’t deliver.

She turned back to him. “You’re giving me too much credit.”

“I’m not,” Andrew said, and there was an urgency in the way he said it—a conviction that felt rare and almost dangerous. “You rebuilt Madison’s story. I’m just rebuilding the building.”

They stood in the quiet, letting it settle. Footsteps echoed from somewhere upstairs, then faded.

She asked, “Do you ever get used to the feeling of being outnumbered?”

He smiled, lopsided. “You learn to like the echo. It makes your voice sound bigger.”

They both laughed, and the distance between them seemed to shrink, not physically but in a way that made the air less oppressive.

"So, that's it? You just type up a report and start begging the state for money?"

Andrew howled at her innocent question. "We've got some issues with the roof that I'm worried about. I've still got a couple of nooks and crannies up there and in the cupola that I need to look at in detail before I can completely sign off on them. Oh, and then there's a wildlife report that we have to complete. Compared to the headaches you two-legged pests have been giving me, the wildlife portion should be a breeze."

Olivia frowned. "Wildlife? You mean a family of armadillos living in the Judge's chambers at night?"

He chuckled at that. "Yeah, something like that."

He shifted the portfolio to his other arm, and as he did, his hand brushed hers—just a featherlight touch, enough to register but not linger. Olivia felt a jolt, a surprise that wasn't unpleasant.

She looked at him, really looked, and saw not the architect or the outsider but someone who had—without ever saying so —staked his reputation on her side of the story.

"Thanks," she said, the word feeling both too small and exactly right.

He nodded, then added, quieter: "We make a good team."

Neither of them moved to leave. The silence stretched, charged, and Olivia wondered if he felt it too—the sense that something new had opened up, not just in the town or the committee but in this exact sliver of space.

She thought about the builder's marks, the hidden initials, the proof of hands on the work. She wondered if maybe this was a mark, too—this moment, this brief but undeniable connection.

Andrew's hand hovered next to hers, a question in the space between. She didn't pull away.

Outside, the sky finally cracked, and a thin line of rain traced the window. The sound was soft, but it carried.

They stood like that, side by side, until the lights clicked off and the janitor's cart rattled in from the stairwell.

Olivia smiled, then turned to go, but not before letting her fingers brush his again—this time, deliberate.

The echo followed her all the way down the marble hall.

Chapter Twenty-Five

Inside, the foyer of the Verde County Museum was almost unrecognizable. The stifling hush she remembered from her first visit in elementary school was replaced by a low thrum of voices: laughter volleying in English and Spanish, the scrape and shuffle of shoes on freshly buffed linoleum, the whistle of children who hadn't yet gotten the memo about "indoor voices." Half the crowd were old Madison families—most in ranch denim and pearl snaps, a few dressed up for the occasion. The rest, a polyglot of Rodriguez cousins, in-laws, and the stray elders who still called each other by the names of distant, dusty hometowns in Coahuila.

Olivia stationed herself at the double glass doors, rehearsing her smile in the warped reflection of the entry. Every guest brought with them the scent of late summer—damp stone, cut grass, a trace of sweat carried in from the parking lot. With each handshake, she felt the weight of their expectations shift from their palms to her own.

At the center of the foyer, on a round dais, stood the focal point: a block of courthouse limestone, two feet high, shot through with caramel and ash veins. Olivia's hands quivered as she checked the exhibit one last time, fussing with the table skirt, smoothing the card stock into place. The block was the same one Andrew had unearthed during the foundation survey—a cast-off, its edges imperfect, its top marked by a single, looping "C" and beneath it a date, almost illegible in the pitted surface. Her grandfather's signature, more honest than any gold-plated plaque.

Beside the stone, Andrew had installed a steel music balance, meant to keep the heavy block from toppling if (when) some overexcited child tried to climb it. Olivia brushed invisible lint from the velvet drape, the gesture more a tick than a necessity.

People crowded close, cell phones primed for the moment. Teresa Alvarez caught her eye from the far side of the room and offered a quick thumbs-up. Elena stood just behind the rope line, lips pursed, hands clasped as if holding a prayer.

The crowd pressed in. Olivia heard the clip of Carmen's heels—sensible, patent leather, the kind that belonged to a woman who'd spent her life standing on concrete floors. Carmen wore a deep blue rebozo, hair netted tight, and as she edged through the gathering, the knot of Rodriguez kin parted in automatic respect.

Olivia cleared her throat and stepped to the mic. "Thanks, everyone, for coming to the opening of 'Hands on the Work: Stories of the Madison Stonemasons.'" The sound system vibrated her ribs. "It's fitting we're here in the museum, but the actual work started in kitchens and workshops and back lots, where the story got passed down even when nobody thought to write it down."

She could see Andrew lurking at the far edge of the crowd, as close as he dared to the exhibit without being drawn into a conversation. His arms were folded, eyes fixed on the stone, a look of guarded pride on his face.

"I'll keep this short," Olivia went on, "because the people who did the work would have hated a long speech." A flicker of laughter. "This stone came from the courthouse, but the mark—" she gestured at the "C,"—"that's from the man who cut it. He left it so he would be paid for his work, paid by the stone he successfully carved. Failing that, he left it so that we would remember."

She grabbed the corner of the drape, felt the tremor up her wrist, and yanked it free. The velvet dropped, pooled at her feet. The mark was brighter than she'd remembered; Andrew had brushed the surface with water before the crowd arrived, just enough to bring out the contrast.

A collective inhale—not quite a gasp, but the sound that meant people saw it, and were processing what it meant.

Olivia swallowed. "The exhibit is about the truth that lasts longer than the people. But also about giving back a name to the hands that made it."

She stepped back from the podium, heart hammering. She hadn't prepared an ending, so she gave herself permission to leave it unfinished.

Carmen took the cue, moving slowly and deliberately to the stone. She placed both palms on the surface, then lifted them toward the crowd.

"In the old country," Carmen said, voice clear as bell metal, "the stonemason's blessing was to make something that outlived you. A wall, a house, a church." She glanced at Olivia, her eyes fierce, then spoke in Spanish, letting the syllables roll over the room: "Que su trabajo siempre dure, que su nombre nunca se borre." May their work always endure, may their name never be erased.

She drew a breath, then continued in English. "This is not just history. It is our proof."

Carmen bowed her head for a second, then turned to

Olivia, palm out. Olivia set Ric on top, and the two women faced the crowd together.

From the corner, Teresa Alvarez advanced, the legal pad in her hand a comic counterpoint to her tailored suit. She took the mic, voice warm. "Some people thought Olivia would come back and just take. Take a piece of history, take the old stories, and run back to Houston." She eyed the room, letting the crowd catch the line. "But she came back to give. She gave us back our story. Even the parts that hurt."

There were a few murmurs from the older crowd, a shifting of shoulders.

Teresa softened. "She didn't have to come home. She could have left it to the Chamber, or the next investor. But she made us visible, not a mascot." She paused. "That's worth more than any grant check."

A few heads nodded. Someone from the back muttered, "Damn right."

Teresa ceded the mic, and the room wobbled on the edge of polite applause until, out of nowhere, Stuart Morrison—last seen in the local paper arguing with the school board over homecoming mums—raised a plastic cup of cheap white wine.

He called out, "To Stirling's investment! Brought good things." The room stiffened, unsure if it was a backhanded compliment. But Caleb grinned, gesturing at Olivia. "Good for her! Not bad for a city girl."

This time, the applause was genuine. It started slowly, then picked up, spreading through the room in uneven pockets. Some clapped, others just smiled and nodded, but the sound carried and built, and Olivia let herself stand in the center, the echo of hands meeting hands a physical force in her bones.

For the rest of the evening, she drifted from knot to knot, listening to elders argue about who's mark belonged to which cousin, watched kids try to poke holes in the velvet rope with pencils, fielded questions about how the stone had survived a hundred years without being noticed. Every time she circled the exhibit, she found Carmen nearby, keeping an unofficial guard. Once, Olivia caught her running her thumb along the "C," as if to make sure it hadn't vanished.

Andrew lingered at the edge. When Olivia tried to catch his eye, he just smiled, shook his head and faded back.

It wasn't until the last family had taken their cell phone photos, the last cup of punch was drained, and the janitorial crew hovered by the doors that Olivia finally let herself sit on the dais edge, ankles crossed, skirt bunched at her knee.

She traced the mark with one finger, letting the cool stone bite into her skin.

It was proof. And for tonight, that was enough.

❧

THE CROWD FADED, replaced by the slow, shuffling cleanup of after-party hands—folding chairs dragged into neat stacks, finger-food trays scraped down to their last resilient grape. Olivia ducked behind the water cooler, rubbing her palm where the stone's rough edge had pressed a pale crescent into the skin. She let herself breathe, and in that silence, caught sight of Andrew.

He lingered near the exit, hands folded across his chest, scanning the room with the careful patience of a man surveying a building for hidden cracks. He'd kept his distance all night—never stepping into the arc of a conversation, never offering a word that could draw attention. When their eyes met, he smiled, slow and unscripted, then nodded toward the refreshment table.

Olivia found herself drawn toward him, the clatter of the museum staff fading with each step. She reached for a bottle of ginger ale just as he extended a champagne flute, their hands colliding. A fizz of static, not unpleasant, danced up her fingers.

."Congratulations," he said, voice pitched for her alone. "You turned your pitch into reality."

She laughed, breathless. "I barely remember the speech. Did I even say anything?"

"You said enough." He hesitated, then glanced toward the now-exposed stone. "You gave them proof. Even the ones who didn't know they did it."

She looked at the line of guests, most already drifting into the hallway. "You did half the work," she said. "Maybe more."

He shrugged, modest and genuine. "Not my story to tell. I just built the frame."

She wanted to say more, to ask him if he'd always been this careful, this precise with his words, but the feeling in the air—alive and trembling, like the foyer just after a thunderstorm—made her shy. Instead, she accepted the glass from his hand, fingers brushing. He lingered, not moving away, his thumb grazing the rim of his own cup.

"I heard about the booking calendar," he said, sotto voce. "Looks like you'll need more rooms soon."

She rolled her eyes and , grinned. "Only if you can find me the historic paint to match the old hallway."

He tipped his glass, soft as a promise. "I'll source it myself."

For a moment, it felt like a secret pact—a thing they'd built together, but that no one else could see.

The Limestone was dead quiet by the time Olivia returned, the parlor dark except for the glow from the front desk lamp. She walked behind the counter, toeing off her shoes, and spotted the envelope propped against the mailbox. It was thick, the paper a shade richer than anything from the local print shop.

She opened it, careful not to tear. Inside, a single card: "You delivered something better than I imagined. — A.S."

A check, too—smaller than the last, but enough to cover the final retainer. Alex had made it official: she owed no one but herself.

Before she could process the relief, Elena barged in, cheeks still pink from the night's wine. She held two champagne flutes, the good ones Olivia had wrapped in a towel to keep from chipping, and grinned a wolfish grin.

"I brought the emergency stash," Elena said, "but looks like we won't need it after tonight."

Olivia took the glass, letting the cold and the weight anchor her. "Did you see Carmen's face?"

Elena nodded, her own eyes shining. "She was proud of you. Really proud." She sipped, then added, "You earned this. Not because of the money. Not because of Alex, or the Board, or even the town. You earned it because you finished the work. You made the story real."

Olivia looked down, unsure what to do with the heat in facial skin. "I wasn't sure it would last. I thought maybe people would just—forget."

Elena set her glass on the desk, pulled Olivia into a tight hug. "People don't forget the truth. Not when you put it in stone."

They stood there, a minute or two in the hush of the sleeping inn. Then Elena grinned, switched on the computer, and pulled up the reservation page.

"Take a look," she said, jabbing at the screen.

The spreadsheet was lit up with color: every weekend slot blocked out, rooms reserved for reunions and birthdays and, in three different columns, "wedding party." The calendar was full to next March.

Olivia stared at it, something fragile and electric swelling in her ribs. Then, as she scrolled down, a small red dot popped up in the inbox.

She clicked: "Request for Interview — Hospitality Trends Magazine. We're fascinated by your approach to sustainable heritage tourism in small towns."

She blinked , then read it again. The words were real.

A laugh snuck out, tired but genuine. She looked at Elena, who just shrugged. "Told you. You built it. Now you get to decide how to tell it."

The two women sat there, sipping champagne from the good glasses, letting the glow from the monitor and the soft whoosh from the old radiator fill the space.

It wasn't about being in the spotlight anymore. It was about the work, and the proof, and the way a thing could last longer than the people who started it.

Olivia leaned back, closed her eyes, and let herself feel the weight of it—the story, the legacy, and, for the first time in a long while, the absolute certainty that she'd earned her place.

Long after Elena had gone, and the echo of clinking glasses had died away, Olivia settled herself at the desk in her office. The parlor lamp cast a pool of light across the spreadsheets, the check register, the letter from Alex with its flat, final signature. Outside, the night was a murk of distant crickets and the hum of the courthouse floodlights. In here, all she could hear was the soft tap of her nails against the calculator.

She paged through the numbers: bookings for the next eight months, catering deposits, the new line item for "museum docent" stipends. The math wasn't just working; it was thriving. She double-checked the totals, then clicked through to her bank's portal and scheduled the final transfer to Stirling's account. Three months early. She took a slow, deep breath, watching the numbers flick from red to black.

For a minute, she just stared at the screen, letting the reality bleed in. No more payments. No more borrowed time.

She picked up her phone and dialed Alex's number, a tight, almost ceremonial act. He answered on the first ring.

"Ms. Cuellar," he said, voice as brisk as always.

"Paid in full," Olivia said, savoring the shape of the words. "As of ten seconds ago."

A pause, then the rustle of him sitting back in his chair. "Congratulations. That took less time than you expected, I bet."

She smiled, then made herself say it: "Thank you for believing in the vision."

His response was immediate, but softer than she'd ever heard from him. "I never doubted the vision. I doubted you'd believe in yourself. Glad I was wrong."

There was nothing else to say. She let the call end, then sat in the hush, heart slow and even. Not once did she think of Houston, or the old job, or the stories that had once made her feel small. She thought only of this: the old building, the new stone, the story she'd anchored in place.

She closed the computer, stood, and padded through the quiet hall. The place felt different now. Not empty, not heavy, but whole. She ran her hand along the banister; the wood was smooth from a century's use and now, finally, free of the nail-head burr that had always snagged her sleeve.

She stopped at the window in the upstairs hall, gazing out at the square. The courthouse dome glowed under the flood-lights, pale as a pearl, its lines unbroken. Around the base, a ring of lawn chairs sat abandoned by the day's last visitors, like sentries keeping watch over the sleeping town.

A knock at the side door startled her. She checked the clock—10:40, the hour when even the hardiest local had called it a night. She went down, thumbed the latch, and there was Andrew, damp from the mist, hair askew.

He smiled, small and sheepish. "I was in the neighborhood," he said. "Thought I'd check on the garden."

She grinned. "It's holding up. The roses are already plotting a takeover."

He nodded at the air, then gestured to the night. "Walk?"

She slipped on the old cardigan by the door; the elbows faded from years of service. They walked side by side, across the porch and onto the gravel path that wound around the inn. The night was thick with the sweet, watery scent of cut grass and something floral. Somewhere down the block, a dog barked, then gave up.

They reached the garden beds—the ones that, eight months ago, had been a mound of crushed brick and debris. Now, the beds were edged with limestone, the soil rich and dark. The salvage roses planted on a gamble were not only alive but thriving.

Andrew crouched, brushing his fingers over a blossom. "You did a good job," he said. "Most people would have paved it over."

She squinted, eyes adjusting to the half-light. "I didn't do it alone."

He shook his head, grinning. "You finished it. That's what I mean. Most people stop at the plan."

They stood like that in the wet, quiet dark, and Olivia felt a contentment she didn't have words for. Not pride, not relief, just a gentle, rooted satisfaction. It felt right.

A firefly blinked, then another, and soon the beds were lit by dozens, tiny pulses of green and yellow floating above the petals. Andrew watched them, then looked at her, a question in his gaze.

He offered his hand, tentative. She took it without hesitation, neither hurrying the moment.

They walked the rest of the loop in silence, the path solid beneath their feet, the future less a blank and more a line she could follow. When they reached the front steps of the inn, she stopped, let herself lean against his arm, head against his shoulder.

He didn't speak. He didn't need to.

Across the square, the courthouse dome and the inn both glowed: one stately, public, a testament to the men who'd cut its stone. The other a testament to the future she'd cut for herself.

Olivia looked at the two together, their stories finally side by side.

And she knew in that moment that she had built something that would last.

Afterword

This book and the series that it belongs to has been a long process for me. What I initially wanted to be a contemporary romance series hit a roadblock several months in when I realized to my horror that I was not, in fact, a romance writer.

That realization kept me in creative freeze for longer than I'd care to admit as I debated abandoning the Madison County Courthouse renovation idea, and the idea of just leaving fiction for a while while I figured out what I wanted to do creatively.

Eventually, I managed to figure out that what I wanted to do was tell a tale of women who were trapped in the dilemma of "no good deed goes unpunished," and if there were some romantic elements in the book, all the better. I'm so sorry Andrew, I feel you got shortchanged.

I'm eternally grateful to my critique partners and my ARC readers who were generous enough to sit with me while I figured out what I wanted to do with this series. Their advice and support has been an incredible source of support for me at a time that other aspects of me life were in turmoil. Unfortunately, Madison, Texas suffered during that time and it took me longer than I'd initially hoped to get their stories in order.

This series came to me years after I sat in a conference room and presented to a room full of County judges who were going through the process of applying for the Texas Historical Commissions's Historic Courthouse Renovation project. THC was generous enough to invite me as a records management pro to present the State Records Center's requirements for records management.

Prior to that morning, I had assumed that my state agency was the only one driving the good people of Texas' local government to drink. I was very, very wrong. The process is long, and THC has done a commendable job trying to ensure that the process is done in the most transparent and responsible manner possible. As I write this, almost all of the courthouses in the state have finished this process, and that day I got a firsthand look at how frustrating that process is.

As much as I love to give my fellow Texans crap, I sincerely sympathize with their real life experiences of "no good deed goes unpunished." Historic preservation is an often a fell-good story that plays well on a Hallmark movie, but rarely do we see the unexpected and expensive downsides of preservation. All of the scenarios in this series are fictional, and I fully admit to exaggerating some parts for dramatization. That's my living out the fantasy of us sitting around, circa 2008 and fantasizing about how "somebody should write a book about this; nobody would ever believe it." Once a harried, underpaid, under- funded government employee, always a, well...

I love my home state of Texas. And since I love my home state unconditionally and I am an adult with an adult's view of the world, I have no qualms about honestly criticizing something that I love unconditionally. Love does not equate enabling. Texas is an incredibly diverse, multicultural state, and we as a state have done incredibly cruel things to our neighbors though indifference greed, selfishness, and malfeasance. I'll continued to love and criticize I love, in the hope that looking at it honestly it will do better next time. I criticize Houstón all of the time and I will fight you over it as soon as I can hand someone my purse.

As long as I'm able, I plan on exploring the good and bad of my hometown and the fictional corners of Madison and Verde County. Few things give me more creative pleasure than to say I created my own Texas county. I would literally do this for free.

I lost a dear friend during the writing of this book, Tom Sharp. I was devastated to hear of his passing. I am going to do as much as I can to sprinkle in things to name in his honor and honor his memory in this series and afterward. Between the two of us, he was the only Native Texan, and I'm sure he'll be haunting me soon for daring to name things in his native state after he's gone.

Get over it, Tom. Sam Houston was an immigrant. I miss you terribly.

Laura

An Adopted Texan and a really mean spirited Texas Woman

About the Author

Laura Finger writes steamy contemporary romance and women's fiction. Her Madison, TX and Houston series are set in her home state of Texas, and reflect her years of bemusement at her fellow Texans.

Before becoming a writer, Laura worked as an archivist for the Houston Public Library and Rosenberg Library Systems and later as a records manager for the Texas State Records Center.

She spends her spare time very slowly running marathons and squeezing in yoga sessions. She is the exasperated and mediocre owner of a Siberian Forest Cat, Gretchen.

Laura's book are available in electronic, print and audio on all major retailers.

Connect with Laura on her website.

Also by Laura Finger

Lara's books are available on all major retailers and at her website, laurafinger.com

Saving Madison, TX Series (2025)

The Heart of Madison, the town's beloved community center, is threatened by a greedy developer looking to turn the town into a tourist trap filled with high priced condos. Refusing to roll over and take it, the town fights back, and along the way hearts are at risk.

The Royal We Series (2025)

Princesses are made for fairytales, but what about the people who surround a princess? See the people behind the royal facade get their own happy ever afters in the series.

Restoring Madison, TX Series (2026)

The people of Madison, TX are finally able to renovate their crumbling courthouse. But life and nature keep throwing curveballs at the project, along with chances for romance. See if the good people of Madison can complete the project with their sanity intact and without losing their hearts in the process.

Blueprint of the Heart

Taking Flight

What Remains

Coming soon:

Midlife in Mississippi (2027)

www.ingramcontent.com/pod-product-compliance
Lightning Source LLC
LaVergne TN
LVHW050927080826
845145LV00001B/234

* 9 7 8 1 9 5 0 5 7 1 1 8 5 *